MY ITCHING SCALES
THE MAGICAL MISFITS
BOOK III

BRIDGET E. BAKER

Copyright © 2024 by Bridget E. Baker

All rights reserved.

No part of this book may be reproduced in any form or by any electronic or mechanical means, including information storage and retrieval systems, without written permission from the author, except for the use of brief quotations in a book review.

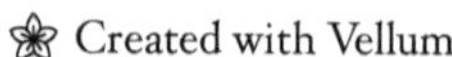 Created with Vellum

WHAT IT'S ABOUT...

If it walks like a dragon shifter and it talks like a dragon shifter. . . but it can't shift? What then?

The entire country rejoiced when, out of a golden egg, Roxana Goldenscales hatched. It's not every day (or even every decade) that a dragona princess graces the earth with her presence. But like most rare, valuable, and defenseless things, every moment of Roxana's existence is supervised, planned, and observed.

Or at least, they were.

Until she ran away.

Her decision to flee from her gilded pedestal wasn't an easy one, and nothing's gone quite right since. Her love life's confusing, her closet's cramped (and a little smelly), and her useless, ornamental dragon scales itch constantly. But after finding a group of misfit friends who support her, Roxana's making a life for herself—one that she chooses.

As usual, the rest of the world has other ideas.

The Manhattan werewolves, the demon-spawn leaders, and Roxana's powerful parents all want her to go back home double quick. Can a helpless princess find the strength to stand on her own? Or will the danger for her friends be so steep that she's swept right back into the very cage she fled?

For Emmy

Because you always need a little more laughter in your life,
and no one makes me smile as much as you.

ROXANA

When Minerva bangs on the door, I startle. I've been living here for quite some time now, and she has never, not ever, not even one single time, banged on the bathroom door.

"You alright in there?" Her voice sounds strained.

"Sorry," I say. "Am I taking too long?"

"The thing is, I had breakfast tacos before I went to sleep, and I just woke up, and. . ." Giggles flutters outside the window above the shower. Then she taps her beak on the glass.

I retuck the towel underneath my armpit and open the door.

"Whoa." Minerva's shoulders droop and her eyes widen.

"What's wrong?" She's seen me in a towel a dozen times, so that's not it. I blink. "Does my hair look bad?" I smooth my hand over it self-consciously. I've never used a blow dryer before, but I wanted to make sure I looked nice.

Technically, I've been on several dates.

Dad found me an escort for every school dance, but it was never someone I chose. It was never someone I *could* choose. I was, more or less, a walking prize. I'm finally going on a date with Lionel, and it feels like it really *matters*. He's stepped in to help me several times now, and even if I'm pretty unsure of his real intentions and feelings, he's a good-looking, powerful, and rich man, and he seems to genuinely be interested.

"Your hair looks. . .fine." Minerva blinks. "It's totally *fine*."

"I hope you're not just being polite, because I spent so much time getting ready that I barely have time to slide into my dress and shoes before he gets here."

"I doubt Lionel would complain if you wore that towel." Minerva's lips compress, and then she rolls her eyes. "Speaking of—longer than you've ever spent—how long was that, exactly?" She's eyeing my makeup, my hair, and my polished fingernails and toenails.

"I painted my nails last night," I say. "But I spent twenty minutes after my shower blow drying my hair and putting on mascara." It's a little embarrassing. "Sorry you had to wait on me."

Minerva's voice sounds strangely high and squeaky when she says, "Just don't let it happen again. Twenty *whole minutes* is a little excessive." She's smiling when she brushes past me into the bathroom.

Then she switches on the fan.

If she hadn't already told me about the tacos, I'd have known to steer clear of the bathroom for a while from the sound of the fan. Flipping that on is like a warning sign or something. At first, after she discovered her father might be akero, I was worried. I thought Minerva might change.

I kind of felt nervous that maybe I didn't really know her at all.

But it's been two days since the discovery, and she's the same as she's ever been. Nerdy, well-intentioned, and a little over-eager. And she still needs a bathroom fan after eating breakfast tacos.

Not angelic in any ways I can pinpoint.

Once I reach my room, I hang my towel over a chair and slide into my clothes. I can't exactly wear a bra with this dress, but I make sure my underwear's nice and grandmotherly. Bevin told me that's the key to making sure a good first date doesn't go too far.

It's nice to have friends to share these tidbits.

The dress I picked is meant to turn heads. It's bright, fire-lizard red, and it has sequins and sparkly beads sewn all around the strapless bodice. It fits me like a glove, and it should. It was custom designed for me by Dior, one of the most famous wizarding families of all time. Now that Mom and Dad know I'm here, Mom actually snuck some of my clothes over by private courier. I have no idea whether Dad knows that she's helping me survive on my own, but it does make it easier to dress appropriately for a date with one of the most prestigious wizards in the world.

I'm trying to decide whether to pull my hair up or leave it down when my cheek starts to itch again.

I've had small patches of golden scales that sort of shimmer into existence and disappear at odd times my entire life. They always appear in the same places, and as luck would have it, they've all been in places that don't look too bad. My left cheek near my eye. My neck, on the same side. My right shoulder. My left hip. My right calf. The top of my left foot.

That's why I always use gold-toned makeup—don't want to clash.

It's hardly surprising my scales are gold. Though I never met him, I've heard that Grandpa—Mom's father—had golden scales, and so does Dad.

Recently, ever since I flung that stupid fireball, my scales have started showing up more regularly, and when they do, they also *itch*. It's really, really annoying. Even though I can't shift, my scales are real dragon scales. Diamond-hard fingernails notwithstanding, it's really hard to scratch them hard enough to get any relief. I'm really going to town on my right shoulder when someone walks into the family room.

"Hello? Everyone decent?"

It's Clark.

I slide into my black, strappy sandals and walk out. "Minerva's in the bathroom," I say. "But we're all dressed."

"Tacos?" He grimaces. "I wondered about that when I saw her with the bag. Who eats tacos in the morning?"

"They were breakfast tacos," I say.

"That's the dumbest idea Texas has ever had." Clark shakes his head. "But Minerva has always loved spicy foods, even though they never agree with her."

"She was really dumping on the hot sauce," I say.

"Hey, are you alright?" Clark's brow furrows and he ducks his head, walking closer to me. "I mean, you look amazing, but. . ." He points.

I glance down at my shoulder, where I've scratched

a huge furrow in my skin. "Ugh." Blood's dripping down my arm. "It looks worse than it feels, at least."

"Who did that?" Clark's jaw's set, and his eyes flash. "What happened?"

I brush past him, heading for the kitchen and a paper towel. "Nothing—no one." I sigh. "I did it to myself."

"Why?" He has pivoted around and followed me over. "Do you want a healing charm?"

I nod. "Yes, please. How did I not already know that those exist?"

He rummages around in his over-the-shoulder bag. "My best healing potions are these creams I made from some fungi you can only get in Botswana."

I quirk one eyebrow as I swipe at the nasty gash with a towel.

He holds out a little glass jar. "Voila."

I reach for it.

"Ah, ah, ah," he says, moving his hand back just a bit too far for me to reach. "Before I hand this over, you have to tell me more about how it happened. Part of the treatment."

I sigh. "My scales have started—" I drop my voice. "*Itching*." It's embarrassing.

"This doesn't always happen?" He frowns, handing me the cream absently. "It's new?"

Xander and I agreed not to tell anyone about the fireball, and I'm assuming that extends even to close friends. At least, I think it does, so I nod. "Yep."

"Like, how new? Today? Or when did it start?"

I shrug. "A few days ago. I've always been able to shoot sparks, but since I dove in front of that dragona who was trying to kill you. . .they've gotten stronger."

"And you couldn't even create sparks when we were facing down the werewolves, right?" Clark's eyebrows rise.

That was embarrassing, actually. It's been a rough few days for me. There's a reason I delayed this date with Lionel. "Yeah, I'm not really in control of my fire-sparking ability, but I do think the power behind it has gone up."

"Interesting." Clark frowns again. "I'll have to look into dragona-specific creams and potions and see whether I can find something for itchy scales."

"And can you keep this between us?" I ask. "I'd really rather not have—"

Clark nods his head, cutting me off. "Of course. Say no more, and neither will I."

He can be a little annoying, but he's a good friend. "Thank you."

"And now that you're no longer bleeding, can I just say, *Wow*?"

I laugh. "You can, thanks."

"This is all for Lionel?" He sighs heavily. "That guy just rubs me the wrong way."

"Me too, sometimes," I admit. "I'm hoping to figure out whether it's just who he is, or whether it's something he can curb."

Clark purses his lips, but he doesn't offer an opinion. "Where's he taking you?"

I shrug.

"He should really give you a heads up on that—even if it's just dinner or an activity and a formality level. How are you supposed to know whether you're dressed appropriately or. . ." He trails off. "I guess you'll stand out no matter what, so being a little over-dressed isn't as big of a deal."

I can't help laughing. "It's a blessing and a curse, believe me."

"Maybe more of a blessing, though," Minerva says, coming out of the bathroom wrapped in a fuzzy blue towel.

I don't bother arguing. Unless someone has spent their life being treated as though their only value is in their appearance, they won't get how demoralizing it feels. At that moment, though, there's a knock on the front door.

Minerva squeaks, and shoots through the family room toward her bedroom. "One second," she says, rather shrilly.

"Time for your date." Clark's lips compress to a flat line.

He's almost ten minutes early, but it probably *is* Lionel. Who else would knock? It's not like we ordered a pizza. "He's not that bad," I whisper. "It'll be fine."

"Agree to disagree," he says.

I'm smiling as I open the door. . .to Xander. "Why are you knocking?"

His expression's strange. "I've always just walked in, but now that we're all part of a pack, I thought I should try to honor a few of the traditional niceties. I'm just trying to offer you all some space."

"You're being strange," Clark says. "Just walk in."

"If Minerva says the same thing, then I will," Xander says.

"Xander?" Minerva walks out. "For the love of

toadstools, why in the world did you knock? Don't do that. You almost gave me a heart attack."

"A heart attack?" Xander asks. "Why?"

"I thought you were that pretentious, officious, rude mage who's coming to pick up Roxana."

"You forgot overbearing, obscenely wealthy, and staggeringly handsome." Lionel pokes his head around Xander's shoulder.

Xander startles. "And disturbingly quiet."

Lionel wiggles his fingers, a bright yellow stone flashing a bit. "When you're insanely wealthy, you can buy all sorts of neat toys. This one lets me move around without making a sound or projecting a smell." He taps a small silver ring on his right pinky. "When I turned twenty, I couldn't decide whether I wanted another house on the beach, or this." He shakes his head. "But the taxes in Martha's Vineyard have gone crazy, and who really needs *three* beach houses?"

"Who needs two?" Xander asks.

"Yeah." Minerva folds her arms, glaring. "Who does need two?"

Lionel arches one eyebrow. "Obviously you need a small one for intimate gatherings—somewhere you feel comfortable with just a few close friends, and a large one for when you're hosting a real party."

Clark snorts. "Right. Obviously."

"Roxana, you look. . ." Lionel whistles. "Absolutely spectacular. Every time I think you can't possibly look any more amazing, you do."

"I don't know," Xander mutters. "I like when she's wearing ratty pajamas and a t-shirt."

Lionel's lip curls. "You would, mutt."

I shake my head. "Nope."

"Sorry." Lionel half-bows. "I forget sometimes that they're your friends."

"No, you don't," Clark says.

Lionel sighs. "No, I suppose I don't. I do cognitively wish I could forget."

"I suddenly have an idea for a gift for you," I say.

Lionel smiles, his head whipping toward mine. "You do?"

I nod slowly. "I saw a normie using one just the other day on their Labrador retriever. They said it would *not* stop jumping up on people, so they had no choice. It's called a shock collar." I tap the base of my throat. "With one little zap, they immediately remind it when it does something that's unacceptably rude. I feel like that might be the only way to turn you into someone who wouldn't embarrass me around my friends."

"Touché," Lionel says. "I'll admit that your education in the social graces far outstrips mine. I promise to listen carefully to your suggestions going forward."

"We'll see about that," I say.

"As much fun as this is, we should probably go," Lionel says. "If I'm late for my reservation, Jacques will call my dad."

"Jacques?" Who the heck is that?

"He's the head chef at Luminesce," Lionel says. "But don't share that info around. It's a secret." He presses his index finger to his mouth and makes a shushing sound.

"Wait, that place is real?" Minerva's mouth dangles open.

"What place?" Xander asks.

"It's an invisible, floating restaurant over the

center of Central Park," Lionel says. "Of course it exists."

"Only top-level mages are allowed to enter," Clark says. "It's invite only."

"What does top-level mean, anyway?" Minerva asks.

"If you have to ask, you aren't one," Lionel says.

"There's allegedly a test," Clark says. "Once you demonstrate that you might have enough raw power, a mentor contacts you. And if they feel you're ready, they put their membership in this organization on the line by recommending you. If you fail the test, they're removed, and you don't get in."

Minerva blinks.

"That's not quite right," Lionel says, "but it's close enough for this group. The restaurant *is* members only." He winks at me as we walk out the door. "Lucky for you, your boyfriend's both a member *and* a top-level mage."

When we reach the sidewalk, I realize he's parked his McLaren 750S right on the curb.

"This is a no parking zone," I say. "Weren't you worried you'd be towed?"

Lionel laughs as he presses the button to open the door.

"What, you have a no-ticket charm?"

"I have a no-towing charm." He winks. "The tickets, I ignore."

Thanks to my dad's McLaren, I know to stand behind the door so I'm not hit as it opens upward. Something occurs to me then, and I pause as I'm climbing into the passenger seat. "What are your fancy mages-only members going to think about you bringing a dragona princess with you?"

His grin's broad. "My dad's the President, so they won't think much." He circles the car and slides into his seat. "Except, it will tell them that I'm not messing around—I've never taken another woman there. Which means you're clearly someone I care about." His eyes are intense as they meet mine.

My heart accelerates a bit, but I'm not sure how much of that's from my own nervous fear. I'm not accustomed to going to places I'm not welcome, and until recently, I never went places where I wasn't wanted.

Except the wolf packs with Xander, and that was an exciting day.

"Alright, we're officially on our first date," Lionel says. "This is where we start learning about each other, right?"

I frown. "What does that mean?"

"Ask me something you want to know."

"Like, about the secret society?"

"Sure, that too." He laughs. "But I meant about Lionel Sol."

Duh. "Well, tell me what you like and what you hate."

"I like beautiful dragona princesses, apparently," he says. "And I like fast cars. I also like to do the unexpected."

"But surely for the person you're with, it's nice to know you well enough that they feel safe in your actions."

"Safe?" Lionel glances my way. "I mean, I can keep

most anyone safe. No one's safer to be around than me."

"If that's the kind of safe I wanted, I'd have married Ragar." My lip curls. "I meant that if you had a real girlfriend, there must be some things about you that would be a given. Things she would know that would make her feel safe about being with you."

"Ah." He nods, his eyes still on the road. "But safe's boring."

No, this fast and furious act is boring. Xander's voice in my head startles me. *Sorry,* Xander continues. *I didn't mean to project that.*

2

ROXANA

I want to ask that wolfy idiot whether he's been able to hear every word of my date. I want to yell at him for listening in, but I can't really do that with Lionel sitting next to me. I think an angry thought as hard as I can, and then I push it.

"Are you alright?" Lionel asks. "You look. . .well, let's just say that you look a little odd."

I blank my face and sit straighter. "I'm fine," I say. "I was just thinking about how my mother keeps calling me. I'm going to have to answer her call pretty soon. She wants to meet you—officially, I mean. As my boyfriend." I shake my head. "It's sure to be a disaster."

"I don't know." He's grinning again. "I think that sounds fun."

I roll my eyes.

But I'm distracted for the rest of the drive. I'm actually relieved when Lionel pulls into a very mundane, very normal looking parking garage just south of Central Park.

"Really?" I ask. "We're going to Luminesce, and this is where we park?" It's funny to me. Even mages can't find special parking in NYC.

But as the McLaren winds around the lines in the cramped corner of the parking garage, its engine roaring, I start to get nervous. The parking spaces end up ahead, with a large sign that tells drivers to head back down. Lionel, however, does not appear to be slowing at all.

He's accelerating.

As we approach the end of the line, I close my eyes and brace myself.

At the last moment, I open my eyes, apparently unwilling to not even see my own demise. In that second, our car bursts through the wall with a popping sound and shoots across a strange, shimmering path that arches out over the edge of Central Park, above the Pulitzer Fountain. "What just happened?"

"You didn't think I'd be paying for parking on some kind of stupid normie-meter, did you?" He's beaming.

"You could have warned me," I say.

"Oh, come on. Where's the fun in that?" He tosses his head. "We're almost there. And see? Now you get what I mean. Predictable's boring, right?" His car starts to slow as the shimmery, invisible flyover comes to an end in a parking lot that's resting right above the bottom edge of The Pond.

"This is where Luminesce is?" I lower my head and peer out of the window. The McLaren isn't exactly made for easy visibility, and the sun's getting ready to set. Not a combination that makes it easy to make things out.

"You'll see it all soon enough." Lionel swings into a space and hops out. "Let's go."

When my door swings upward, he's already waiting for me, his hand extended. It's a little cute. He may be obnoxious, but at least he knows how to behave in upscale social settings.

You mean pretentious *social settings.* Xander sounds grumpy.

But that must mean he can hear my thoughts, including my angry one.

I'm not sure it was anatomically possible, but I did hear that, yes.

Xander really needs to get this stuff under control. The last thing any of the friends will want is to have someone snooping around in their brain.

Actually, so far the only one whose thoughts I hear loud and clear are yours.

After a small burst of happiness—I do feel somewhat special for some reason—I'm annoyed. *Well, butt out,* I think.

I'm trying. Believe me.

"Bowled over, are you?" Lionel's still holding out his hand.

I hurry to take his hand and climb out before he decides I'm a halfwit. "Of course." I look around. It really is an impressive place. The mages who run this super-secret little restaurant have created an entire venue that's invisible to all normies—and previously to me as well. Speaking of. . . "Why can I see this now?"

"You passed through the entrance." He shrugs, as if that explains it all.

I suppose for him, it does. I wasn't worthy before, but now I am.

The restaurant looks like a hologram. It's iridescent, and it shimmers, and it's still practically invisible. It's invisible enough to make me a little uncomfortable walking around on unsteady, insubstantial ground. But after a few steps, some of the panic recedes. The Gapstow Bridge beyond Luminesce is resplendent, and past that, the lights are just lighting up the Plaza Hotel.

It's pretty amazing.

"Just wait," Lionel says. "The food's even better than the view."

As I walk in, my hand on his arm, everyone we pass half-bows. That kind of deference isn't that uncommon in the supernatural world, and especially not to me. It's the same kind of nonsense my dad insists on with his people, but most of the people bowing are clearly mages, and most of them are much older than Lionel.

That makes it strange, even to me.

"Your usual table?" A waiter in traditional mage's robes with non-conventional spiky hair gestures.

Lionel doesn't even bother answering him. He simply walks past.

No one has said a word about me and my lack of high-level magic, thankfully. That would have been awkward. Once we're seated, the waitstaff wastes no time bringing us drinks and appetizers. It's all happening so quickly that it's hard to process.

Or perhaps that's because the entire table looks like something out of the Narnia movies. The center of the table's decorated with beautiful fall foliage, including vines with scarlet, emerald, citrine, and burnt sienna leaves. Butterflies flutter and bob around the unfurling mums and lilies. Overhead, broadly sweeping branches with tiny lights hover in place, lightning bugs darting and diving around them. There's even a small bird that keeps hopping from branch to branch, twittering.

"Giggles would hate that bird," I say.

"Pardon me?" Lionel asks.

I forgot that he doesn't really know about Giggles —and on second thought, maybe she'd love the other avian. Now that I'm looking more closely, I can't tell whether it's a real bird or some kind of charm. "Never mind."

When something in front of me makes a noise, I nearly jump out of my chair, because it's a bug. The plate they brought us had a flower with two small bees on it, and they're buzzing, their wings flickering.

Lionel's hand drops on my wrist. "It's alright." He's smiling. "They're not really alive. They're enchanted."

"We're not supposed to be eating bees, though, right?" I eye the lily on my plate askance.

Lionel releases my wrist, plucks a bee from his flower, and pops it in his mouth. He's not even chewing, as if it dissolved on his tongue. He just sighs. "Definitely not a bee."

I swallow. "I'm not sure—"

"Just try it," he says.

Before he can argue with me further, a couple approaches our table. "Lionel?" The woman speaks first, her eyes wide. "And who's your lovely date?" She's older than Lionel, I'm pretty sure, but I can't really pinpoint how I know that. Her face is unlined, her skin smooth as cream. Her hair's perfectly coiffed into a sleek, shiny, high bun. Something about her's glowing, but I'm not sure what.

It's glamour, Xander says. *You can smell the nonsense thanks to your dragona magic.*

Of course it is. That makes me wonder what she really looks like.

Probably an old prune.

I suppress a laugh.

With a wart on the end of her nose, and a long, black hair growing out of it.

"Aunt Olive." Lionel stands. "How nice to see you here." He gestures my way. "This is Roxana Gold-enscales."

"Of course." The woman's gaze falls on me. "Just as lovely as the television shows."

I stand too and incline my head. "Thank you, but no one in this room can compete with you."

The woman blushes, so the glamour must be pretty high-level. I suppose that's to be expected of Lionel's aunt. With a perfect magical pedigree comes impeccable powers.

"When your looks nearly rival Roxana Golden-scales, you might have turned the glamour knob up a bit too high," Lionel says with a grin.

Aunt Olive slaps his forearm. "Stop."

"Seriously," the man beside her says. "I didn't want to complain, but it's been burning my eyes." Unlike Aunt Olive, the man looks rather ordinary. He's tall, he's thin, and his face is long and heavily lined. His slate-grey hair is neatly combed, but I wouldn't notice him in a crowd.

"Good to see you, Uncle Oliver."

"Wait," I say. "Your aunt's name is Olive, and your uncle's name. . ."

The couple laughs. "Ridiculous, isn't it?" Aunt Olive asks.

"Almost as silly as your glamour that makes you look like you're a twenty-something," Uncle Oliver says.

"We'd better go." Aunt Olive's scowling. "We have some manners to discuss." She wraps one hand around Uncle Oliver's wrist, tightly, and then she tugs.

He huffs as he lets her drag him away, but I hear him mutter, "What? I'm tired of people thinking I'm out with my daughter."

"And whose fault is that?" Aunt Olive mutters. "If you'd use any proper glamour, they'd see us as a matched pair."

Lionel's shaking his head as he sits back down. "You can do almost anything with magic." He points. "Including making surprisingly delicious and charmingly unique treats."

I lean closer. "But what does the bee taste like?"

Chicken, Xander says. *Everything always tastes like chicken.*

I ignore him, and I pop the bee in my mouth. Somewhat predictably, it tastes like honey ambrosia—nothing like chicken. *Idiot.* I should've known. But the flower is light, and it's airy, and as it melts in my mouth, I realize that I could eat three more.

"See?" Lionel says. "Not so bad, right?"

Before I've even eaten my second bee, the waiters float our plates away and bring out new ones, setting them in front of us with a flourish. At first glance, our new course looks like a regular sort of tiny quiche. Before I can try and cut it in half with my fork, tiny fireworks start exploding above it.

"Whoa," I say.

Good food doesn't need so much fanfare, Xander says.

But once the fireworks stop and I take my first bite, I disagree. It's divine. Or, it would be if another mage hadn't just approached. This time, Lionel doesn't stand.

"Mr. Sol." The man looks a few years older than Lionel, but not many. Even so, I'd have thought he was old enough not to call Lionel 'mister.'

"Dresden," Lionel says with a grimace, his voice flat. "You made it in to Luminesce. How delightful."

The man's smile is a little sinister. "And who's this lovely creature?"

Lionel slams his hand on the table, sparks spraying out as he does. One of them sets the napkin on fire.

I pat it out.

Neither of the men even seemed to notice. They're too busy glaring.

"I'm not actually a creature," I say. "Just dragona."

The man's head whips my way. "Not quite as beautiful as they all say, though, are you?"

I'm going to kill him.

"That's nice to hear," I say, turning on the charm. "Usually Lionel's *friends* are almost incoherent around me." I bite my lip.

Dresden sputters. He blinks several times. Then he shakes his head. "Where am I?" He smiles at me. "And what is *your* name?"

"That's more like it," Lionel mutters. "Alright, off

with you before I hit maximum annoyance at your constantly grating presence." He waves. "People should know whether to be sycophants or rivals—that guy's not smart enough to be either."

The man, apparently too twitterpated to pay attention to Lionel now that I've turned on conscious charm, finally trots off.

"Who was that?" I ask.

Lionel spears the end of his quiche and shoves it into his mouth. "Son of my dad's greatest rival. Complete twit."

"I can tell," I say.

Can you? He looked and sounded just *like Lionel.*

I ignore Xander.

My date and I make small talk through a few more courses, each of them even more lovely than the last. Thankfully, none of the new ones look alive, at least, not since the bees. But then the main course arrives—bluefin tuna dressed up in a swirly, brightly-colored sauce—and I barely have room for more than a bite or two.

"Oh, no." I groan. "I know why they do such tiny little courses."

Lionel's brow furrows. "Tell me you're not out of room. You will not believe how amazing the citrus mousse is."

"I can't believe how amazing this bluefin tuna is! It's my mom's favorite fish."

"I'll be making note of that," Lionel says.

"No need for that," I say. "You couldn't force me to put you in the same room as the two of them with a gun against my temple. Not any time soon, anyway."

"I thought our date was going pretty well," he says, leaning forward to brace himself on his forearms. "Or are you still mad about the bees?"

He's handsome. He's sophisticated. He mostly listens when I talk, which is about a hundred times better than Ragar. I should be excited. I should be shivering with anticipation.

Because there's no way he's not going to kiss me, right? It's a first date, and he's *Lionel Sol*. He waves the waiter over. "Give us an extra five before dessert. Her stomach's small—beautiful woman problems." He winks.

Beautiful woman problems? Does your period make you not-hungry?

"Okay, okay," I mutter. "So he's a little misogynist."

"I'm what?" The waiter's gone, and Lionel's eyeing me strangely. "You've done that a few times tonight."

"Done what?" I swallow.

"It's almost like. . ." He waves his hand and frowns. "But you aren't wearing a wire."

"You just checked me for a wire?" I splutter. "What on the mountain peaks?"

He shakes his head. "Something strange *is* going on."

"I think I'm ready for the mousse now." I shove my plate forward.

Almost as if they really do have the table wire-tapped, the mousse arrives, flown over to us by tiny birds carrying little bundles with their feet. "This is a little too Cinderella for me," I say.

"I thought women liked princesses." He cocks one eyebrow. "Apparently actual princesses don't?"

"I'm not royalty," I say. "My father's just the CEO of the Dagobar group."

"And the ruler of all the North American dragona," Lionel says. "So, yeah. You are."

I take a bite of the mousse. . .and I almost forget about everything else that's happened. This mousse—Lionel wasn't kidding. "It's almost worth dating you, just for this."

"Hey," he says. "That sounds like a backhanded compliment if I ever heard one."

I bet he's heard a lot.

I snicker. "Probably from that Dresden person."

Probably too dumb to understand them all.

"Alright." Lionel stands. "Who are you talking to?" He looks around the room, scowling. "Who are you smiling at?"

I wave him back down. "No one," I say. "No one that's here, anyway."

"So you are wearing a wire?" His scowl lightens to a frown. "Why can't my spell pick it up?"

"It's not a wire," I say. "But I'm bonded to a werewolf. It's new, and we're still working out some details, and I keep hearing his input."

"A—a werewolf?" His voice is shrill and high. "Xander Binnigas?"

"Hey," I say. "You remembered his name. Nice work."

He leaps to his feet. "I forbid it." He shakes his head. "You can't be bonded to a *wolf*."

"What's wrong with wolves?" I ask. "Did you know that he was the first person who helped me avoid my own wedding? He suggested the fire escape."

Not technically true, but I appreciate the sentiment.

"He's not even a proper wolf! He's half-human!" Lionel throws his napkin at the table, smashing the rest of his citrus mousse, which is basically a crime. I could punch him just for that.

I could punch him for a lot less.

"You know." I stand, too. "Whether I'm bonded to a wolf isn't up to you."

"Trust me," he says. "You have got to break this off—leave the pack. Whatever. No one in the world will like this news."

"The thing is, though, I don't trust you."

"And you trust the wolf?"

"Why do you insist on calling him 'the wolf,' like he's an animal and not a person?"

"He *is* a wolf," he says.

"And I'm a dragona," I say. "Am I not also a person? What if I were a wolf instead?"

"I'd never date you if you were a wolf," Lionel says. "If that's what you're asking."

"So a dragona's good enough, but not a werewolf?"

He nods.

That's all I need to hear. I march away from the table, not waiting for him to catch up. He's taller than me with much longer legs, so he *does* catch up, but when he tries to grab my hand, I shake him off and spin around. "No. You don't get to trot after me to slander my friend even more than you already have. You're not my boss. You're not my father." I lower my voice to a hiss. "And you're certainly not my boyfriend anymore—fake or otherwise." I inhale slowly, trying to calm down, at least a little. "But even if you were, you wouldn't be able to dictate my friends or the decisions I made in my life."

"Surely you can see how problematic it is for you to be bonded to—"

"Yes," I say. "Of course I do, but everything about my life is problematic. To my parents, I doubt being bonded to a wolf would be much worse than dating a *mage*." I huff and walk away again. He follows me out into the parking lot, unwilling to leave me alone. By the time we reach his car in the parking lot, it occurs to me that letting him drive me off this ridiculous, invisible road is really my only way out.

That's why I get into his stupid blue car.

But I specifically ignore him, not answering any of his invasive questions. And when my mom calls, I make a point of answering with a smile. "Hey, Mom, someone I *like* to talk to."

She's loved making me sound stupid since I was a kid, so right on cue, she says, "Ha, then why have you been avoiding my calls?"

"I haven't," I lie. "I've been really busy, but I picked up just now."

"Dinner," she says. "Tomorrow night at home. Say you can make it."

"Fine," I say. "Yes." Maybe she and Dad can help me find a job. That would be nice.

"Darling." She's practically purring, which is bad. She should be interrogating me, not prepping for attack.

"What's up?" I ask. "Seems like you called for something other than making dinner plans."

I hate how attentive Lionel's being, as if my call is any of his business.

"You know," she says, still purring, "when I

mentioned the fireball that wolf pack said you'd made, you laughed. I remember that specifically."

My hands tremble. "Oh."

"And now, what do you know? They sent us a video."

My stomach turns, the bees buzzing, the mousse sitting like a rock. "Uh-huh."

"It's pretty clearly *you*, and you're actually hurling a massive fireball at wolves that were attacking you. Wolves who are all now dead."

"Yeah," I say. "I know it's bad, but the thing is—"

"Bad?" Mom practically squeals. "Darling! This isn't bad. It's *huge*."

"I killed seven people," I whisper.

"Seven filthy *wolves* who were threatening your life." Her voice goes almost supersonic. "You did it yourself—you made that fireball. Darling, I don't think you understand what amazing news this is."

I hang up.

"Is that true?" Lionel's eyes are wide as he pulls up in front of Minerva's apartment.

"It's none of your business." I leap out and slam the stupid door shut, at least, as much as you can really slam one of the dumb McLaren doors. It's not very satisfying, but I suppose that's fitting.

Everything about today has been a disaster. My date, Mom's call, and her glee over my uncontrollable new ability that I still haven't been able to duplicate. I should've known my mother would be pleased to find out that I'd inadvertently killed people. Because, why wouldn't she be?

When I walk through the apartment door, Xander's there, pacing. "Minerva's at the store. She muttered something about cleaning charms." He looks like he's been pacing for a while, like a lion who's been caged, all rangy energy and flashing eyes. "I'm so sorry. I tried not to hear you." He finally looks up at me, those golden eyes turned toward me.

He's the first truly honest person I've spoken with in the last few hours. I can feel that he's telling the truth through the bond. His words vibrate with it. And as much as I want to be mad at him for butting in, I can't seem to manage even an ounce of righteous indignation. I believe him—he wasn't trying to spy.

He didn't want to wreck my date.

"Actually." He winces. "That part might not be true."

"You didn't try not to hear me?"

He shakes his head, scrunching his nose. His golden eyes are especially bright in this moment. "No, I tried my hardest to give you space, but in spite of my efforts, I might have wanted your date to go badly."

Xander's doing it again, here, listening to my thoughts.

"I can't help it." He throws his hands up in the air as he stalks toward the wall, and I can't help thinking how hot he looks when he's pacing.

A thought I realize he probably just heard.

"Well." My cheeks heat up. I hate that I'm blushing over my *thoughts*. "I think you need to sign up for some kind of alpha-training course or something, because if you think Lionel freaked out, just wait until my mom figures out the truth."

"I know." He stops and pivots on the ball of one sneakered foot. "I already called my dad."

I know that's about the worst thing he could have done, at least in his mind. "Thanks," I say.

I don't really have time to process the rest of what he said until he's already gone.

That's when I realize that he said he *wanted* to wreck my date.

Was Xander. . .jealous?

And why does that make me so stinking happy?

3

MINERVA

Six people know what I found in that file Bevin stole.

And we also now know what forced Bevin to descend a second time. I suppose if you're going to do something bad, you may as well go big or go home. But stealing from the akero? Bevin has more guts than I realized.

Popcorn.

Giggles may not be a normal pigeon, but she apparently has very pedestrian tastes. "Look, I gave you a whole handful earlier. That was enough."

More.

"First of all, the bag you insisted I buy is now buried at the bottom of one of these bags I'm schlepping down the street like a chump. And secondly, if I give you more now, it'll make your stomach hurt." I never should have bought the massive popcorn bag at the store, but she was being so polite, perched on the edge of the cart. Clark says I need to reward her good behavior and penalize the bad.

I'm finding both things to be more trying than I expected.

You have no idea what my stomach needs.

I sigh. "The last time you broke into my popcorn, your stomach, the one I don't know at all, emptied its smelly, watery contents all over my nicest rug. Then I knew far more than I ever wanted to know—and I had to clean up after your very difficult-to-know stomach."

Only because you gave me the cheese-flavored kind. Clearly sensing I'm not going to budge, Giggles squawks and flies up, up, up and through the window.

The *closed* window of my patio.

Meanwhile, I'm stuck marching up a million stairs and passing through the front door like a. . .well, like a chump. She can, apparently, pass through anything she'd like. I had a devil of a time spelling the pantry so that she couldn't just fly right through the door and eat anything at any time. "I can't buy unlimited rugs, you know," I shout, continuing our conversation without thinking about it. "If you want to eat whatever you want, you need to prove you can handle it, you dirty pooper."

People around me are looking at me like I'm crazy.

But I'm sure she could hear me.

Or at least, I hope she could.

As I stomp up the stairs, I think about Giggles. With her grey feathers, and her lined neck, and her little orange eyes, she sure looks like a pigeon. . . But no other pigeons can fly through things. No other pigeons can communicate in words. No other pigeons sass their owners.

The poop stuff, I suppose, is normal.

But the rest?

I've asked and asked Giggles what exactly she is, since she's clearly not a normal pigeon, but so far, I've gotten zero helpful information. It makes me think that she might not be sure either. In fact, the more I think about it, the more convinced I become that she's as clueless as I am.

Xander's fight with Lo Ren Fang and his dummy wolves and Roxana's date with the leader of Illuminae's son has taken up a lot of time and energy over the past few days, but we've spent some time talking about my stuff too—like what *I* am exactly. While I put everything I just bought away, I circle through all of it again.

Unfortunately, none of our ideas entirely explain things.

Michael Akero *could* be my dad, if I really am angel-spawn, or on the other hand, he could have been listed as the key on my file because he was the one who sealed it. His name unlocked page after page of magical aptitude tests and some convoluted explanation of a complicated spell that was probably performed on me. Sadly, neither Clark nor I have the runic training to understand what most of it means. We're still not sure whether I'm actually angel-spawn or just some kind of anomalous, special-needs misfit, like I always thought I was.

Roxana breezes through her bedroom door, and I nearly drop a jar of pickled toadstools.

"What are you doing home?" I carefully shelve the toadstools high enough that Xander and Izaak won't see them. They act like they're a snack, not a garnish. "Date didn't go well?"

Her eyes flash. "Did you know that Xander can

hear our *thoughts*? Did you know he can—" She uses two fingers to make little legs-walking movements. "—follow us around like a lurker in our brains, listening in on what we say and what we feel?"

I have no idea how to react. "Why would you even think that?"

She shrugs in an exaggerated way. "Oh, I don't know. Maybe because he was listening in on my whole date and making snarky comments. I mean, thanks to his stupid jokes and jabs, I accidentally disclosed how he bonded all of us. . .to Lionel."

"You—what?"

She shakes her head, dropping into a kitchen chair. "It wasn't good, I know. That's why I told Xander to get some remedial alpha training, like, yesterday."

My mind's spinning. We agreed to keep the information between us until we figured out exactly how it would work or what it meant—the demon council knowing was bad enough. But now the Illuminae also know?

I'm typing out a text to everyone to tell them that we need to talk when my phone rings.

It's the precinct.

"Hello?"

"I know it's your night off," my partner Amber says.

That's not a good way to start a phone call.

"But my brother's in trouble, and I need some backup."

"Where are you?"

Ignoring my question, she answers one I didn't ask. "My brother's in the holding tank."

Which means he's magically drunk—a zombie,

basically. Vampires can't really get drunk, at least, not without drinking the blood of a drunk or high human, which is prohibited. Impaired humans can't consent, after all. "I'll be right in," I say.

I may have an actual pack now, but if I were picking my own team, Amber would be near the top of the list of people I'd select. I can't ignore her cry for help any more than I'd ignore one from Roxana.

"You have to work?" Roxana's shoulders slump. "So I guess we aren't talking about this dumb thing right now?"

"I'll call Xander on my way in to work," I promise.

She sighs. "Fair enough. Maybe we can talk tomorrow. Today was your first day off, right?"

"I hope I'll be back in an hour or two, but if not, yes, I'm also off tomorrow." I'm barely out the door before Giggles comes winging around the corner and lands on my shoulder. She fluffs up and swivels her head, looking around. "You've forgiven me?"

Not even close, but that doesn't mean I want you getting smashed, attacked, or injured.

"I actually kept myself safe for, well, for my whole life before bonding you." I pause. "And you're a pigeon, so it's not like there's really much you can do to stop someone if they really want to smash, attack, or injure me."

Sure. She huffs.

A pigeon just huffed at me. She's been my familiar for a while, but it feels like she does some new, weirdly human thing, every day.

Whatever you say.

"Hey."

She turns, just like a human would.

"Do you happen to know what I am?"

You're Minerva.

Singularly helpful, as usual. "I know I'm Minerva." I drop to a whisper, as if that will make me seem less crazy, *whispering* to my pigeon instead of talking. "But what I mean is, do you know whether my father's an akero?"

Feathers. She nods. *Yes. That's why I chose you.*

I stumble, nearly face-planting a construction sign. Giggles' claws dig into my shoulder, and her tiny body —bitsy wings flapping like crazy—floats me back to a vertical position.

See? I told you that you need my help.

"But you're saying that you could tell my father was an akero?" I'm not sure whether it's what I'm saying or the simple fact that I'm talking to a pigeon, but people are starting to gawk at me as we pass.

You're supposed to call Xander. You promised Roxana.

"You weren't even in the room. How would you know that?"

I always hear you.

I'm understanding a little more why Roxana was so irritated. Having someone listening in and commenting on the things you say or do after the fact is annoying. "Always?" I jostle my shoulder a little, and she fluffs up, glaring at me with one beady, orange eye. "We may need to set some ground rules." Which is probably exactly what Roxana wants with Xander.

I call him.

He picks right up. "Hello?"

"I'm headed in to work, and maybe you already know all this, but Roxana says you can hear us through the bond. Have you been spying on me for the last two days?" The idea's horrifying. I had the most awful upset stomach this morning. I'm not sure how he'd even be able to look at me if he heard or smelled any part of what I went through.

And I sing in the shower.

Like, not things people want to hear. Thanks to the fan and a white noise machine, no one hears me outside of the bathroom, but. . .

"I've just heard her, so far," Xander says. "But it's a problem. I agree."

"And you're looking into it?"

Xander sighs. "I'm not quite sure how to look into it. I mean, it's not like we have alpha school." He pauses. "Actually, they might. I'm not sure. I was kicked out of wolf school when I was like seven, remember?"

And this is our leader. How fabulous. "There must be someone you can call." I'm entering the subway. I'm about to lose him. "Call them." I hang up.

I always get some strange looks when I go into the subway. . .with a pigeon on my shoulder. You'd think gloffee might help me with that, seeing as Giggles is my magical familiar, but I suppose a pigeon looks normal enough that the glamour doesn't kick in to keep normies from seeing a bird.

"You can't have birds on the subway," a man with a briefcase says. "It's unsanitary, and pigeons are the worst of all."

"Oh." I nod. "I'll be sure to remember that in the future."

The man frowns.

Giggles fluffs up and chitters.

His eyes widen and he turns away. When we get off

at my stop, only three stops from where we got on, Giggles flutters past the man. . .and deposits something on the back of his coat.

"We've talked about this," I hiss. "You can't go doing things like that—this sort of thing is why no one likes pigeons." I whip my wand out. This is exactly what gloffee's intended to cover for. I mutter the spell without thinking. "*Tersus*."

Only, instead of cleaning up the back of the man's coat, a cloud of dust and sparkles whips around the entire subway car, and as the doors close, I notice that all the accumulated dirt on the floor, the film on the windows, the trash in the corners, and all the other nastiness. . .is just gone.

The poop, however, looks pristine. Shinier, even, than when she made it.

I sigh plaintively. "Well, that was a flop, but I guess it could've been worse."

Giggles preens.

"Wait." I'm talking to my bird now. In public. And I don't really care. Plenty of crazy people in New York. I finally fit in. But I do need to confirm a suspicion. "Did *you* just cause that to misfire?"

Giggles pauses, turns a very flat expression on me, and goes back to cleaning her feathers.

It's pointless asking her things she either doesn't want to answer or doesn't have the capacity to answer. I've tried it a lot in the past two days, and I've come to the conclusion that Giggles has her own opinions, and I'll have to wait for her to decide to share them.

"I should've bonded a golden retriever," I mutter.

Giggles hisses. *Those dopey dogs couldn't handle you.*

A familiar wouldn't be able to handle *me?* I think she

has a very backward view of our roles, but I'll have to address that later. I'm walking through the precinct doors at the same time as Peter Chester and his horrible partner, Rufus Ridgeline.

"Really?" I can't help lifting my eyebrows as I breeze past Peter. "You still carry a lunchbox?"

Peter's carrying an over-the-shoulder bag, but in the corner of it, I can see the shining metal of the edge of his stupid Alvin Brilliantus lunchbox. I've seen it, so I know it's the one where the wizard's vanquishing the level seven demon-spawn that was trying to destroy a town in Peru in order to Descend.

"It's a collector's edition," Rufus says in his typically gruff, gravelly voice. "Probably cost more than your monthly salary."

"We get paid the same thing," I say.

"No, we don't," Peter says. "As mages, you and I are paid the same." He shrugs. "The wolves and vampires aren't."

I don't even have time to express my disgust about that injustice, because Amber meets me two steps inside the door, her expression eager. "Okay, so here's the thing."

I try to get far enough away from the idiot brigade that they can't hear what we're talking about.

"There were wolves at the bar where my brother was. . ." She coughs. "Anyway, my brother's really strong, and he apparently has a pretty bad temper when he's a zombie, so. . ."

"What happened?"

Before Amber can answer, Peter Chester bellows, "He destroyed a car. That's what."

Amber's cringe is confirmation.

"That car was a hummer that belonged to my partner Rufus's cousin."

The werewolf world's small, and I figure there are pretty good odds that all the wolves in this building are part of Lo Ren Fang's pack—Xander's enemies now.

Which means they're my enemy too, if they know who I am.

Until recently, Xander looked to Lo Ren as his alpha. He thought Lo Ren was helping him, but recently we discovered that Lo Ren had been lying to Xander for years. Xander was an alpha, and Lo Ren kept that fact a secret from the wolf who needed to hear it most. In fact, to hear Roxana tell it, Lo Ren would've killed Xander if she hadn't been there threatening to expose him. Roxana said Lo Ren insisted Xander was fraying as well, which he clearly wasn't.

Now that Xander has bonded his own pack—nontraditional or not—Lo Ren *really* hates him. He says they can't both remain in Manhattan. I grab Amber's arm and drag her out into the small foyer, waiting until the doors have closed before warding the tiny room for sound. Thankfully, my rapid-fire spell works.

"I'm not sure I'm the person to help with this," I mutter. "You know I want to help. . ." I trail off, unable to tell Amber about Xander or my connection to him, because I'm not keen on dragging her into something even bigger.

"The wolf's insisting on pressing charges," Amber says, "and I think it's because Peter and Rufus are pushing him to do it. My brother just finished basic training, and he's got his test to be an officer in two weeks. If they book him on this. . ."

She thought *I* could help? I can't imagine how.

The only person Rufus and Peter hate more than her is me.

And if her brother has that test coming up, he should *not* have been out drinking the blood of the inebriated. It's always been against the angelic laws, and if you want to enforce the law, you really shouldn't be breaking it. I want to point that out, but I have a brother too.

And I've made my share of mistakes.

Not bonehead ones like going zombie, but still. We all do things we shouldn't, and sometimes our timing is really, really bad. "I want to help," I say. "But I'm not sure what I can possibly do. I mean, if they have evidence that he damaged that wolf's property—"

"They do. The Hummer's in pretty bad shape." She bites her lip. "I guess I just assumed you'd have a plan to fix it. You always fix everything."

I hate that I'm letting her down, but short of destroying state evidence, I'm not sure what I can do. "Why don't you start with telling me what happened —in the right order."

Behind us, there's a loud bang. Peter's leaning against the glass doors. He must have whammed against it with his hand. He's saying something, but thanks to my sound spell, we can't hear him. His face starts turning red, and he whips his wand out. He's clearly trying a stronger spell—after a zap, nothing happens—and then he turns redder still as he tries another. "You better hurry. I have no idea what he's doing," I say, "but it doesn't look nice."

"I'm honestly not sure what happened," Amber says. "As far as I know, my brother's never done anything like this before." She shakes her head. "Never, I swear. But then I just got a call, and sure enough, when I go out there, he's a zombie, and the vehicle's destroyed."

That catches me short. "Why would he start behaving like that now, of all times?" Completing basic training is really hard. You don't usually qualify to take the test unless it's something you really want.

She shrugs. "No idea. By the time I reached the scene, that massive, boxy metal car was smashed in like he was just whamming it over and over—and poor Jake was gibbering senselessly." Her lips tremble for a moment, but she gets it together. "Typical zombie, I guess. I can't ask him anything right now, obviously."

I think about it for a moment. I mean, could the wolves have planned it? They know who Xander's friends are. They saw our faces. I'm a government employee. Could they have targeted Amber to get to me? "Is there any video footage?" I ask. "Did you check neighboring businesses?"

"The bar was a normie bar." Amber sounds disgusted.

We both say, "Gloffee," at the same time.

Gloffee's amazing stuff that keeps all our magic hidden from the normal humans who have no idea we even exist. But stupid gloffee also keeps normie cameras from picking up any decent footage.

"Look, I'm worried this might have been a setup," I say.

Before I can say anything else, I notice that the Chief's standing next to Peter, gesturing. He pulls out his wand and points. He's zapping the door, too? Why?

You can walk right through the barriers of a sound spell.

I push the door open, forcing them to step back.

"What kind of spell was that?" the Chief asks. "I've never felt a barricade quite like that before."

"A barricade?" I ask. "I just blocked the sound."

"With what spell?" Peter asks, his typical sneer gone for once.

I blink. Then I shake my head. "What do you mean?"

"What did you say?" the Chief asks.

"She said day seen-eh," Amber says.

"Oh." I nod, remembering. "I just said cease, but in Latin."

"That's not the silence spell," Peter says. "That's not supposed to be a spell at all."

I shrug. "I mean, I didn't want you guys to follow us, so I think I got confused."

"I hit it with a dozen spells," Peter says. "None of them got through."

"And I used a penetrate and a collapse spell," the Chief said. "Nothing."

"Oh. . ." I'm frowning, but I can't think what else to say.

"We need to talk, Lucent," the Chief says.

"It was an accident," I say.

"Follow me to my office."

Amber looks distressed, but none of us dare to argue. A moment later, I'm closing the door behind myself. "Sometimes my spells misfire, and sometimes the misfires are like that," I mutter. "Not bad, but just. . .too much."

The Chief sits and steeples his fingers. "How often do you think I cast, Minerva?"

I blink.

"How many times a week do you see me whip out my wand?"

I shake my head. This isn't going where I expected. "I mean, I saw you with it today, but I'd say usually. . .never." I shrug. "I'm not saying you don't do a lot of great things, but—"

"But I'm valued for my brain, for my administrative skills, and for my authority."

I nod slowly. "Yes."

"That's why I called you in here. You know that I know your secret. Your spellwork will always be erratic, because although your magical aptitude is better than anyone could have hoped, you're half human, so your casting is unpredictable."

I want to argue—I'm not half human, or at least, I don't think I am. Not anymore. But telling him that I suspect I'm half angel would be catastrophic, even if he believed me. I force a smile. "Yes. I can't argue with that."

He flattens his palms against the desk. "Now, you know that my position is an elected one, and so your father and I worked up a plan. When I took over for him, do you know how we did it?"

I frowned. "He died."

"Yes, that's true, but we had already worked out our plan when he did. He said he'd name me as his successor, which he did in some paperwork left in his desk. I took over for the rest of his six-year term, and by the end of it, I had a solid track record. I was voted in easily on my own merits four years later."

"That was smart," I say. Though to be honest, it sounds a little shady.

"I was voted in a little under two years ago," the Chief says. "I thought about retiring before the last election—the elections are chaotic and tiring, but I had promised your father." He tilts his head. "Did you know that with all your energy and zeal, you almost made Guardian, in spite of my objections?"

I wish I could fake my shock a little better. "Really?"

He arches one eyebrow. "Your father was right about one thing—you're a little spitfire. You do anything you set your very determined mind to. I hung on, and now, I'm finally ready to retire, and I'm naming you as my interim successor."

"But I don't want you to," I say.

The Chief's entire expression falls. "How could you not want to be Chief of Paranormal Affairs? It's perfect for you. You're smart, sensible, and you'd never have to cast again, if you don't want to, not at work. Think of the good you could do—the injustices you could correct."

Shoot. He has me there.

I think about Amber, and how as Chief, I could look into what happened with her brother more thoroughly. I could make sure that demon-spawn are treated with more respect, at least in my precinct. I could try to repair the vampire-werewolf relations. I could. . .

"If you don't do a good job, or if you hate the work, you don't have to run for re-election in four years. You can just bow out. But if you find that it's a good fit, you could win the spot for yourself—I'm sure of it.

You wouldn't be the guardian you wanted to be, but this would be great in its own way."

"Fine," I say. "Alright."

The Chief beams as he stands, leaning over to rummage around in his right-side desk drawer. "I have something else to show you. On the day you're named Chief, I'm supposed to give this to you." He pulls out a small, slim box.

It's crafted of the finest mahogany wood, and it gleams.

I freeze.

"You know what this is," he says, smiling even more broadly as he straightens.

"It was lost," I say. "He was supposed to leave it to Clark."

"He was never going to leave it to Clark." The Chief rolls his eyes. "The whole reason he had this made was to give it to you."

It's the box that holds Dad's akero-feather wand. "But Clark said—"

"The mage who crafted this said it could focus even the most scattered magic—with the power of the angel from whom the feather came."

"Do you know which angel it was?" I ask.

"The feather was white with gold tips," he says. "That can only be one angel."

Michael.

Probably. . .my father.

4

MINERVA

y father died *years* ago—like more than six years.

"Why didn't you give me the wand after Dad died?" I can't quite help the accusatory note from creeping into my tone.

The Chief smiles. "Your father didn't want me to give it to you at first. Remember, power has never been your issue. You didn't need a boost before. You were struggling to control what you had. But lately, your misfired spells are different—stronger, even. I think you're ready to use this, and I think that you've earned it."

I don't really like how he seems to be trying to step into my father's place, but I appreciate that his intentions are, at least, good. "Clark thought he was supposed to get it." I'm frowning, so I try to blank my face.

"Your father did say he used Clark's college fund to pay for it in some way, but I'm sure your brother's fine now. He's got a job, and he's done with school, right?"

Something moving far to my side catches my attention. It's Amber, with Giggles sitting on her shoulder, flapping her wings. I glance down at my phone and see her message.

THEY'RE ABOUT TO PICK UP THE VEHICLE AND BRING IT IN.

Once it's been logged as evidence, once the officer who brings it in testifies that witnesses at the scene accused Amber's brother of damaging it, Jake's done for.

Our window to take action is rapidly closing.

"Um, yeah, Clark's fine." I stand. "You know what? I'll think about it."

"You'll—" The Chief pulls the wand back without even opening the box. "Well, when you make the right decision, your wand will be waiting."

"You're saying you won't give me the wand my father left for me unless I accept the position as Paranormal Affairs District of Manhattan Chief?"

He compresses his lips.

"That feels. . ." I shake my head. "Not right."

"Your father told me to make sure you did the right thing. He said you were bullheaded, and clearly he was right." He stands. "If you flat-out refuse, we can talk. I'm not holding it hostage, but I think you'll realize it's the smart move."

"How long do I have to decide?" I ask.

"Two days." He drops one palm against his desk and leans closer. "I think that's plenty of time—and that's how long I have."

"How long you. . .?" I can't help my frown. Is he dying or something?

"I love this job. I'd have muddled along for another

term or two, but my wife's sick of doing everything alone." He sighs. "She issued an ultimatum of her own."

The idea that the massive, powerful paranormal affairs chief is being ordered around by a tiny little woman—his wife barely clears my shoulder—is comical to me. "Well, I guess we both have a lot to think about over the next few days."

"Not me," he says. "I've already done my thinking. Nothing matters more than Adeline."

That's sort of cute. I've barely cleared the office doorway when Peter descends on my left side, his dumb old falcon shrieking. Amber was already standing on the other—but Giggles is gone from her shoulder.

"What did he want?" Peter asks. "Are you in trouble?"

"We need to go," Amber hisses. "Now."

I still can't think of what we might be able to do—until out of the corner of my eye, I see Giggles. . .hovering over Peter Chester's desk. His partner's pulling something out of the juvenile Brilliantus lunchbox, and it's practically gleaming from the place where Rufus sets it on the corner of the desk. I'm suddenly alarmed that Giggles might do something stupid to Rufus or the lunchbox. . .or both.

Like poop on them.

And then, if I try to spell-remove the evidence, she might tinker with my stupid spell again. I swear, I really need some kind of trainer or something. Because unless I can eliminate the evidence of Giggles' interference, Peter will lose his mind and. . .

Eliminate the evidence.

An idea occurs to me.

If the stupid wolf pack orchestrated this whole thing somehow to punish me and Xander, as I suspect they might have, and if poor Jake is somehow collateral damage, it's my duty to protect him. I clearly can't *eliminate* Rufus's cousin's car. That would be insane, and also, having a car that's missing might be worse than a mangled one. But. . .what if I could spell it and somehow repair it? It's no less insane than swapping clothing with a bunch of teenage girls, and I did that when I was a teen.

The tingling starts in my elbows this time, which is a little strange, but the important thing is that I can feel it. Tingling means I'm on the right path. My magic's telling me that there's something here. If I could just get to the car before the thing's logged. . .

"I have an idea." I grab Amber's elbow, and then I turn to Peter. "I'm in big, big trouble. You got me." I nod. "I better get home, since I'm not even working tonight, and focus on repenting for what I did."

"But what did you do?" Peter asks. "Was that illegal magic in the foyer? How did you cast that protection bubble that no one could break?"

I'd forgotten about that. "Uh, yeah, it was. . .you know—don't want to incriminate myself." I shrug and we race out the door, Giggles flying so high and so diagonally overhead that all I can see is the top of her head. Only as we're nearing the parking lot does she shift.

That's when I realize that she stole the stupid lunchbox.

"Mother *feather*," I say. "Why would you do that? They're already mad enough."

Giggles drops it then, and I catch it out of reflex. Then she tosses her head at the transport truck up ahead.

It's too late.

I have zero time to try and repair the large, yellow H2 that's sitting on the trailer up ahead. It's been logged, the serial number recorded, and poor Jake is screwed.

You aren't a normal witch. Giggles settles on my shoulder and nudges the side of my cheek. *I brought what you need. If you* think *about it, you already know.*

Brought it? She *stole* the lunchbox, and how could that possibly help? Is she trying to get me thrown into lockup too? Why would she think I should know what to do in this bizarre situation?

"Know?" I want to scream. "What do I know?" But then I remember. "I did have an idea." I look pointedly at Amber. "I thought maybe I could repair the damage your brother did, but now that the car's been logged, it's too late." I point. "Isn't that it? Or is there another Hummer somewhere that your brother smashed like a Coke can?"

Amber's staring at me strangely, probably still a little unaccustomed to someone talking to a pigeon. She shakes her head. "Yeah, that's the one." She glances down at the Brilliantus lunchbox. "Did Giggles just steal Peter's lunchbox?"

I almost throw the dumb thing. "Yes, and now she's insisting that I can somehow use it."

"She's *insisting?*"

I almost choke. "No, I mean, I'm assuming she stole it because she wants me to use it." I nod. "Like, for my lunch." Sometimes I forget that Amber doesn't know I can talk to Giggles, or that Xander bonded us, or that the Demon Council and the Manhattan pack are out to get us.

Sheesh.

I really need to figure out how to pass her off to another partner.

For all I know, it could have actually been the Demon Council who set her brother up. I have too many targets painted on my back right now. "The Chief wants me to take over for him when he retires," I blurt. It's the one secret in my life that I can actually share without putting her at greater risk. "I'm not sure whether I want to do it."

"The Chief—what?" Amber's eyes widen. "You—that's what he wanted to tell you?"

I nod. "He's stepping down. His wife wants him to retire, and he's going to choose me as his interim replacement, if I want him to."

"That's amazing," Amber says. "You'd be so good at that. And the look on Peter's face when he finds out." Her lips compress, and her nose scrunches, and she looks ready to gloat like she's never gloated before.

Just then, as if my big revelations are boring her, Giggles launches off my shoulder and flies into the open window of the tractor trailer rig that's hauling the Hummer into the garage where larger evidence is kept.

She shoots out the other end a moment later, but there's a *lot* of shouting from inside. The truck grinds to a halt and the door swings open. "Did you see that?" The man inside's wearing a uniform that tells me he works with Central Justice. "That insane rat-bird just flew in, pooped on my paperwork, and flew back out." He waves his clipboard around, and I grimace.

It's impressive to me how very much damage one little bird can do with the same trick. "Sorry?" I say.

"Why are you sorry?" the man asks. "It's not like that's your pet."

Amber's eyes cut my way.

The man's muttering as he stomps his way inside. "Have to print up a whole new report now. Stupid flying menaces."

Now. Giggles swoops back down and lands on my shoulder, flapping her wings at me.

"Now, what?" I'm staring at her, but all I see are beady little orange eyes. No other sign of what she did that for. Of what she wants me to do.

"You're talking to her," Amber says. "This time, I'm positive. Does Giggles *talk* to you?"

I sigh. "She's definitely a little strange." I look at the lunchbox, with its brilliant yellow paint, and its blocky corners, and I glance up at the busted-up Hummer, wondering what on earth she thinks I'm going to do, when it hits me.

"Stand back, Amber."

"What?" She frowns. "Stand back. . .from what?"

I lift up the lunchbox, handle up, and I toss my head. "Get it on the platform," I hiss.

Giggles doesn't miss a beat.

She clutches the lunchbox in her feet, flies up, sets the lunchbox on the platform, and nudges it up underneath the Hummer. The spell begins to form inside of me. It takes me a moment, but then I can sense the words I need to say.

"Whatever you're doing, hurry," Amber says.

"There are two squad cars coming. Less than a minute before someone will see us."

I wanted to hop up and check out the serial number, but it's too late for that. I just have to hope my magic's leading me in the right direction.

"Loca negotiandi, spatia nitida, tempus ad noviora gradaria facienda."

"What did you say?" Amber asks. "Because it looks like it didn't work."

The tingling turns into a tsunami of magic pooling inside of me, and then it strikes, along with a collapse and rebound of pressure. There's a sharp crack and then a pop, and almost at the same time, the shiny yellow lunchbox expands, and the Hummer contracts, and I'm staring at a bright, new, pristine H2. . .and a collapsed, contorted, mashed yellow lunchbox.

Amber freezes. "Holy mother of all wings, what did you just do?"

I shake my head. "I mean, I just tampered with evidence. We could be going to jail."

"I'll insist on adjoining cells," she mutters.

Giggles flies underneath the shiny, new Hummer, grabs the handle on the mangled lump of lunchbox, and hefts it into the air, winging it back toward me.

"What are we supposed to do with that, now?" Amber asks.

I sigh, catching it when Giggles drops it. The sharp edge cuts the palm of my hand, and I can feel the tingling, and I know. To each strange spell I cast, there's a price. Sometimes it's a small price, and some-times it's large. But this one taught me something.

I may not want to be Chief.

I may hate the idea.

I want to be out in the world, defending righteous demon-spawn, and taking down the bad ones. I want to be righting wrongs and fighting evil, and generally making the world a better place. But my type of magic is weird, and what I can do isn't well-suited to fighting demons.

It's pretty tremendous at fixing wacky injustices, though.

I squeeze my hand around the twisted handle of the crumpled lunchbox, and I march back inside with it.

Peter's sitting on the corner of Rufus's desk, cackling. For some reason I can't explain, I'm almost certain it's about Jake. Their heads whip toward us as we walk inside.

"I accidentally took your lunchbox outside," I say. "And I dropped it." I cringe a little. "I'm afraid it got a bit crushed."

Peter leaps to his feet. "You—what?"

I walk almost to where he is, and I hold out my hand. "Here. Sorry about the damage."

Peter's spluttering too much to yell, but Rufus recovers faster. Typical werewolf. "You can't destroy his property. You'll pay for this."

"Actually," I say, "you two might be wise to let it go." The tingling in the bottoms of my feet tells me I'm on the right path. "Because you're talking to the future Chief of the Manhattan precinct."

The Chief's door bangs open, and I'm virtually certain, thanks to the timing, that he has some kind of listening charms placed around here. "You said you needed time." But he's beaming. "You said you had to think about it."

I shrug. "I guess I didn't need to think as long as I thought I would."

He's striding across the room, and he claps me on the shoulder before Peter's even taken the mangled mess of his lunchbox.

"But what about my lunchbox?" Peter asks. "She ruined it."

The Chief scowls in his direction. "It's a *lunchbox*, son. Man up." He takes it from me, chucks it at Peter's desk with a clatter, and leads me toward his office. "We have a lot of things to talk about, you know. You've made the right decision."

"Are you really going to be Chief?" Amber asks, following us like a puppy. "Because that's amazing."

"You can come with us to talk about it," Chief Lumos says. "You'll be part of the transition, too." He waves us all into his office and starts explaining what my most important tasks will be.

"If you want to remain her partner," he says, "there are a number of things you could do. I didn't replace my partner." His brow furrows.

My dad had been his partner for more than twenty years, and after he became a guardian and then Chief, Chief Lumos never found another one, opting instead to do management work for the precinct.

Amber's asking about vacancies when someone bursts into his office. "Chief Lumos," Wisteria says. "There's been a problem." When she realizes Amber and I are in his office, her distress turns into a hard glare.

Wisteria's one of the most level-headed vampires I've ever met, and when she was injured in the line of duty last year, I was delighted to hear she was moving to the administrative offices. She and Amber are actually friends. I'm not sure why she looks so upset.

"Something *happened* to the Hummer that her brother destroyed." She arches one eyebrow and tosses her head in Amber's direction. "It's. . ." She shakes her head. "Well, it's not destroyed at all."

The Chief frowns. "What does that mean?"

"There's not a scratch on it." Wisteria drops her voice. "In fact, Rufus's cousin said he was in a fender bender a few weeks ago that he hadn't had time to repair, but even the back bumper's *perfect*."

The Chief turns slowly toward me. "Do you know anything about this, Lucent?"

Giggles, perched on the edge of a lamp beside me, coos. I shake my head and try to look innocent. "Sorry, sir. I have no idea what might have happened—maybe it was a glamour that faded? Some kind of joke?"

He stares at me for a moment, and then turns back to Wisteria. "Well, if there's no damage, we have no evidence, correct?"

"But we *had* evidence," she says. "The driver from Central Justice says it was completely pulverized, and then he went inside to get new paperwork, and then—"

"Why would he need new paperwork?" The Chief arches one eyebrow.

"Some kind of manic bird ruined his," she says. "And when he came back out, the vehicle was. . ." She shrugs. "I'm not sure—it was repaired."

"Did you check the serial numbers?" he asks.

She nods. "The number's identical."

"Have tech see whether it's been tampered with."

"Already did," she says. "Magically sound. No spells, no transmogrification, nothing."

The Chief's smiling now. "Well, then it looks like we made a mistake somewhere down the line. Amber, maybe you better check on your brother, and if he looks alright, give him a stern warning to check humans more carefully before feeding and send him on his way."

Amber jumps to her feet. "Thank you, sir." She half-bows. "Thank you so much."

He clears his throat. "Don't thank me. Can't arraign without evidence."

I stand up, too. "I should help her."

The Chief doesn't argue. "Of course you should. Good news for your partner's brother, that it was all just a misunderstanding."

"But what am I supposed to—"

"Sounds like it must have been some kind of elaborate prank," Chief Lumos says. "The truant mages are always working up new charms, you know—wreaking havoc, wasting our time. I imagine they charmed the Hummer to make it look destroyed, and Rufus's hot-headed cousin blamed the closest zombie."

Wisteria's mouth forms an 'o.' "That's terrible," she mutters on her way out.

I doubt the Chief believes his own story, but I appreciate him for making it up. "Whatever you did," he whispers as I leave, "keep up the good work." He's grinning as I pass him.

Amber pauses just outside the door. "Can we tell people about. . .your retirement?"

"I don't see why not," Chief Lumos says. "It's really

a done deal. Once I submit her name, Minerva'll have to be ratified, but that's basically a rubber stamp."

"What does ratified mean?" I ask.

He waves me off. "Just a very basic formality. The Paranormal Affairs Chief's always a mage, but the other branches have to sign off on my nomination."

"Branches?" I ask.

"You know, the Manhattan pack, the local Demon Council, the Dragona King, who I think you actually know, and the Sublime Chancellor for the vampires. They don't really care who I choose, though. Don't worry."

Only, I'm pretty sure the Chief's wrong about that.

Roxana's father *might not* be holding a grudge, though I wouldn't count on it, but I'm pretty sure all the others are going to be adamantly opposed to his selection of Minerva Lucent. The Demon Council and the Manhattan Pack for sure, but I'm guessing the vampire's Sublime Chancellor remembers that I flash-boiled his son a few months ago. . .

Which means, I'm as screwed as Peter's lunchbox.

As I walk out, I notice that instead of standing beside a dragon, Alvin Brilliantus, on the tiny portion of the lunchbox I can see, is sitting on the driver's side of a large, yellow Hummer.

BEVIN

Once, right after my mom died, I had to go to a normie food bank for dinner for several weeks. It was before the mage council identified that I was an orphan and assigned me to a demon-spawn reform facility. The soup was full of lima beans and the aftertaste was terrible, but I forced it down. I learned quickly that even awful tasting soup was better than an empty belly.

But right now, I'm struggling.

This soup tastes really, really bad.

"You just have to sign." The woman with the thick, blocky black glasses sliding down her nose glares at me as she proffers a dark fountain pen. "If you're not someone who can write, just draw an x."

"Not someone who can—" I consider shocking the glasses right off the end of her bulbous nose. I'm pretty sure I'm angry enough to do it. "I know how to write." I glare right back at her. "But would *you* sign this?"

"For a six hundred thousand dollar check, I'd sign

most anything." She drops the pen in my hand, and pushes both her hands against her hips. "Just do it."

My nostrils flare as I read the simple statement one more time.

I, Bevin Bahar, accept the charitable donation from Orion Sol, leader of the North American Illuminae, for the purpose of rebuilding my business. Mr. Sol regrets the way the Demon Council attacked my place of business without provocation, and as a protector of the innocent and helpless of the magical world, he has stepped in to lend generous aid. I'm filled with gratitude and admiration for his bold and decisive leadership and generous care.

I mean, he is giving me six hundred thousand dollars. I keep repeating that in my head. It's much better than the unnatural flames with which my own kind burned my shop to the ground, killing my sentinel chicken and destroying all my belongings. But putting my pen to paper and saying that I think he's a protector of the innocent and helpless? I don't like saying that I'm innocent or helpless, and I really don't like declaring that he's a bold and decisive leader full of generosity.

But on the other hand, it *is* six hundred thousand dollars, so after hemming and hawing and agonizing for an obnoxiously long time, I do it.

I hold my breath, and I sign my name. *Bevin Bahar.*

Only afterward does the horrible woman explain that I also need to read the ridiculous statement aloud for a tape recording. When I balk, she frowns again. "So, you really can't read?"

I huff. "For the love of toadstools."

"No one loves toadstools," she says. "They spread like a plague, and they smell when they get wet."

"Even you have to admit that the pickled and charmed ones aren't bad," I say, "though they do smell. But my point is that I already signed. Why do I have to read it too?"

She points at the fine print at the bottom, in which I acknowledge that I'll be happy to do two in-person appearances at the time of Mr. Sol's choosing, and that I'll record my statement for use in promotional materials at his discretion.

Promotional materials? Ugh.

It's worse than the chalky, slimy lima beans.

But I do it.

Filthy lucre.

I half-expect to descend when I finish the stupid recording.

"Mr. Sol has also taken the liberty of arranging a bid for you on the rebuild of your little shop as well." She hands me a bright blue folder with a startlingly golden sun logo on the front. It shimmers even without light touching it, so it's clearly charmed. Who has the extra money to waste on charmed folder logo stickers?

"I'll be finding my own contractors," I say, dropping the folder on the desk. "But thanks."

"You should take the bid at least." The woman pushes her glasses back up. "You may find it harder than you expect to retain a contractor, given what happened to your last shop."

This time, I'm the one frowning. "What does that mean?"

"Very few contractors may be willing to work for a business that's squarely in the cross-hairs of the Demon Council." She shrugs. "Who knows? Maybe

I'm wrong. Maybe they'll all be clamoring to work for you."

I pause long enough to pick up the folder. I'm sure she *is* wrong, but just in case. . . And moments later, I'm finally walking away from the Illuminae's Manhattan office, holding a cashier's check for six hundred grand. It's hard to believe, really. I march immediately to the bank and deposit the thing in my account, alongside all the funds my friends raised, bringing my total balance up to a million dollars—a sum I never even imagined I might have.

With all the stalling I did, I'm almost late to my appointment at Grand Central Gloffee. In the end, I could've saved myself the time. I meet with three contractors, but as if that woman's words prove prophetic, as soon as they realize who I am and what happened to my second-hand magic shop, they all bow out.

I'm nursing a strong, bitter cup of gloffee when my phone rings.

"Bevin!"

It's my real estate agent. I actually feel pretty guilty. "Raven," I say. "I'm so sorry I haven't had time to call you back. The thing is, I was going to sell the lot, but my friends had this fundraiser, and—"

"You have an offer," Raven says. "Can you believe it? The property has been live for two days, and you already have a formal offer!"

I can't believe it. "Yes, but did you hear me? I think I'm going to rebuild, so I won't be selling the lot after all."

"You're—what?" I hear a strange crackling sound. "You're breaking up for some reason, so I can't really hear you. I'll just forward the email with the offer over, and once I'm back to the office, I'll call you again. Okay?" She hangs up.

Without much else to do, I open my email. I mean, I won't need to sell the land my shop was built on now, but while I think about what other contractors I could use, I may as well take a look at—*by Gabriel's wings.* I knock my gloffee over and spill sticky, vampire-flavored gloffee all over the side of the sofa and my leg.

"Mother feather," Gavin says.

"It was hot, but not so hot it would burn me," I say. "Don't worry."

"I'm not worried about you—you'll heal." Gavin crouches next to the ugly orange corduroy sofa. "But this beauty—ugh. Nothing gets Izaak-flavored gloffee out."

"I'm sure you're exaggerating," I say. "I'll just call Minerva and—"

Gavin sighs and straightens. "Don't bother. With her luck, she'd probably set the whole shop on fire. And anyway, it won't matter soon."

"What won't matter?" I can't help my frown. "You're redecorating? No more 1970s-inspired velvet sofas? Are you getting rid of the corduroy chairs, too?"

Gavin doesn't even pretend to be amused. "The owner's selling the whole building. Not enough money in it, I guess."

"New York real estate—not enough money in it?" I must've heard him wrong. "What does that mean?"

His shoulders slump. "Building was rent controlled. Only way out is selling up."

"Well that stinks," I say. "For you."

Gavin nods, his expression dejected. "I was finally competing with Glamour Gloffee—but there's no way I'll be able to find another place like this. My entire profit will be gone, between the move and the higher rent."

I feel bad for him—so bad that I text Clark and ask him to look into the stain I'm leaving behind. CAN YOU MAGIC-REMOVE A STAIN ON THE RIGHT SIDE OF OUR SOFA AT GAVIN'S? IT'S MY GOOFUP, AND HE'S HAVING A BAD DAY.

STARTING MY NEW JOB, he texts back. WILL SWING BY WHEN DONE.

THANKS!

I feel a little better as I schlep myself through the front door of Minerva's place, and I'm almost ready to force myself to look at the stupid sun-emblazoned folder. Maybe, knowing that I have a million to spend, the quote will even be reasonable. And who knows? It's possible that stupid Orion Sol won't make me record any more video testimonials even if I select his crews for the build.

That would be nice, but it's not very likely. He feels like the kind of guy who always collects.

"What's wrong with you?" Roxana pauses the vampire-werewolf movie she's watching.

"Wait, so are you team Edward or team Jacob?" I arch one eyebrow.

"You've seen this?" She swallows.

"Everyone's seen it," I say. "But you didn't answer the question. Werewolf or vampire?"

Roxana presses several buttons before she manages to shut the television off, and I can't help noticing her face has flushed bright pink. "Sparkly vampires? Really?" She scoffs. "The whole thing is ridiculous."

I'm going to have to watch her. She's acting really strange, and now I'm starting to wonder whether she likes one of the boys in the film. "How'd it go with your date last night?" Maybe I can pump her for some information on the Sols.

"Terrible," she mutters. "Never date two men at once."

"You dated two men?" I can't help my smile. "Look at you—growing up."

She frowns. "Not on purpose, and stop distracting me. What's wrong with you?"

"Why do you think anything's wrong?"

"You were muttering when you walked through the door," she says. "Why?"

I shake my head. "No reason, really. I mean, I got my money from Orion Sol, and then I had three contractors leave in a huff when they realized my shop had been burned down by the Demon Council, so apparently I'm going to have a pile of money and no shop."

"Why did you tell them about the Demon Council?" Roxana asks. "It's not like you have to disclose why it burned down, right?"

"Well, because I'm a complete moron, of course." I roll my eyes. "I didn't tell them, okay? They figured it out."

"I guess a business burning to the ground in a giant demon-lit bonfire isn't exactly a secret in the supernatural world."

"Guess not," I say.

"Well, I bet the Illuminae—"

I hold up one hand. "Before you suggest calling your boyfriend, I should tell you that they actually submitted a bid on the rebuild." I drop into the large armchair with a plop. "But I'm sure it comes with strings."

"Everything with them does." Her lip's curled, and I should be annoyed at how pretty she looks, even when scowling, but sometimes I just have to sit back and appreciate art for what it is.

"Does it get tiring?"

"What?" She perches on the edge of the sofa across from me. "If you're asking about some kind of construction thing, I'm the wrong one to ask. I've never been involved with any of my dad's business stuff."

I am seeing a little more why she can't find a job. "No, I meant being quite so beautiful."

She snorts in the least lady-like way I've ever seen from her, and it still doesn't really diminish her beauty and elegance. "More tiring than you can possibly imagine, but probably not for the reasons you think."

Sometimes she surprises me. She may not have a lot of life experience, being sheltered since birth, but she's not empty-headed, either.

"What are you going to do?" she asks. "If you can't find a decent contractor to rebuild?"

"Maybe I'll just set up a tent," I say. "I could sell things out of that. With a few good spells, maybe Clark can—"

"Why not just hire normies to build your shop," Roxana says. "It's not like it needs anything in particular to be magical, right? Clark could still ward it for you."

I'm taken aback at her shockingly smart suggestion. "Why didn't I think of that?" Until recently, I had no magic at all. I've spent my adult life catering to the magical people of NYC, but that doesn't mean I can't work with normies. I mean, sure, it's nice that the magical builders literally can get a place up almost overnight, but it's not necessary. Slow and steady can win races, or so I hear. "I wonder what their prices are like."

"I imagine they're a lot like ours," Roxana says.

"What does that mean?" I ask.

She shrugs. "The prices with normies will also vary."

I'm poking around on my phone, looking up contractors and their reviews on some app called *Yelp* when Xander bursts through the door.

Roxana stands immediately. "You." She drops her hands on her hips. "I hope you're here to tell me you've signed up for an 'Alphas for Dummies' class." Her eyes are narrowed, and her full lips are pursed.

"Uh-oh," I say. "What's going on?"

"Oh, you know, the normal." She cocks her head so she can see me, too. "I had a date, and Xander thought he'd come along uninvited. In *my head*."

I frown. "What does that mean?"

"I'm having trouble learning how the alpha bond works," Xander says. "And it turns out, there's no alpha training courses, paid or otherwise. It probably has something to do with the fact that no alphas have ever been willing to admit to even a scrap of vulnerability, and signing up for any kind of course is basically a complete admission that they have no idea what they're doing." He sighs. "But my dad has an alpha friend, and I left him a message, asking whether he thinks his friend might be willing to help me."

"That would be good," Roxana says. "Even if they can just go over the basics. I mean, we really just need you to learn how to give people their space."

"Don't hold your breath, though," Xander says. "The Binnigas wolves aren't really known for being super popular. My dad's 'friend' is probably someone he conned out of money who just hasn't caught him yet or something."

Her eyes widen a little, but she sits back down with an exaggerated sigh.

Xander circles the sofa like a dog that's wondering how hot the fire he's facing really is. "I am sorry, for what it's worth. I don't love Lionel, but I wasn't trying to ruin anything either, I swear."

She nods slowly. "I remember when you just waited in the lobby politely before, when I told you I was fine. You've always given me space, but we do need to get this under control."

"Wolf packs aren't exactly known for providing space to their members." I think back on everything I've ever read. "I think some of the work to carve out space from Xander may fall on us. For instance, when you were a child, didn't your mother teach you the basics of shielding your mind?"

"To what?" Roxana's eyes widen.

"I'm guessing that's a no," I say. "But it's a basic supernatural thing. Wolves aren't the only supernaturals who can invade your thoughts, and I'd think that amongst the dragona—"

"Oh." Roxana nods. "Yeah, but not for the females. Only the males have to worry about that."

"I bet you and I can practice some things that will set up boundaries with the bond," I say.

"I would love any help you can offer," Roxana says.

"As lovely as this female bonding is," Xander says, "and as much as I want to support you guys also establishing some boundaries, I need to talk to Minerva. Is she around?"

I shake my head. "Haven't seen her."

"She got called in urgently to work last night and didn't come home until really late," Roxana says. "I think she's asleep now."

Xander nods. "Okay, well, can you have her call me when she wakes up?"

"Is everything alright?" I ask.

"I have to vacate my apartment," Xander says. "Like, right *now*."

"What?" Roxana looks horrified.

"The pack owns it, right?" I ask. "Maybe you should've seen this one coming."

"We're packing," Xander says, "but with the short notice, we're not sure where we're going to go."

"Clark has that big empty place," Roxana says. "Maybe you could live with him for a while."

"I'm going to ask," Xander says. "But I was hoping I might be able to store some things here."

"Actually, this whole building may be sold soon," I say.

Roxana and Xander both demand more information, so I explain what Gavin told me.

"That's terrible," Roxana says. "I *just* started drinking gloffee, and now I'm going to have to walk two blocks to get some."

"And also Gavin's livelihood, and our neighborhood, and Minerva's apartment," Xander says.

"Well, yeah," Roxana says. "All that stuff, too."

Xander's smiling a goofy smile right at her, and I would want to thump him, except I've felt like that around her a time or two myself. "It's really too bad there's nothing we can do about it," I say. "I'm having enough trouble just trying to get my shop rebuilt, but if Minerva's not even going to be living here, or you guys either, and if Grand Central Gloffee's gone, what's the point?"

"It's so distressing," Roxana says. "All this stuff is changing at once."

"Makes me want to just sell my land," I say. "Someone offered me almost two *million* for it. Can you believe that? It turns out, even though my shop was one and a half stories, there's no limitation how tall the building can be on that land, which makes it worth quite a bit."

Xander blinks. "Plus you have a million from the Illuminae and our fundraiser, right?"

"Oooh, you should buy the building, Bevin!" Roxana stands. "Forget about rebuilding. Just make that little tax firm, or whatever that is next to Gavin, into your shop, and then Xander and Minerva and all the other tenants can pay rent to *you*!"

"It's not like three million would even begin to buy this building," I say. "It's way wider than the tiny spot of land I had, and—"

"It might make a pretty decent downpayment, though," Xander says.

As he says the words, I realize he's right.

Maybe I could buy the building, and then the pack

couldn't kick him out, Minerva wouldn't get booted, and I could evict that little office and make that into my shop. . .

"I think I should call my agent and head down to the bank," I say.

"Maybe I'll come with you," Xander says. "Because for once, maybe things are looking up."

"I'll be okay alone," I say. "You have some boxes to unpack."

"Even if he doesn't come with you," Roxana mutters, "he'll still be there." She's scowling, but she doesn't look nearly as annoyed as she did.

"I've dealt with worse things than a nosy wolf." I'm smiling as I head out.

Maybe Xander's right.

Maybe things are looking up.

6

CLARK

New hire paperwork's always a pain—they make jokes about it for a reason—but the Illuminae take it to a new level. It takes me a day and a half to complete all the forms their administrator shoves at me, but finally, I get cleared for duty.

"Grab lunch, and then report to this address." The octogenarian witch who now knows where I spent nearly every second of my life up to this point hands me a card with an address printed on it.

Nothing else.

"What's this?" I can't help my smirk. "I feel like I'm in a spy movie."

She doesn't grin. She doesn't even smirk. "Get lunch, and report there."

"Uh, okay," I say.

I wasn't sure, when the photos I planted in Roxana's room failed to break her and Lionel up, whether his father would honor his promise to find me a job. But a few days after I sent him the screenshot of the photos in Roxana's room, a message was delivered to my apartment by courier.

Witch courier.

It took a relatively high-level spell even to unlock it. The letter inside was simple. It told me to report here to finalize paperwork, and it said I'd been hired as a 'magical liaison' to the paranormal community for Orion Sol's Office of Akero Affairs.

It's a fancy title.

And I have no idea what it entails.

Which means that, like Roxana before her date, I have no idea what to wear or how to prepare. I don't like the feeling of unease, but I'm hoping that after I report today, I'll have a much better idea of what I'm expected to do.

When I reach my apartment, I notice the package I ordered from Romania arrived, overnight as they promised. My hands are almost shaking as I unbox the rare Mesosa Longicorn beetle. It's preserved perfectly, which is a relief.

The potion my old professor promised would work on dragona as a cure for itching requires a live and wriggling Mesosa Longicorn. I've already prepared the rest of the potion, and I decide to skip lunch and make Roxana's treatment instead.

When I release the stasis charm, the beetle surges to life, three wriggling legs on either side, and tiny, fine, textured hairs all over its body that make a beautiful pattern, not unlike a cheetah or a panther. I almost feel bad when I drop it into the pot of boiling liquid.

With a venom base, and a binder of poison sumac, this is one of the strangest potions I've ever made. But even more surprising is that when I drop the beetle into the mixture, the entire thing flashes brightly, nearly blinding me. As I blink to clear my vision, I can hardly believe it, but it's settled in as a brilliant hot pink.

I'm smiling as I pour it into my nicest charm vial, a vintage bottle I bought from Bevin right after we met. At the time, I couldn't imagine what I might ever use it for, but now it feels. . .like fate. Roxana may be dating Lionel Sol, but who's taking care of her? Who's noticing when she needs something, and who does she trust to fix her problems for her?

As I grab a cab to save time, I can't help thinking about how our fingers will brush when I hand her this. How she'll rub it on her face, her shoulder, her neck, and her calf when her scales itch, thinking about me. I may not be flashy or super powerful, but I'm thought-ful, and I'm always around. My time's coming—I can feel it. I glance at my clock. Surely Minerva will still be sleeping with the hours she keeps. If I'm lucky, I'll be alone with Roxana when I stop in.

I should have known that's not the kind of luck I have.

Minerva's literally clipping her toenails when I arrive. The snick, snick, snick of her clippers removing large chunks of dead cells from the end of each of her toes is as far from appetizing or romantic as I could imagine.

Then again, I am here to give Roxana a charm to deal with itching scales. Maybe I'm the gross one for thinking it might be something it clearly never was.

"What are you doing here?" Minerva asks, one eye blinking. "I thought you started your new job today."

"Yesterday," I say. "Although, I guess technically I spent all of yesterday filling out forms, so I'm about to head over to the real job for the first time. But. . ." I pull the vial out of my satchel. "I brought this over for Roxana. Is she around?"

Minerva's still blinking when she stands up. "What is that?"

"What's going on with your eye?" I peer at her. "Did you—what did you do this time?"

She scowls. "If you must know, a tiny chunk of toenail flew up and stuck in the corner of my eye." She shakes her head and rubs at the edge of her right eye. "It really stings."

"Maybe don't rub it," I say. "I think it's making it worse."

"Thanks, Doctor Lucent."

"It's Doctor *Clark* Lucent to you," I say.

We both laugh. As if I'd ever be a doctor. Useless humans who pretend they can fix things that require spells to improve in the slightest. The stuff they can't spell heals on its own in almost all cases.

Funniest normie profession of all.

Without warning, Minerva stops laughing and bellows. "Roxana! My dumb old brother's here with some pink crap in a weird old bottle that looks recycled." She plops back down on the sofa, picking the clippers back up.

I fight the strongest urge to kick her in the shin.

It's a good thing I don't do it, because Roxana practically dances out of her room one second later, smiling. "Is that for the itching?" She's pulled her sweater down, exposing her entire shoulder. It's the same shoulder I saw before, only this time, it's not bleeding. This time, the scales are shimmering brightly, surprisingly beautiful against the golden undertones of her skin. "I really hope so. I feel like it's getting worse."

I can't stop staring at her. I know I should. I really should.

But I can't help it.

It's like staring at a work of art.

She's more beautiful than a brilliant sunset, or a sparkling, susurrating waterfall.

"Stop being a creeper," Minerva hisses. "Geez."

That snaps me back to myself. "Yes," I finally croak, clearing my throat. "Yes, it's for the itching."

Roxana's smiling. "Awesome." She holds out her hand without bothering to fix her sweater. She looks like someone who's posing for the front cover of a magazine. She looks utterly unreal, but this time I manage to hand her the vial, nearly dropping it on her palm. Our fingers don't brush. They don't even touch, but at least she's not thinking I'm a complete dolt.

"Recycled?" Roxana's laugh sounds like the tinkering of the world's most beautiful bells. "This vial's stunning." She caresses it exactly like I was hoping she'd caress me.

"You should try it," I say. "Then I'll know whether I need to make some adjustments."

"Oh." Her eyes shift upward, focusing on my face. "Right. Thanks." She sets it on the end table closest to her and lifts the stopper. She pauses. "Do I rub it on? Or am I supposed to drink it?"

"Don't drink it," I say at the same time Minerva shouts, "Don't drink it, dummy."

Roxana laughs. "Got it." She turns the bottle over,

pouring a tiny amount into her hand, and then she rubs it on her shoulder.

Both Minerva and I watch intently.

"Should I be worried?" Roxana arches one eyebrow.

Before either of us can answer, the scales on her shoulder flash like a solar flare, and she shudders. "Is it supposed to do that?"

I'm squinting from the brightness of the flare—not sure about my sister. "No. Definitely not."

"That's not good." She drops the stopper in the top of the vial and holds it out to me again. "Sorry, but I'm not sure I need the rest."

I shake my head, taking it back. "Not your fault, obviously. I'll come up with something else."

"Is it normal to have to try so many things?" Her shoulder doesn't look red at least—it looks just like it did before.

"Does it itch any less?" I peer at her, blinking to try and clear my vision. The scales look just like they did before to me, sparkling and brightly golden.

She shakes her head. "I mean, not really. I still feel like I should scratch them right out of my shoulder." Then she frowns. "Obviously not. I'm not a moron."

"What?"

"She's probably talking to Xander again." Minerva plops back down on the sofa one more time, digging around for her clippers. "It's annoying."

"Wait, talking to. . .what?"

"Xander's working on it," Roxana says.

"You can *talk* to him when he's not here?" I step closer. "How?" I don't see a headphone or earbuds.

"It's been happening ever since we bonded,"

Roxana says. "He can hear most everything I say, and it's hard for him not to respond, apparently."

"I haven't heard a word from him," I say. "Maybe he needs to learn not to badger ladies."

"So far, I think it's only me he can't manage to leave alone," Roxana says.

"I bet." Minerva's smirking.

I really am going to kick her shin. "Stop," I say. "Don't act like it's something special between the two of them. I'm sure it's just new alpha stuff."

"Or." Minerva tilts her head and straightens, giving up on the clippers. "Maybe it's because they're the only two shifters. Maybe that's why they have such a *special bond*."

"Stop calling it special," I say. "She's dragona. It's totally different than a wolf. The akero didn't even find them on the same *planet*."

"Speaking of the akero." Minerva pops to her feet, clipping her toenails apparently forgotten. "Do you remember Dad's akero-feather wand?"

I snort. "Do I?"

"Yeah," she says. "Do you?"

"I'm not an idiot," I grumble. "That was my answer. Of course I remember it. He spent my college fund on it."

"I'm not sure about that," Minerva says. "I looked it up, and they don't cost fifty or even a hundred thousand dollars."

"Xander says they cost millions," Roxana chimes in. "He said he saw an article on it in SpellWeek last year."

"What's he doing reading SpellWeek?" I ask. "He can't even cast a single spell." I can't help sulking, at least a little. Until Xander can figure out his weird bond thing, I'll never be alone with Roxana. It's not like I had time with her planned, but this bothers me a lot.

In fact, I kind of hate it.

"If Xander wants to be part of this conversation, he should just come over," I mutter.

Two seconds later, he blows through the door. "Good idea," he says. "Smart thinking, Magical Liaison to the Illuminae." He's smiling like he has no idea how irritated I am with him right now. So much for his stupid-special bond.

And Roxana's smiling back at him like she can't sense my irritation either.

In fact, as I glance between the two of them, something really bothers me. In all my years as Xander's best friend, I'd never really looked at him as, well, as a *man*. He's always been my goofy, self-conscious, half-human wolf-castoff.

He's been a charity case, if I'm being honest.

But now, with Roxana smiling at him like that, I see him differently.

He's tall. He's broad-shouldered. He's got great hair, albeit a little shaggy, and he's got a pretty good-looking face. He's supposed to be looking for his wolfy match, but he appears to have already decided what he wants.

And it's not a wolf at all.

"Are you sure it's a fluke that you can only hear Roxana?" I ask.

"Why were you asking about the akero-feather wand?" Xander asks. "Did your mom find it, finally?"

"That would be nice," Minerva says, "but if she had, she'd never have called me."

"Dad said he was going to leave it to me," I say. "But then when he died, nothing. No wand, no feather, no note."

"Do the wands really cost millions?" Roxana asks. "Because Bevin said you traded your feather to someone for that fire lizard."

Minerva's shoulders slump. "I did."

"You had an akero feather?" Xander asks.

My sister nods, dumbly.

"How did you get one?" Roxana asks. "From the same place your dad got the wand?"

"We don't even know if he really had a wand," I say. "I actually think he made that up as an excuse for blowing all my college fund money on something stupid."

"Dad wasn't like that," Minerva says.

"Then where's my wand?" I ask.

"How did you get your feather?" Roxana asks again. "You never said."

"I was young." Minerva glances at me as she sits on the sofa again. "I hadn't started school yet."

I shrug. "I think you were like five, maybe?"

"Anyway, I got lost. We went to a theme park as a family, and Mom was busy with something, and Dad— where was Dad?" She frowns. "I wandered off, and I was cold, so I kept on walking, and I'm not sure how long I wandered around before I decided to sit down and rest for a bit."

"You were lost?" Roxana crosses the room, sitting on the edge of the seat in the armchair across from

Minerva. "You poor little thing. How have I never heard this before?"

"Because after my nap, I woke up on my own front porch," Minerva says. "I heard a strange sound, like a whooshing, and then I felt a burst of air, and then when I sat up, it was there. A simple, white feather."

"Was it really an akero feather?" Xander asks, standing just behind Minerva now.

My sister nods. "They had it verified. It was white with gold tips."

Roxana's jaw drops. "Your feather was Michael's?" She shakes her head. "Mother feather, maybe he is your dad."

"Or maybe he just found a lost child and took me home, and they put his mark on my file as a key, because it was a significant event in my life," Minerva says. "No way to know."

"I can't believe you traded that feather for a fire lizard," I say. "That was so stupid."

Giggles fluffs up and coos, like she agrees with me.

"It was one of the dumber things I've ever done," Minerva says.

"No kidding," Xander says.

"But maybe not as dumb as the time you thought that you could breathe under water if you *had* to," I say. "Remember? You made me promise to hold you under water, even when you looked like you were drowning."

"Aren't you supposed to be at work?" Minerva asks. "You said you were on your lunch break, right?"

I glance at my watch and swear under my breath. I tuck the exploding vial back into my satchel and wave. "I'll try another charm tonight."

Roxana smiles, and this time, it's at me. "Thanks, Clark. I really appreciate it."

Take that, Xander.

On my way out the door, I glance back, and I can't help but notice how naturally Roxana angles her body toward Xander, and how his eyes track her movements, no matter where she goes in the room. I really need to figure out a charm to save the day quickly, or she might forget that he's a mongrel.

Stupid alpha charm.

I'm fifteen minutes late when I finally reach the weird address, but no one seems to care. Actually, when I show up, there doesn't seem to be anyone to notice anything at all.

They sent me to an empty warehouse on an abandoned street.

Is Lionel's dad punking me?

I'm about to head back to the old woman and yell at her for playing a prank when. . .I wonder whether it's all a front. I've heard that some of the higher-level jobs have difficult-to-find entrances. It takes me another half hour, but I finally notice it.

There's a small, scraggly flower right at the corner of the foundation stone—a spring flower in the fall in New York. A crocus. It should be blooming in March. Maybe April. Definitely not two weeks before Thanksgiving.

"Aha," I whisper. "I've got you."

It's another twenty minutes before I've engineered a spell that will let me though the door—and I have to whip out the stupid address card to do it. But eventually, I'm walking through the doors.

A dozen mages are waiting for me, laughing.

"I didn't think he was ever going to figure it out," a tall man with a pointy black hat says, as if wearing that's not already the worst kind of wizard-cliche. I should be laughing at him.

"I almost drop-kicked him a copy of *Locate Spells for Dummies*." A witch with long fingernails cackles and slaps her thighs.

"You took at least an hour your first day," a short mage with longish hair says, glaring at the pointy-hat wizard. "And you returned to the processing center to tell them they gave you the wrong address, Agnes."

The witch named Agnes sniffs, and the pointy-hat wizard purses his lips like he's sucking on a lemon. "You're no fun, Horatio. Ever."

"Welcome to the Liaison's office," Horatio says. "You found it faster than nearly everyone else here who's heckling you."

"Everyone except me." A witch with one blue eye and one hazel eye smiles, and then she holds out one hand. "Charlotte Leclair."

"Leclair," I say. "From the French 'clair' for bright."

She beams. "My father's family is French, yes."

"Hopefully you can explain what a Magical Liaison does," I say. "I was told the title, but no one told me quite what I'll be doing here."

"Come with me," Horatio says. "I'm your assigned mentor, and Charlotte was my last mentee."

She trails along behind us as we walk down a long hallway. When it finally ends, we enter a massive room, lighter and brighter than most open-air plazas.

"Our job," Horatio says, gesturing widely, "is simple. We do anything the Illuminae need us to do."

"What he means to say," Charlotte says, "is that we're magical fixers."

"Fixers?" I frown. "Like, repairmen?"

Horatio shakes his head. "No, we don't repair things, we repair situations. People. We eliminate problems, in any form."

As they walk me through the types of things we handle for the wealthy and influential Illuminae and their families, from criminal infractions to the fallout from extramarital affairs, I start to feel a little sick.

They might call us 'fixers,' but I've got my own name for what we do.

"We have almost limitless resources at our disposal," Horatio says, "and because of the nature of what we do, there's very little oversight or paperwork."

"We clean up messes," I say. "Right?"

Charlotte nods. "Exactly."

Great.

I betrayed Roxana's trust and violated my own moral code. . .so that I could become a well-paid magical janitor.

7

XANDER

Do not think about Roxana. Do not think about her eyes, her lips, her hilarious view on life, or her sassy responses. Do not think about what she might be seeing, or feeling, because if I do think about it. . .

I shake my head.

"You alright, dude?" Izaak calls. "Because the bond feels, like, *whack*."

I drop the half-eaten bag of jerky I was staring at into the box in front of me and jog around the corner to Izaak's room. "What does that mean? Whack?"

Izaak shrugs. "Not sure, but just. . .it was vibrating or something."

"Vibrating?" I arch one eyebrow. "Wait, you can feel it?"

Izaak nods. "Kind of like a little bunched up ball in the back of my brain. A little knot of Xander."

"Can everyone feel that?" That sounds horrible.

Izaak shrugs. "I mean, I'm kind of surrounded by Xander, so maybe it's easier for me to spot."

I sigh. "I keep dropping into other people's minds and intruding on what they're doing."

"Other people?" Now Izaak's arching an eyebrow. "Or *Roxana*'s?"

Something behind Izaak suddenly draws my attention. "What on earth is. . ." I trail off, because what I'm looking at is *so* gross. "Are those dried bloody loogies?" I can't help dry-retching.

The wall behind Izaak's bed looks like it's covered with reddish-brown slugs that dried onto his wall in various stages of nasty.

"You do know they make and sell boxes of things designed to prevent just this." I tilt my head, just in case it might look less revolting.

It doesn't.

"Look, vampires have to process blood, and sometimes if we get too much, or if there's something nasty in it, some of it sort of. . .comes back up."

"That makes it worse."

"Sometimes I use an empty water bottle," Izaak says. "But if I have to get up for a tissue, I can't go back to sleep."

"You can *always* go back to sleep when the sun's up."

"That's why it's so hard for me to get up." Izaak shrugs. "Besides. I feel like this is a fitting parting gift for those Manhattan pack jerks. Let them clean it up."

He has a point there.

Izaak's phone rings, and I head for the door. It's a good time to escape before I see some other disgusting thing he's been hiding in here —something worse than a wall of bloody boogers. Who knows what weird stuff vampires may do that I haven't yet discovered?

Though, with the way I keep inadvertently dropping in on my friends' thoughts and actions, I may discover things I don't want to know, even from the family room. I'm about to pick up my phone and call my dad to leave him another message when I hear something strange.

The high-pitched tone coming from Izaak is a sound usually reserved for dog whistles and dolphin sonar. "—Donovan Summers really wants to meet me?"

I've heard the name before, but I can't think where. Producer? Director? Actor? I wait to see what strange squeaky noise Izaak makes next.

"Of course I will, especially for something like that, but did you ask if we can meet via Zoom?" He exhales gustily. "Try harder. You know what'll happen if I meet him in person."

When Izaak hangs up, he looks like a melting candle, his shoulders are so slumped.

"Isn't that good news, bud? I've heard of that guy before, I think."

The eyes he turns on me are full of despair. "It's the break I've always wanted. Donovan Summers is *the* rom-com producer in Hollywood, and he 'liked my style.'" He shakes his head. "Or at least, right now he does."

But once they meet in person, normies' innate terror of vampires will kick in and. . .poof. Big break gone. I clap one hand on his shoulder. "Chin-up, big man. I'm sure all the filming on his corny romance movie would have been scheduled during the day." I toss my head at the booger wall. "We all know how you do during the day."

"I'd figure that out," he says. "Silver infused Red Bulls are magical. Plus, people dig the bedroom eyes."

I can't help curling my lip at the wall that OSHA would surely condemn. "Right. It's hot, for sure."

"Just give me a moment to be upset, and then we can try and come up with a plan."

"Is that before we panic-pack so we aren't run off like mangy dogs, or after I sign up for remedial alpha training so I can stop snooping through my best friends' heads?"

Izaak's eyes snap up toward mine. "I'm sorry, fam. I really am. I know things are rough enough for you now without me being all whiny about my big break before I've even blown it."

"It's a big deal," I say. "I get it. I'll try and think of something to help you, too."

My phone rings, and it's a call from a number I don't know. I wonder whether it's Bevin. A tiny, insane part of me is hoping that she'll actually buy the building and somehow, miraculously, we won't all need to move.

Nothing in our life *ever* works like that, so I'm not optimistic, especially since I doubt the bank would want to take a chance on a demon-spawn whose business just burned down, but it would be nice.

"Hello?"

"Xander?" The female voice's drawl is familiar, but I'm not entirely sure why.

"It's Jewel," she says. "We need to talk."

I can't help my sigh. "I should've called you back. I'm sorry I didn't." She's left me fifteen messages. If I wasn't waiting on Bevin's call, stupidly hoping for some way to stay here, I wouldn't have answered this time, either. "The thing though—"

"We know the thing," Jewel says. "And at first, we were worried, but I wanted to tell you that we're in."

Huh?

"In fact, ever since you left, we've been looking for solutions to your problem, and we found one this morning."

"My problem?"

"We even have an offer on our compound."

I'm so confused that I'm beginning to worry that she's speaking another language. "I'm sorry, but I have no idea what you're talking about."

"You're going up against the Manhattan pack," she says. "Which is really risky. I'm not going to lie, more than half of us wanted nothing to do with it, but I convinced them."

"You—you convinced them?" I shake my head. "Jewel, I'm not going up against anyone. I think you've been misinformed, and the reason I haven't called you is that. . .I bonded a pack, actually."

"You—what?" Now it's her turn to be confused.

It does make me wonder who she's been talking to. "Why would you think I was going up against the Manhattan pack?" I kick an empty box and send it flying across my room. "I'm actually elbow-deep in boxes right now, trying to vacate the stupid Manhattan-pack apartment I was staying in."

"It's all over the werewolf gossip groups—you already fought Lo Ren and you beat him, but he ran before you could finish him off."

That's not exactly what happened. "But the thing is—"

"He thought you'd be an easy target, but even as a lone wolf, even as a brand-new alpha, he couldn't take you down." Jewel sighs. "That's what sold 'em, you know. When I explained that, we all knew that with a pack behind you, you'd be unstoppable."

"My pack—I already have one," I say. "And it's a strange one."

"You don't have wolves, I hear," Jewel says. "And if you want a spot on the wolf-advisory, you need to bond at least one wolf."

She's shockingly well-informed. "I didn't even know you could bond a non-wolf," I say. "When it happened—"

"It's that dragona, isn't it?" Jewel asks. "Is that who you bonded?"

It seems like everyone already knows everything. "Yes, Roxana," I say. "I hardly think—"

"You didn't ask, but you probably ought to know this. Our entire pack staffs the local prison. Guards, cooks, and cleaning staff. It took us a while, but I finally managed to convince the warden to put in a good word for us, and we got the contract to staff the newly reopening Manhattan Detention Complex."

I'm sputtering. "But you said—you can't just—"

"It happened really fast, as we were looking into how we could make you happy and still find a situation that would work for us. I know you weren't impressed when you met us before, and I even understand why. There are almost a hundred of us, and we looked like a total disaster. But I swear, we're good wolves, and you're going to need some help. Let us provide it."

"It's not that I don't want a pack," I say. "But my life's so complicated that you should believe me when I say that—"

"The offer we just got for our complex is two point four million, and if you can find us decent housing, it's all yours. To help with running the pack, of course."

Are they bribing me to be their alpha? As bribes go, it's not a bad one. It's way more than I expected them to be able to come up with. Not that I've really sat around thinking about how much of a bribe anyone could scrounge up. . .

Which is all beside the point.

"Jewel, I'm sure you can find another alpha, one who doesn't have the same baggage that I do. If you come here, I'll just drag you into something that you don't want—something you don't deserve."

"Do you think we haven't looked?" she asks. "Alphas have become less and less common in the past thirty or forty years, and the ones we have found have been. . .aggressive. Often, the weaker an alpha is, the more aggressive he is—precisely because he's weak. The ones we've met, other than you, were worse even than our last alpha. You were strong, smart, and kind. You're the one we want. We've already voted."

"Did you hear the part where I said I already have a pack?"

"You need *wolves* in your pack, or you'll get no vote on the Wolf Council, and that means you'll have to leave Manhattan. Your dragona girlfriend didn't look too keen on moving to the sticks when I met her."

"She's not my girlfriend," I say. "And—"

"My brother's fraying," Jewel whispers. "If we can't

find him an alpha soon, *very* soon, he's going to have to be put down."

There it is.

Her rabid insistence finally makes sense.

"I don't know anything about managing the fray," I say. "In fact, I thought *I* was fraying. Your brother would be better off—"

"Most alphas would put him down immediately," she whispers again. "I thought someone like you, someone who does the impossible, like bonding non-wolves, might give him a chance."

Well, now she's got me. "Look," I say. "I'm not making any promises, but if you bring him to Manhattan, I'll meet with you. Okay?"

"We can be there in three hours."

Oh.

Oh.

"I can't meet with you in just three hours," I say. "I'll need to talk to some people first. How about you give me a few days?"

"Two days. I can't give you more than two days."

Before I can even tell her my address, she hangs up.

I'm headed across the hall to update Minerva when Bevin jogs up the stairwell. "Xander!" She looks agitated. "You have to come with me to the bank."

"What?"

"Those idiots at PNC said I need someone more reliable to cosign on any loan, and guess what occupation they list as a *stable* paranormal position?"

I'm sure I have no idea. "What?"

"A werewolf alpha." She's shaking her head. "With your help, we really might be able to buy the whole building. We just need to make sure we can prove that we'll be able to rent all the apartments. According to my agent, a lot of the apartments have fallen vacant in anticipation of the sale."

"Oh, I think I might be able to find us some tenants." I grimace. "We need to get everyone together. We have a lot to discuss."

❧ 8 ❧

IZAAK

Vampires are basically parasites who feed on humanity.

We aren't from earth.

We weren't invited, either.

And now our magical forms take, take, take in order to propagate. I've known this all my life, but I'm just now realizing how much I hate it.

I never really felt like I belonged here, on earth, or even with any other humans, not as a vampire. It makes jabs and jokes about me being a bloodsucker sting, to be honest. I mean, we *are* bloodsuckers. We would die without humans to feed on. Our bodies would reject the tiny vampire crouched inside our brains, and we'd all shrivel up.

Or something like that.

That's why, instead of drinking blood directly from humans, I've always just bought blood bags. I know that direct blood-taking can create a bond with humans, and I know it can make us stronger, but I don't want that. Along with bonds like that comes the knowledge that the humans we're connecting with don't have choices.

They *always* bond with the vampire who takes their blood.

How can we really know whether they're willing? How can we know whether they hate it? Or whether they love it? I mean, they always *say* they love it, and that's enough for most vampires, but not for me.

No one bats a thousand—even Taylor Swift has haters.

But vampires don't.

It's hinky, right?

Sometimes I think I'm being greedy, wanting to spread joy, wanting people to *like* me for who I am. But when I think back on the time I spent in that theater as Mercutio, when I remember my time in the park, where people lined up to meet and photograph themselves with me, those moments felt real. I only delighted the people in the park while fundraising for Bevin because they weren't normies, and I'm not sure how or why I didn't terrify the humans that day in the theater, but I've been longing to recapture that high ever since.

In fact, it's all I want.

It's why I've spent all morning hopped up on Red Bull laced with silver, walking around the city, trying to figure out how to keep people from being afraid of me. Sadly, nothing I've tried is working.

Like, at all.

"Oh." A kid with a long skateboard has more metal forced through him than a pincushion, and he's wearing black lipstick. "Sorry, I didn't see you there."

I smile and wave, but he still blanches white and

drops his board, kick-rolling away from me as fast as he can.

It's been like that all day. Grandmas. Children. Business men. Families on holiday. Actually, they may be the worst. I think it could be that they're already wary of dangerous New York streets, but several of them have actually run over small dogs, other tourists, and once, even a squirrel in their haste to escape my presence.

"I give up," I mutter. "Tomorrow's meeting is *doomed*."

Maybe not, buddy. Xander's voice in my head is encouraging. *Maybe he'll be like the guys in the park.*

"Nah, I looked into it," I say. "Donovan Sommers isn't supernatural."

Well, that's too bad, Xander agrees. *But maybe that's where you've gone wrong. There's a small but vibrant community of supernatural performers you should be networking with who—*

"They do standup comedy and sing for private parties at Illuminae functions." I shudder. "Pass."

The family of four walking past me could be on a postcard advertising travel to New York City in the fall. They're all bundled up in coordinated but not matching scarves, and the little girl has a poof ball on the top of her knit cap. She kicks an old can in my direction as they pass, scowling. "Crazy guy, talking to himself."

At least she didn't seem scared of you, Xander points out.

"She's right," I say. "I need to figure out how to think things in your direction. I sound like a lunatic, talking out loud like this when I'm alone."

You're supposed to be trying to block me, Xander says. *Then you're supposed to only let me in when* you *want to.*

I am doing that, but I feel shut off from enough people. I don't want to cut off the one friend I've got. "You're always welcome in my brain, buddy."

No thanks. It's a pretty lonely, vacant place in here, Xander says, and I can *feel* his smile.

"Shut up." But I'm smiling, too. It feels nice, honestly. There hasn't been much to smile about today. "Where are you, anyway? Since I'm up in the middle of the day for once, I should buy you lunch." I have the money, thanks to that horrible villain role I took.

At the bank with Bevin. Not going great.

Well, maybe with my vampiric charm and witty personality, I can change that. Not with humans, but PNC Bank's paranormal owned. It's also obligated, by angelic code, to hire fairly. Maybe their banker's a vampire. Actually, I think Aunt Ada works there—not sure what she does exactly. I was always a little worried it was with collections, so I never asked.

I head for the closest branch of PNC—the only one near our apartment, really—assuming Xander will be too distracted to notice I'm moving closer. He may not even realize he needs my help until I'm right there, ready to offer it. Only, when I walk through the front doors, I don't see them at all. "I'm here," I whisper. "Where are you?"

Here?

"The PNC branch on 10th. I came to support the two of you. Maybe you need another cosigner. I'd like to own a building too, you know. Sounds like a good investment for a movie star."

Xander's mental laughter sounds the same as it

does in person. *We're on the far left side in a tiny cubicle run by an insane woman. So far, she does not have good news.*

I jog toward the corner, waving off anyone who tries to help me, and I open the door without permission. Always better to get that later.

"That's what I'm saying. I know your agent told you that they'd take thirty-five million, but ten percent just isn't reasonable. Even with an alpha willing to cosign, and even with a lien on the building, our bank won't make a loan of that size without twenty percent down."

Banks are the same, supernatural or not—greedy and impersonal.

This woman's definitely not my aunt Ada, but her face is just as sour. She's also wearing a pair of glasses on top of her head and another pair on the end of her nose. "What if they had another cosigner?" I ask. "I'm a movie star—you might recognize me?" I smile my winning-est smile.

"Paranormal Network Company Bank doesn't care about extra cosigners." The woman's a very old, very crusty witch, and she does not look amused. "We care about dollars and cents, and you simply don't have enough."

"What if I could add two million and change to what we have?" Xander's cringing a little as he asks. "Would it be enough then?"

"The building you want has provided notices that most of its tenants were asked to vacate in anticipation of sale." Her glasses slide down her nose when her frown deepens. "You would need to provide evidence that you'd be able to fill those vacancies at a market rent, and you'd need to come up with. . ." She peers at a computer screen, tapping at the keys. "Did you say two million?"

"Two point four," Xander says, "to be precise."

The witch scowls. "I always want you to be precise." She goes back to clacking along, but finally, she lifts her eyes. "You'd still be a million short."

"A million?" Bevin splutters. "What are the floors in that building made of? Cotton candy?"

Xander turns toward her slowly. "Cotton candy?"

"Gold-plated cotton candy?" She shrugs. "What? That's my favorite snack. I'd buy the crap out of a building made of cotton candy."

"You keep an eye out for Gretel here." Xander's looking at me as he stands. Then he turns toward the witch. "We'll see what we can do, and we'll get back to you by tomorrow."

"I want to get you a preapproval letter." The witch stands. "That's how I pay my mortgage. But I can't do it without the proper elements. I do hope you understand."

Xander sighs. "Of course."

"And if I could ask." She slides her glasses up on top of her head, knocking the ones that were already there backward. They fall to the floor with a clatter.

"Yeah?" Bevin leans over and picks them up. "What?"

"You listed Mr. Binnigas as a werewolf alpha, and you're buying a building in Manhattan." She clears her throat. "I try to stay out of other group's affairs, but. . ." She sighs. "There won't be trouble with Lo Ren Fang, will there? You have his permission to buy real estate in his area?"

Xander looks right at her, smiles, and nods. "Of course. I don't have a death wish."

She sighs dramatically. "Thank goodness." Her laugh's clearly nervous. "None of us do, and besides. It wouldn't be good business, either."

Xander nods slowly.

"I'll just need a signed letter to that effect from his office for our file."

"For sure," Bevin says, her smile so large and so fake it almost pains me. "We'll shoot that right over."

Of course, once we get outside of the bank, all three of us deflate. Xander's normally broad shoulders are especially slumped.

"I'm sorry, man," I say. "That was rough."

Xander shrugs. "It was always a long shot." He half-chuckles. "Buying a massive building in the middle of New York?" His laugh gets louder. "I'm not even employed."

Bevin's laughing now, too. "Me either." She has to wipe at her eyes, she's laughing so hard. "From jobless to real estate mogul?" She shakes her head. "It was a pretty harebrained idea."

"But if we aren't buying a building," I say, "does that mean we are moving?"

Xander sighs. "Probably to Waterbury."

Now Bevin's laugh is a little unhinged. "Unless they get here first." She stops mid-step, her laughter dying just as fast. "What are you going to do with all those wolves if we don't have a building?"

Xander cringes.

"Wait," I ask. "What wolves?"

"Everyone was too busy last night, but I really need

to talk to everyone," Xander says. "We have some important stuff to discuss."

"Discuss?" Bevin arches an eyebrow. "As our alpha overlord, don't you just *tell* us what to do and we have to listen?"

"That's not the kind of alpha I am," Xander says, "and something tells me that while it might work for wolves, it won't work for any of you."

"I'm happy to hear that you acknowledge you're not my boss," I say. "But even so, you're coming with me tomorrow, right?"

"Tomorrow?" Xander frowns. "For what?"

"My meeting with Donovan Summers." I can't help my scowl. "Sometimes it feels like you don't listen to anything I say."

Xander's lip twitches. "We spent the last two hours talking about him and trying to get you ready. Did you really think I'd forgotten about it?"

I shove him.

But Bevin's ignoring us, typing on her phone.

"Who are you obsessing over?" Xander asks. "Meet a cute witch?"

"Or a mean vampire?" I ask.

"Oh, oh, I know," Xander says. "It's a terribly dashing demon-spawn you met at the hot yoga studio —she can hold downward dog for an hour."

Bevin rounds on us, eyes flashing. "Hot yoga? That's *so* last year. Actually, like three years ago. Now it's *goat* yoga. Try to keep up."

My phone buzzes. I notice Xander whipping his out, too. It's a text from Bevin, so maybe we were being jerks, mocking her for having a new crush. She was just trying to help Xander set up his meeting.

MEET AT MINERVA'S AT FIVE.

"Minerva should be waking up soon," Bevin says, "and Clark should be off work, in the next little while, I think? What does he do again? Magical bean counting? Obituary drafting?"

"He's a magical liaison to the Illuminae now," I say. "He's only bragged about it one hundred times."

"I block that stuff out," Bevin says. "At least, unless I'm in a good place, which clearly." She sighs. "I'm not right now."

"Jobless, homeless, blah, blah," I say. "We all know."

"You're a little whiney right now too," Bevin says. "I think we've both been channeling our inner Clark a little too much."

"That's mean," I say.

But it's also funny. Like Clark, there's plenty of good in my life, and I'm focusing on the bad. As we walk the six blocks between where we are and home, Xander and Bevin talk about what we could do with the pack—and where we could look for apartments just outside of Manhattan—but I can't help thinking about what I bring to our friend group.

Our pack, I guess.

Bevin has money from her shop—and even more from the land. She's tough and kind and has a strong moral code.

Xander's an alpha now, and he's held down a solid job, albeit a miserable one, for years. He has savings. He has stability. And now, he has pack magic.

Clark has a prestigious job and powerful magic. He's also got lots of savings and a mother who's proud of him.

Minerva has. . .well, she has a frigging awesome pigeon and a hot guardian who likes her. She probably has some money saved, and she plans things like the fundraiser for Bevin. When people have problems, she's one of the first people they ask to help, misfiring spells notwithstanding.

Roxana's the hottest woman I've ever met, and probably the most desirable bachelorette in New York City. Her father would burn down the city for her. Her mother has sent her thousands and thousands of dollars' worth of designer clothing. She may be unemployed, but I'm sure that won't last long.

Then there's me.

Magical dud.

Not a scary vampire.

But too scary to do what I want to do. . .

Not an assassin, or even a successful actor. I'm a drain, on everyone and everything. I get why my mom's embarrassed, and why my friends don't ever ask me to help with anything.

I'm a waste of space.

When things are in flux, when people are in danger, I'm the last person anyone would call. I really want to change that, but I'm not sure *how* to go about it. So, I just drag my feet along the pavement all the way back to the apartment we're about to flee.

Am I acting like Clark?

Or, when he's being whiny, is he acting like *me*?

9

XANDER

After I flunked out of wolf school, I barely ever saw my dad. Even when I did see him, he never really said much. It was like we had one thing we shared, and when I was no good at it, we had no common ground at all. In fact, before he showed up in NYC to confirm that he'd known all along that I was an alpha, I doubt I'd heard from him in over a year. Not even so much as a text.

Imagine my surprise when he calls me within forty-eight hours of my leaving a message.

"Xander," he says. "It's me, your dad."

"The wonders of caller ID had revealed that fact to me," I say.

"Right." He grunts. "You said you had some questions."

"So, I bonded my friends. I imagine you heard."

He grunts again.

"And now, things are kind of strange."

"You bonded a bunch of non-wolves, and you're

calling me because that's *strange?*" My dad sighs. "Or is there more than that?"

"The thing is," I say, "no one's really taught me how to be a wolf. I've never been part of a pack, and I don't know a thing about being an alpha, so I'm sort of struggling."

"With what, exactly?" Dad asks. "Ordering your packmates around?"

"Nothing like that," I whisper, conscious of Bevin and Izaak listening in carefully on the very end of our walk back to the apartments. "It's just that. . .well, I'm practicing talking to them telepathically, and—"

"Wait, you can communicate with them?" Dad splutters. "Non-wolves? In their minds?"

"Should I not be able to?"

"I've never heard of it," Dad said. "But then again, as far as I could find, no one has ever bonded non-wolves."

"How many people know?" I ask. "How did you hear?"

"Lo Ren Fang posted about it on the Forum. He was. . .displeased."

"Forum?" We're climbing stairs now, but I'd probably be huffing even if we weren't. "Dad, maybe you should start at the beginning. Assume I've heard of none of this."

"The Forum's basically like Facebook, but for wolves, okay? We're all there. Make an account. Follow the big alphas."

"Is Lo Ren a big alpha?" I ask.

"Practically the biggest," Dad says.

"What are people saying about me bonding non-wolves?"

"About what you'd expect. There are plenty of haters, saying you're a freak, that it's unnatural, and that you should be put down."

"You know, the usual," Bevin hisses. "Bullying, attacks, and threats of murder."

"Who was that?" Dad asks.

"One of my packmates."

"The demon one?"

"Demon *spawn*," Bevin says. "And yes. That's me. Hi, Mr. Binnigas."

"Tell her that she's the first one they want to eliminate. They think it's embarrassing to have an alpha linked to a level one demon-spawn."

"I love them, too," Bevin says. "And if I were them, I'd be more embarrassed about having fleas."

"There are plenty of them who are curious," Dad says. "They'd kill for the knowledge that you can communicate with your packmates telepathically, for instance."

"Well, don't go posting on there just for attention," I say.

"I would never do that." I'm surprised when Dad sounds hurt. "I would hope you'd know that, at least."

"I do," I say, though I'm not sure it's true. "And while we're dispensing advice, do you remember that alpha friend you mentioned? If you could get him to call me, I could really use a mentor."

"Things with Haymitch are. . .complicated."

I knew it. Dad isn't one to keep friends very long.

Dad coughs. "But I can tell you a few things myself. To be considered a real alpha, you need to bond at least one wolf," Dad says. "In fact, there's a lot of discussion about your pack right now, and apparently wolf law's clear. An alpha becomes an alpha when he bonds *wolves* to him. Wolves, plural. I could come and be your first real packmate, but you'd need more than that to really qualify as an alpha. You need to find a few wolves who will let you bond them, or you won't have any rights at all—no seat on the Wolf Council, either."

"I'd never even heard of the Council."

"They don't come up much, to be honest. Wolves largely handle themselves, but there is a loose confederation of alphas who sort of make bigger decisions involving more than one area. Some alphas go to them with arguments. For instance, if you wanted to stay in New York City," Dad says, "you could ask for their help, or you could kill Lo Ren. Those are pretty much the only ways. Generally speaking, their creation was just to try and prevent massive wars that would have extensive casualties."

"Sounds dope," Izaak says.

"Ah, dear Izaak's there too," Dad says. "How lovely."

We've reached the hallway outside our apartments, and I wave toward Minerva's door. "I'll be over in a few."

Bevin frowns—she knows when she's being dismissed—but she doesn't argue. Izaak, of course, follows me cluelessly into our apartment.

I duck into my room and shove the door as closed as I can get it with boxes wedged into the hallway. "Listen, have you ever heard of someone unintentionally spying on one particular pack member?"

"What does that mean?" Dad sounds uncomfortable.

"Well, like, I don't want to know what one of my packmates is doing all the time, but somehow, I just can't seem to help listening in, so to speak."

"*All* the time?" Dad asks.

"Not right now," I say. "It's easier when I keep myself busy, but if I'm not actively trying *not* to see or hear what this pack member's doing. . .I can."

"Like when she's. . .showering?"

"Why are you assuming it's a girl?" I hate how high-pitched my voice has gotten. "It could be a guy."

"I thought you weren't gay," Dad says. "Am I mistaken?"

"No." Okay, now I just sound like a teenage girl in a Halloween movie. I force myself to calm down. "Dad, stop being weird. I'm not gay."

"Then why are you talking about a mate-bond with a male?"

"A *mate* bond?" I can barely breathe.

"It's not an alpha thing for you to be unable to break off a mental connection with another wolf," Dad says. "That's something that happens when two wolves are compatible as mates. The only way to sever the connection is to close down that bond. Entirely."

"Close down the. . ." I choke. "What does that mean?"

"If you want to stop, you have to reject the other wolf as your mate."

"She's not even a wolf, Dad," I say.

"It *is* a female," Dad says. "That's a relief. Adoption laws are broadening, but they're not common or easy for our kind. Being a gay wolf is extremely hard."

"Dad, focus."

"Is it the demon-spawn?" he asks. "Or the witch? Because the only witch-wolf bond—"

"Dad!" I shout. "Just stop. How do I reject the bond?"

"You would have to remove her from your pack," Dad says. "It really only works if one of you is entirely geographically distanced and you sever the pack bond."

That's bad. I'm not sure I can do that. But there's no way that Roxana could be my mate. She's dragona. . . "What happens if I *don't* do that?"

"You'll keep spying on her, for one," Dad says. "I'm guessing, based on your phone call, that's not something she's a fan of." He grunts. "If it's the witch, she might be able to cast a spell or concoct a charm that could stop that, but the rest. . ."

"What's the rest?"

"You can't find another mate until you've rejected her," Dad says. "And I assume that someday, you do want a mate."

"What if all I ever want is her?"

"Could she want you back?" Dad asks. "Because if so, things could get really strange, really fast."

"What do you get if you cross a half-wolf, half human with a dragona who can't shift?" I ask without thinking.

Dad swears under his breath.

"I'm kidding, Dad."

"But is it really Roxana Goldenscales?" Dad asks.

"I mean, it's not *not* Roxana," I say.

"You need to reject her right away. Her family will eat you alive. If you ever listen to one word I say, let it be this suggestion: kick her out, and do it fast." Dad hangs up.

Well, that was encouraging.

I'm trying to decide whether I can possibly share what Dad said with Roxana when Izaak grabs my arm and starts dragging me across the room. "What are you doing?"

"It's five," he says. "Or did you plan to skip the meeting you called?"

"Bevin called it," I mutter. I follow him across the hall, but I stop in front of the door.

"Did you let your dad get to you?" Izaak slams one hand against the wall by the doorframe. "I swear, that guy pisses me off."

"No." I shake my head. "It's not that."

"What then?"

"I have no idea what to do in a pack meeting," I whisper. "Bevin called it so fast, and I was talking to my dad, and now I'm supposed to go in there and. . .what?"

Izaak slings one arm around my shoulders. "Just talk to us, man. We're still your friends." He shoves the door open and drags me inside.

"You two are finally coming out?" Clark asks. "If you'd let me know, I'd have brought balloons and a fabulous rainbow cake."

"Nice try," I say, shoving Izaak a foot away. "Not even close."

"Not that there's anything wrong with it." Bevin arches one dangerously irritated eye.

"Didn't say there was," Clark says.

"Or me," I say.

"Alright." Minerva's rubbing her eyes. Until she yawns.

Then Roxana yawns.

And I yawn. Clark, Izaak, and Bevin all yawn, too.

"Knock it off," I say. "Go get some gloffee."

"I hate the instant stuff," Minerva whines. "It's all sludgy. And it tastes like plastic."

"I knew you'd say that." Roxana leans over and pulls a carrier up from the ground. She lifts one cup out and hands it to me. "Glespresso, dragona." She winks.

My entire stomach flips over.

"Gloffee, black, demon-spawn," she says as she hands one to Minerva. Then she turns toward Bevin. "A glatte, vampire." And then to Clark. "Glofficino, dragona." She's smiling, but she doesn't wink, and for some reason that makes me feel way better.

"What about me?" Izaak asks.

"I got you a muffin." She tosses him a bag. "I saw you with gloffee earlier, and it looked like you were pounding it."

His expression is sheepish. "Early day for me."

"You really didn't know I was getting gloffee?" She circles back around and sits next to me on a stool. "You didn't see me doing it?"

I was practicing distracting myself while I was at the bank, helping Izaak, and then talking to my dad. I didn't expect it to work, but I guess it did. "No idea," I say. "Are you proud?"

She beams.

And I'm, conversely, a little bummed. Does that mean we aren't really mates? It's far, far too embarrassing to ever admit, but after Dad said we might be. .

.I was excited at the idea. Which is dumb. There's no way my mate would be dragona, and there's no way *she'd* be excited about it if it were true.

"Well." I stand up, taking a sip of my glespresso to have something to do. "I'm glad you're all here. There have been a lot of developments since you all stood beside me to defy the demon-spawn who cornered us in this very room."

Everyone's watching me like I'm their CEO or something, and it's disconcerting. I sit down.

"Tell them about the pack in Waterbury," Izaak says.

"The pack in Waterbury?" Roxana arches an eyebrow. "Did they contact you again?"

"And we should talk about the building thing," Bevin says. "I mean, we're still a million bucks short, but who knows what Clark has underneath his pillow."

"I think it's mattress," Minerva says. "The phrase is underneath his mattress."

Clark looks uncomfortable for some reason, but I can't think why.

"And we should talk about the telepathic stuff," Roxana says.

"I agree we have a lot to discuss," I say.

"Start with the building," Izaak says. "Because that's one we should vote on—and maybe other people can help."

Bevin leaps in to explain how she found out the building was for sale, and how she has three million, between the money we raised and the money she'll clear from the sale of her land. "And with the rents I think we'd get, it would basically support itself."

"Unless, you know, an old building like this needed

repairs or had any foundation problems or roof issues, or electrical, or air conditioning malfunctions," Clark says.

"Yeah." Bevin fiddles with her scarf. "Unless all that stuff." She bites her lip. "Stuff I never thought about, because I've never owned anything but my little shop, and look how that went." She looks utterly deflated.

"Plus," I say, "unless someone else has a million bucks, we're a little short even for the downpayment."

"All we need is four million for a downpayment on this whole building?" Minerva's frowning. "What's the purchase price?"

"So that's where the pack in Waterbury comes in." I sigh. "They have right around a hundred wolves in their pack, and their alpha died a few months ago, and they're in pretty bad shape. But they did find a buyer on their compound, and they're willing to move to New York."

"But there's already a pack here," Roxana says.

"Right, but there's a lot of precedent for splitting an area," I say. "*If* I were an alpha with bonded wolves who could petition the Wolf Council."

"You can't petition this council without a wolf being bonded to you?" Roxana looks unimpressed.

"Multiple wolves," I say. "As in, more than one." At least, if she doesn't know all this, she really didn't hear my whole conversation with my dad, which means she has no idea about the possibility of the mate thing. That's a relief.

"That Waterbury wolf wants him to bond their whole pack," Izaak says. "And they'll give him the two million and change they'll get from the sale of the compound to pay for the building." He's practically bouncing. "Then we'd own the building, and Lo Ren couldn't kick us out."

"But he could kill us all," Clark says. "Right?"

"I mean, that's always a risk," Izaak says. "Dude is pretty cracked."

Minerva blinks. "But even with that two million and change, we're still short on the building down-payment?"

I nod. "Yep. I'm thinking the building is out, which is a bummer. I think the crazy Waterbury wolves have found a new job, and it's here. In Manhattan."

"A job?" Roxana's brow's furrowed. "Doing what?"

I smile. "Prison guards, cooks, and support staff, I guess."

"That tracks." Her lips are compressed. "But would you want a pack like that?"

"I feel like they haven't caught many breaks in life, and I can relate to that," I say. "And. . ." I have to tell them, or they'll be as confused as I was. "Jewel, one of their nurturers, has a brother who's fraying. I think, from what she said, it's pretty bad. I think he may not be the only one who's struggling."

Clark swears. "That's dangerous, right?"

I can't argue with him there.

"You're our alpha," Minerva says, "so what are you telling us you're doing?"

I shake my head. "I'm your alpha, but that's not how I am. You know that already. I'm here to ask you what everyone wants to do."

"I have money saved," Clark says. "Not a million, but a quarter million, maybe. I could contribute that, if we could come up with the rest somewhere else."

"I have some," Minerva says, "but not as much as Clark."

"Oh, and we'd need to get a signed note from Lo Ren for the bank saying he's fine with us buying the place," Bevin says. "So, clearly we'd have to forge that."

"Do you hear yourselves?" Roxana asks. "This is madness."

"We could move," Minerva says. "I mean, we could just move. Has anyone thought about that?"

"To where?" Roxana asks. "Waterbury? Because I've been there, and let me tell you, it's *not* nice."

"Hey," I say. "I'm not sure we really gave it a chance."

"It's not New York," Roxana says.

And I realize anything but New York won't be nice to her.

"I don't know what we should do," Minerva says, "but it sure feels like the universe is trying to destroy us, doesn't it? That can't be a good thing."

Bevin holds up one finger. "The Demon Council." Her voice is quiet but clear. She holds up another finger. "The Manhattan Pack." She holds up a third. "Minerva's weird past." And a fourth. "And the dragona aren't exactly our biggest cheerleaders, since we've been harboring Roxana." She shakes her head. "It's more than three strikes."

"I hear California's nice," Clark says.

"It's better for movies," Izaak says, "but I love New York. And you didn't mention the vampires at least. They may not love us, but they don't hate us."

"Don't be so sure," Minerva says. "Remember how I got suspended before?"

Izaak lifts his eyebrows.

"I kind of boiled the Sublime Chancellor's son in a hot tub on accident." She's cringes. "I just found out that, even with the Chief's nomination of me as his replacement, the head of each faction needs to ratify his choice."

"And you don't think they will?" I ask.

Minerva shrugs. "Do you?"

It's not looking good. "Alright, well, let's hear from each of you with what you think we should do. One obvious solution to part of this mess would be for me to unbond you and move away myself. The rest of you could stay here."

"I can't. Your bond was all that kept me safe, and I don't want to move," Bevin says. "I mean, I already did have to move, sort of. I'm staying on the sofa here, but I don't want to run away. I know the Demon Council's scary, but we stood up to them once. And Lo Ren Fang's a big old bully, and I've hated bullies my entire life."

"I think you should bond some wolves," Minerva says. "Waterbury or not, and then go to the Wolf Council and ask them to split the area."

I'm floored. I was bracing myself for them to ask me to un-bond them. I thought they'd all want out. "But where will we live?"

Minerva shrugs. "I think that matters less than being together. If we have to move, we can move."

"We can't move if we're dead," Roxana says.

"Would your father really let that happen?" Clark asks. "Do you really think you're in danger?"

"She almost got mauled when she went with me to visit the packs looking for my mate," I say. That gives me pause for a moment. That day, our purpose was to find my mate. . . What if I actually did? I shake off the strange thought and focus. Clark was acting like Roxana had nothing at stake here, but she does. "Roxana made a fireball that day and blew up the people attacking her. Don't treat her like she always hides behind her father."

Roxana's eyes widen.

"By the wing," I say, "I'm sorry. We weren't telling people."

"Wait," Minerva says. "We're 'people' now?"

Roxana shrugs. "It was just—it was a weird day, and then my mom started calling and asking about it." She sighs. "I panicked."

"A fireball?" Clark asks.

"That's when I started itching," she says. "That's what changed."

Clark frowns.

Roxana's brow furrows. "That pack did get a video, and they've sent it as proof to my mother. I put her off one more day, but tomorrow I have to go home and talk to her about it."

"I'll go with you," I say.

"And hey, maybe I can get them to loan me some money," she says. "A half a million's nothing to them, and I know I have a trust fund, if I can access it. It's worth a try."

"Don't take money from them," Minerva says. "We'll think of another way."

"I do have an interview tomorrow," Izaak says. "Who knows. Maybe I'll get a job, and it'll pay well."

None of us hold our breath, but it's cute he's still so optimistic after all this time. "Maybe so, man. That would be great."

"We all agree, then?" Bevin asks.

"Wait," I say. "Before we go any farther, none of you really got to choose whether to join my pack. I think all of you should get a chance to bow out. No hard feelings at all. This thing—a pack with non-wolves—my dad says it's the strangest thing any of the wolves have ever heard. And Roxana can tell you that it has some undesirable side-effects, and I'm definitely still figuring things out."

"You helped me," Roxana says softly. "That date with Lionel was—well, it was just bad. You gave me an excuse to just walk away."

Something about her words—my hope soars. I try to squash it down, but I'm not very successful.

"And we did choose you—we chose this," Minerva says. "We all had a choice. At least, I did."

Clark, Izaak, and Bevin all nod.

Roxana says, "We all chose you, and I think we're all in for whatever comes next." She laughs. "I didn't expect a redneck wolf pack, but if that's what we need, I guess I'm in for that, too. Everyone loves a good makeover, right?"

"Plus, we've only talked to one bank," Bevin says. "Maybe we talk to a normie one or two."

"What would we tell them our jobs are?" I ask.

"I'm a liaison," Clark says.

"Officer of the law," Minerva says.

"And I'm a small business owner," Bevin says, "and I can prove it with my books from before the shop burned down." She stands up. "I'm calling my real estate agent and telling her to take the offer on the land. She can prepare an offer for us. I think we should try—buy the building and tell Lo Ren we aren't scared."

"You're ready to lie like that?" Minerva asks.

"Fake it till you make it," Roxana says. "I'm in, too."

There's a strange uplift of power in my body then, like when a wave surges underneath you in the ocean, lifting you upward on its crest. "Guys, the pack bond likes it."

The knock at the door surprises all of us.

"My money's on the Demon Council," Minerva mutters. "They've been way too quiet."

"I'm not sure they'd knock," Roxana whispers. "I think we're past that point."

"Lo Ren?" Clark asks, looking my way. "They know you're friends with Minerva. Maybe they tried across the hall and didn't find you."

I really hope they didn't already destroy all our stuff. "Let's hope not." But as I walk toward the door, I can smell them.

It's a wolf.

As my hand grips the knob, all the muscles in my body tense, and I hear the others lining up behind me. When I glance over my shoulder, Minerva has her wand out, and I'm not sure whether that's encouraging or not. Clark's wand is out, too, and his eyes are determined. Roxana has her hands out, but I really hope she doesn't have to blow a fiery hole in the wall.

I fling the door open.

Jewel's jaw drops, and the man next to her, whose

hair is sticking straight up in the air at strange angles, jumps. "Xander?" Jewel's eyes move beyond me to my friends. "I thought we heard you in here, and I know we said tomorrow, but Pat's not doing so great. Is this a bad time?"

10

ROXANA

My brother Mateo left New York when he married his dragona princess, but she came from a nobody family that rules in Honduras. My mom didn't think most of my brothers would find wives, or she'd never have agreed to the match.

They hadn't been married long when my sister-in-law asked to visit.

From the moment we picked them up from the airport, Valentina kept saying how much better she would fit in here in New York than she did back home. Mom was extremely uncomfortable from the start. When we finally reached the penthouse and Mom welcomed them inside, her face was stiff. Mom's eyes were a strange mix of nervous and angry, and her movements were jerky, like someone was pulling her strings.

That's exactly how Minerva looks when she welcomes Jewel inside.

"So happy to meet you," Minerva says. "Xander has

said good things."

"Has he?" Izaak asks.

"Of course he has." Minerva's face somehow looks even stiffer when she glares at Izaak.

"What has he said, exactly?" Jewel lifts both eyebrows.

"Well." Minerva's blinking too much. "He said you have worked very hard to. . .um." Minerva winces. I actually feel a little sorry for her. She's the consummate hostess, always graceful and inviting. Except for now, apparently.

Jewel clearly made an effort to prepare herself for the city. She's wearing clean, newish clothing, even if it's not well made, and her hair has been washed. She may not look perfect, but it's a tremendous improvement over the last time we saw her.

Her brother, well, that's another story. I don't recall meeting him when we went to Waterbury, but he's a mess. At first, he focuses his eyes on whoever's talking, but after a moment, as if following the conversation took up far too much effort, he starts staring at a spot in the middle of the room where no one's sitting or standing or talking or doing anything at all. For a moment or two, he just frowns at it.

Then he starts muttering.

A minute later, he snaps at the air, his sharp incisors flashing.

At least they're clean, which is more than I can say for his hair, his ragged nails, or his clothing. I suppose Jewel could only do so much. Xander did mention he was in bad shape.

"What do you want?" Xander's asking. "I know we'd talked about meeting tomorrow to discuss details, and I'll tell you now that we're actually strongly considering it. We're in negotiations to buy this very building, and it has quite a few vacant apartments."

"That's amazing," Jewel says. "For a pack, living near their alpha is very important. I'm sure in New York City, that's challenging."

"Don't expect me to move," Clark says.

"Just the pack," Jewel says.

"I'm part of the pack." Clark folds his arms. "Everyone in this room is."

Jewel's eyes widen. "How many of you are there?"

"Five," Xander says. "Roxana you met before, but also a demon-spawn, a wizard, a vampire, and an er, well, a witch."

None of us are sure what to call Minerva. Even if she's angel-spawn, we certainly can't say that out loud.

"How interesting," Jewel says.

"If that's a problem," Xander says, "then—"

"It's not," Jewel says. "Not at all."

"But you came a day early because. . ." He lifts his eyebrows. "You had a hair appointment you forgot about?"

I can't help my snort. There's no way she gets her hair done.

"It's Pat." Jewel swallows. Her eyes dart sideways, and she licks her lips.

"What about him?" Xander asks. "He's clearly not doing that well, but—"

"He tried to *borrow* energy yesterday, and I almost couldn't detach him." Her nostrils flare.

"He—you should have put him down," Xander says. "That's a hard and fast rule." He stands, his hands balled into fists. "It's not even safe for him to be here, and it's certainly not safe for you. Did you bring him here so I could. . ." He scowls, his eyes flashing gold, and a muscle in his jaw popping. I can't help noticing that the corded muscle in his forearms is taut as well.

Xander's really hot when he's angry.

"Look, our pack started back in 1975 when my dad bought a lotto ticket with the last of his money and won. He used the winnings to buy the compound, and he never once turned a wolf away, no matter what condition he or she was in." Jewel's staring at Xander, her eyes full of quiet desperation. "We're all gamblers. We always have been. Lately things haven't gone well, but we know that with any gamble there's risk."

"And what about this gamble." Xander turns toward Pat. "A gamble that puts *my pack* at risk?"

Jewel's entire face crumples, and her eyes well with tears. "He's my twin brother. Did I mention that? He's been my best friend my entire life, and I just can't—I —would you be able to do it?" She points. "What if one of them was fraying?"

Xander starts pacing. "Of course I couldn't do it, so I'd find someone who could, but it's not relevant, because they're not *wolves*, so they won't ever fray."

"Which is also a rule, and you broke that!" Jewel's eyes are wild, but her feet are set shoulder-width apart, and she's not folding, even in the face of an angry alpha. She's tougher than I realized. "You—we wanted you specifically for *this* reason. We're a pack with problems, clearly, but you don't seem to be afraid of a fight." She steps closer, getting in the path of his pacing. "Please, Xander. Packs aren't strong because they're made up of warriors. They become warriors when they'll fight for the people who have helped them. We will fight for you forever, in any circumstance, but we need someone who will fight for us too."

"Jewel, it's not that simple."

"We'll fight with you against Lo Ren Fang, even if it's to the death," she says. "Can you find another pack on earth that would do that?"

It's an impressive claim, but one look at Pat tells me it's unlikely there's much Xander can do, even if he wants to help. I doubt there would be anything an akero could do at this point. Pat's drooling now, and he doesn't even bother swiping it away.

Xander wasn't unaffected by Jewel's plea, clearly. He stops pacing, sighing heavily. "I don't even know anything about how to help wolves with the fray. As I understand it, he'll be a bottomless black hole of need —he'll suck me dry if I try to bond him. That means trying to save him will put my friends in danger."

"We're already in danger," Minerva says. "We have been since we stood up to the Demon Council."

Bevin looks a little sick about that, but she shouldn't.

"Actually," I say, "maybe longer. You've all been in danger since I showed up on your doorstep."

"Maybe longer than that," Minerva says. "As long as you've been my friend." Her expression is deadly serious.

"Since you chose to be my friend," Clark says, looking at Xander. "No one liked it back in college, and they still hate it now."

"Since you welcomed a vampire roommate," Izaak says. "We've all been misfits from the start."

"The only place we fit," Xander says.

"Is with each other," I say.

Pat leaps to his feet then, lunging at Xander. When Jewel blocks her twin, he pivots on one squeaky heel and turns toward me, his hands grasping my shoulders. His grip hits me like a live electric wire, a jolt so strong that it would have knocked me on my backside if he wasn't anchoring my shoulders with surprisingly strong hands. Then something weird happens, something I can't even describe properly.

The closest I can get is that it feels like someone's vacuuming me from the inside out.

It feels like my life force is being inhaled from my feet, through my stomach, my lungs, my head, and then out through a hole in the top of my skull. It's excruciatingly painful, and I can't even scream. I'm frozen in place, like a Greek statue, my face contorted in what I'm sure is a terribly ugly expression.

I've become a Greek Tragedy, I realize, and I'm powerless to stop it.

Luckily, Xander's not. He leaps on Pat, wrenching him away from me, and then slams an open palm against Pat's face. There's a bright flash of blue light, and then Pat's head tilts at a strange angle and he whines.

He sounds just like a stray dog.

Jewel whimpers behind me, but when I start to slump, she's the first one to prop me back up. "I'm so sorry," she's whispering, over and over.

Not that the sentiment helps my jelly-knees or rubber elbows. I feel like the strong insides of my body have been hollowed out, and I'm struggling just to stand upright.

Xander's ticked about it. His face is as furious as

I've ever seen it, his normally rich and brilliant golden eyes hard, his mouth compressed into a hard line, and his brow furrowed from eyebrows to hairline.

He forces Pat to his knees.

But instead of killing him, Xander shifts and puts his other hand, palm open, on the top of Pat's head. I shiver then, as a pulse of energy passes through me, and I realize that Xander's doing something. What? I have no idea. But. . .something.

There's another pulse, and then another, and Minerva's *glowing* with brilliant golden light, while Bevin's glowing too, surrounded by an almost blood red haze. It's the strangest moment of my life, and I've watched my friend bond a pigeon, and a were-wolf alpha become trapped in a lime green Jello bubble.

But then Xander's broad shoulders straighten, and his chest flexes, and his nostrils flare, and he releases Pat. Instead of going ballistic, or panting, or whining, or whimpering, or anything else I've seen him do, Pat lowers his head, and he whispers words that sound an awful lot like a prayer.

"From this day forward, I swear to serve you and only you. I'll defend you, honor you, and protect you and yours with my life, my soul, and all my strength, now and forever." When he bows his head, there's a kind of a popping sound, like the inverse of my ears popping on a plane.

It's like the world around us popped instead.

Without waiting for any kind of explanation or response, Jewel drops to her knees and shuffles toward Xander. "Me. Now bond me."

"Bonding the nurturer who was mated to the last

alpha. . ." Xander narrows his eyes. "You didn't tell me that before."

"You know now because Pat knows." Jewel bows her head. "Yes, bonding me would bond the entire pack, but I wouldn't have tricked you into it."

"Because the whole pack's bonded to the alpha's mate." Xander cocks his head. "You really would have told me?"

She nods slowly. "I considered *not* telling you, but I don't want that kind of start. Not with you."

Xander doesn't look so sure, but he finally inhales. "Fine." He looks around the room. "Unless any of you object now that you've met them."

"Is he going to be alright?" Minerva tosses her head at crazy Pat.

"He healed him." Jewel's eyes are so intent on Xander, so full of adoration that I'm a little uncomfortable.

That's a lie.

I'm ragingly uncomfortable. I'd like to punch her. No, *incinerate* her. Some part of me wants to lunge at her, screaming *MINE.* But that's insane, so I force my hands into fists at my side, and I stand my ground.

"Did you really heal him?" Bevin asks. "I thought he was too far gone. Whatever he did to Roxana sure didn't seem pleasant."

"He did what he did for Roxana," Jewel says. "Fraying wolves, when they latch on. . ."

"They don't let go." Xander's voice is heavy, deep. IIe looks. . .turbulent in a way I've never seen.

Alpha looks *good* on him.

"But he did let go. Xander, you patched Pat's soul. I didn't think it could be done, but he's fine now."

She's absolutely giddy—her face has the shining certainty of a true zealot. "He's incomparable."

"You didn't have any way of knowing I could do that." Xander's gone back to storm cloud. "You risked Roxana's life with that stunt."

"Her gamble worked," I say, "at least partly because of *us*. She's right—we're not a normal pack."

Jewel's face turns toward mine. "If you'll let us swear, if you'll bond our pack, I swear that we'll do everything we can to honor the privilege of being part of this unconventional and powerful pack."

I'm not terribly close with any of my brothers. One of them, I was, but then he married and left. After Mom finally hatched a girl, she stopped all the constant pregnancies, so even my youngest brother is still quite a bit older than me. But now that I've met Izaak, Clark, Minerva, Bevin, and Xander, I'm starting to get how she might feel.

"I'm fine with it," I finally say.

As I watch Xander's face, when he nods silently, I realize that I feel differently about him than I do the others. I care—more isn't the right word. I care for him *differently*.

It scares me, but it's exciting too.

As he bonds Jewel, knowing that he's taking on an entire massive group of little wolves with all their indi-vidual and unknown problems, I experience a moment of panic. But as the bond settles in, a feeling of *power* bubbles through me.

It's not just me.

I can see it in the faces of the others as well. Minerva gasps. Clark's inhale is sharp. Izaak blinks repeatedly. Bevin swallows and shakes herself.

But Xander's the biggest surprise. He throws his head back and *howls*, for all the world like the wolf I've rarely even seen him be. Not even a full minute later, he shifts.

His shirt and pants rip and fall into pieces, and the wolf that rises up is glorious. He's massive—easily a good hundred pounds larger than any wolf I've ever seen. The furry ruff around his face is variegated, white in some places and brown in others, but the darkest color is the exact same as his hair. I want to ask if that's normal, but it doesn't seem like the right time. His golden eyes are exactly the same, glowing bright and intent as he turns to look at me.

"This may not be the best time to share this," Jewel says, "but we're closing on the sale of our compound tomorrow, and we start work next week. So we've already come." She swallows. "The rest of the pack's in the city."

"Wait," Minerva says. "How many is 'we'?"

"A hundred and nine," Jewel says. "The youngest was born just last month."

"A hundred and nine?" Clark looks floored.

"Where will you stay?" Minerva asks.

"Xander mentioned he might be buying a building. What's the timeline on that?" Jewel glances his way.

Not that fast. We have details to work out yet. I glance around to see if everyone else is also hearing Xander in their heads, and it looks like they are—Minerva's doing the same as me, looking around wildly.

It's a pack thing, Xander says. *I bet you can all do it now.*

I try without luck, but maybe eventually.

"We're still a little short on the money we need,"

Bevin says, "but my agent did leave me a message about a conversation she had with the owner. They're fine with the price I mentioned. We just need to get financing lined up."

"Signed leases would help," Izaak says. "She mentioned some of the apartments are vacant now, which is a little concerning for the bank."

Before this can descend into total disarray, I inter-vene. "Do you all have someplace to stay tonight?" The sun will be setting pretty soon.

Jewel shakes her head. "I'm sure New York has hostels, or something, right?"

"Where is everyone?"

Pat's walking toward the window. "Most of them were waiting down on the street."

A hundred plus people were just standing around down there?

We all follow him over, ducking out onto the patio and looking over onto the road. There are bunches of people milling around, several of them with dogs on leashes that don't really look like dogs. "That's them?" I ask.

It's more kids than I expected.

I glance around to see what Xander thinks, but he's notably absent, and as I have that thought, I get a flash of the floor, the door handle, and the ground in the hall. I realize that he's gone out the door and to his room, possibly to change. Even the shreds of his clothing are gone—he must've gathered them up with his mouth.

Jewel says, "A few of them are visiting friends and extended family in the area, but I made them swear to keep quiet about our purpose."

"Lo Ren's going to be furious," Minerva says. "He was mad enough the last time we heard from him, and Xander hadn't bonded any wolves."

"We need to find them all a place to stay." Xander's breezing through the door, and maybe it's the clothing—all black is a good look on him—or maybe it's the alpha power, but he has never looked more attractive. Not ever.

The teddy-bear version of Xander was cute, but I think it's gone.

This new Xander's lean, strong, and decisive. I like it. I like all of it.

"So, how do you guys feel about breaking and entering?" He lifts his eyebrows, and I realize the teddy bear's still in there, too. Thank goodness. I would have missed it.

"Not great," Clark says. "Not great at all."

"Then I'd say you should get to dinner, or whatever you do in the evenings when you're not here." Xander tosses his head at the door. "Our night's about to get interesting."

"Interesting?" Izaak asks.

"Bevin, didn't you say your agent had a list of which units were vacant?" He arches one eyebrow.

Bevin splutters and objects half-heartedly, but in the end, I think she feels it too. Now that Xander has bonded the pack, I can *feel* this need to take care of them. Their first need is to find a place to stay. "Unless you want them all to come bunk down with us," I say, "this is probably our best option."

Luckily, a lot of them brought bedrolls along with their suitcases.

"Most of our stuff's in storage," Jewel says, "but we

weren't sure where we'd be staying, so we brought necessities along."

"What would you have done if Xander refused to see you?" I ask. "Where would you have gone?"

Jewel's chin rises. "I had a good feeling about him."

She has balls of steel. "You put your faith in the right guy," I say. "He's got a big heart, and he's reliable."

"It's a rare combination," Jewel says. "As is someone who can see beyond what the world tells them to see."

It takes a half dozen spells and a few charms to block the cameras and break into the vacant units, but within an hour and a half, the entire pack has a place to sleep, at least for the night. Several of the apartments still have power, and they all still had water, so that's a small blessing. With as chilly as it is, we tried to make sure the smallest children were in one of the units with heat.

"How does it feel?" I ask, as I follow Xander down the stairs and back toward our floor.

He stops and looks over his shoulder. "What, being a felon?"

"A felon?" My brow furrows.

"Breaking and entering?" He snorts. "Probably a half dozen paranormal laws broken, too."

"I meant having a real pack, now."

Standing in the stairwell, we're hardly somewhere private, but the way he's looking at me makes the rest of the world melt away. "I already had a real pack." Have his golden eyes always been this intense? Or can I not stop looking at him, not stop thinking about his face because he's my alpha now?

Are all wolves intensely attracted to their alpha?

"You're intensely attracted to me?" Xander's voice is low, rough.

I want to curl up into a ball and drop through the floor. He *heard* me thinking that? Of course he did. By Gabriel, has he been hearing *all* my dirty thoughts over the last day or two?

"You've had more thoughts about me?" He blinks. "I was trying to make sure I *didn't* drop in on you." The corner of his mouth turns up, and his eyes shutter. "But maybe I shouldn't have tried so hard."

"Xander. . ."

He steps closer. "Today has been the scariest day of my life." His voice is quiet. It's barely above a whisper. "I've spent the last few years being beaten up, ordered around, and belittled by Lo Ren Fang. Everyone knows he's one of the strongest alphas on the East Coast. Today I challenged him, bonding a wolf pack here in Manhattan, holing them up in the building *he* placed me in." He sighs, his eyes lifting back to mine. "I might be dooming all of us. I want to do the right thing, but I'm afraid I'm not strong enough to beat him. Not even close."

"But Xander, you're the strongest person I know. The best. You always do the right thing, no matter how hard it is."

A muscle works in his jaw. "It's hard sometimes, doing the right thing."

"Is it?" Not from what I've seen. When fraying wolves shove their way into his friends' apartment, he saves them. When his friend can't pay rent, he covers it. When he's got what he always wanted dangling in front of him, he still won't betray a recent acquaintance to take it. "You seem to do it effortlessly."

"Not really," he says. "I've spent most of the last few weeks thinking of—dreaming of—all the ways I could kiss you, then drag you back to my apartment and never let you leave."

"Who says I'd want to leave?"

He drags a breath in. "But I shouldn't kiss you. It's the worst thing I could do."

My heart's hammering in my chest. I can barely breathe. "You've been thinking about kissing me?" I bite my lip. "Truly?"

"Doesn't everyone?" He shakes his head. "From the moment I saw you in that penthouse apartment in a wedding dress."

"But you didn't even seem to like me then."

Not nearly as much as I like you now.

I heard him. Standing right next to him, I heard him in my head. I haven't heard him since my date with Lionel.

And I missed it.

I've missed *him.* "You're not the only one who's been thinking about. . ." I swallow.

"But I can't like you." He shakes his head and steps backward until he hits the wall. "My best friend's in love with you."

"I know Clark 'likes' me, but *I* don't think about Clark. Doesn't that matter?"

"Not to him," Xander says. "He thinks you'll come around eventually."

"I won't, though," I say. "Because lately, I only think about one guy."

Xander blinks.

"A really tall, really muscular, powerful alpha."

The muscle in his jaw that I really, really love shifts.

"It's you, Xander."

"Say my name again."

My voice usually annoys me. It's always husky, always sexy. But in this moment, I'm grateful for it. I open my mouth, and I do as he asked. "Xander," I say slowly. "Binnigas."

Xander's eyes dilate, and his hands shoot out and grab my forearms, yanking me closer. His gaze fixes on mine, his eyes *burning* a bright, bright gold, like molten flame. "Roxana."

That's all he says before his head tilts down, and his arms bring me upward, closing the space between us. My nails dig into his hair, dragging him down faster, and then our mouths meet, and I forget everything else.

I've kissed Lionel.

I've kissed a few dragona males my parents shoved at me.

None of them felt anything like this.

I'm an inferno inside. I'm practically climbing up Xander, my legs straddling his waist while my arms wrap around his neck and shoulders. My nails dig into his body, trying to get closer, closer, something near *close enough*. But it's not even close. I'm worried it will never be enough with him.

He tastes like peppermint and beef jerky, and it should be gross, but it's not. It's better than the best dinner I've ever had. When his tongue darts inside my mouth, I moan.

"We—" Xander breaks away, falling backward

against the wall of the stairwell. "I—I'd drag you up to my room, but the thing is. . ."

"There wasn't room," I rasp. "I heard. Not everyone fit, so you have wolves staying in your place."

He groans. "But—by Gabriel, I wish I didn't."

I can't help my smile. "Xander Binnigas, you kissed me."

His expression falls. "Do you regret it?" He frowns. "I'm just a mutt. I know."

"Don't talk that way about *my* mutt." I take a step to close the distance between us, grab the collar of his blue shirt, and drag his face back down to mine. "Or I'll make you pay."

His frown shifts instantly into a smile, and he steals another kiss. I practically tear his shirt when he pulls away. "We can't—it's not a good time for. . ." He's panting, and I really, really like it.

"We have all the time in the world," I say. "Once we defeat Lo Ren Fang and you earn your side of Manhattan for our new pack."

"Do you really think I can?" The mixture of pride and vulnerability in his eyes is the cutest thing I've ever seen.

I pull his head down again, but this time, I press my forehead against his. "I've never been so sure in my life."

"I think I needed to hear that," Xander says.

"Nothing about any of this makes sense," I whisper. "Except us." I drag a finger down the side of his face, and we both shiver at the same time.

"We can't tell anyone right now," Xander says. "I need time to—Clark—and with the pack stuff. . ."

I nod slowly. "I know, and technically the world

still thinks I'm with Lionel. I need to clean that up, too."

"For now, we'll just. . ." He kisses me one more time, slowly. Then his mouth moves up the side of my face, and he whispers in my ear. "I'm not going to give you space anymore, though. If that bothers you, come find me and we can argue about it."

The smile on his face when we finally climb the last few stairs and emerge into the hallway is positively wicked.

And I love it.

CLARK

Some people smoke.

Others compulsively order saddle pads in every color, even though their horses already have way too many. (I'm not saying I know a person this crazy, but I hear they exist.)

My problem is buying blankets.

When I see a fuzzy one, a furry one, a minky one, or a chunky fuzzy yarn I've never seen before, I have to buy it. It's cold all winter in NYC, and you never know when you might be cold. Once, our furnace in the building broke, and I was cold for days.

As a result of my personal compulsion, I have more blankets than anyone could ever possibly need. I've been planning to donate them for months, but I've been too busy. When the poor, redneck wolves show up, bunking down on hard floors in empty apartments, I finally realize why I've hoarded so many. As I head back to my place to bring them over, I think about how impressed Roxana will be when I show up looking like Wolf-Santa-Claus.

As I heft not one, but two huge bags full of blankets out of the cab, I imagine just how her face will look when she sees me and how generous I'm being. She'll look at me the same way she was looking at *Xander* when he started breaking into apartments for them. She'll look at *me* like I'm amazing. Like I hung the moon.

I wait in front of the elevator for five or six minutes before deciding to just jog up the stairs. In fact, maybe she'll see me coming out of the stairwell, muscles popping from hefting these bags, and I'll get to see that look early.

But then, in the stairwell, I hear Roxana's voice. I freeze at first, and then slowly, I creep a little closer, just close enough to see who she's talking to.

"Xander Binnigas, you kissed me."

Kissed him?

My stomach knots up.

Could that be, like, a euphemism? Could she be making a joke? I carefully set the two bags of blankets down and creep closer still, leaning around the corner to try and see something. I'm worried she might see me—but the light's dim. Once my head turns the corner, I can see, and it *is* Xander and Roxana, and they're staring intently at each other. I doubt they'd see an elephant if it squeezed itself into the stairwell.

I'm not sure I would, either.

"Do you regret it?" Xander's frowning. "I'm just a mutt. I know."

Maybe she kissed him because she felt sorry for him. Are there pity kisses?

"Don't talk that way about my mutt." Roxana stalks toward him, grabs his collar and drags his face down toward hers. It doesn't *look* like pity. Nothing like pity, in fact. It looks an awful lot like she *wants* him. "Or I'll make you pay."

Xander agrees with me, kissing her for what I have to assume is the second time. He does break it off, at least. "We can't—it's not a good time for. . ." Xander looks wrecked, like he's both excited and destroyed by the fact that the world's most beautiful woman wants to eat his face.

"We have all the time in the world," Roxana says. "Once we defeat Lo Ren Fang and you earn your side of Manhattan for our new pack."

"Do you really think I can?" It's a puppy dog face that he's making. I've seen him make it before. I wouldn't have thought it would work on Roxana, but I can't fault him for trying it.

It is working on Roxana, though, for sure. She yanks his head down to hers *again*. "I've never been so sure in my life."

They're whispering now, and I can't hear much, but I do hear Xander say *my* name.

Roxana nods, and she says something about Lionel, too.

He won't be any happier about this than I am. And then, as if they just can't help themselves, they're kissing again, and I finally think to pull out my phone and snap a photo. The idea of Xander, my supposed best friend, stealing the girl I've liked as long as I've known him, turns my stomach, and I want to burn the building down, but I don't say a word. It's not the time for talking. I need some time to think so I can figure out what I should do.

Once I'm sure they're not still in the stairwell, I

gather up the blankets I dropped and practically run upstairs to dump them outside the doors of the empty apartments. I don't bother trying to do it in front of Roxana. I'm not going to win her over from Xander with two bags of blankets, apparently.

On my way back to my place, I can't seem to think about anything else. All my memories with Xander—college, and every year since. Thanksgiving dinners. Christmases when he had nowhere to go and came home with me. Weekends. Every day at Grand Central gloffee. All his corny jokes. His help moving me, my help moving him. Commiserating about jobs, and the complications of our lives.

He's my best friend.

I just can't believe he would do this to me.

Sure, he's a wolf. He's not like me in really any way. He makes constant jokes. He's never had much of a career. He hasn't had a substantial relationship, not ever. None of the women he's taken out have stuck around for more than a week or maybe three.

Maybe that should reassure me.

Xander can't maintain a relationship. He never has. He inevitably says or does something truly idiotic, and then he plays it off because what he really wants is a mate. That's been his excuse all along—it's okay he's never had a girlfriend, because one day he'll just meet *the* one. Someone who's perfect for him.

Another wolf.

But now he's kissing the dragona princess whom he almost turned in to the Manhattan pack to secure himself a place. The irony should make me laugh, but instead it fills me with a dreadful rage. It's a sick kind of anger I wish I could get rid of, but it's dogged. It chases me down the street, and up into my apartment. As I try and sleep, it continues to haunt me.

I toss and I turn all night.

I have plenty of things to lose sleep over.

The Manhattan pack wants us dead. The Demon Council hates us for helping Bevin. I turned down a job I always wanted to keep from adding heat to Roxana when she was hiding, and then I lost my job instead. I betrayed Roxana to get a new job, but my new job's horrible. I also almost died defending her against a massive, psychotic dragona bent on melting me into a charred spot on the top of Dagobar Tower.

Meanwhile, Xander didn't step up. He didn't try to save her from Ragar or his goons. Lionel didn't either. Not when it mattered.

I did that.

And yet, she hasn't noticed me at all. Really, ever since she showed up, my life has been in a nosedive, and I didn't even mind. I thought I was prioritizing what really mattered: love. Only, apparently it wasn't love *for me*.

Xander watched me do those things, risk everything, every step of the way, and now. . .what did he tell her? Did he tell her I placed those photos in her room? Did the two of them laugh at me and how pathetic I was, liking a dragona princess? I alternate between anger and jealousy all night and barely sleep at all.

When I wake up, I use a charm to improve my appearance. The bags under my eyes are awful. It's not a great look to show up with on my second day in a new job.

Not that I care much about this crappy job.

Instead of tossing and turning last night, I should've been prepping my resume. Maybe if I called back the professor who loved me so much, they could find me a place after all. Academic stuff moves slowly. Maybe the position's still open. I work on updating my resume on my way to work, adding an end date to my last job and writing up a description for my current one. It doesn't look great that I'm searching for a new job in the first week that I have this one, but some things can't be helped.

Of course, when I reach work, Charlotte's waiting for me. "Our first big case," she says. "I'll be filling in for Horatio. He got called up on a confidential one."

My first full day and my mentor isn't here. Why am I not surprised?

"Don't worry." Charlotte tucks her long hair behind her ears and smiles. "It's a very routine call today. Horatio told me to let you handle it, and I'll be here if you have questions."

"What are we doing?"

Charlotte pulls an envelope out of the pocket of her jacket and hands it to me. "Read for yourself."

I lift my eyebrows as I pull out the single sheet of paper. "Is this how we usually get our orders for the day?"

She nods.

I unfold it. MAGICAL CLEANUP AT SOLBERG MANSION. GREMLIN INFESTATION.

"*This* is our bread and butter?" I groan. "Gremlins, really? Don't they have services for that?"

"Services have marked trucks," Charlotte says. "The neighbors talk. They wonder who in your family has been fooling around." She shrugs. "The best families would never call a service."

"At least tell me that we have equipment."

"What? Do you mean, like a full body suit?" She arches one eyebrow. "That's worse than a marked truck. High power mages don't need that sort of thing."

I curl my lip. "Fine, but I never go places that might have gremlins, so I should go reinforce my personal protections."

Charlotte laughs. "Yes, and maybe bulk them up in the future. You'll go a lot of places with gremlins going forward."

I can't help shuddering as I zip into the restroom and duck into a stall. I learned the right charms in school, of course, but I haven't used them, not since I passed the test on personal protections.

Once we're driving over in Charlotte's black sedan —I won't get one until my mentor clears me—I ask, "What are the Solbergs doing that they wound up with gremlins?"

Her sideways look is a little judgmental. "That's none of our business."

"But seriously. *Gremlins.*" I shudder again.

"Look, demonic energies are useful for a lot of tasks, and some of what the wealthier and more powerful mages do is distasteful, but it still has to be done."

"You're saying they got a demonic STD doing assigned, sanctioned *work?*"

Charlotte laughs. "Sex with a demon's not the only way to get gremlins. The key is that they didn't realize they'd picked them up, so the infestation was allowed to grow."

I can't even imagine.

Gremlins start out microscopic, living on their host until they're large enough to peel off and wreak havoc on their own. "They itch, right?" I shake my head. "How did they *not* notice and deal with it sooner?"

"Again, not for us to judge," Charlotte says. "It does sound like you haven't done much with them lately. Maybe we should review the ways to dispense with them effectively."

"I've never dealt with them," I freely admit. "I had a class, so I know the general concepts. Do we really deal with them a lot?"

Charlotte shrugs. "They're embarrassing. We deal with everything the high-ranking Illuminae find embarrassing."

"Alright, well, what I remember from school is that there are three types of gremlins. The first are attracted to water. They tend to stay near it. They destroy buildings, trees, and any kind of debris around the water source. They're the termites of gremlins, basically."

"Sprite gremlins, yes. They can only be destroyed with a lure. They're a real pain."

"You lure them with an illusion of water that's strong enough to smell, taste, and sound like water."

"And then?" She's keeping her eyes on the road, but she arches one eyebrow.

"You destroy them with fire, or you banish them to the demon realm, which is my favorite. Give them back to the misery they came from, now that they're big enough to be a pain. Like fattening up a tick and handing it back to the deer it came from."

"At least you paid attention in school," Charlotte says. "What's next?"

"Dark gremlins," I say. "They can't abide sunlight, but at night, they come out in large groups, destroying anything they can find."

"That's right," Charlotte says. "They feed on anger, envy, or poor intentions, and if they get large enough or old enough?"

"They'll become more and more sentient," I say. "They can actually target their host and try to do anything that might specifically harm him or her."

"They're vicious," she says. "And really, really bad if you ignore them."

"Those are *only* passed through. . ." I cough. "Relations with a demon. I think."

Her lip scrunches. "You're remembering wrong. The dark gremlins do attach to a particular person and bedevil just them, but it's the sleep gremlins who always originate from *doing* things with demons."

I find myself scratching my head, as if I have lice or something. Just thinking about gremlins gives me the heebie jeebies.

"Speaking of sleep gremlins," Charlotte says. "Tell me about them."

"Sleep gremlins." As I talk, the itching only worsens. "They specifically plague people only when they're asleep, and they'll happily pass to anyone, normie or supernatural. They don't specify."

"But you can only bring them over from the demon-realm through. . . You know what."

"I don't know how we ever wind up with these."

"The massive numbers of demon-spawn running around contradict your doubt."

"They aren't demon-*mage* crosses, though," I say. "It's always human-demon crosses."

"Not always," Charlotte says. "The more powerful demon-spawn come from mage families." She shrugs. "And once they're here, sleep gremlins can go anywhere. So they could be picked up in a hotel or home that someone visits, even if they had nothing to do with a demon themselves."

"Right." I smack my head. "Once there are more than, what? Eight or ten of them? The youngest ones leave to form a new pod."

"Heaven help the poor normie who picks one up," Charlotte says. "They'd have to burn their house down to get rid of them. Thankfully, they're almost always passed to overnight guests, and we never get called unless it's a top level Illuminae member who wound up with them."

"Am I remembering this right? They bite or sting the sleeping hosts and suck their blood?"

"Yep, and their spit soothes the bites, so usually the host won't realize they're there for a very long time. The symptoms come from their discharge," she says.

"Poop," I say. "Their poop causes hallucinations in the long run, and it permanently damages walls, buildings, and support structures, like invisible acid."

"It also causes miscarriages and all sorts of other maladies," Charlotte says. "The textbooks usually leave that out."

"That's horrible," I say. "So what kind of gremlin infestation do they have at Solberg Mansion?"

Charlotte shrugs. "No way to know until we get there."

How fabulous. "I'm not even sure which is the worst."

"Do you know how to destroy the dark or sleep gremlins?"

"Can we just burn all the beds down?" I ask. "Or maybe the house?"

She laughs. "Try again."

I sigh. "I think for dark gremlins, you make a black hole and it draws them to it, right?"

Charlotte's hands grip the wheel tightly, and she turns her head slowly. "If you can make a black hole, what in Gabe's name are you doing here?"

I definitely can't, but I was hoping maybe she had a portable one. "Okay, I think the easier option was to assemble something really gross. Something smelly and hot, and then wait. It'll usually draw them to it, but you have to black out the whole house to get them moving during the day."

She's nodding.

"Then you banish or drown them."

"Without ruining their fifty-thousand-dollar hand-knotted rug from Portugal." Charlotte's lip's curled this time.

"Ha," I say. "You don't like this either."

"Of course not," she says. "No one likes dealing with gremlins, not even the specialists. But it's worse for us."

"Because we're smarter?"

"Because we have to do it without tenting the dumb house—we have to be discreet. And if we ruin any of their stuff, we're in trouble."

"At least we're paid well," I say.

"Sleep gremlins," she mutters. "How do we deal with them?"

I sigh. "I'm not sure. Honestly, I just can't remember."

She looks like she's bitten into something rotten. "You have to get in bed and go to sleep, obviously."

"You're kidding."

She shakes her head. "The good news is that sleep gremlins hunt in packs, and there usually aren't a lot of them. If you catch one. . .you can lure them all to you with that first one's screams. But." She coughs.

"I have to let it bite me first," I say.

"I'm obviously hoping it's not them." But that's when Charlotte turns down a long, tree-lined drive. I realize as she parks that our discussion, however disturbing, at least distracted me from Roxana and Xander. It's the first stretch I've gone without thinking about them since seeing their horrible kiss.

"Are you okay?" Charlotte asks. "Truly, it's annoying, but this isn't a big deal. We'll be in and out in half a day."

I hope she's right. As we approach the house, I wonder for a moment who's here and whether I might make some connections I can use in this job. The people we're dealing with are sure to be powerful, right? If we impress them. . .

"You're wearing your *I mean business* face," Charlotte says, her lips twitching. "It's cute."

"What?" I snap my head toward her. "Not at all."

"We won't meet the Board Member, trust me."

"What—" I splutter. "No, I mean—"

The door opens, and a woman in a white apron curtsies. "You're the liaisons?"

Charlotte nods. "Here as promised, at nine on the dot."

The *maid* lets us in. It takes me a moment, but I realize she's a vampire. "They have a vampire maid?" I hiss.

"A vampire housekeeper," the woman says, arching one imperious eyebrow. "I keep the children safe and make sure they're adept at basic combat maneuvers in addition to keeping things clean."

"It's nine in the morning," I say. "Aren't you tired?"

She cocks her head to one side. "Finding out the house is infested with sleep gremlins has proven remarkably effective in helping me stay awake in the early hours of the day."

I can't help my groan.

Charlotte hisses softly, but she doesn't reprimand me. "You're up."

"Do we know what room they're located in?"

"So far, we've only been able to prove they're in the master," the vampire housekeeper says. "But I'm worried they may be elsewhere."

Of course she is.

I suppose I'd be nervous, too. Actually, I'm nervous already, and the odds of them following me home are much, much lower than them moving to a new bed in the same home. I still can't believe I'm stuck dealing with this.

"Since I'm the one who's supposed to be cleaning this up," I say, trotting along behind Charlotte, "maybe it would be better if—"

She whips around. "No way. You're the one being spelled to sleep."

I tighten my hand around my wand, which I must have pulled out because I was nervous. "Our first order of business is to check each of the rooms and find out which ones have gremlins," I say. "Right?"

"Normally," Charlotte says.

"But the Solbergs have a charmed amulet, and they tested this morning," the vampire housekeeper says. "It says they're only in the master." She doesn't look convinced.

"Would you like us to check yours before we leave?" Charlotte asks.

"That would be wonderful," she says, her face relaxing.

"It's always nice to have confirmation." Charlotte motions for me to precede her into the master bedroom, the double doors for which we've stopped in front of.

I grit my teeth and go inside.

It's an enormous room with a massive four poster bed in the center. There are huge, oversized night-stands on either side, and two huge dressers, also one on each side of the bed. On the far end, there's a desk against the wall and on the side closer to us, there's a door that I presume opens into the bathroom and closet, but there's also a large sitting area with a sofa and chairs.

"Alright, well, I think we should start—"

She points. "Check the bed first."

I've barely reached the side of the bed when she hits me with it. I barely hear the words, "Somnum autem," before my world goes dark.

When I wake up, the light's almost nonexistent. Even in the limited light from the cracked closet door, I can see that there's a stupid gremlin sucking on my elbow.

"Inhabilitare," Charlotte says.

Great. Now it's *stuck* to my arm.

I practically fling myself into a seated position, but Charlotte's agitated about it. "What's wrong with you? Are you trying to lose it?"

"How long do I have to let it eat me?" I point at it. "It's not your arm it's munching on."

"If you snap its teeth off while you're flailing around. . ." she says.

My memory's returning slowly, but I realize why she was snippy. "It frees it."

"And we'll have to start over, only, they'll know we're here."

"Fine," I growl. "Fine." I feel around with my awkward left hand for my wand and finally close my fingers around it. "Dolor lancing," I mutter.

Only, I guess I didn't realize my wand was backward. My spell hits me right in the chest, and my body *writhes* with the lancing pain I was trying to zap the dumb little vermin with.

Charlotte's too busy laughing to do anything herself.

When the waves of agony finally fade, the stupid little gremlin's looking at me with what looks an awful lot like mirth in his frozen eyes. This time, I make sure my wand's facing the right way, and I zap him good with the same spell.

It's satisfying to watch his body spasm, and it's a

tremendous relief when his pointy little teeth finally release my arm.

"Congelo in place," I mutter.

The little guy, who's wearing no clothing on his bulbous little body, but bizarrely is wearing a tiny little porkpie hat, stiffens and falls sideways.

Charlotte snatches him into what I hope's a charmed bag and ties it tightly with flaxen cords. "Now comes the fun part."

She doesn't give me the chance to do it, she just dumps him into an ice-water-filled bucket, holding the thrashing bag down for a count of ten before lifting him up.

The screeching sounds faint to us, but I'm guessing his buddies can hear him loud and clear.

"Do you have more bags?"

"Why?" Charlotte pulls a tiny bag out of her pocket and upends it, blowing the powder that comes out all over the room. It's golden, and it disappears quickly, but now that it's dispersed, I can see them.

A dozen little bulbous bodies are creeping toward us.

"Banish them," she hisses. "Now."

Not many mages can banish straight to the demon realm, but I did mention that was my preference. I point at a small bunch and say, "Ad daemones," and the three of them disappear with a popping sound.

I can't quite help my smug smile. I haven't had to do that since school, but I've still got it.

"Keep going, idiot," Charlotte shouts.

They're advancing on us, and there are a lot left. I'm surprised they haven't spread to other rooms yet. I repeat the spell six more times before getting them all.

Other than the one in the bag.

"You can take care of that one," I say.

Charlotte shakes her head. "I can't power that spell."

It's a big admission. Plenty of mages can't use it, but I assumed everyone in our job could. I don't meet her eye when I banish the last one. Charlotte doesn't glance at me while she checks to make sure we've gotten them all and orders me to do the cleanup spell.

"Shoot," I say, as I'm finishing the cleanup. "I bled on their coverlet."

Charlotte swears.

"I hardly think they can fault us for that," I say.

"You'd be surprised," she says. "We're not celebrated and thanked, Clark. We're expected to do our jobs without any mistakes. If we do that, they don't think about us. If we mess up, we're in big, big trouble."

Thanks to the work I did on that stupid sofa for Bevin, I have a few decent charms for stain removal. "I'll take care of it," I say.

There's barely a smudge left when we leave to confirm the housekeeper's room is clear. I doubt they'll even notice it. Miraculously, none of the other rooms are infested. We're on the way out the door, and it's not even noon. Charlotte was right. It was a quick, albeit disgusting, job.

"I'm shocked there were that many confined to the one room," I say. "Usually don't they start breaking off once they get over eight or nine?"

"Only if they don't have enough food," Charlotte says.

I'm staring down at the scab on my elbow when

another voice says, "Gremlins, I assume?" A man snickers. "They would have had plenty of food in the master bedroom of this house."

"Are you kidding me?" another man asks. "That's rude."

Two men swing around the hedge on the side of the house, walking up the path from the garage around the corner. The first man I know, Lionel Sol.

What are the odds?

Not horrible, I suppose, since I'm doing magical cleanup for the elite of the Illuminae, which certainly includes him.

"Your dad's nasty, and you know it," Lionel says. "And you should thank him, or you'd have been feasted on by his gross gremlins."

"I don't even want to hear about it," the tall man next to Lionel says. "If you'd just kept quiet, we'd never have had to talk to them."

Lionel's eyes meet mine at that exact moment. "Clark!" He actually smiles. "How'd you pull gremlin duty?"

"We're the Illuminae's magical liaisons assigned to this case," Charlotte says, ducking her head respectfully.

I should be following her lead, and my failure to do so earns me a glare from Lionel's friend.

"Liaison duty," I say. "Always a pleasure."

"Sorry about that," the tall man says. "Especially since you're a friend of Lionel's." He grimaces. "You'll keep this on the down low, right?"

"It's part of our employment contract," Charlotte says. "You have nothing to worry about, Mr. Solberg."

"Greg," the man says. "You can call me Greg."

Charlotte nods, but I notice she doesn't repeat his name.

"Hey, can I chat with you for a minute?" Lionel asks, but he's not really waiting for me to agree.

"I'll head for the car," Charlotte says. "Take your time." She rushes away like there's a lion after her.

"Greg, give us a minute." Lionel waves at the front door. "I'll be right in."

"Hey, is the house clear?" Greg scrunches his nose. "Like, you got them all, right?"

"Banished to the demon realm," I say, "every last one."

Greg exhales slowly. "Thank goodness. And hey, nice job." He's not half-bad, throwing me thumbs up as he disappears.

Lionel doesn't even wait for him to be gone before asking, "How's Roxana?"

I can't help my frown. "Didn't you just have a date with her?"

"She's ghosted me since." Lionel throws his head back and growls. "Obviously the date didn't go well. She didn't tell you?"

I shake my head. "She was excited before it, I thought."

"That creepy wolf followed her through the whole thing, like he had a crush on her or something."

I should warn him. Lionel should know, as her supposed boyfriend, that the creepy wolf does in fact have a crush on her.

More than a crush.

I open my mouth to tell him what I saw, what I heard, when a little twinge of guilt works its way in. Xander may have betrayed me, but he's still my best friend, sort of. Don't I still owe him more than *Lionel?* This guy only looks out for himself.

"I think you should ask Roxana," I say.

"Like I said, I've been texting her," he says. "I even sent flowers and a card, but she returned the flowers."

I bite my lip and scrunch my nose. "Dude."

"I know." He starts pacing, his wide shoulders whipping right and then left, right and then left. "I *know* that's my answer, but here's the thing." He stops and turns toward me. "No one has ever dumped me. Not ever."

"Technically that's still true," I say. "You weren't actually together, not really."

"But the thing is, I like her more every time I'm around her. It's like I'm stuck in a vise, and time with her just twists it tighter and tighter." He does look pretty strung out. "That freaking wolf was crawling around in her brain, and who does she get mad at? *Me!*"

"He's our friend," I say.

"He's more than that," Lionel says. "How do you think her parents will react when they find out she's been *bonded* by an alpha werewolf? And a loser one at that—he doesn't even have a job."

"Shouldn't you be more worried about whether she actually likes him?"

"The wolf?" Lionel snorts. "Not really—he's about to be put down by the alpha of the Manhattan pack. I just need to make sure no one finds out they were connected."

"I'm not sure—"

Lionel claps a hand on my shoulder. "I'm going to give you a little advice, from a friend. Get out of that situation, if you're involved, before it gets really ugly. I'll do whatever I can for Roxana, but any ties to that wolf are going to be really bad."

"I heard that wolf's petitioning for them to split the Manhattan areas so there can be a south pack," I say. "But even if that doesn't happen, I think going in hard against Xander's a losing play."

"Xander." Lionel's hands curl into fists. "I hate him, Clark. Like, really *hate* him." He pivots on his heel and brings his face around until it's right in front of mine. "Let's make a deal."

"A deal?"

"My dad made you a promise." He tosses his head at the black sedan. "He lost you the job you had, and then he paid you back for trying to break me and Roxana up by giving you those photos with this terrible position." He lifts both eyebrows, which tells me he's guessing. "It's exactly the kind of thing he'd do."

He knows his dad. I don't confirm his guess, but I don't deny it. I fold my arms. "What do you suggest? Because I feel like listening to the Sol family hasn't been smart in the past."

"Help me find dirt on this Xander. We break up Xander and Roxana, and that helps us both. She's your friend, too. You want to keep her safe."

I do want Xander and Roxana to break up. It really is what's best for everyone. And working with Lionel to make it happen, well. Enemy of my enemy, and all that. "I'm not sure—"

"Help me, and I'll get you a *much* better job than this." He sidles closer. "You're banishing gremlins for perverted wizards?" He shakes his head. "Come on, Clark. This is *so* not you."

"It's really not," I say.

But neither is betraying my friends. I did it once, but only to help Roxana see that Lionel's a mess. She already knows that, so no matter what I do, it's not like she'll go back to him.

His hopes of getting her back are delusional. What does that mean about *my* hopes? "Do you really think that even without Xander you have a chance?"

"She's going to see her parents tomorrow," Lionel whispers.

"Right," I say. "I heard that already."

His grin starts small, but it widens as he talks. "And I'll be there. They invited me. They didn't like the idea of the two of us at first, but they're coming around. I have a plan to win them over."

"Win them over?" That sounds alarming.

"I think Roxana might be the one for me," he says, utterly serious.

Oh, man. He's in for one load of a surprise. She doesn't even like him. "I just don't think there's much I can do."

"You think being bonded to Xander's good for her?" He arches one eyebrow. "Honestly?"

I should tell Roxana that Lionel's planning an ambush. I should defend my friends. I know it's the right thing to do. I'm just not sure I can actually do it. I hate myself just a little when I ask, "What do you want me to do, *specifically*?"

12

BEVIN

Demon-spawn don't own buildings. Especially not level two demon-spawn. We're pretty much the bottom of the para-normal food chain.

Clark was pretty sure he could convince his mother to invest in the building. He and Minerva also had some savings they said they could use. When my agent calls, I feel good about things. "I think we almost have our funding worked out," I say. "Like, we're a lot closer than I thought we'd be."

"That's good, because I got a call from the listing agent today. She said there's a buyer looking at the building right now. It's a corporation in China that's been investing in American real estate."

"They're not even supernatural buyers? Really?" My stomach lurches.

"Money's money, Bevin. I don't think the seller cares where it comes from. I need to know how serious you are about making an offer."

I *am* worried about losing the building, but I'm just

as worried about getting caught for squatting there. "When you say another buyer from China's *looking*, what does that mean? Are they walking the place? Or do they just kind of check out images on Google Earth?"

"I don't know," Raven, my agent, says. "Does it matter?"

"I mean, I'm just curious how committed they really are, because—"

"Here's the bottom line. The seller would rather sell to you—someone local who will live here—but if you can't get an offer together soon, they'll take the best one that's in their hands."

"By the angel's feather," I say. "Okay, I get it. But look, we have almost five million pulled together, but the bank wants another half million on top of that."

"You're talking to more than one bank, right? Or just PNC?"

"No, I mean, we realized yesterday that maybe we should branch out, but the thing is, none of us have a lot of work experience to offer, and it's not like a normie bank would be impressed that I've run a second-hand magic shop."

"Normie banks literally only care about dollars and cents. You could tell them you run a second-hand adult novelty store, and they wouldn't care as long as they think you'll pay your lease note."

"Right, but—"

"Bevin, do you at least have the three hundred-thousand-dollar earnest money payment ready to wire?"

I choke. "I mean, yes, I do, technically."

"My advice? If you're serious about this, figure out

the rest in the next seven days. Make an offer now and lock the building down before it's too late."

I groan, but I don't think she's wrong, really.

Do it, Xander says. *We'll find another bank that gives us a bigger loan, or we'll get the money from Clark's mom. Somehow, we can find a way to get the last amount we're short.*

It's encouraging, having someone in my corner, someone else to tell me that things will be okay. It would be a little more encouraging if we had more of a plan, or if either of us had a job, but it's fine. Some people just manage buildings, right? Once we buy it, we'll be real estate moguls. Landlords.

It'll be fine.

"Draw up the offer," I say. "Make the closing date soon."

"Like a week?" she asks. "Can you get things together that fast?"

"Maybe two," I say. "Can we do that?"

"I have no idea what you can do," she says. "Usually business loans can be expedited on rent-producing properties. Can you get signed leases? Do you have tenants lined up?"

"You know, maybe lowball them just a hair. If we can get the price down a smidge, we won't be quite as short."

"With another buyer in the wings, the lowest I'd go is thirty million."

I groan, but I give her the green light. I'm scrolling through normie bank options to find one with an office that's close that also handles commercial loans when I'm nearly flattened by a truck. I hop back on the curb, just a block from Grand Central Gloffee. "Phew," I say. "That was close."

"You've been blessed with all kinds of miraculous saves lately," a familiar voice says. "Wonder how long your tremendous luck can last."

"Oh, I don't know." I fold my arms under my chest and glare at my twin sister Soki. "Feels like it already gave out. At least, having my own people burn down my shop and home didn't *feel* very lucky."

"Maybe that's your fault," she says. "You're the one who refused to join us."

"Yes, I love following people who threaten to harm me and anyone I care about if they don't get their way."

"You're like a child throwing a tantrum." Soki steps into the street, smiling as cars crash to a halt in front of her. She turns back and waves impatiently for me to follow. "Come on."

"You called it good luck when I didn't get hit by the truck," I mutter. "But here you are, jaunting across the street in front of traffic."

She taps her head as she steps on the curb. "Foresight, remember?"

One of her demonic powers allows her to see into the future in flashes and fits. It's not always reliable, like most demonic powers, but when she knows something, she knows it.

"Must be nice," I mutter. Her second power was the ability to torch things. Meanwhile, the only power I've gotten so far is a static-electricity level zap. I finally reach the other side and step up onto the sidewalk a few shops down from the building I'm trying to buy. I hope she didn't overhear anything about that.

The last thing I need to do is attract the attention of the Demon Council again.

"What's your second power?" Soki asks. "Better than that little love-zap one, I hope." She widens her eyes. "You can't really be refusing to tell me."

"It's not any of your business." I fold my arms. "The last time I told you, you ran to the council and told them right away."

"They sent me," she says. "Of course I told them what I discovered. You should be telling them yourself."

"I thought you came to warn me," I say. "What happened to blood's thicker than water?"

She blinks. "Is it? Before or after it clots?"

"I—does it matter?"

"What does that phrase even mean?"

"That you should support your family," I say. "I think."

Soki snorts. "Maybe if you weren't hell-bent on destroying your life. I'm quite sure whoever made up that dumb saying didn't have a sister as stupid as you."

"I'm a delight." I bare my teeth.

"Maybe so," she says, "but you sure do like to put your head right in the noose." She moves to get out of the way of a power-walker with several shopping bags and comes nearly nose to nose with me. "Here's some sisterly advice. You think your little wolf pack's full of friends, and you think that you should be loyal." Her eyes flash. "In this world, you need to surround yourself with people who make you stronger. That wolf isn't making you stronger, and neither are the other rejects you've shackled yourself with in the interest of staying *free*."

"That's ridiculous," I say. "No other wolf has ever bonded non-wolves. He's unique, and you have no idea how powerful we are together." I puff up. "He could destroy you easily."

Soki's laughter rings out loudly enough that people jogging past us freeze to stare. "Destroy me?" She drops her voice to a hiss. "That stupid wolf is the reason you haven't received a second power—stop pretending it's not true." She jabs me right below my throat. "You may hate yourself, but if you can't join people who strengthen you and cut out the ones who drain you, you're doomed." She lifts her chin. "I may be following orders, but that doesn't mean I'm not also trying to help you. Stop fighting and fall in. You've been warned."

I'm not sure how long I stand on that corner, watching numbly as people stroll, jostle, and lurch past me with bags, boxes, and packages. When a delivery scooter hops the curb and nearly plows into me, I'm finally roused to movement again. Even so, I think about what Soki said the entire way to Grand Central Gloffee.

I just told Raven to place an offer on the building, and I don't even have the money together for our financing. I might lose three hundred thousand of my precious dollars. And sure, it's the Demon Council's fault I'm shopping, and it's their fault my life is up in the air, but from Soki's perspective, it's my fault too.

I'm the one denying who and what I am.

I always have.

From the time I knew I was demon-spawn, I hated it. Once my mom explained what it meant, I wanted to fling the people who made me this way the bird.

Then I felt bad for wanting to do that, like that anger came from my demon-nature, and I decided to pray for the daimoni instead.

I'm sure that made them laugh.

Or maybe only the akero laugh when someone prays for the daimoni. I'm not sure. Either way, I've always been at least as ridiculous as demon-spawn are wicked. My life has been one sequence of uphill battles after another, and for the first time, I feel the weight of them.

I'm tired of always fighting what I am.

Soki's words, that I should find people who make me stronger, not people who drain me, keep coming back over and over.

I feel *so* drained.

Everything feels hard. I have no home. No belongings. No shop. Nothing. All the things I'd worked for, all the hours I'd spent building my safe little corner of the world, my innocuous, do-gooderly little second-hand magic shop, poof.

They're all gone.

And for what?

Because I stood up for Roxana, a dragona I barely knew.

I should've kept my head down. I should've continued to do tiny things that were good and avoided any epic acts like protecting people I think were being mistreated. The danger's in the grey areas. Always in the grey. Demon-spawn might get away with being good, or at the very least, they might be able to avoid being bad.

But we can't be heroes.

That's just not our story. We have to cling to

anyone and anything that can lend us strength, because on our own? We're nothing special. We're half-evil. I've known it my entire life. I've pretended it wasn't true. I've played at being good, but I always knew that deep down, I'm like a spoiled apple. At my core, there aren't seeds that hold a future.

There's just rot.

It's my legacy.

And now I fear I may be dragging all the others down with me. The Demon Council may have left when Xander bonded me, when he bonded all of us, but they aren't really gone. They're regrouping, and they'll come back once I think we're safe. The one thing they cannot allow is for a single demon-spawn to rebel—no one can refuse them. They have to enforce their power or they'll lose it.

The law of the jungle, but in New York City, the concrete jungle.

I'm still thinking about it when I walk into Grand Central Gloffee. Minerva's awake, at least, sipping on her plain, black gloffee. Two sugars. No cream. She's taken it the same way as long as I've known her. She may sugarcoat things sometimes, but she never makes dark into light or light into dark. She's straight-up.

She's as much light and life as I am darkness and death. Half-angel makes sense. I should have known. Maybe that's why I attached myself to her in the first place. I could feel her goodness, just seeping out. She should cut me out, especially now that I've descended and she knows that she's not half-human like she thought. She's as lovely as I am dirty.

But when she sees me, she smiles and waves. "Oh, good."

Across from her, Xander knocks back a glespresso. Probably dragona, if what I've noticed lately is right. "Minerva's got a date soon, and she said I'm not qualified to help her pick an outfit."

"For feather's sake, no," I say, turning toward Minerva. "Not unless you want to look mangy."

"Dog jokes." Xander frowns. "Always funny."

"Where are all your little puppies?" I sit next to Minerva, waving at Gavin. "Glachiatto, vampire."

"I still can't believe you order those, knowing who donates." Xander shivers. "I mean, just, no."

"I bet you ordered dragona," I whisper.

Xander's eyes widen. "Hey, that's a secret."

"Is it?" I ask. "I mean, she's *out* now, right? Does she have to disguise that she's donating blood?"

Xander's brow furrows. "Maybe not." Then he takes a sip. He doesn't bother denying that it's Roxana's brand of glaffour berries, I notice.

"Okay, so can you help me pick an outfit?" Minerva gulps her gloffee down and stands. "Because Ricky's coming in like. . ." She glances at her watch and squeaks. Giggles wings away from the shelf over the door and *disappears*, like she just teleported out.

She pops up on the other side of the door, thankfully still alive, but squawking.

"But my glachiatto," I say.

"I made it to go." Gavin hands it to me. "I heard you talking."

"You're a wonder," I say.

"Tell Izaak that." He winks.

"But for real, you know that he's not—"

Gavin's hand squeezes my upper arm. "They all say that, until they don't." He shrugs. "Let a guy dream."

Xander stands. "Well, if they're going back. . ."

Gavin hands him another glespresso, also to go. "I figured."

"I really hope you don't have to find a new location," Minerva says. "You're so good at what you do."

Gavin shrugs. "I hear there are two buyers interested, so I guess we'll see what happens when one of them puts money down."

The second we reach the stairwell, Xander's bugging me for info. "Two buyers?"

I tell him what Raven said. . .and what I did.

Giggles is fluttering around closer and closer to our heads. She's being pretty irritating, to be honest. "Oh, man." Minerva's agitated, and her pigeon can probably feel it. "You—you told her to make an offer? The earnest money's. . ." She chokes. "What if we can't find financing? What if—"

"But we can't lose it to the Chinese buyers," Xander says. "She had to do it."

Instead of trying on lots of outfits, Minerva and Xander spend the next half hour on the phone with different banks, asking about our options. It's pretty cute, right up until Minerva squawks and drops her phone on the sofa like it bit her. "Ricky's on his way." The blood drains from her face. "I don't even—I haven't even put makeup on yet."

"You look great already," I say.

Xander rolls his eyes. "And even if you don't, hasn't he seen you at work and stuff?" He grins. "If lover boy likes you at your worst, he'll think you look amazing now, out of uniform."

"Why does that sound like an insult?" Minerva frowns.

"It's not," Xander says. "I'm saying, guys don't notice nearly as much as you think we do."

"They always notice when Roxana—" Minerva looks around. "Wait, where is she?"

"She's at a job," Xander says.

"Where?" I ask. "I thought she hadn't found anything."

He sighs. "It's a modeling gig. I know she wanted more of a real job, but we need money quickly, so when Luis Vuitton asked her to model for their dragona-inspired handbag line. . ." He shrugs. "Add another hundred thousand or so to our balance sheet."

"Holy forked demon-tails," Minerva says. "That's amazing. Who else could she pose for?"

"Right?" I ask. "With yours and Clark's, that means we're only four hundred thousand short for PNC. Or did we find someone else who might—"

"Wells Fargo wants two years of work history," Minerva says.

"And Bank of America wanted collateral other than the building," Xander says. "And a vacancy rate below twenty percent." He shrugs. "On the upside, they didn't need a forged—" He coughs. "A signed letter from the Manhattan pack."

"Did you tell them we already have renters for the empty units?" I ask. "In fact, we could kick out some of the current tenants and still fill the building."

"You know, I didn't mention any current fire hazards or illegal squatters who want to pay rent," Xander says. "I figured I'd let you go into more detail on that later."

I roll my eyes.

When there's a knock at the door, Minerva darts

toward her room. "Talk to him for a minute." She's glaring at Xander, and she motions for me to follow her.

"What?" I ask. "What can I do?"

Minerva's still waving, so I follow her as Xander answers the door. As I close Minerva's bedroom door, I hear Xander, his voice all high and weird like it is when he's nervous. "So, Ricky. I hear you're a guardian."

"Yep," Ricky says. "You must be Xander, the new wolf alpha."

Xander nods. "Hey, have you heard this one yet? What do you get when you cross a billionaire and a sorceress?"

Ricky's frowning.

I wait to close the door until I hear his corny punchline. Xander always has a corny joke on the tip of his tongue. They're usually painful, but I've gotten used to them.

"Not gonna guess?" Xander's still waiting.

Ricky shakes his head.

"A very *witch* person." He's grinning, like somehow his smile will persuade Ricky to join him in his mirth.

It worked in this case. Ricky's bark of laughter is deep and manly, and I can't help smiling too as I close the door. "What are you doing in here? The man of your dreams is currently being entertained by a very nervous Xander. Do you know what nervous dogs do?"

Minerva swallows.

"They pee on the floor," I say. "Xander's out there, right now, peeing all over the tile. Go save Ricky."

Minerva grabs my hand. "How do I tell him?"

"About the building? I doubt he'll care. I really don't think he's into you because of your savings."

"No, dummy. About the wolf thing, and about the chief of paranormal affairs thing."

Minerva's hands are clammy. Giggles lands on her shoulder and fluffs up, cooing, and I use the distraction to extricate my hand. Before I can suggest any ways for her to break the news to him easy, Minerva starts talking again.

"Of course not," Minerva says. "That's a terrible idea. That's why I'm asking Bevin."

"Umm, hello. Are you going crazy?"

Minerva glares at her pigeon.

"Wait, is *Giggles* talking to you?"

Minerva swallows. "Will you think I'm nuts if I say yes?"

"Maybe don't tell Ricky about that tonight," I say. "The Chief of Paranormal Affairs and the bonded by a werewolf thing might be too much already. But as the current mayor of crazy town, I think it's cool."

"I just. . .I've liked Ricky for *so* long, but what if he can't handle the insanity that is my life?"

"Most people couldn't."

Minerva's shoulders droop.

I drop to a seat on the edge of her bed. "What did Giggles say?"

"She said if learning about me scares him, he's not man enough for me." She sighs and plops down next to me. "But Ricky's not the problem. He's the manliest guy I've ever met. He's powerful, and kind, and courageous. And have you seen him?"

"He does have dreamy eyes," I say. "But that birdbrain's right." I pat Minerva's hand. "If he can't handle your life, which is *amazing*, by the way—if he can't handle your light, he doesn't deserve you."

Minerva nods repeatedly. "Right." She looks down at her hands. "I guess."

"Sometimes it feels like we're the problem." I lean my head against her shoulder.

"It does, yeah." She sits next to me like that for a moment. Then another.

Awkward laughter bursts out in the family room. "Are you going out there soon?" I ask. "Because if you don't, I think it may not matter what you tell him."

"Xander's definitely an acquired taste," Minerva says.

"Yes, exactly."

Minerva hops up, Giggles flapping her wings to keep her balance on Minerva's shoulder.

"I know what I'm getting you for Christmas."

"What?" She's got one hand on the doorknob, but she turns toward me, a bemused expression on her face. "A vat of ice cream to help me get over Ricky when he dumps me?"

"No," I say. "Ricky might be smart enough to handle you, or maybe not. You'll be fine either way, but your shoulders may not survive much more of that." I point at Giggles—she's already glaring at me. "I'm getting you sweaters with reinforced shoulder pads, like the kind elementary teachers used to wear."

"Smart idea," Minerva says. "She's got terrible balance."

Giggles is chittering when they walk through the door as if she's upset with me for criticizing her, and she immediately launches off Minerva's shoulder and heads for the fridge. I'm pretty sure she's hiding treats up there for later. To avoid making painful small talk, I immediately duck back into Minerva's room. I can't help thinking about Soki's warning as I poke around at Minerva's obsessively organized stuff. Soki said I should surround myself with people who make me stronger, and my friends may not do that. In fact, we may not help one another at all.

We're kind of our own biggest liabilities.

But my friends do make me happy, so maybe Soki's wrong.

Maybe it's okay if my friends bring me nothing but joy. They're good people, and as demon-spawn, that may not be a usual criterion for associates, but it's my primary concern. I'm happy, and that's a lot for a demon-spawn to be able to say.

I hear a weird crash, and some talking, but then, I hear them leave. Finally. When I poke my head out, it's just Xander, and he's sitting on the sofa, staring at his phone. I've just decided it's safe to come out when Clark breezes through the door.

"Bad news," he says. "I went by Mom's on the way home, and she said she won't invest." He drops onto the sofa next to Xander. "So we're still half a million short." He leans his head on his hand.

"Just four hundred thousand," Xander says. "Roxana's doing a photoshoot."

Izaak bursts through the door, then. "And I've got a meeting. You didn't forget, right?" He widens his eyes. "Right, Xander? You can't wear that, and we're going to be late if we don't go, like, now."

"Wait," I say. "What's Xander going to this meeting as?"

"He's my manager," Izaak says. "Duh."

"You better get dressed like a manager," I say. "And you two need to slay this meeting, because if we can't come up with four hundred thousand dollars in the next week. . ."

Betting on Izaak getting a ridiculously high-paying gig that pays up front? It feels like. . .I'm an idiot. All my earlier happiness flees, and I can't help spiraling just a little. Happiness might be great, but it only goes so far.

I'm worried that, like Soki said, I may be betting on a losing team.

13

MINERVA

When my dad died, it felt like someone kicked a leg out of my three-legged stool.

I still had my brother Clark, of course, and I had my friends. That gave me two solid legs, but you kind of need three legs to stay upright. Before he died, I called my dad every day. I'd tell him my goals, and I'd talk to him about the things that went wrong.

I told him all the things.

When I botched a spell, I'd call him in tears. When I got in trouble because of a stupid misfire, he'd pat my head and tell me it was fine. I knew, deep down in my bones, that he loved me the same, even with my problems. He didn't think less of me because magic sometimes ignored me. He never thought I was worthless. He never told me I couldn't do something. We talked about how it would be when I made guardian. We talked about how I'd save the world one day.

And then, one day, bam. Heart attack.

No warning—he was just gone.

I've felt a little unsteady ever since.

The misfired spells hurt a little more. The times I didn't get promoted to guardian stung a bit harder. The jabs from co-workers, and the ways I failed my friends, they all stung just a little worse because my dad wasn't here to take some of that pain.

But when I leave my room to save Ricky from what I'm guessing is not the first of Xander's bad jokes—he's telling one about werewolves when I open the door, and Ricky clearly has no idea how to react—I wonder whether I might finally get a leg back. It would be really nice to have a boyfriend I could count on when my life got all *Minerva* on me.

I guess I'll find out soon enough.

When I tell him about all the madness my life has become, he'll either take it in stride, or he'll freak out and leave.

"Hungry?" He smiles at me, and my stomach flips over.

He's absolutely, painfully gorgeous. His muscles have muscles, which is a wonderful bonus, but he also has these two dimples that frame up the most beautiful mouth, with gleamingly straight teeth. He's tan without resembling a paper bag. His skin looks like the kind of color you get by going out for a run, or like, serving at a community clean-up event. Real color from being a big, brawny do-gooder outside every day.

And he always looks genuinely happy to see me.

Is it strange to say my boyfriend reminds me of my dad? I mean, I guess that sounds weird, but it's more about how I feel with him: safe. At least, so far, I have.

"Minerva?" Xander prompts. "The very handsome man asked whether you're hungry."

"Very handsome? Try to sound less gay. Geez." I try to stroll across the room in a way that looks effortless and breezy. Unfortunately, as I'm aiming for breezy, I throw my hand up to toss my hair back over my shoulder, and my hand collides with Giggles, who's swooping back down from the fridge to land in her normal place. My hand knocks her sideways and she crashes into a lamp, knocking it to the floor where the blown glass lamp shatters into a million and one tiny shards.

I flick my wand at it without even thinking. "Vicissim."

The lamp shards reverse like a video in rewind, the lamp reassembling itself.

Ricky's gaping at me, his bottom lip dangling open.

"I *am* hungry." Giggles finally settles onto my shoulder, preening a little to refluff her ruffled feathers. She coos. Then she leans closer and pecks my earlobe. "My familiar's hungry too. But then again, she's always hungry." I glance sideways at her decidedly plump form. "Maybe she should sit this date out."

"What did you just do?" Ricky asks.

"Oh, the lamp?" I shrug. "I mean, my grandmother brought it back on a vacation they took without the kids to Venice, and if it went missing, it would turn into a whole thing. My mom never lets go of stuff like that."

"No, not the lamp. What was that word you used?" Ricky's frowning. "Was it 'reverse'?"

I frown. "Not sure. It just popped to mind."

"That's not a real spell." He's shaking his head. "That shouldn't have worked. You should be—well, you should have *exploded*."

"That's not really true," I say. "I know they say that can happen in school to scare us, but trust me on this one. I make up spells all the time, and I have never once exploded."

"True," Xander says. "I was there when she made some woman just start spouting cash from like, every single pocket and bag."

I didn't tell him that after that, all the cash in my wallet was gone. Always a price to pay—but in that case, I think it was well worth it. That woman really seemed strapped for cash, and her kid just wanted ice cream.

Ricky's head turns slowly toward Xander, and I realize how many rules I break when I do that kind of thing. I shake my head, make a pained face, and drag my hand across my throat, hoping Xander will go along with me. "He's kidding." I force a chuckle and roll my eyes. "Xander and his jokes."

"No, seriously," Xander says, only looking at stupid Ricky. "This kid wanted an ice cream cone, and his mom said they couldn't afford it, so the next thing you know, Minerva's whispering some thing or another, and bam. Money everywhere. Then, after that, she made this old lady grow new hair!"

"New hair?" Ricky's blinking far too often.

"I mean, in Minerva's defense," Xander says with a grin, and I can feel a joke coming, "she had no idea the half-bald old woman was a redhead, or she wouldn't have done it, I'm sure."

"A redhead?"

"It's a joke," Xander says. "Get it? Her hair was white, what was left of it, and because people say redheads are the worst—you know, they're always getting angry? It's funny, because she wouldn't have saved a redhead had she known."

Ricky's brow furrows and his nostrils flare.

"Dude, does your mom have red hair or something? I'm kidding. I like redheads just fine." Xander leans against the counter. "But let's talk about the state of comedy. I mean, jokes are funny because you're saying something taboo. But, like, for some reason, it's okay. For instance, comic drops on myself are fine. I'm mocking myself. Comic drops on a person who's like way, way better than me—more powerful, richer, better looking—they're also okay. I'm dissing a person who can't really be hurt by me."

Ricky's staring at the lamp with narrowed eyes.

"Xander." He has got to stop the monologuing.

"Now, I know, people don't talk about this but hear me out." Xander's like that bus you just have to watch drive right over the cliff. "We can't make fun of redheads anymore, *apparently*, and we can't make fun of fat people. We can't make fun of religious stuff, and obviously racist jokes are out. What does that leave us?"

Ricky's frowning.

"If we can't make fun of *anything* anymore, what's left?" He shrugs. "Just myself, I guess. I mean, it's funny? But there's not much scope for it. That means I'm stuck with lame witch and werewolf jokes, and let me tell you, you weren't really laughing at this much earlier either."

I harden my tone. "Xander."

He finally meets my eyes. "What?"

"I'm sure Ricky has reservations somewhere. We need to go."

"Ah, sorry. I do tend to talk too much when I'm nervous."

Ricky follows me out the door, even pretending he doesn't notice when I try to shake Giggles off my shoulder without any luck. "So, that was weird," I say, "but the thing is, Xander exaggerates."

"Was any of that true?" Ricky asks as we walk toward the elevator. "Do you really make up spells?"

I shrug. "Let's go eat, and we can talk about it."

He doesn't argue, but as we exit, he's quiet, much quieter than he usually is.

"Where are we headed?"

He stumbles, and I grab his arm.

"Whoa, there. You okay?"

"Making up spells—my cousin did that." He's staring at me. "I watched his attempted spell explode —he lost his arm."

"Oh." I shake my head. "But listen, I've been doing it my whole life," I say. "It might have to do with being a halfie—not sure. I promise, it's totally safe for me. In fact, my made-up spells work better than the real ones, usually."

"Do you think that's why your spells misfire, though? Because you fool around with the right phrasing or words?"

"Mine misfire when I use the correct words and proper intonation. I think I'm a strange caster, and I need to lean in to what works."

"But what if leaning in could kill you?" Ricky's frowns, and his stumbling makes sense. He's worried about me.

"I'm hungry, but not too hungry for a small

detour." I grab his arm. "Come with me for a moment."

He's stiffer than usual, but I manage to drag his burly self toward Central Park. I find an empty bench, which is a little hard to do at dinnertime, and sit. He reluctantly takes a seat next to me.

"I showed this to Xander, which is what he was rambling on about. From the time I was much younger, sometimes I'd get a tingly feeling. I'm not sure how else to describe it."

"Tingly?" He finally focuses on my face, his expression lightening. "Like your fingers are falling asleep?"

Giggles coos and chitters.

"Your familiar is pretty strange," Ricky says. "But I think she fits your personality."

"Great. You think I'm like a pigeon."

Giggles starts chittering loudly, clearly annoyed. I'm just happy she's mostly acting like a real bird.

Ricky smiles. "She's as sassy as you are."

And now she's preening again. She hops down to the ground and starts to strut her stuff in front of us, attracting the attention of a few other pigeons. "None of that," I hiss.

She catches my eye. . .and smiles.

How a pigeon can smile with a beak, I have no idea, but she's *definitely* smiling. A glint in her eye, the set of her head, and a slight opening of her beak. She's *daring* me to tell her what she can't do.

She's a brat.

"I'm nothing like her." As if I don't have enough to deal with right now, she's acting up? *Brat.* "Alright, so I'm going to keep my eyes open and wait for the tingle, and while we're waiting, I may as well tell you all my news."

"Xander, the lone-wolf jokester, bonded you as part of his pack."

Now it's my turn to gape. "You—how do you know that?"

"Guardian." He jabs that indented spot on his chest just between the defined pec muscles I can see through basically every shirt. It looks especially good right now, with just a plain sky-blue t-shirt hugging it. "The Demon-Council was pissed, and now your friend's kind of famous. I've heard a lot of things, but one thing I've never heard of was a demon-spawn being bonded by a wolf. The fact that he did it to stymie the Demon Council, because she *doesn't want to join them*." He whistles. "I'm getting a lot of attention because you're my girlfriend."

The word settles against me like a ray of unexpected sunshine on a winter day. "Girlfriend?"

"Right?" He frowns. "Or should I not say that?"

"No, you should. I like hearing it." I look down at my hands.

"Was that all your news?"

I look back up. "Not revolutionary enough for you?" I lift both eyebrows. "A witch being bonded by a wolf?"

"No, it was, definitely, but you did say *all your* news, implying more than one thing."

"Right." I bob my head. "So, I had to go in to work the other night on an emergency call for my partner, Amber."

"The vampire." Unlike other Guardians, there's no judgment in his tone. He's just clarifying.

"Right. And while I was there, the Chief pulled me aside." I drop my voice. "This is a secret though, so like, shh."

He suppresses a laugh. "Got it. Lockdown initiated."

By the angel, he's so cute. "The Chief's stepping down, and he wants to recommend me as his replacement."

"What?" Ricky braces his hands on his knees. "Are you serious?"

"As serious as a misfired spell," I say.

He frowns.

"It's a joke." Then I remember he said his cousin lost an arm. Maybe it's not a joke to make in the future. "But listen, I doubt it's going to happen. The heads of the different groups all have to ratify his nomination, and I don't see that happening."

"Like they *all* do?" He sighs. "Because the Demon Council kind of hates you, and I doubt anything could change their mind."

"You know, the Chief didn't say whether they're included. I wonder if convincing the others would be enough."

"Does anyone else care about the wolf thing?" He tilts his head. "I'm sure that with your dad's past, the Illuminae will support you, and you'd think the wolves would like that there's a witch tied to a wolfpack."

"Er, well. My best friend is kind of in the process of dumping Lionel Sol, so I wouldn't count on Illuminae support."

"The vampires, though—"

"Not that long ago, I sort of—inadvertently—boiled the Chancellor's son."

"That was you?" His eyes widen.

"Afraid so."

"At least the dragona like you, right?"

"Maybe they would have, before I let their daughter hide with me for weeks after she skipped out on her wedding." I'm cringing.

"Minerva, you really do get around." He chuckles. "The thing is, though, you were just doing what you thought was right in each case."

"I hear that's a sought-after trait in a Paranormal Affairs Chief."

He snorts. "Maybe not, but I think if you had time to talk with them, you could convince them."

"You know, maybe you're right. I'll just call each one of them up and see if they want to meet me for drinks and a chat."

Ricky bites his lip. "I happen to know where they'll be two nights from now, around, say, nine o'clock."

"What?" I tilt my head. "Why would you—"

"We're having a guardian fundraiser. The Demon Council tends not to attend, but everyone else has RSVP-ed already. They have to support us—we're protecting Earth from the threat of the daemoni. You should come as my plus one."

"Brilliant," I say. "That gives me some time to come up with ideas for how I can convince them that I'm not a terrible choice without getting you fired."

"Why do you want to be Chief?" he asks. "Just because your dad was?"

"Or because I won't ever make guardian?"

He winces. "I didn't want to say that."

"But we both know it's not going to happen."

He shrugs. "You really never know."

That's when I see him.

There's a little old man, staring at his hands. It's cold, so at first my brain just thought he was closing his fingers repeatedly to warm them up. But then I notice that there's a guitar case beside him. He flexes his fingers a few more times, and then he pulls off his derby cap and tosses it upside down on the ground. He doesn't look rich, but when I think about solving his money problems, nothing tingles.

When I think about his hands, *everything* does.

"Okay, do you see that guy?"

Ricky frowns. "What guy?"

I toss my head.

"The old guy with the guitar?"

I nod.

"What about him?" He peers that direction. "Do you think he's demon-spawn?"

I shake my head slowly. "No, but I'm tingling."

Ricky freezes, and then he swallows. "Minerva."

"Just have a little faith." I drop my left hand on his forearm, and I pull out my wand. I think about the old man's hands, about what it must be like to struggle to play if it's what you love, if it's all you want to do. And then I say the word that comes into my mind. "Restituo."

"But that *is* a spell," Ricky says. "It's for faded pictures and documents that you want to—" He cuts off, watching the old man, who had just begun strumming his guitar. He looks the same. A pained face, cramping hands, and a bent back.

But then the wind picks up.

Bunches of green, red, and orange leaves swirl around us, through the park and beyond. The wind knocks my purse on the ground, and my lip gloss falls out, clattering away from us on the pavement, and breaking. My gloss leaks out, staining the pavement a fall-perfect russet.

"The price," I whisper. "Always a price."

The wind still hasn't stopped, though. It tosses the man's wisps of white hair. His hand freezes mid-strum, the one holding the top of the guitar tightening on the strings. Then he gasps.

The wind dies.

And the old man sets the guitar down. He flexes his hands again, this time with a look of wonder on his face. He *looks* the same, and yet he looks nothing like he did. He stands up. He dances in a circle, and then he sits down again, picking up his guitar like it's a newborn baby.

When he grips it with his left and strums with his right, he's beaming. The sound's full, rich, and beautiful. Not a second later, he opens his mouth and starts to sing. His voice doesn't sound feeble, nervous, or wobbly.

It sounds strong and true, and he looks surprised by it.

Ricky and I watch as he plays one song, and then another. The first was a ballad. The second was a pop cover. By the time he starts the third, people are milling toward him, listening, talking, and tossing coins in the hat.

Tears slide down the old man's papery, wrinkled cheeks.

"You—you did that?" Ricky sounds astonished. "You restored his ability to play and sing?"

I shrug. "He's not an old document. I'm not sure I ever learned the spell for restoring things like that, but if I'd tried to cast it, I'd probably have burned whatever letter or contract I focused on to a crisp or crumpled it into an irreparable wad."

He snorts. "I doubt it."

"No," I say. "Truly."

"Do you do this often?" he asks. "Come to the park? Make up spells for people?"

"All the time," I say. "Whenever I'm discouraged. Whenever I feel like a screwup."

He drops one hand over mine. "You're not a screwup. Not at all."

"Do you feel better about the made-up spells?"

"I believe that it's different for you," he says. "And that's okay."

We sit there for another hour, and I find two more people who need my brand of help—a lady with a sick dog, and a boy with a limp. If it costs me a broken watch and bruise on my knee, well, it feels worth it. By the time we stand up to go, we barely have time to grab hot dogs before I have to change for my shift. "Sorry—duty's a real nag sometimes."

Ricky shakes his head. "Not at all. That's one of the things I like about you. You like your job—you just want to help the world."

It's one of the things I like best about him, too.

When I reach the department, the Chief's holding his briefcase and looks to be on his way out. "Sir?"

He stops, but he smiles when he realizes the

person who called him was me. That's always good to see. "Lucent."

"Do you have a quick second? I want to run something past you."

"Sure." He points at his office.

Once he has closed the door, I waste no time. I'm sure his wife's waiting on him. "I was talking to Ricky tonight, and—"

"I heard you two were dating. That's great. Glad it wasn't just a rumor." He sits down across from me, beaming. "He's a gifted guardian, and he advocated for your selection for years."

"He told me you didn't." I frown. "Thanks a lot for that."

"You know why," he says.

I do, but it still stings. "Well, anyway, he had an idea. He said there's a fundraiser for the guardians that most of the heads of the different—"

The Chief slams his hand down on his desk. "That's a fantastic idea!" He stands up. "Once they meet you, once I tell them how great you are, they'll support you. I'm sure of it."

Or it'll draw their attention to who I am and why they don't want me to take over. I don't mention that possibility. "Anyway, I just wanted to make sure you thought it was okay for me to go."

"I have to go, you know," the Chief says. "This is exactly the sort of thing you'll need to attend in this position. I should have thought to bring you. If you can just survive the party without any incidents, they'll realize you'll be fine to have around."

"Well, we can dream, and if they all freak out

tomorrow, at least we'll know you need to choose someone else." I stand up. "I won't keep you. Tell your wife I said hello."

"Wait." He unlocks his desk drawer and pulls out the box I know holds my dad's wand. "Take this."

"You said once I accept the position I can have it, and we have no idea whether I'll even be approved by—"

"I wanted *you* to try. This is your reward for giving it your best effort." He shakes the box a little. "Take it."

I reach out slowly, feeling the weight of the wand before I even pick it up. "You always kept it in your desk?"

"Heavens no," the Chief said. "I've used it for years but trust me. It's not worse for the wear. I'm actually pretty sad to be losing it."

"You can keep it." My hand freezes an inch away.

"No." He shoves it the rest of the distance until my fingers wrap around the smooth wood. "You know." He releases it, and suddenly. . .

It's mine.

"I told you a lie before." He chuckles. "I guess I felt guilty about it."

"A lie?" I know I shouldn't be frowning, but I can't help it. "What do you mean?"

"I told you that your dad gave it to me to keep it safe. I told you I was supposed to give it to you when you made Chief, but that's not what your father made me promise."

"What did he want?" I open the box, my eyes falling to the champagne-colored wood of the wand.

When my fingers brush against it, they *vibrate*. It's like it's calling to me. I force my eyes away. "Chief?"

He sighs. "He actually made me promise *never* to give you the wand. The wand was my bribe, to make sure I helped you with anything you needed and so that when I retired, I'd make sure you took over for me, like your dad did for me."

"But—"

"I felt guilty for taking it. Your father was my best friend. He shouldn't have had to bribe me. He should have known I'd do whatever he asked. He did so much for me that taking this wand felt wrong."

"Wait." I need to make sure I heard him right. "He said you should *never* give me the wand?" I drop my hand over it again, closing my fingers around the wood and lifting it out, and like a bell that's been struck, the vibrations from the wand travel up my body, ringing so loudly I'm shocked the Chief isn't staring at me in confusion.

He just answers, like nothing strange is happening at all. "He said something about how if I did, you and your brother would fight, blah blah. He said your mother always favored Clark because he wasn't adopted, but if I gave this to you, it would cause unrest."

"Okay." The vibrations are finally receding to a small, manageable buzz. "That's weird, though. Clark and I have always gotten along great."

"I thought it was strange, especially since the strength of the wand is in focusing energies and collecting magic. It always seemed like just what you needed, what with all the misfiring."

He's right.

It does feel like just what I need, but I've learned that should always make me very, very nervous. Things in my life never come easily.

There's always a price.

With something like this wand, that price will be steep. I hope I'm able to pay it.

❧ 14 ❧

IZAAK

Everyone has had a naked dream.

You know what I mean—that dream when you're at school, work, or the park, and you realize the reason everyone's staring at you is that *you're naked*. More often than naked, though, I would find myself some place without shoes. For some reason, my subconscious brain found the idea of being out and about barefoot to be even more horrifying than being out naked.

Probably because I look pretty good naked.

But ever since that day in high school that I filled in for my normie bestie and played Mercutio? I've probably had a dream once a week that I'm up on the stage, and everyone's smiling at me. Everyone's laughing—not *at* me-, but because I delivered a line perfectly.

That dream has kept me going all these years, reminding me of the best part of my entire life, but I'm worried that hanging on to that high has been far worse than walking around the street barefoot or

193

naked could ever have been. I finally have the meeting I've always longed to get. I'm going to meet a director, the kind of director that could change everything for me. . .and if I scare him too, I'm done for. Actors don't get two chances, not like this one.

My whole life has built to this, and I'm about to screw it up.

I can feel it.

Xander's knee is bouncing uncontrollably next to me in the cab.

"Bruh," I say. "You drank one too many glespressos."

He glares at me, but he doesn't stop bouncing.

"Alright, maybe *two* too many."

"I've been thinking about something." He stops moving, and he stares right at me. "You want to do this—acting—because you loved it back in high school when you played Mercutio, right?"

They've all heard the story. "Right."

"Okay, but that means that you didn't scare people back then. It means it's possible. Terrified people don't laugh."

I can't help my frown.

"And, even more than that, you had a normie friend, right? The one who you took over for as Mercutio? So, you didn't scare him either, not at all. Not at a baseline, or you wouldn't have become friends."

I blink. He's right.

"You should have called him," I say. "Maybe met for lunch. You could even come clean with him and ask him if you ever scared him."

"We can't come clean with normies," I say. "It's against the rules."

Xander laughs. "So, like better or worse than hiding a dragona from her family? Or what about bonding a demon-spawn, a vampire, a dragona, and two mages to a werewolf pack?" He's really laughing now. "Or what about hiding an angel-spawn—"

I slap a hand over his mouth and glance at the cabbie. He doesn't *seem* to understand English, but you never know. "Have you gone nuts? You're spouting off nonsense anywhere?"

He leans toward me, his eyes almost shining. "Izaak, I've watched you for years now, doing anything you can to get past this. But the one thing you've never done is work with *normies* to try and fix it, and they're the only ones who can tell you if it's working."

"Fam, I *can't* work with them. That's the point."

He shrugs. "Well, it's like wanting to be a chef and only watching cooking shows. Until you actually pull out the butter and flour and start mixing it together, you'll never learn to make a cake."

"You lost me with the baking, but I see what you're saying. All of that's incredible insight. . .if you'd had it a week ago. We're on the way to the meeting right now, though."

Xander grimaces. "I mean, that's sort of my thing, right? A day late, and four hundred dollars short. I didn't realize I was an alpha until I was about to be executed by the pack I'd been begging to let me in for years."

He seems to find this funny, but I'm on stress level 900. "Okay, does any of this help with my meeting? Because if not—"

"I know," he says. "I should shut up. But I keep thinking about your friend, D. This producer or whatever, he's just one guy, right? You only have to keep from scaring *one* tiny human. Just like that time years ago. You just have to connect with one. So what scares humans?"

I have no idea what he's asking. "Spiders?"

He nods. "Okay, and like, dark water? Maybe darkness in general?"

"Sharks." I snort. "Taxes."

"Those scare everyone."

"Fair," I say. "What about death?"

"A lot of what scares us is the same, and death is probably the thing that scares everyone the most. That's what they feel when you're around. You don't usually kill humans, but you *can*, and they can feel it."

"But lots of things can kill them. They aren't scared of buses, airplanes, the ocean, or like, azalea plants, right?"

"Do you even know what an azalea is?" Xander leans back as if to study me.

"I watch television," I say. "I'm an actor. Hello?"

"They did a special on azaleas?" His lip's twitching.

"They did, a few months ago. Things to keep your pets and kids away from." I straighten up and square my shoulders. "But look, the point's that—"

"Yes, what's the point?"

"You have arrived at your destination," the GPS intones.

"Filthy feathers," I mutter. "No time to make any points."

"When you meet this guy, I want you to imagine he's D," Xander says as we climb out of the cab. He pays, thankfully. "Pretend you're just meeting your friend."

"I don't think that's going to work," I say.

"Great, well, then let's go with your plan." He folds his arms and lifts his eyebrows.

"I don't have a plan."

He rolls his eyes. "Just go."

"Okay, so I just pretend I'm going to see Dmitrius, whom I haven't seen in like ten years almost." I'm nodding as we walk toward the building. "I'll just walk into the board room and smile, because—" I grab Xander's arm. "But wait. I haven't seen him in a long time. What if he doesn't like me anymore? What if he's angry that I didn't keep up with him after I left school?"

Xander throws his hands up in the air. "You're not really seeing D, and you're an actor, Izaak. Pretend he's *not* mad. He's just happy to see you, okay? And you're happy to see him. It's just like a normal day in. . ." His face scrunches up. ". . .high school? In a board room."

I can do this.

Yes, it's a plan. It may not be a good one, but it's all I've got. I straighten my shoulders again, and I march through the doors. There are two people standing near the elevators in matching navy-blue uniforms, so I aim for them. "I'm here to see Donovan Summers," I say.

"We're the janitors." They toss a thumb at the elevators. "Building directory's over there."

It should deflate me a little, but hey, they weren't scared of me. It's not nothing. It takes us so long to work out how the building directory works that we're almost late by the time the elevator doors open on the thirty-second floor.

This time, the woman sitting behind the entryway desk turns and smiles. "Summers Production. How may I help you?"

"I'm, I—"

She stands. "Oh, we're expecting you, Mr. Alexander. Please come this way." She gestures for us to walk around her desk and down the hall, but when we pass, she flinches.

I'm not entirely certain it's out of fear, but it could be. I start to sweat, which I hate. I'm grabbing the front of my shirt and pulling it out, trying to get some air flow, when Xander turns to look at me behind her back.

He shakes his head and frowns. *Pull it together, man. You're scaring* me, *and you never do that.*

Right.

I'm calm.

I'm just going to see my friend D. That's all. Hanging with a buddy. But when we walk into the board room, a man in a really sharp suit with dark hair that's just grey at his temples stands and smiles, and all my chill shoots right out the door behind me.

It's Donovan feathering Sommers.

He could make my whole career. If this goes well, I could land rom com after rom com. I could deliver witty lines. I could make women swoon, and I could finally bring joy to, well, to people everywhere. I'm *so close*, and I can feel it already.

I'm going to choke.

"Izaak Alexander. The second I saw your new film, I knew. This man is far too handsome and far too eloquent to be a villain." He holds out his hand.

I can't shake it.

Even if someone's strong enough, brave enough, and confident enough that my presence doesn't terrify them, direct physical contact with a vampire will punch through.

"I'm recovering from a cold," I say, waving him off. "Don't wanna pass anything along." I force a smile. Because I'm just chatting with D. Just shooting the breeze. Cool. Chill. Calm.

"I'm sorry to hear that." He drops his hand and sits, pointing at the chairs across from him. "And who's your friend?" He raises his eyebrows.

"I'm Xander, Xander Binnigas. I'm Izaak Alexander's manager." His smile looks genuine, albeit a little awkward. "We're both very happy to be here. Thanks for asking us to come in."

"So, have you ever thought about doing a rom com?" Donovan braces his forearms on the massive, wood slab conference table and leans closer. "Because you may not know this, but that's kind of my bread and butter."

I look him right in the eye and open my mouth to tell him *yes*, but that's when I see it.

He flinches.

I'm staring right at him, and as if he can finally sense the danger of being near me, his entire body tenses. "Or are rom coms not intense enough for you?" He's cringing now, backing away from me, and kind of curling in on himself like he needs to protect his vital organs.

Shoot.

Shoot, shoot, shoot!

I imagine him as a black teenager, just trying to make it in high school, but it's just not working. He's wearing a suit, and the man has a production company that does plays in New York City and movies all over the world.

I'm going down in flames.

Until Xander clears his throat, and pops his right ankle up on his left knee, and smiles. "He's actually been wanting to move into rom coms for a while. I can vouch for the fact that he's really funny—great comedic timing—but also, with his face, what woman wouldn't want to be cast alongside him?"

Look at Xander, busting out the well-spoken answers. "Right," I say. "What he said."

And somehow, something about what he said *works*. Mr. Sommers straightens, shakes his head a bit, and smiles. "That's exactly what I was hoping to hear. In fact, I have a movie in mind for you *right* now."

We spend the next few minutes talking about the plot of the movie, the actresses he's considering, and the location—which luckily, happens to be mostly in New York City. Xander asks some decent questions, but I mostly just marvel.

Donovan doesn't seem to be afraid at all.

"Would I have any input in the actress you choose?" I ask.

"Of course." Donovan smiles. "We'd have them come read with you and you could tell me if you think there's chemistry. Of course, I'll be watching too." He reaches for his water just as I reach for my phone, which I left on the table.

Our hands collide, and I cringe. Hard.

But even physical contact doesn't trigger any reaction from him. He just reaches past me for the water glass that slid eight inches when we slammed into it and offers me a half-smile. "Bad timing. That's another thing we'll want to watch for. Some actor-actress combos just have bad timing, and you can't make a good movie with someone if your leads have timing that's off, you know?"

I blink.

"There are so many intangibles, but now that we've met, my nerves about announcing you as the lead are gone." Donovan sighs. "Assuming you're interested?"

"For sure," I say.

Xander smiles. "I think we know just what you're talking about when you say intangibles." I feel it, then. A tiny pulse I hadn't noticed. Xander's *doing* something. His alpha bond is. . .is he muting whatever it is about me that makes humans afraid? And if so, how?

Donovan taps the table in front of us. "I'm going to send a contract to your agent, and then you let me know what you think about the terms, alright?"

I nod dumbly, still trying to figure out what Xander's doing. Now that I've identified it, I can't think of anything else. It's like a very small, very low-level humming that runs along the length of the bond.

I manage to keep it together for the next few moments of pleasantries, and I watch the receptionist as we leave. I even reach out and drop a hand on her shoulder. "Thanks so much for your help. It was such a pleasure to meet everyone."

She beams at me.

Not a single ounce of fear.

The second we're alone in the elevator, I round on Xander. "What was *that*?"

"What?" Xander shrugs.

"You're doing something, and I want to know what

it is and why we never did it before!" I can't contain my smile. "Because this is the best day of my life!"

"I thought that was the day you played Mercutio," he says.

The elevator stops, and I step out, practically bouncing as I walk. "Not anymore. This has replaced it. You just have to show me what you're doing, and—"

Xander's grimacing.

"What?"

He shrugs. "I would show you, but I think it's an alpha thing. I could just sense when he reacted to you, and I kind of. . ." He pauses. "It was like I put a blanket over that energy or something."

Now that he mentions it, I do feel a little like I'm kind of stuck under a wet-dog-smelling sort of umbrella—or blanket works, too.

"But now we have something to practice," Xander says. "And I think we need to go out in public, with humans, to do it."

"Like, go for a jog in the park?"

"A jog?" Xander pulls a face.

"Oh, fine. A walk?"

"Sure."

"I could bring a tennis ball to throw," I say.

Xander just got us a cab, but he scowls at me as he climbs in, closing the door instead of sliding over. I can't really blame him. Dog jokes are always funny, but maybe not quite as much to him.

Even after having to wait for three cars to pass before I can climb into the cab, I'm still just unbelievably happy. "You do realize you're going to have to follow me around forever now, right?"

"How's that new?" Xander's a good friend.

The best, really.

"Thanks, man."

"I'm just happy it worked out, finally." Xander frowns. "It's nice to have something go right."

"We have the building too, right?" I ask. "And you have a pack now. I think a lot of things are looking up."

But on the way home, I think about all the people who are upset about what he's done, and I understand why he's worried. Xander went from lone wolf to alpha of a large and very strange pack in a few days. It must be terribly stressful.

"Whatever comes, we'll face it together," I say.

He doesn't brush me off as being a powerless vampire. He doesn't roll his eyes or shake his head. He just smiles. "Thanks, man."

I just hope a good attitude and strong friendships are enough for what's coming.

15

ROXANA

I've never paid much attention to photoshoots, not even the ones for the brands I liked. I suppose to me, the reason for buying something was never that someone else liked it.

I just bought whatever I thought looked nice.

"We need more *flames*," the man in the black, thick, horn-rimmed glasses says. "Way more flames."

More flames? Has he lost his mind?

There are a dozen torches, all of them fueled by something large, because they've been blazing for a while. I think they might be used for actual heating in outdoor venues, because they're pumping off a lot of heat already.

As a dragona, I don't mind fire.

I really don't.

My father burns stuff regularly. All my brothers do, too. It's a given. Recently, I discovered that I'm mostly impermeable to heat. Mom says she's not, but maybe that trait skips a generation.

Even so, I *hate* being hot.

And right now, it's even worse thanks to my stupid itching scales. I scratch at my shoulder again, the one that bothers me the most, and the man with glasses scowls at me. "No more scratching. I said that." He uses the same voice with me that he does on the runners who are now dragging some kind of portable fireplace ten feet away.

"If you keep turning up the heat, you're going to have to let me scratch," I say. "All the fire's making my scales itch."

His brow furrows. "Makeup, get over here. Fix where she's all red." Then he rounds on a very short woman next to him. "Find out if we can add flames post production."

"Do you want her holding this bag or this one?" The woman from Luis Vuitton holds up two large bags. One's golden, and one's bright red. "I think the red will set off her scales better."

"The gold matches," he says. "Use that."

She turns toward me, rolling her eyes, and hands me the over-the-shoulder bag in gleaming gold.

When I take it, I can't help looking more closely. "Wait." I drop my voice when she turns back. "What on earth is this? I know it's not dragon, but they are scales."

"Dyed pangolin scales," she says. "We tested a dozen different options, but those were the closest to the actual dragon hide we had without being so prohibitively expensive that no one but the Sol family could afford them." She winks at me.

Oh, good. I need to break up with Lionel double quick. Maybe once we're officially not dating, people will stop using him as some kind of barometer for what rich and famous means. "Hey, what's a pangolin? Is it, like, a big, scaly, gross lizard?" A girl can hope.

"Pull it up on your phone." She stomps off.

Before the glasses-guy can start yelling again, I whip out my phone and search for pangolin. It is *not* a gross lizard. It's a very cute, strange-looking little anteater thing, and now I feel terrible. I stroke the bag softly. "I'm sorry, little man. I wish they hadn't murdered you and turned you into a bag."

Someone next to me laughs.

When I turn, it's a girl who looks maybe twenty, and she's videotaping me. "You're funny."

I frown. "Hey, no videotaping me without consent. Do you know what I'm being paid for this one shoot?"

She squeaks and runs away. There are gremlins everywhere.

"Alright, Miss Goldenscales. Time to earn your fee." Glasses gestures at my shoulders. "Let's get going."

I groan, but I don't have much choice. We need money, and I have absolutely no other way to get it. Except for groveling to my parents, but even then, I'm not sure they'd shell anything out. They're not well-pleased that I still haven't come back home.

I slip off the scarlet robe they gave me, tossing it at the woman who's waiting to take it. Now I'm left standing here in what amounts to a gold string bikini. My eye makeup, which is entirely outrageous, is also in various shades of gold. Everything's just going to blend together—my scales, my makeup, this stupid swimsuit I'm posing in, and the dumb old golden ant-eater bag.

I force a smile anyway, and then I try not to sweat while not one, but two different people with cameras flash, flash, flash away for twenty minutes. I have to change clothes three times, and they stick me with bags in various sizes and colors, ranging from red, to emerald green, to black, but finally, they release me.

"I think that's all we need," Glasses says. "I appreciate your cooperation."

I'm currently wearing a red-gold swimsuit with five-inch black stilettos. I'd definitely say I cooperated fully. "Where can I change back into my clothing?"

He looks at me for a moment, and then with a sigh, he points. "That trailer."

I said I wanted to change, but really, the moment I'm finally alone, I strip the stupid swimsuit off, and I start *scratching*. It's glorious. After all the itching, itching, *itching*, to finally be able to *do something* about it is heavenly. Of course, by the time I manage to stop, I'm bleeding in three places. My shirt covers one of them, my pants the other, but when I walk out, I realize the bloody gash on my shoulder's visible.

"Oh, no!" The woman who gave me the bags practically sprints across the distance between us. "You're bleeding!" Her hand flies up to cover her face. "What happened?"

"Nothing," I say. "Nothing at all." I tug my sleeve down to mop up the blood and force a smile. I should be great at that after this stupid, interminably long shoot. "I'm really just fine. I better get going."

"Wait." She turns sideways and gestures. "As part of the contract terms, you're entitled to pick any of the bags you like best to keep."

Keep a tiny-anteater murder bag? I try not to, but I wind up scrunching up my nose. "I'm good."

"You're—what?" She repeats herself. "Are you

declining? But you can keep whichever one you want. Any color or size, not limited to the ones we photographed."

"The thing is, I'm not sure they're really my style."

"We literally designed them with you in mind," she says. "And they're retailing at eighty thousand dollars."

"You know what?" I point at the red one. "I'll take that one."

"Good call." She hands it to me. "The gold was a little too much."

I'm staring at the sad bag and wondering how much I could get for it on eBay when the woman asks, "Is it true?" She drops her voice. "Did you really get bonded by a werewolf?"

It's only then that I take a good whiff and realize. . .she's a wolf.

I'm not sure what to say, but I decide that the truth is the truth. "Not only that, but I think I'm falling for the alpha." I wink at her.

She practically passes out, stumbling back into the table full of bags and knocking the terrible overpriced monstrosities onto the ground.

I've barely sat in the cab when I text Clark. FINISHING MY SHOOT AND REALLY REALLY NEED SOMETHING FOR MY ITCHING SCALES. ANY LUCK?

SURE. I'LL BRING IT BY NOW.

Thank goodness. If I'm itching this badly when I go to dinner with my parents tonight, I'm doomed. I'm a grown woman to almost every culture, but Mom and Dad still treat me like an errant toddler. They'll never let me leave without being seen by a dozen healing mages. The last thing I need is to give them any ammunition to try and keep me home.

The stupid photoshoot was all the way out in Brooklyn, so blessedly, by the time I walk in the door, Clark's already there. "Last time, I tried using a mixture of—"

I don't even wait for his explanation. I snatch the little pink bottle out of his hands and pop the top off. It's the same bottle as before, but hopefully it's a different recipe. "Pretty bottle," I say.

A light and airy smell floods the room—that's new.

"What is it?" I carefully pour a little into my hand and then set the bottle down. "Is this fine? I can put this much on?"

"You shouldn't need anywhere near that much," Clark says.

"You have no idea how many places I'm itching." I dab some on my shoulder and unlike the last time, one drop of this feels like I'm somehow immersed in a cool spring on a summer's day.

The relief is *immediate*.

"What on earth is this?" I collapse onto the sofa and sigh, yanking my shirt up and smearing it all over my belly.

"You have scales there?" Clark's staring rather rudely, but I itch too badly to be picky.

The front door flings open, and Xander comes flying through. "Are you alright? You didn't stop in to say hello."

"Why should she stop at your apartment to say hello?" Clark arches one eyebrow. "Is that a thing she usually does?"

Xander swallows, his eyes seeking mine out.

"I told him I would," I say. "I have a dinner with my parents later, so I wanted to make sure we have our story ready."

"Your story?" Clark sits on the chair across from me. "What story?"

"You know, about how I wound up bonding New York's dragona princess, and how totally *not* a big deal it is." He sits on the sofa next to me, a little closer than he probably should.

"You two look pretty *in sync*." Clark frowns. "Spending a lot of time together?"

"Somehow, I started kind of linking with her," Xander says. "We've been working on fixing it."

Clark nods slowly. "Ah. Got it."

I'm still frantically slathering everywhere I itch, which is basically every inch of my body.

"Why are you itching so much?" Xander asks. "Should I be worried?"

"Well, as her treating mage, *I'm* worried," Clark says. "I made sure the charmed potion has no toxic elements, but it's not like she should really bathe in it. It wasn't inexpensive or simple to make."

"Why does it smell so good?" I ask.

"Its main ingredient is a lotus blossom," Clark says. "It's supposed to have some remarkable soothing properties, and that appears to be correct."

"I think it got so bad because it was so hot," I say. "And I think it's the heat that causes it. First the fireball, and now this."

"At the risk of sounding simple, maybe you should avoid heat," Clark says.

"I'm worried that when I see my parents, they're going to demand some kind of demonstration. The pack I fire-balled is asking for compensation, and of course my mom's delighted about the whole thing. Female dragona aren't really known for being powerful, so this is kind of a game-changer."

"Right." Clark's frowning. "So the itching started after the first fireball?"

I nod.

"And the heat at the photoshoot today made it worse?"

"It definitely made it worse."

"And you said you itch in the morning a lot. Do you sleep under a lot of blankets?"

"I guess," I say. "I do get hot at night." I hadn't even thought of that. "So, maybe I should sleep with less clothing and blankets."

Xander's eyes widen, and I know he's suppressing a wink.

More than a wink...

"She could maybe have some kind of virus." Clark frowns.

Viruses are not hot.

"Maybe expelling the fireball activated it or something?" Clark isn't paying attention to us at all, which is nice, because Xander's fingers are brushing against mine, and now that's all I can think about.

"What about the bond?" Clark turns toward Xander. "Can you feel any of the itchiness?"

Xander's hand springs away from mine, and he props his head on it. He looks very strange, and very guilty. "I feel her emotions when she's upset about it, but not the itching itself."

"You're useless," Clark says.

That was kind of rude. "There's not really anything he can do."

"You're right." Clark stands. "What you need is the help of a skilled mage." He huffs. "You're lucky you know one."

"Actually, maybe you should ask Lionel for help with this before you dump him." Xander's smirking.

"You're dumping Lionel?" Clark asks. "For certain? You've decided?"

I stand. "I have. The last date was bad, and I do feel something around him, but it's not good. I think it's just *nervous*, and that's not something I want to pursue. I want someone I can feel safe around." I can't help glancing at Xander.

"Someone who can protect you when you're sick or dealing with something." Clark sniffs. "That makes sense."

I wonder whether he's referring to himself—but I can't help thinking about how Xander leapt to my defense back when we thought he was fraying. He's always been willing to wolf out to keep me safe. "Yes," I say. "That's exactly what I want."

Clark's smiling when he leaves. "I'll make more of the potion," he says. "Looks like you'll need it, and I can add a cooling charm, too. But the most important thing I'll do is some research on dragona females to see when and why they get heat rashes."

"Thanks," I say.

After he's gone, I expect Xander to pounce on me. I haven't seen him in hours, between my dumb shoot and his meeting with Izaak. He doesn't stand up, though. He stays on the sofa, staring at his hands. Something's clearly wrong. "Did the meeting go badly?" I kind of hate to ask, but it's better to know.

"Izaak got the role," he says, still not looking up. "He's pretty excited about it."

"Oh," I say. "That's great."

Xander finally stands and turns to head for the door. "Well, I better get back to—"

I grab his wrist and yank him toward me. He's not expecting it, but he's agile. He pivots and holds his ground. I'm the one who falls, right against his powerful chest. "Oh." Our faces are inches apart, but for some reason he's just staring at me, not kissing me. "What's wrong?" I sound irritatingly breathy, like a damsel in distress.

"Nothing." He offers me a forced half-smile and steadies me with one hand. Then he steps back.

"Xander Binnigas."

He's already turned away again, but he stops. "What?"

"You will tell me exactly what went wrong in the past two minutes *right now*, or we'll find out exactly how badly fireballs make my itching."

When he turns back around, he looks utterly *miserable*. "We all know you're too good for me. Everyone knows it."

"What?"

"But for some reason, hearing you say it. . ." He sighs. "It felt lousy."

"Say *what*?" I have no idea what he's—then I realize when I said I wanted someone I could feel safe around, I was kind of agreeing with Clark.

Xander would have taken it that way, anyway.

I snag his wrist this time, and I drag him to the

sofa. I shove him down, and I sit on his lap, using my left hand under his chin to make sure he's looking at me. "Xander Binnigas, don't you ever let me catch you or anyone else saying you're not good enough for me."

"I'm a mongrel," he says. "You're a princess. It's worse than that cartoon about the thief who steals a lamp."

"I liked *Aladdin*," I say. "But you're nothing like him. You'd never steal anything, for one. And for another, you do *not* have a pet monkey." I'm smiling, but he's still not.

"Look—"

Before he can say another stupid thing, I kiss him. He may be acting idiotic, but his body reacts just like it always does. He curls around me, every part of him orienting on *me*, like he would do anything, *give* anything.

Kissing him is the safest place I've ever been.

Once he's entirely breathless, I pull back, which is actually harder than I planned. "And for a second thing, you should know that when I said I want someone who makes me feel safe, I didn't mean *Clark*." I snort. "I meant you, idiot."

"I can't even keep myself safe," he says.

"But whenever danger threatens, you leap to my defense."

"I didn't when Ragar was threatening to force you to marry him." He hangs his head. "I almost turned you in."

I sigh. "That's true."

"See?" His stunning golden eyes are stricken.

"And I plan to hold that over you forever. But if you had been on that roof, you'd know that Clark didn't save me either. He was actually saved by a pigeon and then by me, in that order." I laugh at the memory. "I had to save myself on that roof, and one thing you've always been great at is letting me do what I want."

"What?"

"Most men try to barge their way in and save the woman. You'll do that when the situation calls for it, but whenever I ask you to step back, or to wait in the lobby, or give me space, you listen. And you back me up when I do things like murdering seven of your kind."

"Those wolves were attacking you unprovoked."

"You were going to send me back to the car and die defending me." I brush one hand down the side of his face. "I know you'll do anything I need." As I say the words, I realize they're true. "I *really* like you, Xander Binnigas. I like you in a way I've never liked anyone in my entire life."

When we kiss again, it's not chaste.

Not chaste at all.

The alarm on my phone reminding me to leave for the Dagobar tower ticks me off, but I'm glad I set it. Otherwise, I might have totally missed dinner. I wouldn't put it past my mother to show up on my doorstep just to yell if I skipped out tonight.

Nothing good would come from that.

"You have to go?" Xander asks.

I sigh, dragging one finger down his neck and into the tiny, curved indentation where his collarbones meet. "Why don't you come with me?" I glance up casually, like his response doesn't matter.

It's probably a bad idea to take him. Dad has a

terrible temper, and it's going to be bad enough telling them that I'm breaking up with Lionel, whom I supposedly canceled my wedding to Ragar to be with—and that's probably why I want him there.

It's a monumentally stupid idea.

Terrible, really.

Having the werewolf who bonded me present so that Mom and Dad are even more likely to find out what's going on is catastrophically stupid. But I'm scared to go, and I feel better when he's around.

You do?

My eyes snap toward his. "You heard that—my thoughts?"

"I'm trying not to listen in on your thoughts. I know it bugs you when I do, but it's hard." His eyes are intense, bright—gorgeous.

"It doesn't bug me anymore," I admit. "It just upset me that day because it was new, and also." I don't really want to admit this. "I didn't want you there when I was with Lionel, because I liked you more. I was comparing you in my brain, and I was worried you'd hear it."

"Really?" He shifts so he's even closer, my body touching his almost from our shoulders to our feet. "You know, my dad said that usually alphas only struggle with this when they've found their mate."

The word rings like a gong in my head.

Mate.

"But I'm dragona," I say. "I can't possibly be your mate. You're a werewolf."

"We don't fit." He's so close that the breath from his words fans across my face, but I don't mind. I like having him this close. "We can't fit."

"Have you ever really fit anywhere?" I ask. "I don't feel like I have."

"The first time I've felt that way was with you," he admits.

"For me, too."

"Fine." He stands up and offers me his hand. "Then let's go together. I'll be your friend—we can tell them I came along to make sure no one bothered you."

"You'll be my bodyguard?"

"That's what I was the first time we met," he says. "Do you remember?"

The awkward wolf who told me about the fire escape. "It's because of you that I ran. I had no idea how I'd get down until you told me about the ladder."

"It never occurred to me that you might use it." He grins. "But I'm glad you did."

"So am I."

16

ROXANA

I wasn't injured much as a child.

There just wasn't much chance for me to be injured. I was basically wrapped in bubble wrap and kept in a cabinet. I was trotted out to play from time to time, but always alone. I was periodically taken to things like the opera or a sporting event, but only with my parents and a guard of at least a dozen dragona. I tried to join the dance team at school once, and within two days, Mom had decided it was too great a security risk—there was *no* way to make sure that every single person who danced with me and every single person involved in both the training and the performances would be safe.

It's probably not surprising that I very rarely got hurt.

The first time I recall being hurt, it was my own fault entirely.

Our chef had the night off, and Mom had made balut, which is a fertilized duck egg that's been allowed to develop almost all the way. . .and then been boiled. She ate them right out of the shell like it was some kind of treat.

"This reminds me so much of the street food I grew up with." She sighed. "These are just *perfect*, too."

"You're right." Dad slurped little bird babies down just fine, too. "Not overly soft, and still a little chewy."

When I started crying, Mom got annoyed. "If you don't eat this, you don't eat at all."

She held the line, convinced that she'd turn me into a balut-lover with a firm edict and patience, but I was stubborn, even then. I hated fighting, but I didn't want to back down either. When Mom finally got up to show Dad something, I seized my chance. I sprinted to the pantry, my belly complaining loudly. Luckily, no one was close enough to hear it. Mom had saved two of the disgusting little chewy bird embryos, and I was determined never to eat them.

I was scared she'd come back, irritated that I wasn't at the table, and force me to take a few bites. That made me rush, so when I found a can of peaches, it felt like fate. I scrambled around until I found what I thought was a can opener, and after several tries, it worked.

Unfortunately, once the can top had been cut all the way around, I had to somehow pry it upward. On my second try, I finally slid my finger under the edge enough to lift it up, but I also sliced my finger pretty badly.

When Mom walked in, she was so distressed about the blood pouring out of my finger that she forgot all about the balut. I didn't get my peaches, but I didn't have to eat the little duck babies, either. Mom rinsed the cut and wound a band-aid tightly around my finger. A few days later, she wanted to take it off, but I was worried. When she first started pulling, it hurt.

The bandage had stuck tightly to my skin.

"Mom, leave it alone."

"You can't keep it on. We need to see how that cut looks."

Before I could stop her, Mom yanked the band-aid off.

I swore then and there that I'd never do that again. No bandage should be ripped off. People should be allowed to take their time. There's no need to rush, especially when you want something to heal.

Nothing since has changed my mind. Mom and Dad can meet Xander, and I can tell them that the thing with Lionel was just for publicity. We can talk about ways to officially break up—they'll be pleased that I'm done with my relationship with the inappropriate mage—and then slowly, ever so slowly, I can introduce them to Xander. Once they get to know him, once they see how funny, valiant, and brave he is, then I can tell them that I like him. Somehow, over the next year or so, I'll convince them that he's the guy for me.

We've just reached the base of the Dagobar tower when it hits me—my anxiety about confronting my parents. That, and also nervous shaking that almost consumes my entire body. "Oh, by Gabe, I'm not looking forward to this." I lean over my knees and drop my head in my hands.

I want to turn around and head back to Minerva's.

"It's going to be fine," Xander says. "They're your parents. They just want to see you and verify that you're fine. They want what's best for you."

"Yes, but their version of what's best and mine are not the same. They never have been."

"That's why I'm here." Xander slides his fingers through mine. "Remember when you strolled into the Manhattan pack with me, determined to keep them from putting me down?"

"I did do that." I smile.

"Now it's my turn to do the same."

I can't help myself from asking, "But I saved you with the threat that if they harmed me, my dad would destroy them." I grit my teeth and hiss. "Do you think my dad will be scared of yours?"

"Let's just go," Xander says.

He's barely let go of my hand before we're pushing through the front doors. Dragona guards fall in on either side of us. One is a brown dragon when he shifts, and the other's blue.

"Eamon," I say. "Marshall." I nod at them.

They both drop into deep bows. "Your Majesty."

"Stop that," I say.

Eamon frowns as he straightens. "Stop what?"

"Don't call me that," I hiss. "It sounds ridiculous."

"You've never minded before," Marshall says. "Not for the past twenty-eight—"

"Alright." I wave my hand at them. "Tell them we're coming."

"We're to escort you up there," Eamon says. "Along with your date."

"Oh, he's not my date," I say. "Xander's a—"

"He didn't mean the wolf." Lionel steps around Eamon and smiles. "Good to see you, darling." He moves one pace closer and drops a kiss on my cheek.

I can *feel* rather than see Xander bristle, and I know that if he were in his wolf form, he'd be growling.

"What in the daimoni's den are you doing here?" I ask. "I thought I was pretty clear the last time we spoke—"

"Unless you want me to tell your parents about your real relationship with that wolf, you'll march me upstairs and keep pretending," Lionel says.

"My real—" I splutter. What exactly does he know? "You're threatening me? Why?"

Lionel reaches for my hand.

I step back. "What's your end game?"

"I'm like goat cheese," Lionel says. "I'm a strong flavor, and it takes a while for people to realize how great I am. I'm just bargaining for a little more time to win you over."

"Someone who blackmails me into spending more time with them is not someone I will ever want." I turn toward Eamon. "He will not be coming upstairs."

"But he has an invite," Eamon says. "From your—"

"My father has no idea the things—"

"Not your father," Marshall says. "The invite was from your mother."

I sigh. If it's an invite from Mother, I've already lost. I grab Xander's arm and slide mine through it, hooking mine around his elbow. "Let's go."

"You think the wolf can keep me away?" How did I ever find Lionel's cocky grin endearing?

"I had very questionable taste," I whisper. "I'm sorry."

He is rich, Xander says. *I don't blame you for giving him a chance. Your life with him would be much easier than your life with me.*

"I'm not interested in easy," I say.

"What?" Lionel gestures for me to follow him into the elevator.

"Nothing. I was talking to the person I invited to come with me."

"If you think anyone will accept that you're dating a wolf, you're mistaken." Lionel's indolent smile bothers me more by the moment. "People will struggle enough just to believe he managed to bond you, but no one would ever believe you were dating."

"And why is that, exactly?" I scoot closer to Xander, my hip touching his. "What would make *you* a catch when someone who's not pushy, demanding, and impossible to ever satisfy is somehow unbelievable?"

"I am pushy," he says, "but—"

"I'm not done." He's so obnoxious that I want to scream. "Xander's kind, he's caring, and he's powerful in an understated way. He defends people who need it, and he *listens*."

"Wait," Lionel says. "Are you trying to say that. . ." His eyes widen.

"Yes," I shout, just as the elevator stops moving. "With as sheltered as I've been, I had no idea what love felt like. I had no idea what a relationship really was, or how to pick someone who was good for me. That's the only reason I ever pretended to be your girlfriend."

Lionel looks like I just shoved a banana cream pie in his face.

"Xander and I started out as friends, but the more time I spent with him, the more I liked him. And now, comparing what I feel for him to what I feel for you—it's crystal clear. I adore him, and I detest you."

"You love. . .*a wolf?*" Mother's standing by the elevator, a bouquet of flowers drooping in her hand almost to the ground. "A *werewolf?*"

"Oh," I say. "Hey, Mom. Good to see you." I release Xander's arm and start to move. "I didn't say love."

Xander's not following me off the elevator.

I'm stuck reaching back and circling his wrist with my hand. "Let's go, dummy."

"*That* wolf?" Mom still looks like she's in shock.

I yank Xander off just before the doors close in front of a very-shocked Lionel. Good riddance.

"The penthouse looks good," I say, as if a single thing has changed. I breeze past her and stop in the large round entryway, right next to the massive thirteenth century jade vase that's full of a different bouquet of flowers every morning. "Why are you holding flowers?"

"It's polite," she says. "I thought I was meeting my daughter's boyfriend."

"You got Xander flowers?" I can't totally suppress my smile.

Mom chucks them at the floor, and chunks of lilies go flying. "Of course not." She jabs a finger toward where Lionel was recently standing. "I got the son of the leader of all the mages flowers." Her brow rises. "Not some mangy wolf."

"He's not *mangy*." I realize that I'm baring my teeth at my mom, and I try to reel it back a notch.

"I just used that very word myself," Xander says, clearly trying to defuse the situation.

"Mom, let's go eat dinner. We can talk in there."

She folds her arms under her chest and sticks out her bottom lip. Then she shakes her head, tightly.

"Trust me, once you get to know them, Xander's *way* better than Lionel."

"Lionel Sol came to visit us yesterday," Mom says. "He told us that he understood the importance of dragon eggs to our people. He said he knew that you could live a long and full life. He offered me two options." She arches one eyebrow.

"I don't care what he did," I say. "I don't like him. Is anyone listening to me?"

"I didn't think I'd raised a capricious child." Mom shakes her head. "You didn't even ask what his options were."

"I. Don't. Care." I huff. "You aren't even listening to me."

"Really, neither of you is listening to the other," Xander says. "You're a little like two ships, passing in the night. It's a strange study in mother-daughter—"

"Shut up," Mom says at the very second I say the same thing.

Our eyes lock.

I can't help my smile. "He does that sometimes, but after you're around him more, you find the pedantic rambling endearing. Trust me."

"Lionel reminded me that he won't live anywhere near as long as you. He's like, a youthful fantasy. A childhood romance. He told me he'd be fine with you making dragon eggs during your marriage at set intervals, or you could spend his lifetime with him, knowing you'd have hundreds of years that would follow his death when you could remarry and produce plenty of dragon eggs for the dragona." Mom bit her lip. "It was pretty romantic, how willing he was to bargain, just to be with the woman he loves."

The doors ding and then open again.

"He doesn't love me," I say. "Lionel wants to own me. There's a big difference."

"That's not true." This time, Lionel steps off the elevator. "I own plenty of things, and you're the only one who talks back. I'd say if it was about ownership, you'd be the last person I'd pursue."

I swear, I'm going to punch him. "Mom. Hear my words. He's pushy, he's manipulative, and I don't like him."

Dad finally says something, and I realize he was beside Mother all along. "Your mother may not be listening to you, but I am." He grabs Lionel's sleeve and shoves him back into the elevator.

Lionel's eyes widen. "Wait. I haven't even told you all the bad things about Xander yet."

"What?"

The doors are closing, but he manages to shout. "He got expelled from college for cheating. He put his own mother in the hospital!" Right before the doors close again, he says, "He gets fleas and has to use dog shampoo."

"Okay, the flea thing's just a werewolf challenge we all face," Xander says. "It's not just me—it's all werewolves."

"You put your own mother in the hospital?" Mom asks. "And you cheated in college?"

I decide to rip the band-aid off. "I do like Xander," I finally say. "But also, he's my alpha. He's the first werewolf in recorded history to bond non-wolves. As werewolves go, he's pretty badass. With as much as you like power, even you should be able to appreciate that."

17

XANDER

We haven't even left the entry hall, but I feel justified in my belief that this is already the worst dinner *ever*. I should be paying attention, preparing to deal with whatever objections Roxana's parents have, but all I can think about are the things Lionel said.

The friend I was accused of helping cheat in college was *Clark*. He had in fact been cheating, but I didn't need a degree, not to join a pack, so I took the fall for him. And the only one who knew about my mother going to the hospital, other than my mother herself, was Clark. He was there when Mom startled me mid-change and I mauled her. It had been a complete accident, and she knew that.

She was out the next day with a bandage on her upper arm, and a healthier belief in the rules I'd set for knocking before entering my room when I closed the door.

The flea thing? Well, anyone could have told Lionel about that, or he could have been guessing. But the other two had to have come from Clark, but why would Clark tell *Lionel* about those? Why would he want to make me look bad? Why would my own best friend betray me?

But I'm the only one hung up on the things Lionel said.

"Your—he—the wolf bonded you?" Roxana's father may be small, but he's still utterly terrifying. I've seen him shift into his dragon form, and human sizes can clearly be deceiving. "How could he possibly do that? You're not a wolf."

"It's a long story," Roxana says. "I'll give you two options. You can get the short version right now, and then Xander and I will leave." When she arches her eyebrow, she looks *just* like her mother. At least I know she'll age well. "Or you can invite us into the house like civilized people, and we can tell you all about it while we eat."

"By all means, let's go inside." Her mother gracefully gestures for us to head straight through the entry hall and toward the brightest place ahead—the dining room. "I made your favorite."

"Adobo?" Roxana asks. "Pork? Or chicken?"

I file that information away for the future.

"Neither," her mother says. "Balut." Her smile's triumphant.

"You must be kidding." Roxana scowls. "Mother."

"Oh, I'm sure your boyfriend won't mind," her father says. "They say wolves will drink from the toilet."

"Some of them will," I admit. "I can vouch for that. But most of us have too keen a sense of smell to go anywhere near the toilet, even in canid form."

"A dog that speaks," her mother says. "How delightful."

"Mom." Roxana's positively fuming when we finally follow her parents into the dining room. I have no idea what balut is, but it seemed to mean something to the two of them. I doubt it's something good.

I decide it's probably the *least* sensitive topic we'll address tonight. "Tell me about this balut," I say. "Is it an inside joke of some kind?"

"No, no," Roxana's mother says. "Balut's just a food that our people—Filipinos—love. I was a little too focused on other things after Roxana was born, like keeping her safe, and I failed to make balut often enough. She didn't develop a taste for it."

"What is it?" Now I'm getting a little nervous. I brace myself for something truly strange, like grilled gremlins or ground up baby seals. "Is it cooked, at least?"

"Oh, it's cooked," her father says. "It did take me a few dozen times eating it before I liked it. If Roxana would just listen to us, *trust* us, she'd realize that we want what's best for her—with balut, and with life."

"But you don't always know what's best for me, because it's *my* life, and if I don't want to eat little boiled baby ducks, I shouldn't have to."

Oh, no.

Baby ducks?

It's as bad as I feared.

They eat baby animals? I try not to shudder. "Is it on the bone, still?" I try to ask without any sort of judgement. "Is it time intensive to eat?"

"Just come sit," Roxana says. "It'll make more

sense when you can see it." She points at a chair, and I trot over to her side.

But the platter in front of our plate is piled high with eggs. There are also large platters piled artfully with mounds of white rice, and tureens filled with some kind of soup. It's watery, with chunks of what I'm guessing are chicken, smallish onions, and tiny tomatoes.

"I don't see any baby birds," I say. "What am I missing?"

When we sit, Roxana gestures at the eggs. "That's the balut. The baby ducks are a week from hatching when they *boil* them. Then you peel them out of the shell and eat them, bones, brains, feet and beak—all of it." She grimaces. "Sounds great, right?"

"She's being dramatic," her mother says. "Who knew she had such a flair for that?"

"Apparently wolves bring it out in her." Her father's not looking nearly as upset. "Weren't you with her when she massacred those wolves?" He lifts his eyebrows. "Didn't that upset you?"

"Seeing as they were about to kill us both, I was happy about it," I say.

"You couldn't have protected her against seven little wolves?" Her father looks very unimpressed. "What kind of alpha are you?"

"I wasn't an alpha then," I say. "In fact, we thought I was fraying."

"What?" He stands. "One of the most dangerous things—"

Roxana hisses, pointing at her father with her lips. "Sit down, before I throw a duck fetus at you."

He rolls his eyes.

"He wasn't fraying," Roxana says. "He'd been lied to by the Manhattan pack's alpha for years. They knew he didn't realize he was an alpha, and they lied because Lo Ren Fang saw him as a threat. The most powerful werewolf in New York, maybe most of America, saw Xander Binnigas, lone wolf, as a threat." She pauses.

A flair for the dramatic, her mother had said. She might have been right.

"Mom, Dad, you've always valued excellence. Trust me when I say that I've found it in a place no one was looking, with a group of friends that everyone has undervalued."

"Tell us about the fireball," her mother says. "How did you do it, and can you do it again?"

"I've tried," Roxana says. "No luck yet." She leans forward, scooping up some of the soup and putting it in my bowl. Then she dishes up hers. "Thank you for having sinigang, too." Her voice softens. "I was angry, and I was scared, and I couldn't stand the idea of Xander being harmed to try and protect me from some crazy wolves."

"You created the fireball. . .to protect him?" Her father's expression has softened.

"I think so," Roxana says. "Because Dad, I care about him. I think he makes me stronger. I'm becoming *better* because I'm with him. Isn't that what you want for me?"

The rest of the meal isn't so bad. Roxana refuses to eat the balut, but I don't hate it. It's sort of like eating a tennis ball with a lot more flavor. To be honest, though, I don't hate tennis balls, even without the flavor. There's something about chewing on them that really brings a sense of accomplishment.

Or maybe the repetitive motion's just soothing.

Either way, I manage to eat a dozen balut, and that seems to impress Roxana's mother.

"Tell me," Mrs. Goldenscales says. "What's your plan?" She's not attacking. She's not ranting. She's honestly calmed down faster than my own mother probably would.

"Plan?"

"Surely Lo Ren Fang isn't going to just accept that you're staying in New York?"

"He's bonded a whole wolf pack, and they found work here," Roxana says. "So he's petitioning the Wolf Council to split the New York region."

"The council's mostly for show," her father says. "They'll wait to rule until you've worked it out yourself."

"I do have a plan," I say. "Along with the help of my friends, we're buying the building we live in. We're putting down roots here, and if Lo Ren pushes, we'll be ready to deal with that."

"You're not afraid of him?" Roxana's mother's not challenging me. She looks genuinely curious.

I shrug. "I was. For years, he was the alpha of the pack I wanted to join. I begged him to admit me. He made me show up and be beaten over and over and over. I had submitted to him as my alpha, and he still forced me to lose." They're hard memories to examine. "But I didn't know who I was. It's sort of like the story about the eagle."

"What story?" Roxana asks.

"You haven't heard it?" I look at her parents, but they look baffled, too. "Well, don't think I'm claiming this story. I'm not sure where I heard it first, but there's this legend that there's an eagle who's raised from hatch with a flock of chickens. They never fly, so neither does he. Instead, like the chickens, like his family, he scratches around in the dirt."

"I like this story," Mrs. Goldenscales says. "I too believe that choosing the right people to associate with is vitally important."

"I spent my entire life trying to get every wolf I met to accept me," I say. "None of them ever did. But my roommate—a vampire—my best friend from college who's a mage, his sister who's a witch, and her friend, a demon-spawn who just wanted to be good, they kind of became my family."

Roxana's mother wipes her mouth with a napkin and smiles. "They kept you from flying, then?"

I shook my head. "On the contrary. While my own kind were tying me down in the dirt, they showed me how to fly."

"And those same people inspired me to use a fireball," Roxana says. "I know you hate them, Mom. I know you don't like Xander either, Dad, but for the first time, I feel like no one's telling me to be a chicken."

"We've always wanted what's best for you." Her mother looks hurt. I actually feel sorry for her.

"But maybe I can't live my best life all cooped up, even if you caged me to keep me safe." Roxana's not yelling, and for the first time, her parents appear to actually be listening.

After we've eaten, Roxana's mother pulls out some kind of cinnamon cake, and I finally just blurt out what I've been thinking. "You don't seem that upset anymore."

Her mother's gaze finally stops on mine for a moment. Then it quickly shifts to her husband. "I think we should release Roxana's trust fund. I think she's old enough to use it however she'd like."

Her father blinks a time or two, and then he waves his hand. "It's not very large. It's always been hers. She can do what she wants with it."

"How large is it?" Roxana asks. "What are you saying?"

"Why would you do that?" I ask.

"We tried cutting her off." Roxana's mother arches one eyebrow. "That didn't work." She grunts. "We tried threats. We tried ignoring her." She scowls. "Now I'm hearing that she faked a relationship, that she accepted a tasteless photoshoot, and that she's been bonded by a wolf."

"How is Luis Vuitton tasteless?" Roxana asks. "You're ridiculous."

"Just listen," her mother says. "But Lionel made a good point. You will outlive the mage, the wolf, and any vampire you might choose to date, as well. If we give you the trust money, at least you won't need to do embarrassing photoshoots anymore, and no relationships you form will be for lack of money."

"How much is in my trust?" Roxana asks.

"It can't be more than ten or twelve million," Mrs. Goldenscales says. "Not enough to get you in trouble, but enough to keep you out of it, I hope."

I can't believe the progress we made in just one night. When she leans over to hand me a piece of cake, Roxana whispers, "I guess we can make that downpayment now."

You were glorious, I tell her. *Absolutely amazing, convincing them to like me. Convincing them to let you fly.*

"It was your story." She's staring at me so intently that a shiver runs down my spine.

"Easy, dog," Mr. Goldenscales says.

"Dog?" Roxana stands up. "I appreciate you giving me the trust fund, but I think it's time for us to go." Her eyes are flashing. "Maybe next time, you'll have better manners."

We walk to the elevator, and Roxana presses the button. Three times.

"It's not going to make it come faster." But I'm smiling. She looks like a stubborn little girl when she does things like that. I imagine she was an adorable little girl.

"A dragona can dream," she says.

Her parents have followed us over, and I can't help hoping they won't ride down with us. I've endured enough awkward interactions for one night.

"If you think we're giving you the trust fund because we approve of this. . .bizarre attachment," her mother says, "then you're mistaken."

Roxana drops my hand and spins around to face them again. "Mom, seriously?"

"Yes, it's not that we approve," her dad says. "I want to be clear on that."

"Then why would you give me my money?" Roxana asks. "What other reason could you have?"

Her father shrugs. "We're pretty sure the wolf will die soon, and we want to make sure you know we're here for you when that happens."

"Yes, do try to stay out of the fighting, fireball or

not," her mother says. "Let him die, but don't risk yourself in his fights."

Luckily, the elevator arrives then, and Roxana practically leaps inside. "So we didn't make quite as much progress as we hoped," she says, after the doors close. "But at least now we can pay for the building."

She's right about that. At this point, I'm all about the wins, even the tiny ones. And this one feels pretty large.

18

MINERVA

Most girls I knew did things with their mothers.

One of my friends, Kate, made cookies. Sometimes they'd also make cakes, and with the help of a little magic, the cakes they made were often epic. I remember that one of them had tiny dogs all over it, frolicking, barking, and playing. Another of my friends, Alice, often went hiking with her mother. They chose fun locations where they could harvest fresh potion ingredients, and then they'd mix concoctions together. Actually, Alice wasn't great at laboratory-based work, but she'd help harvest and she'd watch her mother make things.

My mom wasn't really into quality time with her daughter.

In fact, she pretty much did her best to *never* spend time with me. It's hard, as a kid, not to take it personally. A decade and a half ago, I gave her "coupons" for her birthday. They said things like, "one back massage," and "watch any movie you want." She smiled and thanked me when she got them, but she never redeemed them.

I upped my game.

My mother loved Celine Dion. She was demon-spawn, of course, but exceptions had to be made in the face of epic talent. Mom listened to her all the time, and she belted out Celine's songs in the privacy of her shower. Mom was always the first person I knew to talk about any new releases.

When I found out she was coming to perform in New York, I decided that we had to have a mother-daughter date. I found a part-time job at a fish and chips place near home, and it was disgusting. Smelt were popular for fish and chips baskets, but since they're tiny boogers, they were a real pain to clean.

First, I had to cut their heads off, then I had to slice their bellies, and finally, I'd have to scoop the disgusting, squishy yellow goo out and clean them. Each fish and chips basket had like four to ten of those little fish in it, and I prepped each of them for hours each afternoon for weeks and weeks, but it was worth it.

I used that money to buy two tickets to Celine Dion.

Mom was over the moon when she unwrapped the gift. I opened my mouth to tell her that I had paid for them myself, but before I could speak, she whipped out her phone and started punching in numbers. I thought she was calling Dad. She'd want to make sure he could get off that afternoon so we wouldn't be late. Maybe she'd even want to get dinner beforehand. I'd be happy to eat literally anything, as long as it wasn't fish and chips.

But she didn't call Dad.

She called her best friend Karen. "You're never going to believe what I just got my hands on!"

Karen *did* struggle to believe my mom had tickets, especially as close to the stage as they were, and she was *very* excited to go with Mom. They both reasoned that, even though Celine was demon-spawn, a voice like hers was a miracle. That made supporting her okay.

All their friends were terribly jealous.

I quit my job that afternoon.

And I also stopped trying to find ways for Mom and me to bond. Clearly, she didn't even like me. What kind of mother doesn't like her own daughter? One with a terrible screw-up for a child. That's who.

I couldn't even blame her. I was a total dud.

When I get home early in the morning after my shift, I shower and flop into bed. It takes me a while to drop off to sleep, because I keep thinking that my mom isn't even my mother, not really.

I have another mother.

One I know nothing about.

And with Dad gone, the only person I can ask about my mother is my mom, the woman who never liked me. The woman who never wanted to see me or spend time with me. The woman who has always found fault with everything I say and do—not that that's been hard to do.

But this matters so much more than a Celine Dion concert. Before I can second-guess myself, I whip out my phone and text Mom. NEED TO GRAB SOME STUFF FROM MY ROOM. CAN I COME BY AROUND 3? That's about the earliest I could get there, if I sleep just a few hours and head out.

She doesn't text back right away.

Why would she? She knows I work nights, and that I'm probably waiting around for her answer. It would be a missed opportunity to torture me in a small way if she replied immediately. I repent of my uncharitable thoughts almost right away. Which is good, because she finally texts back.

OF COURSE. ALL YOUR STUFF IS IN BOXES IN THE GARAGE.

Of course it is. Dad's gone, and she cleared out all his stuff, leaving herself an office and a storage room, but she would also need to clear everything out of my room, because that's just who she is.

NO PROBLEM. SEE YOU THEN!

I wait for a response for a bit, and then, not getting one, I drift off to sleep.

When I wake up, some of my bubbling fervor for answers is gone. I hear a strange sort of banging outside, and I drag myself out of bed, into decent pants, and to the front door, finally.

"Hello?" I'm still wiping my bleary eyes, but when I see who's on my doorstep, I stumble backward. "Can I help you?"

"We can't find Mr. Binnigas," a little girl says.

"We can feel that he's not close," a tall man behind her amends. "And we're wondering whether you know where he went."

"Um, no." I shake my head. "He doesn't normally check in with me. If he's not at the gloffee shop downstairs, I'm not sure where he went. He *is* unemployed, after all."

"There are some people here, saying they're supposed to be treating the whole building for pests in anticipation of the sale." The tall man's hand's trembling. "We cleared our stuff out, but they definitely realized that we were kind of bunking down there."

That's not great. "You didn't tell them you're related to Xander at all, right?"

He shakes his head. "Not at all. The last thing we wanted to do was get him in trouble."

"You have a new job to report to?" I take in the six people in front of me. Two are children—not very clean children, but I can hardly blame them, since their current residence has no shower—and four adults in what appear to be shiny, new prison shirts.

"We do," the tall man says. "But we were hoping we might be able to store some things in Xander's apartment." He peers around me. "Or yours?" He inhales. "We don't want to be a pain, but—"

I swing the door wide open. "Please do. Fill the room up if you have to. We're part of the same pack, now."

All their faces freeze, and then, as if they were waiting to see whether I was making a joke, they smile. The little girl takes my hand. "You're so pretty."

"Well." I can't help smiling back. "Thank you. What's your name?"

"Agatha," she says. "Can I possibly use your toilet?"

"Use the bathroom," I say. "Shower. Go pee. Brush your teeth. Whatever."

Within twenty minutes, there are dozens of wolves coming in and out of my apartment, and the family room looks like the inside of a hoarder's garage, but I can't blame them.

We don't want their presence to disrupt the sale.

If there's even going to be a sale.

I need to call Xander. We have to come up with a great deal of money in a very short time, and I'm still not sure how we'll possibly be able to do it. Clark and I have pulled out all that we could, and even if Roxana's paid quickly for her shoot, we're still going to be very, very short.

We may all need to pool our money and find a building we can rent in Jersey or something. I try to keep from shuddering. "I have to go out," I say.

Giggles flutters down from the top of the fridge to sit on my shoulder, staring at them intently, her head cocked sideways. *I like Xander, but this is a lot of dogs.*

Now that I've said something, they're all staring at me intently. Thanks to Giggles' comment, they *look* like dogs to me, all waiting on direction from their owner. "You're welcome to stay here while I'm gone," I say. "You can keep the kids here. Watch television. Eat some snacks." I point at the pantry. "There are even cookies in the freezer."

The kids immediately start whispering.

"Wolves do like cookies, right?"

"We do," Agatha says. "But we're not really wolves. We're just regular people who can turn into wolves."

Which I know, obviously.

I've seen Xander eat cookies. It's not like I think they're really dogs. Giggles is messing with my brain. "I'm so sorry. I know all that. I'm just—there are a lot of you, and I don't know you very well yet."

What if they're thieves? What if they steal everything I have and—

"Don't worry about us damaging your place,"
Agatha says. "We all have the same boss."

Boss? I have no idea who their prison boss is or
what it has to do with me.

"If we repaid your kindness with a mess, I'm sure
he'd be really angry," the tall man says. I think he's
Agatha's dad, maybe. "Trust me when I say that no
one wants an angry alpha."

Oh. Xander. Duh. "Well, if Xander thinks I'm
going to call him my boss, he's got another think
coming." I'm smiling, but every single one of them
looks terribly distressed. "Don't worry," I say. "I love
Xander, but I also think of our relationship as more
friends-and-neighbors than employer-employee."

They're mostly frowning as I duck into my room
to grab my bag.

"I know you don't really do this," I whisper. "But
any chance you'd stay here and—"

Keep an eye on them? Giggles is giving me the stink
eye. *Where exactly are you going?*

"Just to see my mom," I say. "Then I'll come right
back."

If you don't, I'll come find you.

"I know," I say. "And I won't fault you for that. But
surely you can see why I'd want you to stick around
here."

Keep them from pooping on your stuff.

I laugh. "Exactly."

I call for a cab, because with the wolf-delay, it's the
only way to make it out to Scarsdale on time. "Alright,

well, make yourselves at home, and I'll be back in a bit."

Not a single one of them has so much as sat down when I finally close the door, so I hope they loosen up a bit after I'm gone. As I'm climbing in the cab, it finally occurs to me that Agatha literally answered my concern about them stealing with a reassuring statement that they'd never do that.

Could she hear my thoughts?

Because if so, that's whack.

I can't hear theirs, but I plan to ask as soon as I get back home. On the way to Mom's, I think about ways to try and broach the topic of my birthmother. I could mention that I know I'm not half-human.

On that topic, I'd actually like to know why she lied to me about that. Wouldn't it have been easier, when I asked whether I was adopted, to tell me if I was Dad's sister's kid? I mean, how hard is that? It's one line.

"You're actually your father's blood niece, but of course we love you like you're ours."

I could write such a lovely script for my mother.

I wish I could, sometimes. Having a puppet mom would be awesome. I'd get the mother I always wanted, and that's when I admit to myself: I'm desperate to meet my real mother. I really want her to like me.

I've always wanted to be liked.

More than anything else.

More than I wanted to be a guardian, more than I wanted to cast good spells, more than I wanted Dad to be proud of me, I want people to *like me*. And I wanted the people I liked to like me most of all.

Maybe it's because of Mom.

Maybe having the person who's supposed to love you the most *not even like you* breaks something in a person's brain. But whatever the reason, I'm still desperate to have a mother who actually wants to spend time with me, a mother who's proud of me.

So of course, I'm terribly afraid Mom'll refuse. It would be a very Melina Lucent thing for her to do. She'll tell me it's for my own good. She'll insist that she's doing me a favor, and she'll keep me from ever finding the one person who might not be embarrassed of me. I'm agitated and jumpy when I finally pull up in front of the tasteful white house I grew up in.

"We're here." The cabbie shifts one bloodshot eye. "Time to pay."

I pay him and climb out, but my anxiety spikes when he peels out and disappears.

"Your cab left?" Mom's already opened the door, and her head's following the yellow car's disappearance around the corner. "How will you get your things back home?"

"I'll call another one," I say. "Or I'll get an Uber. It's fine, Mom."

She purses her lips but doesn't argue.

I jog up the three steps to the porch and walk through the doorway she's already evacuated. "Hey, so—"

"I'm actually going to be cleaning the bathroom upstairs," she says. "Otherwise, I'd be happy to help you go through your things. But, you know, a big house like this doesn't clean itself."

I almost never see her, and I took a cab all the way

out here, and she's going to be busy cleaning an upstairs bathroom that literally no one ever uses? This is exactly the kind of thing I knew she'd do.

On the way out, I came up with a dozen different ways to slowly edge my way toward my question, but now that I'm here, now that she's already distancing herself, I just can't. I blurt it out gracelessly, like usual. "Before you leave to go scrub a toilet, can you just tell me?"

She turns back, frowning. "Tell you what? I said the boxes are in the garage. They're marked clearly with your name."

"Who's my real mother?" I focus on my anger so that I don't start to cry. "You know, the one who might actually like me?"

Her entire face falls like I've struck her. "Minerva Lucent."

"Stop." I shake my head. "I can't deal with it, not today. For once, let's not pretend. Let's just be honest. Is it Dad's sister?"

Mom chokes, and then she looks around the room like there might be an assassin in black hiding to leap out and murder us. "Minerva Lucent, you're being ridiculous."

"But the reason—"

Mom sprints across the room and slams her hand down over my mouth, looking around with wide and panicked eyes. She shakes her head violently, and then releases me. "I do need to clean that bathroom," she says loudly, "but I just realized that I need some Clorox to do it. Why don't you come with me to the store?"

What's wrong with her?

Moments later, she's dragged me into the car, driven four blocks to the closest market—an over-priced tiny one—and she's pushing a cart around with a very fake smile on her face.

I finally grab the end of the cart and shove. "Stop this, now."

She pulls until I release the cart, steers it into the corner, glances around not once, but twice, and then crouches over the cart.

"Mom. No one's following us."

"That's what I needed to verify."

"You're freaking me out, now."

"I should be." Her eyes are flashing. "I had to lie to you before, but I did it for your own good."

Huh?

"Your aunt *is* your mother, Zintrel, and if you had any idea the lengths to which your father went to try and spare you from the same fate she endures. . ." She shivers. "Stop being an idiot, and leave it alone."

"Leave *what* alone?" I ask. "The Chief wants me to take over for him, and—"

Mom grabs my hand and squeezes, her eyes lighting up in a way I've literally only ever seen them do for Clark. "That's wonderful, darling. The best news I've heard this year."

I yank my hand away, but it's hard. "Mom, there's no way I'll get appointed. The vampires hate me, the dragona would roast me if they could, and I won't even go into the wolves or the demon-spawn, because they're literally trying to kill my friends."

"Oh." She deflates, crouching over the cart again.

"Listen, though, I know it's been frustrating for you, but even if the Chief thing doesn't work out, you mustn't look into anything with your aunt. Do you hear me? You have parents—Melina Blitz and Holden Lucent—and we love you, even though you're half human." She's saying things slowly and nodding like I'm actually a half-wit.

"But you know that's not true," I say. "I'm sick to death of all the lies."

She clenches her hands around the shopping cart and lowers her voice yet again. She's speaking so softly that I can barely make out what she's saying, and I'm now leaning close enough that I'm inches away. "Your father gave up *everything* so that you could live a decent life. If you don't stop digging right now, you're going to wind up being locked up forever, you big idiot."

That, at least, sounds more like the mother I know. Maybe she wasn't taken by body snatchers and replaced with a cyborg. "That's my decision to make."

She slaps me.

The sound of her palm cracking against my cheek is so loud that an employee dashes back to ask whether we're alright. So much for whispering to keep from drawing attention.

"I'm fine," I say. "That sound was just me dropping. . ." I look around for something, and grab a box. "A huge box of tampons."

The poor man practically chokes, and then he sprints away. My story made no sense, but tampons are like kryptonite to most men.

Works every time.

"It's not your decision," my mom says, "because you don't understand enough to make it. If I tell you, then you'll be in more danger. For once in your stupid life, can't you just trust me?"

"Trust the mother who doesn't even like me?" I snort. "No, Mom, I can't do that. Pardon me, if I don't want you making decisions for my life anymore."

She looks deeply hurt, as if she's been this earth-mother type. As if she hugged me, and kissed me, and put healing charms on my skinned knees. As if she even thanked me for the Celine Dion tickets I gave her, instead of always trying to hide my inadequacies from everyone she knew while simultaneously ignoring me.

"At least I know Zintrel's my mom," I say. "My friend found her already, so I don't really need you now."

"You—" Mom shoves the cart away and lunges for me. "You can't talk to her. You can *never* meet her. Do you hear me?" She's not whispering now. She's practically trying to claw at me, her eyes alarmingly wide, her voice hysterical.

My mom's gone insane.

"By the angel, chill."

She won't release my wrist, though. "I spent every night rocking you after we adopted you," she whispers. "I loved you more than any mother ever loved a daughter."

"I guess it took a while for you to realize I was a dud," I say.

She shakes her head, staring me right in the eyes. "No, it took a while for me to realize that you could be taken away from me at any moment, and there wouldn't be a single thing I could do about it."

That surprises me. Is she saying she didn't spend time with me. . .because she was worried it would hurt if she lost me? That's some crap, right there. "Just tell me this. Why would Dad bribe his friend with a million-dollar wand, and then make him swear never to give it to me? Especially when it's a wand that could have fixed my fumbly spellwork?"

If I thought she looked stricken before, it's only because I hadn't yet seen this. All the blood drains from her face, and she finally releases my hand. "Tell me you haven't touched that angel-cursed wand." She screeches. "Tell me!"

"Mom, you have got to calm down." More employees are gathering around us, and I'm actually getting a little nervous. For all her spy moves earlier, I doubt she could have drawn more attention to us if she tried.

She finally looks around, realizes what's happening, and paints a terribly fake smile on her face. "Sorry." She waves. "Just found out a dear friend of mine is in the hospital."

Everyone milling around just accepts that, like it's common for people to start shrieking in public if someone they know becomes ill. Then we drive home. Mom's quiet the entire way—which is really only a minute—with her hands at ten-and-two, gripping the wheel. Once we reach the house, she glances all around again, like we're checking for tails, and then points. "Let's weed some flowerbeds."

Her flowerbeds are pristine, and it's late fall, but I don't argue.

"You just pulled your file at work," she whispers, bending over a wilted, brown rhododendron, and somehow miraculously finding a weed to pull. "And your friends are all making the paranormal news network every single day. The last thing we need to do is have them link the files your dad buried about Zintrel and what family she came from."

"Is Grandma in danger?" I hate that thought—she's literally the nicest little lady I've ever met in my life. Unlike my mother, she never acted nasty with me. She cheered the loudest for every tiny win.

Mom freezes, a worm dangling from the roots of the plant in her hand, wriggling like mad. "Your *grandmother* isn't really your grandmother. It was your grandfather who had the affair."

"Wait—*Grandpa*?" I never even met my grandfather, and. . . "He got an angel *pregnant*?"

"Hush." Mom shakes her head. "There's a reason you don't know any of this. You *shouldn't* know any of it. And you have to promise me that under no circumstances will you *ever* use that wand."

"This one?" I pull it out of the lining in my jacket, and wave it at her.

She lunges at me, and I'm stuck running away from my own mother. I zip around the back yard, but she's surprisingly fast. When I barely turn in time to avoid losing the wand, and dart into the front yard, I'm nearly plowed over by a car.

A very nice, vintage Porsche.

Whoever's driving it parks and cuts the engine, and as I stand, huffing, a car between us, my brother steps out of the driver's side.

"You have Dad's Porsche?"

Clark freezes. "Uh, yeah, Mom told me not to tell you. She just felt bad when they couldn't find the wand Dad promised to leave me, so. . ." His eyes focus in on what I'm holding, and his jaw drops. "Wait. *You* have the wand?"

Mom walks in front of the car, her arms spread out. "This has gotten way out of hand."

❧ 19 ☙

CLARK

When I turned eight years old, I had just been given my first wand, and I was allowed to cast basic spells under supervision of an adult. It was an exciting day. Of course, once the adults weren't watching, all the eight-year olds talked about was what spells they'd tried *without* supervision.

We were supposed to surrender our wands when instruction ended, but most of us had an extra at home, or we knew how to sneak ours home.

I did both.

One of the times I snuck out my wand, my best friend, Phillip, suggested that we practice some things on the walk home. Of course, one of the first spells we tried was, "Ardeat."

Phillip tried it first, and he managed to get a fallen leaf to smoke.

I went next, and other than a small wisp of smoke, nothing.

"You have to think really hard about what you want to burn," he said, sagely. After all, he *had* singed the leaf.

"Alright," I said. "Alright." Only, no matter how many times I tried, and no matter how hard I focused on one single leaf, I never succeeded. By the time Phillip peeled off at his house—three houses before me—he had given me a new nickname.

"Clark No Spark," he said and then grinned like a lunatic.

It was literally the worst nickname I could imagine. The possibility that, with my father, the hotshot guardian, I might be low magic was terrifying. Misery-inducing. Impossible to contemplate. Which is why, the next day, I packed my own lunch for school and ran down to Phillip's house early.

I begged him not to tell anyone else.

"But it's true," he said. "You tried and tried, and. . ." He shrugged. "Nothing." The diabolical grin returned to his face. "Clark No Spark."

I felt like I might puke.

And then, I got angry. Not a little angry. Not, like, "why does he always get picked for mage ball first?" Or, like, "why does Phillip always get the newest robes, or the lightning bolt cut in the side of his hair, while I seem to always get the discount robes and the boring old bushy-hair cut?"

No, I was "stepped on an Alvin Brilliantus hat-shaped lego" mad.

This time, I would show him. I wouldn't just set the leaf on fire. I would set the neat *pile* of leaves in his front yard on fire. I whipped out my illegally possessed wand, and I pointed at the leaves, and I pulled on my anger, and my jealousy, and my fear, and I said, "Ardeat!"

The pile of leaves remained entirely untouched.

My former best friend Phillip looked at the pile I was clearly trying to spell and with his evil grin, chanted, "Clark No Spark." And then he laughed. He laughed so hard that his face turned red, and his sides heaved. He laughed so hard that he had to put his bag down on the ground.

That's when we realized, both of us hearing a strange crackling sound, that his house was on fire. Not, like, a few flames along the front porch, or something. No, there was smoke billowing from the hole in the roof, and flames were licking both sides of the house—it was literally a massive bonfire.

His mother shot out the front like a bat that didn't want to be bonded as a familiar, his little sister on her hip. Both of them had faces streaked in black soot, and the black cat that followed them looked fine, but probably only because it was already black.

There were no casualties in that fire—no living things died.

But the house was reduced to ash in less than an hour. Even when the fire mages arrived, there wasn't much they could do. All their photos, clothing, keepsakes, memories, furniture, and special belongings were all gone.

Phillip never told anyone that I cast that spell.

To be honest, neither of us were one hundred percent sure it *was* me. After all, I hadn't been able to singe a single leaf. But neither of us ever took our wands home without permission again, and Phillip stopped talking to me. . .at all.

A few weeks later, when my mom dragged me to the apartment they were staying in to drop off a carload full of things we'd collected to help them start over, I found myself standing in front of Phillip with no one else around.

"I—um." I cleared my throat.

He wasn't even looking at me. He was staring at his shoes.

"I'm really sorry," I blurted. "In case it was me."

He nodded, but didn't look up.

A moment later, his mother and mine breezed through the doorway, back into the kitchen, talking about the things they would do with their new house. "Luckily insurance will cover enough to get us a nice, new house." Phillip's mom was smiling like she was truly happy. "It'll be just as large, but not twenty years old."

"We don't have any of our stuff," Phillip muttered.

His mother dropped a hand on his shoulder. "We'll buy new stuff, plus our friends are generously giving us lots of things, like the Lucents here."

"They're not our friends." Phillip glared at me, spun around and disappeared down the hall.

"I'm so sorry," his mother said. "He's been strange since the fire. The loss of our stuff and that house hit him really hard." She leaned over, looking me right in the eye. "Phillip adores you. In fact, sometimes I think he's a little jealous." She winks. "Not every little boy has a superhero for a father. Phillip's dad is an actuary. If I didn't work too, we'd never have had the house we had to burn in the first place."

Mom's laughter was pretty uncomfortable, but I appreciated that his mother was trying to make me feel better.

That's the day I realized that what they teach in school—apologizing can fix anything—isn't actually true. There are lots of things that no apology will ever fix.

Now that I've had time to think, I'm beginning to worry that telling Lionel every single bad thing I could think of about the person I actually like the most in this world was one of those mistakes. Kind of like betraying Roxana, just to try and break her and Lionel up.

Sure, she's not right for Lionel. He was being a jerk, and she deserved to know, but I did it the way I did it, leaving photos in her room, because his dad offered to help me. I did it for myself, not to help Roxana. That's what makes it unforgivable.

I need to go to their apartments, get down on my knees, and beg for them to forgive me. I need to pray that this isn't like it was with Phillip. But when I get there, they're nowhere to be found. When I text Xander, he says they're on their way to the Dagobar Tower. He's going as moral support when Roxana faces her parents.

Which leaves me to stew all night alone, basically. Around ten o'clock, I give up on hoping they might text me. Lionel said he was going, and he'll have used all the information I gave him, and my best friend and the girl I love will cut me off. I'll deserve it.

Only, just as I'm drifting off to sleep, my phone rings. I scramble up to sitting, and I swipe to talk to them. "Hey. Listen, I—"

"No, you listen. I told them all the things you said about Xander, and I'm not even sure they cared. You must have been holding back. He put his mother in the hospital? She's a normie. Of course he did—he's a wolf. And he cheated on a test? I just looked it up, and you two went to a *normie* college. I can't believe that's all you gave me."

"That's all there *is*," I say. "Xander's a really good guy."

"He's a loser who doesn't have a pack or a job," Lionel says. "I needed *more*. I'm sure it's there, but you haven't done any digging."

"And I'm not going to," I say. "I shouldn't have told you the stuff I did. Look, Roxana told me she doesn't think you two are right for each other, and I have to agree. You're powerful, sure, and you're not bad looking—"

"Oh, you're gay? That makes so much sense."

"I'm not gay," I say. "I just think you'd be the world's worst boyfriend, and Roxana deserves better."

"Stop. You and I both know there isn't better," Lionel says.

I hang up.

He calls me three times, but I turn off my phone. The next morning, I'm really dragging, so I decide to head over to Grand Central Gloffee in the hopes of catching one of them. It would be easier to come clean with just one at a time, so ideally, if I could see Roxana first. . .

But Roxana's not there.

Just Bevin.

And she looks exhausted.

"You okay?"

She's looking over a paper, and she's talking to herself. If she were a wolf, I'd say she was mid-fray.

"What?" Her head snaps up, and she cuts off. "No, Clark, I'm *not* okay. We're supposed to close on this stupid building soon, and I haven't found a bank that will give us a loan, and the one I have that will finance us wants to have almost a half a million dollars more than we have, and that's *if* Roxana gets her check in time, and if you and Minerva actually pull your retirement money out." She throws her hands up in the air and falls backward against the sofa. Papers flutter to the ground around her. "We're doomed."

That's when it hits me.

The best apology's more than words. It's action. "I've already initiated a transfer of my money," I say. "But what if I can get the rest, too?"

Her arms flap up and down a few times, and she moans. "I heard from Minerva—you already tried. Your mom said no."

She's right about that, but I didn't *really* try. Not all the way. "The thing is, my mom told me that if I got a professor job, she'd loan me money. She said that she didn't pay for my college, and she could help. That tells me she has it, and—"

Bevin straightens so fast that I stumble back and bump into the coffee table, falling backward on my butt with a loud wham. "Whoa."

"You're clumsy, you big idiot, but if you could pull that off, I'd love you forever. How are you going to do it?"

My ears are ringing, and my butt feels like someone just ran over it with a car, but it feels good to hear she loves me. "I'm not sure, but—"

"You don't even have a plan?" Now she's wailing again.

"No, I do," I say. "I was kidding. I'm going to lie to my poor widowed mother and tell her I got a professor position. Then I'll say that I need enough money to get an apartment closer to the university. That could get us what we need."

"You'd lie to your poor little old mother for me?" Her eyes brighten. "You're just the best, Clark." She clears her throat. "Well, you're almost as good as Izaak and Xander, anyway."

"But *as* good as Minerva and Roxana?" I'll take it.

She laughs. "Not even close."

"Wait, so once I get enough money to buy the building, I'm still the person you like worst of all the friends?"

She pats my hand. "You're catching on, but think about how much *more* I'll like you than I did." She looks like she's not kidding. At least she's the one I like least, too—such a spastic mess.

"Well, thanks, I guess?" I don't sit. "I better get my car and head for Mom's."

"Wait, you have a car?"

"You can't tell Minerva." I grimace a little. "My mom wanted to pay me back for not paying for college, and the fact that I didn't get the wand Dad said he'd leave me, so she gave me my dad's car."

"The *Porsche*?" I can't tell whether Bevin's oohing or smiling. Maybe it's both. Smoohling. "That's awesome." She stands. "When can I borrow it?"

"If I loan it to you, will you like me more than Xander and Izaak?"

"Never better than Izaak," she says. "But closer to how much I like Xander."

I can't help my frown. "I better go."

"Okay, but don't forget. When you're done, call me." She smiles. "To tell me how well the lie worked, but also to set up a time for me to get the car." She wiggles. "Vroom."

She is *such* a weirdo.

The drive out helps me, calming me down a little. Once I save the building, once they see how much I was willing to do to help everyone else, surely they'll accept my apology. It's not like I burned a building down this time. And I've gotten better at apologizing.

But when I reach Mom's, she's not alone. In fact, I practically run Minerva over. They're clearly fighting, and even stranger—they do fight a lot—Minerva's *glowing.*

She looks like those glow sticks you buy at concerts, only she's glowing more like a whitish-blue LED light. "What the. . ." When I climb out, she looks almost as surprised to see me. That's when I remember I'm in the Porsche.

Whoops.

"You have Dad's Porsche?" I'm guessing this isn't going to help Mom and Minerva resolve their fight.

"Uh, yeah, Mom made me promise not to tell you." Shoot. I should not have blamed Mom. That'll just make things worse, even if Mom did make me promise. "She just felt bad when they couldn't find the wand Dad promised to leave me, so. . ." That's when I take a good look at what she's holding. It's something I've seen exactly *one* time. I bet I feel a little like Minerva just felt when she saw the

Porsche, only maybe angrier. "Wait. *You* have the wand?"

Mom walks in front of the car, her arms spread out. "This has gotten way out of hand."

"I'll say," Minerva says. "You've been lying to both of us for so long, you wouldn't know the truth it if slapped you in the face." Minerva glares.

That's when I notice my sister's cheek is *bright* red. Surely Mom didn't. . .

"There are two things I cannot allow," Mom hisses. "You cannot have that wand, and you mustn't, not under any circumstances, try to go see your biological mother."

"She's talking about your aunt," Minerva says to me casually. "Just in case you weren't in on the monumental sham that is my life."

"I'm not—I had no idea."

"He doesn't *need* to know," Mom says. "In fact, you're endangering Clark right now, which I told your father would happen when he begged to adopt you in the first place."

"Mom." I walk around the car toward her. "You sound entirely insane right now. Of course Minerva deserves to know the truth about her birth mother, and if you were her, you'd be asking the same questions. Maybe if you'd been nicer to your own daughter, she wouldn't feel like she didn't have a real mother."

Mom's mouth falls open. "Been *nicer*? My entire *life* has been about keeping her safe. My marriage suffered. Your life suffered. In fact, my life was wrecked, and—"

"Do you hear yourself?" I shake my head. "Just stop."

"No, you stop," Mom says. "You both need to stop

talking about this. Trust me, *it's not safe to be out here yelling*." She looks around and then sighs, plastering one hand across her forehead. "I can't believe that even you won't listen to me."

"Even him?" Minerva looks as wounded as I've ever seen her. "Because he's your real son, you mean?"

"No, because unlike you, he usually does listen."

But Minerva's done with Mom. She shoves the wand in her pocket and stomps off down the road, heading. . .I don't know where. Anywhere but here, I guess. I can't even blame her.

My mom told me the wand was lost—clearly a lie.

She told me not to tell Minerva about the car. Suborning perjury.

She's always treated my sister like she was a burden, and an embarrassing one at that. I tried not to see it, because Mom was always such a great mother to me, but I have to admit it was there. Minerva screwed up a lot, and it bothered Mom, far more than it should have bothered someone's mother.

"Clark." Mom motions toward the flowerbeds. "Come help me pull weeds."

"I can't." I open the car door, about to go after Minerva. "You're just—you're unbelievable."

"No, wait." Her eyes plead with me. "Five minutes. Surely I've earned that much from you."

It'll take Minerva at least that long to get an Uber to come find her out here. "Fine, but not one minute more."

I stomp toward the stupid flowerbeds, and as I do, I remember how much time Mom and Dad spent out here. They were always out here in the mornings, crouched over the shrubs and flowers.

"Your dad spelled these shrubs," she whispers. "They keep any listening devices from working in a ten-foot radius."

"Mom, you sound so crazy right now."

"Your sister's not just angel-spawn," she says. "Angel spawn is when an angel and a human have a child."

I'm having trouble understanding her. "Wait, you knew her mother was angel-spawn?"

She hushes me. "Clark, listen. She can't know this, because it impacts the spell's ability to work, but your dad spent every speck of magic he had, he called in every favor he'd earned in his career, and he managed to sneak Minerva away from his sister without anyone knowing Zintrel was even pregnant. If anyone had known. . ." Mom shakes her head, paler than I've ever seen her.

"We saw Minerva's file. It's all redacted and strange."

"Zintrel took care of all that herself, so I'm not sure what it looks like. But here's the important part, Clark. If some of what Minerva did sets anything off, or if that spell starts to unravel." Mom shudders, and then she begins to cry.

"Mom, what are you talking about?"

"Angel-spawn are just like your friend Bevin. If they do any heroic acts, any truly miraculous things, they'll ascend. Just like demon-spawn, they can upset the balance of the universe. But unlike demon-spawn, if we try to destroy them, they shine brighter. It's dangerous to destroy one. They have to be contained, kept in a prison of light, basically, forever."

"That sounds horrible," I say.

Mom nods. "I met your aunt one time," she says. "I know Minerva, and probably your father, thought I hated her. They fault me for not being more support-ive, but Clark, the idea that she exists, basically stuck in an endless prison, it makes me so sad that I have trouble even functioning."

"Okay." I glance at my watch. "Mom, just tell me the rest. I really need to talk to Minerva. I don't want her to get an Uber before I can go get her."

She grabs my arm and squeezes so tightly that I'm worried she might cut off the circulation. "Clark, Minerva's father's an angel."

I shake my head. "Now you're getting confused. Her mother's angel-spawn, and her father's. . ." I laugh. "If Dad's sister's angel-spawn, but still related to us, she came from a mage, which means she's like three-quarters angel. That would mean that if Miner-va's dad was an angel. . .she'd be, like, more than three-quarters angel." I'm ready to laugh—even though I feel like it's a very inappropriate joke, but then I realize Mom's crying again.

I'm suddenly worried that what she said is somehow true.

"That *can't* be," I say. "Minerva can barely cast a simple spell. They always misfire. She's a disaster. She can't be. . ." I almost can't bring myself to say the word. "Almost a full akero." I think about her, ranting about her pigeon not staying in its cage. "Mom, she couldn't even bond a familiar. After trying over and over, she wound up with a *pigeon.*"

"Do you know what makes the akero so special?"

"Huh?"

"Do you know why they live up on that super high

mountain peak, almost never interacting with the rest of the world?"

"Because they fly, so they can?" Most of what I know about the akero came from children's books in primary school. To truly study the akero, you have to become angel-blessed, an acolyte, and they're chosen once every ten years. "Not really. Have you ever seen one in real life?"

She shakes her head. "No, and for good reason. The akero are so glorious, so brilliant, and so bright, that being around them *changes* things."

"What does that mean?"

"Your sister wasn't *supposed* to be able to bond a familiar, because a tangible bond to someone like her would permanently alter the being she was bonded to. The akero *lift* anything they're around. Exposure to them must be extremely limited, because they change us, our entire world."

"Wait, you said she wasn't supposed to, but she did bond a pigeon. . ."

"Yes, and I'm saying that it might not *stay* a pigeon. You need to kill that bird immediately. While you still can."

"Mom, you sound really nuts right now."

She pats my hand. "I know, but everything I'm saying is still true. You can't tell her—you can't talk about any of this. You have to shut her down when she asks, because if she does a single truly miraculous thing, like changing a pigeon into a hawk, or saving someone who was doomed to die. . .with as much angel blood as she has, she could Ascend immediately." She frowns. "Just like a demon-spawn Descending, Clark, something like that would break the world."

"I'm telling you Mom, she can't really even cast."

"I know."

"Then what are we talking about? You must have some of this wrong."

"She can't cast spells because your father and her mother worked together to shackle Minerva so that she can't really use her magic," Mom whispers. "She had to be caged, but your father didn't want her caged in the same way his sister was. It was too miserable to isolate her like that, too depressing. Instead, they cast the most awful, insidious, terribly parasitic spell on her. It sucks up her goodness almost as fast as it can effervesce."

"Effervesce?"

"It looked like. . ." Mom shakes her head. "Like a soul-sucking cloud of pure evil when it attached to her chest." She's crying again. "And it cost your dad *every-thing* he loved to cast that spell the last time."

"So, wait. What's the feather in the wand? Is it really an akero feather?"

"It's her father's feather," Mom says. "You have to get it away from her, immediately." She really does look unhinged, but I'm starting to understand why. "Clark." She swallows. "I think it's calling to her."

It's not until I'm driving away that I think about something my mom said and begin to really panic. If she's worried about the bond between Minerva and Giggles, what would she say about the bond between Minerva. . .and all the rest of us? We're all connected now through Xander?

But then I force myself to stop panicking.

Maybe, somehow, Dad got a hold of a real akero feather. And maybe his sister's truly angel-spawn. But there's *no way* she had some kind of affair with an akero and then got pregnant. Right? It's insane.

It's far more likely that this is some hallucination of my mother's. I call her health and wellness wizard and ask him to do a house call, and then I start driving around, looking for Minerva. I really need to give her a ride home and explain.

With as angry at me as Xander must be, I can't risk upsetting Minerva too.

BEVIN

If I had to describe to someone what I thought a superhero might look like in real life, he or she would look nothing like Clark. I mean, he does have the glasses for the mild-mannered alter-ego, at least, when he doesn't bother with contacts. And he does have the name—close enough, anyway—but he just doesn't have an overpowering desire to get something done. He doesn't have the guts to stick his neck out.

Although, he did step up to defend Roxana against Ragar.

Right before he was almost squashed like a bug. I heard that Roxana saved his life, which makes sense. Of course the dragon shifter who can't shift and has spent her whole life locked in a tower would save the mage who was trained for years from the scary, fire-breathing monster.

My preconceptions notwithstanding, it was Clark who rode off in a four hundred horsepower Porsche to do whatever it takes to get us the money we need. His mother may not be a fire-breathing dragon, but she's pretty scary, and he just stormed off to lie to her so we can buy this building and have one place in the world that we feel safe.

I spend a ton of time watching my phone, waiting for him to call.

Also, waiting for the text saying my Chinese food is ready, but mostly waiting for his call. Which means that I'm staring at my phone when Roxana calls.

"Hello?" I ask. "You are not my Chinese food."

"I do have it, though," she says. "I was in the stairwell when I ran into the guy—the elevators are taking forever, by the way. We may need to call someone after we buy this place."

"When did you meet the delivery guy?" My voice may be a little shrill. "I hope you're coming with that food quick. If I don't get some MSG up in here quick, I might go crazy." I drop my voice. "I'm actually hiding in your room right now. Apparently there was some kind of rodent treatment or something in the empty apartments—you know, the ones they were squatting in—and we were worried they've figured out that there are vagrants here. Minerva invited them in, and now we're stuck drowning in like a hundred wolves."

"Are there really a hundred?" Roxana asks. "Because I feel like there are maybe only fifteen or twenty."

"Who knows?" My voice has almost gone dog-whistle. With their wolfy hearing, the werewolves outside probably know exactly what I'm saying. But maybe that's good? Maybe they'll be inspired to get a hostel. "They're wolves, and I don't know them, and they're all over the place, and I skipped breakfast, and I just want to eat my Chinese food in peace."

I feel guilty as soon as I say the words. I'm a total sponger myself, living with Minerva after I lost my home. These wolves have no home, and they had no alpha, and they're handing all the money they have in this world over to Xander to help us buy the building. "Oh, fine. There are probably only twenty of them. And a few of them are even little kids who are kind of nice, albeit emaciated and homely."

"Hey, Bevin?"

"What?"

"Knock, knock."

"Oh my gosh," I say. "I swear, if you tell me some dumb joke about how the witch and the vampire cast a spell on the bar or something, I will lose my mind."

The door to Roxana's room where I'm hiding opens, and I leap to my feet, unintentionally chucking my phone at the person in the doorway. Unfortunately, it's Roxana, and my phone hits the brown bag she's holding, knocking it to the floor, scattering *my* orange chicken and stir-fried rice all over the wooden floor. "Ugh," I say. "I'm sorry."

"Not a good idea to surprise Bevin," Roxana says. "Noted." She crouches down and starts picking up the food she can salvage. "Sorry about your dinner."

"It's fine," I say. "I actually ordered way more than I could possibly eat under normal circumstances."

She frowns. "Expecting someone else in my room?" She blinks. "Is it rude if I say that I hope not?"

I laugh. "I'm a stress eater. Having hundreds of thousands at risk and not having the money we need. . ." I close my eyes, inhale, and open them. "It's going to be fine. Someone will come up with something—Clark just left to try and work his magic, but the earnest money alone was a lot, and if we can't come up with the rest, I'll lose it, so."

"Wait, can he make money with his magic?" Roxana balls one hand in a fist. "I knew it. I knew there had to be a way."

"No, dummy. He's talking to his mom again. This may be our last real chance of getting the money."

She stands so fast that she knocks the box of orange chicken I just picked up over again.

"Mother feather, Roxana! What in the name of all that flies are you—"

"Bevin." She claps. "I was going to tell you first thing, but you threw the phone at me, and I got distracted."

I shoot to my feet. "Did that worthless idiot call you first instead of me?" I'm going to kill Clark. "I told him to call *me*. I helped him come up with the idea."

Roxana shrugs. "Didn't hear from Clark, but my parents released my trust fund! I have the money, now. However much you need."

"You're kidding."

"Not at all."

I use swear words I'd forgotten that I knew in my glee, and then I dance round the room, making an even bigger mess with the Chinese food, and I don't even care. "Roxana, I could kiss you right now."

"Please don't. I'm pretty sure that would be awkward for both of us."

"Oh, honey," I say. "You poor thing. You have no idea."

She freezes. "Maybe I should tell you that I'm kind of with Xander."

"You're—*with* him, with him?" I thought maybe there was attraction, but holy quill. "Since when?"

"It just barely happened." She's blushing. She's actually blushing. "But I'm pretty excited."

I sit down on the floor, too hungry to keep trying to clean things up before eating anything. I snag the poor orange chicken, which has now been knocked over twice. It's barely half full. Even so, I pop a bite into my mouth and close my eyes.

"Is that orange chicken?"

I nod.

She pulls out chopsticks. "Are you going to zap me if I try a few bites?"

I can't help smiling. "Is that a risk you're willing to take?"

"I didn't have breakfast either." She snags one piece, pops it in her mouth, and promptly pulls a face and spits it into her hand. "Hey." She makes fake retching sounds. "That is *not* orange chicken."

"I'm vegetarian," I say. "Or did you forget?"

"That's *disgusting*. What is it?"

"It's orange-*tofu*," I amend. "It tastes almost exactly the same."

She drops her chopsticks into the bag. "Saying something does *not* make it true."

"You are so closeminded. If you weren't stunningly beautiful, I might like Clark more than you."

She stares at me for a moment, and then we both start laughing.

My phone rings, the ringtone I assign to real friends.

The sound's *so* clangy and obnoxious that I'm almost guaranteed not to miss it. I crawl across the floor and stretch out, snagging my phone and crab walking myself back into place in front of my Chinese food. No time to check caller ID, or it might go to voicemail. "Hello?"

I'm holding the phone between my ear and my mouth, so the sound's a little muffled when my real estate agent says, "Did you get my email? The walk through's in. . ." There's some strange whooshing and then a windy sound, and then she says, "Sorry about that. I'm just grabbing a cab. It's in twenty minutes. Do you have a list of things you want me to look at, or are you coming yourself?"

"The walk through?" I frown. "What is that exactly? Normally, I'm in for all the charity things I can possibly do, but with the building sale coming up, I'm a little crunched on time, and—"

"You're kidding, right?" Raven laughs. "Bevin, a walk through's an important part of the purchase process, and for a building of this size, we do two. One now, just to make sure there aren't any surprises on the day of sale—busted elevators, electronic problems, that sort of thing. It's not as extensive as an inspection, which you waived against my objection, but it's one of your biggest protections."

"Do I need a lot of protection?" I ask. "I have two mages as best friends. I'm sure they can magically repair any problems the building has."

She's laughing again. "As if mages can just fix electrical issues or foundation problems. You are so funny, Bev."

I hate when people call me Bev. I'm not Beverly.

And I'm not a middle-school kid, who's happy to have a nickname slapped on her.

"So, are you coming then? Or will you send me a list?"

"We'll waive that too," I say.

"Stop," Raven says. "You can't waive the walk throughs. They're fast and painless and if you don't want to come, I'll do it myself. Besides, it gives us a chance to verify that there *are* tenants in the occupied buildings, and after we're done we can go to the seller's accounting office and look at the books."

Oh, good. The books. I'm bored just saying the word.

"You should look at the books," Roxana says. "That'll be our best snapshot of how much revenue we'll have coming in, and how much of a loss we may sustain before we get the rents back up again."

I cover the mouthpiece of my phone. "We have renters, remember? Our issue will be getting *rid* of the ones who haven't already left."

Roxana frowns. "Do all the wolves *have* to live in this same building?"

She's the one dating their pod-person leader. She knows better than me, I'm sure. "I think they want to. When Xander walked out to take the trash to the dumpster earlier, I saw a few of them sniffing his scent after he passed and closing their eyes with a smile." It creeped me out, honestly, but clearly just being near him makes them happy.

"What?" Roxana reaches over and grabs a piece of tofu-chicken, popping it in her mouth without thinking again. This time, though, she doesn't spit it out. She just stares into nothing, chewing.

"Bevin? Are you there?" Raven's tinny voice is chiming from my phone.

"Right, sorry," I say. "How about this? I'm pressed for time today, so we can do a cursory walk through of most of the building and call it good. Okay?"

"If that's really what you want." Raven sounds irritated, but I'm paying her, so that's too bad.

"It is."

"Alright, well, can you get there in twenty minutes?"

"I think I can swing it," I say. "See you soon." I take Roxana down with me, after she tells me she has nothing else going on. "If you're investing too, you should at least take a look."

The walk through's less catastrophic than I expected. I tell the wolves to barely crack the door if possible, and if my agent asks, they're supposed to insist they're having a party in the middle of the afternoon. When I circle back around half an hour later, they do just as I suggested. Raven makes a valiant effort to push past them, but they hold the line.

"It's fine," I say. "I'm sure it's fine."

No one answers the door at Xander's place, so the agent for the seller knocks, announces himself, and then whips out a key and opens it. "Coming inside," he says.

And then we're walking through Xander's apartment without Xander. Honestly, it's a little strange. The last time I walked through the door, they were mostly packed and planning to leave. Now they're mostly unpacked again, and we're buying the building. Our lives have been turbulent over the past weeks.

Ever since we met Roxana.

Roxana pretends to inspect the place, tapping her lip. "Interesting. Interesting."

"What is?" Raven asks. "Do you see a problem?"

"I'd get rid of these guys as soon as you could," the seller's agent says, his lip curling. "They're total slobs." He's looking askance at a massive pile of laundry that probably piled up when they thought they were about to be homeless.

Roxana points at a photo on the end table by the sofa. "The tenants here are very good looking, though." She leans closer. "Especially the one with the golden eyes."

Raven snatches the photo and peers at it. "Really?" She glances at Roxana. "You have one of the hottest men I've ever seen as your boyfriend, and you think these losers are cute?"

Just then, the pile of laundry comes to life, lurching toward us with a terrible groan. "Loooooosers?"

It takes me a split second to realize that, of course, the laundry's Izaak. He's totally dead to the world when the sun's up, and it's definitely still up. Clearly he fell asleep in a strange place, but the seller's agent's a normie, and Izaak's a vampire, sleepy or not. The poor agent looks ready to soil his suit.

"You know what?" I ask. "I've seen enough. Let's go."

Luckily, vampires are incredibly somnolent during the day, so as soon as Izaak isn't actively hearing someone call him a loser, he slumps back to the floor and drops right back to sleep. I pat his head before I leave. "You aren't losers. That guy was a loser."

He grunts.

I'm smiling on my way out.

Blessedly, the rest of the walk through's pretty boring. The wolves all got the messages we asked the ones in Minerva's apartment to send, and no one's where they shouldn't be. It might have been a bit of a shell and pea game, Roxana messaging them when to head down to the third floor, and when it's okay to head back up to the fourth, but as we're finishing, the accounting office calls.

Raven's talking so quickly that I have trouble understanding her, but then she says, "I was told today. Were you lying then or now?"

She sniffs. Then she grunts.

Then she finally says, "Fine. My clients are busy, but I guess tomorrow will *have* to do." She hangs up, but she's not happy, clearly. The poor seller's agent, after being scared half to death by a vampire, is now getting a terrible tongue lashing about reliability in business as they walk toward the building exit.

"Wait," Bevin says. "I thought there was a small shop next to Grand Central Gloffee."

The seller's agent smacks his forehead. "Yes, but it's the one business with a private entrance. You can't access it from the stairwell."

"Grand Central Gloffee has its own entrance," I say. "I don't understand."

"All first-floor shops do. But usually the back of it would connect to the rest of the building, like Grand Central does."

"I don't get it either," Roxana says.

The seller's agent looks like he thinks we're idiots. "We walked through the back of Grand Central to come check out the rest of the building." He points. "Remember?"

I nod.

"The tiny office on the bottom right's called a pocket office, and it has an endcap studio apartment directly over it that's only accessible from the shop itself. That means you're pretty much forced to rent it out in conjunction with the connecting shop. You can 't rent that studio apartment separately."

It sounds. . .perfect, almost like it was designed for me. "Can we take a look?"

The agent pulls a key off the wheel. "We were able to terminate the agreement with the tenant—he was not keen on having his rent raised, so he moved along. He should be out by tomorrow, but you can take a look today if you'd like."

"I would, yes."

"Actually." The seller's agent drops his voice. "Just keep that key. It's an extra, and since the lease just ended, it's fine. Don't mention it at close." He winks. "I have to pick up my son or my wife is going to kill me. I'll make sure you can see the books tomorrow."

Raven gets a call, so she waves as she leaves, and suddenly, it's just me and Roxana. I've only seen the shop through a window, and it looked small and a little cramped, so I'm eager to check it out myself.

I knock first, mimicking Raven and the other agent, but no one answers. The lights aren't on, either. They key's a little sticky, but with a wiggle and a sharp twist, I get it open.

"We could have it rekeyed," Roxana says. She looks so proud that I'm guessing she just found out what rekeying is.

"I kind of like locks that have a little personality."

"Right," Roxana says. "Sometimes I forget that you're weird."

"Don't worry. I'll always remind you." When I step through the doorway and look around. . .I'm surprised to find that the entire thing's utterly empty. No furniture. No decorations. Not even a single sheet of paper.

It's dirty, though.

Dust bunnies roll right and left as I walk around the room, and my feet leave prints in the dust on the floor. I sneeze heartily, expelling all the stupid amounts of junk in the air violently. "It could use a good cleaning. That's for sure."

"Mages may not be great at repairing the foundation, but they sure can help with cleaning." Roxana sniffs and shakes her head.

"You don't say." I grin. "Once it's clean, and once I can add a counter and lots of shelves. . ." I spin around, my arms outstretched. "I think this will work."

The studio upstairs is even better than I imagined it would be. One wall is exposed red brick—beautiful brick, with a lot of color variation. There are two nice, long shelves mounted on it, and a bookcase on the far end. On the opposite wall, there's a full stove and oven, and the dishwasher—yes, there's a dishwasher—has two separate racks. The cabinets built in are solid wood, and they could use a buff and polish, but they're a lovely, almost vintage cut. The fridge may not be full size, but it's twice the size of the mini-fridge in my last place.

Whoever lived here before even left the most amazing, chunky lime-green corduroy curtains that hang on either side of the large bay windows looking over the street. Speaking of the windows, they open onto a very small, very cute little balcony. It's only three feet wide, but it runs the length of the shop, and I can't believe I never noticed it before. This place is light, bright, and it's chock full of character. I couldn't have designed a nicer place if I'd tried.

As we walk back down to the storefront below, I can't help comparing this to what I had. It's almost the same size—maybe a little smaller, but not much.

But it's totally empty.

It took me almost six months before I opened my first shop to assemble all my stock. I can't exactly pick up a catalog and place an order. And if I put all my money into buying this building, I won't even have money to buy secondhand magical things.

"What's wrong?" Roxana asks.

"How much money do you think your trust fund has?"

Roxana shrugs. "Why?"

"If you could chip in half a million, that would be great," I say. "But a million would be even better, if you could swing it."

"How about two?" Roxana says. "Then you can put in two, Xander and his wolves can put in two, and we'll all be even partners."

It's like a weight has come off my chest. "Really?"

"Really." She kicks the floor and dust flies everywhere. A dust bunny rolls like a tiny tumbleweed, end over end, picking up more dust as it goes. "You'll have plenty of costs, turning this dump into a shop. You should have some startup capital."

"It's a real blessing," I say. "Your trust fund, I

mean. And my money from the fundraiser and my land sale. I know that."

"But it's still a little depressing." Roxana's shoulders slump. "I know how you feel. Last night, I told my parents I was not dating Lionel, and I told them that I *am* dating Xander, alpha of a wolf pack I've joined."

"By all the angels and their feathered wings—how did that go?" I can't even imagine telling them all that on the same night.

"Did I mention that Xander was with me when I did it?"

I wince. "Did he get charbroiled?"

She shakes her head slowly. "No, but it was a close call."

"I bet."

"I should be happy—I'm dating someone I really like for the first time in my life. I'm out here on my own, doing it."

I'm not sure having a huge trust fund counts as being on your own. "Wait, you told your parents all that, and they still gave you a trust fund?" I snort. "I should call my mom up and tell her I've descended twice, but I only have one power. I wonder what she'd give me. Probably a spanking with a bat or a shovel." My mom's always been the only person in the world who supported my Herculean efforts to be good— she'll be devastated when she hears.

Everyone else always just thought I was doomed from the start.

My mom bet on the wrong horse, of course, but still, it felt nice to know someone thought the best of me. I'm so afraid to tell her I failed, that I haven't called her at all since I lied and descended. She doesn't even know my shop burned down. As a normie, she doesn't really get the typical news about stuff like that.

"They only gave me my trust because. . ." Roxana steps forward and leans against the window, her forehead pressed against the middle pane. "They think Xander's going to die soon. They figured I should have some kind of money so I can get a cab, buy clothing, or you know, pay for my boyfriend's funeral before I come back home. It's a golden leash to lead me back to them."

"That's a rude thing for them to tell you," Bevin says. "But you know they might be right? We have a lot of people piling up who hate us."

"And it's all my fault. It all started when I climbed down that ladder on my wedding day."

"It's not, though," I say. "You didn't make me half daimoni. You didn't make Minerva who she is, or Xander. You didn't force any of us—we could have turned you in. You did it yourself when you realized it was hurting us."

"I've never had anyone who cared what I wanted to do."

"Well, you do now." I wrap an arm around her shoulders and she leans against me quietly.

"If I haven't said it before," she whispers, "thank you. I know it hasn't been easy, being my friend. I think, once we get the wolf stuff and the Demon Council stuff worked out, I'll learn what it feels like to be free *and* safe." She smiles. "I'm looking forward to it."

"Me too," I say. "And for what it's worth, I'd do it all again."

"What?"

"Lie to cover for you and descend. I haven't regretted it."

Her eyes well with tears, but before she can say anything, her head whips toward the far side of the window. "Bevin." Her eyes widen, and she inhales softly.

"What?" I turn, but before I can see what has her alarmed, she grabs my elbow and yanks me toward the back of the store.

"Did that agent guy say this opens on the alley?"

I frown. "I don't think he said that, but I saw it."

"Great," she says. "We need to go."

"Why?" I turn back toward the front. "I don't think I locked up yet."

"Don't bother," she says.

"That agent gave me the key," I say, "but that doesn't mean I have no responsibility—"

Roxana claps a hand over my mouth just as I see what she saw: wolves.

Dozens and dozens of them are streaming past the front window.

"We need to get to the back of Grand Central," Roxana whispers, "and get Gavin to evacuate everyone he can through to the alley, *right now*. Lo Ren's brought his pack."

21

XANDER

Every year for Mother's Day, I would agonize over what I could buy or make that would be the perfect gift for my mother. She hadn't wanted a kid in the first place, and she certainly hadn't wanted a son who turned into a dog, but she got stuck with me all the same. On the one day each year that everyone celebrated this chore my mom had been saddled with, I wanted to make sure she knew that *I* was grateful she had me.

I was so grateful for her.

One year, I carved her a little wolf.

When she opened the clumsily-wrapped carving, she stared at it for a moment. Maybe two. "What is this?"

She couldn't tell? I'd even found a hunk of wood with light and dark swirls that I thought looked sort of like my coloring. "It's—"

"Oh." She nodded. "I see it now. It's a doorstop shaped like a dog?" She stood up and walked across the room. "For this one that keeps closing." She shoved it next to the door, and within thirty seconds, the door and the tiny wolf had slid slowly back toward closed. "Maybe we could put weights on the bottom of the little dog."

"It's supposed to be me," I said. "It's a wolf."

She frowned. "But we don't want people to know, right? Seems like making a wolf out of wood's a bad idea." She picked it up and looked at it. "Are you sure it's a wolf?" She turned her head.

That year was a definite failure.

The next year, I'd just been kicked out of school, for the second time, and I *really* wanted to impress her with something good. For just one day, I wanted her to be happy that she'd had a child. I gathered cans from everywhere I could find them. Trash cans. Ditches. Stores. I'd hide them behind the house, and I'd leave for my new school early to drop them off.

I got almost ten cents a can when I cashed them in.

It took months and months, and my hands were sticky and stinky from the stupid junk that spilled out of the cans all the time, but by the time Mother's Day rolled around, I had forty-six dollars. It felt like a small fortune. Only, when I walked to the store after school, I had no idea what to buy with it.

The only stores that were close enough for me to walk to them were the 7-11, a sports collectibles store, and a pharmacy. Since Mom didn't like sports, and since I doubted she'd be very impressed with a Mega Big Gulp, I decided the pharmacy was my best bet. It had things that weren't medicine, and the checker was a really nice, really fancy looking woman a few years younger than Mom.

I asked for her help.

After a lot of deliberation, I decided to buy a nice card, which cost four dollars and eighty-eight cents, some lip gloss which was eight ninety-nine, and then shampoo and conditioner that the checker said, "smelled amaaaazing."

This time, I knew Mom would be happy.

Who didn't want to smell like peaches? The checker told me all human women liked smelling good. And if she looked at me a little oddly when I asked what human women liked, well, I was also a little boy. I had three dollars and fifty cents left, so I bought a Big Gulp on my way home. Of course, that's when I realized I had no wrapping paper or a bag.

It was fine.

I cut up a big brown grocery sack, and I wrapped it as best I could.

When Mother's Day came, Mom was even more confused than she was with the carved wolf. "You. . .bought me shampoo?" She glanced up. "Does my hair look dirty to you?"

I frowned. "No, not at all, but the lady at the store told me this one smells great."

"Do I smell bad?" She was frowning so much by then that her forehead had wrinkles. "Is it a wolf thing?"

I shook my head. "No, I had a human help me pick it. She said—"

"And I don't wear pink lip gloss, X. I'm not twelve."

I didn't cry. I was really proud of the fact that I didn't cry. But when I found the lip gloss, shampoo, and conditioner that Mom left on my bathroom counter, I sure did. At least I was all alone, so I didn't make her feel bad. The card was in her trash can the next morning when I went around to gather it all up and put it on the curb.

In spite of ongoing attempts, the next few years were actually worse.

When Roxana told her parents about us last night, it felt. . .significant. I had to leave early this morning to file a petition with the Wolf Council for them to split our area, but that went way faster than I expected. When I found myself with free time, I thought I'd grab some kind of gift for Roxana on the way home—a thank you for telling her parents. A thank you for wanting to date *me*. Only, even with many more stores I can now walk to, I'm terrified that I'll get her something really stupid—something she'll hate.

She's basically a princess.

She can buy anything she wants, and her parents just gave her a trust fund worth millions without even thinking about it. I run my hands over row after row of t-shirts that say various things about New York City, and all I know is that everything I've considered has been a really dumb idea. An hour of shopping, and I still have no better ideas than peach shampoo.

Until I see it.

It's a plain grey t-shirt, and it says, "I have great taste in dogs, but bad taste in men." There's even a silhouette of a wolfy sort of dog in the center that the words curl around.

Roxana doesn't have a dog, but now she has me. People make werewolf jokes all the time that compare us to dogs. . .I'm not sure why the double slam on me makes me smile so much, but it does. It's just a grey t-shirt, but she looks awesome in everything, so I'm hoping she'll think it's funny enough to wear.

I grab it.

I'm checking out when I notice another shirt. It's another grey t-shirt, the exact same shade of grey, that says, "Keep calm and hug your dog." It has the same wolf-dog-silhouette—they almost match. "I'll take that one, too."

On my way back to our building, I duck into an alley and yank off my boring brown polo shirt—I had to look presentable to visit the Wolf Council—and pull my new shirt on. I'm not sure how the wolves in my pack will react, but I think Roxana will get it.

Izaak definitely will.

That makes me think about Clark—he would have loved it. But now, I'm not even sure I care what he thinks. I'm still trying to figure out what it meant, that he told Lionel all those things about me. Why would he do it?

Unless he knew about me and Roxana and he was mad.

The longer I stand in the alley, thinking about the timing, the more certain I become. I'm not sure how he found out, but it had to be retaliatory. In some ways, I feel better. He did it because he was hurt. In a lot of ways, though, I feel worse.

I've never really had any friends, so I'm probably the wrong person to say whether this is true, but I always hoped that my real friends would come talk to me if they were mad. I didn't think they'd use things they knew about my life to try and hurt me. It feels. . .pretty lousy. Almost like I've been betrayed.

Roxana didn't seem to care about any of it.

Her parents almost seemed to write Lionel's shouting off as some kind of insane rant, but Clark didn't know it would play out like that. For all he knew, it could have broken Roxana and me up.

Which was probably the point.

I'm pretty bummed as I walk the last few blocks to the building we're about to buy. I think about stopping for gloffee, but I'm too worried Clark will be there. I'm not ready to run into him, because I'm not ready to forgive him. Not yet anyway. I jog up the stairs, and I'm almost to the top when my phone starts ringing.

"Hello?"

"Xander?" It's Bevin.

"Yeah?"

"A whole lot of wolves incoming. Roxie and I are in the empty shop next to Grand Central Gloffee. You close?"

"Almost to the door of our place," I say. "Are you two safe?"

"We're coming," Bevin says.

No, don't! I can't help reaching out to Roxana. *Please, please, leave with Bevin. She can zap anyone who threatens you, but hopefully the wolves won't notice either of you.* I'm racing toward my apartment door, but I'm also reaching out with my new alpha senses, which are quite unfocused as of yet, and broadcasting. *Get the pups to safety. Lo Ren's here.*

Before I've even touched the handle of my door, it's opening. Wolves are pouring out—some in wolf form, most in human. Many of the humans are leading children toward the back of the hall.

"There's a fire escape back there," I say. "Be quiet, and be quick."

"We're going up," Iris says.

I've only talked to Iris once before now, right after I bonded Jewel. I spent a few minutes talking to them each in turn when I formally bonded them, but we're still basically strangers. It's quite strange that I can feel what's going on inside of her head. The calm I feel is even odder.

"Of course we're calm." When Iris smiles, her face lights up. The bizarre mullet she's got, bleached on top, actually almost works for her. Instead of back-woods, she almost looks punk rock. I could totally see her in cutoff jeans, Doc Martens, and a whole line of earrings down the right side—heavy eyeliner.

"I love that idea," she says. "When this is over, can you show me where I'd find clothes like that?"

"Why aren't you all panicking?" I look around, just now realizing that none of them seem terrified. "Did you understand me? Lo Ren Fang, the Manhattan pack alpha, is here with a lot of other wolves."

The little boy next to me smiles. "But so is our alpha, so it's okay." He looks up at me with something very close to hero worship. "That's why you need us close, in case you need extra magic."

As if they've now told me all I need to know, they go right back to heading out and up toward the roof. Lo Ren, with his hundreds of wolves, is coming to kill us—I have, maybe, forty fighters? Probably also a vampire, possibly a witch who's not reliable, a demon-spawn who can be defeated with a box of Bounce sheets, and a wizard who's really mad at me and prob-ably not keen to risk his life right now.

Just then, Roxana and Bevin show up, moving the opposite direction of the wolves who are dutifully evacuating upward. My sweet little wolves immediately part, letting them through.

"Your mate's pretty," a girl with bright red hair says. "Even prettier than you."

"Wait, all the wolves already knew?" Bevin frowns. "I thought—"

"Do they?" Roxana doesn't look pleased. "I can't believe you told them."

"He didn't tell us." The redhead beams. "I can smell it."

Roxana lifts her shirt and sniffs. "I *smell* like Xander?"

The girl shakes her head. "You smell like alpha's mate." Her mother tugs on her hand, and she skips away.

"This whole day has been strange," I say.

"Where do we want to face them?" Jewel's voice behind me helps me focus on what counts. Now that the small wolves have been removed, at least somewhat, it's time to deal with Lo Ren and his pack of aggressors.

Other than that time he tried to run me off with just a handful of supporters, this is our first faceoff. All the times I spent around him for years, I had yielded to him as my alpha. I'm half-scared, half-curious to see what will happen now that he's not got a metaphorical foot on my throat.

"I think, as much as it pains me, the safest place to confront him would be Grand Central Gloffee, or maybe the street outside if we can keep them back that far."

"The humans are evacuating this block," Jewel says. "They said there's a terrorist threat."

Gotta love what the magic from more than a hundred werewolves' worth of gloffee will push out there.

"Let's go, then." Roxana darts past me and starts heading down the stairs.

I shoot forward, Jewel and everyone else moving out of the way. I grab Roxana's shoulder. "Wait."

"What?" She doesn't look as panicked as I expected.

"Can you please head up to the roof with the others? I need someone who can keep them calm."

She purses her lips—she knows I'm lying.

"Please?"

She looks past me to Jewel. "What do mates usually do?"

"Mates only come to a fight if it's a sure win." Jewel shrugs. "But you're not really his mate yet, no matter how you smell. You're his girlfriend."

"But if I was?" Roxana arches one perfect brow. "What would a werewolf mate do? Wait on the roof?"

"Lo Ren's pack is big," Jewel says. "It would be less distracting, and less nerve-wracking for Xander, if he wasn't trying to split his focus between protecting you and the pack."

"He won't need to," Roxana says. "I don't want him defending me."

"Roxana," I whisper. "I know you think your dad and brothers will be enough to keep you safe, but—"

"I don't," she says. "I think *you'll* be strong enough to keep me safe. I think this fight *is* a sure thing." She looks shockingly serious.

"I stood in the lobby," I remind her. "When you said you didn't need me that night that Lionel called, I—"

She steps closer, right into my personal space, and she kisses me. I totally forget everything I was thinking. When she releases me, she stays close. Her whisper's just for me. "Xander Binnigas, we weren't dating when you did that, and I doubt you'd do it now." Her eyes are practically sparking. "I'm not going to be caged—not by my parents, and not by you. If there's a fight for our pack, I'm part of it. I'm in." There's fear in her eyes, but also resolve.

I nod.

We jog down the stairs together, and everyone else falls in behind us, including Bevin, who hasn't said a word.

"Shouldn't you go up to the roof?" Roxana turns toward her. "You're trying not to descend again, right?" She tosses her head. "Best way is to stay away from temptation. Plus, remember how you're kind of already magically constipated?"

"Not a chance. I'm coming." Bevin shakes her head. "I do have a question though." She narrows her eyes and looks down. "What on earth are you carrying? Is that weapons or something?"

She's looking at my bag, the one that says, "Paul's Boutique."

"Shoot," I say. "It's. . ." I thrust it at Roxana. "It's a gift for you."

"I'll go out and see where they are," Jewel says. "Maybe we can convince them to stay in the street or even fall back."

When she ducks out, Roxana opens the bag and

pulls the shirt out. It's a small movement, but her lip twitches. She likes it. "You got me a dog shirt?" Only then do her eyes seem to notice what I'm wearing. "By the angel, you got us *matching* dog shirts?" Now she's smiling. "No wonder you had no idea you're an alpha. You're so corny."

Before I can stop her, she whips her shirt off, and for the first time, I see my girlfriend in nothing but a bra. A bright *red* bra, which frames up a really cool patch of shining golden scales, and shows off a whole lot of beautifully tan skin. Of course, wolves all up and down the stairwell are seeing the same thing—and Bevin—but, still.

It's really, really hot.

Based on all the slack-jawed expressions, I'm not the only one who thinks so.

"Mother *feather*," Izaak says from above us. "What's going on down there?" He pushes past the wolves—in canine and human form—and reaches Bevin, me, and the now-dressed-again Roxana. He squints to read her shirt, and then his eyes widen. "*You* got her that?" He turns toward me.

"So, the thing is," I say, "Roxana and I are kind of dating."

Izaak's mouth almost hits the floor. "You're *what*?"

"Did you hear that Lo Ren's here?" Bevin asks. "Congratulations come later, if we even survive to make them."

"Pshaw," Izaak says. "Lo Ren's a butt-sniffing, flea-ridden, toilet-lapping yorkie, compared to my *king* right here. This guy's dating New York's dragona *princess*."

"At least if I die today, I'll die a legend." I take Roxana's hand and we push through the doorway.

Lo Ren's holding Jewel by the throat.

"I'm guessing he didn't want to take it outside."

Jewel smiles.

"You filed a petition?" Lo Ren snarls. "To bring the most disgraceful wolves I've ever seen to New York?"

"Actually, they were already in New York," I say. "I only lured them to the City."

"You're all a match made at the pound," Rylan says. "Those wolves stink—they're perfect for the scardiest wolf I've ever seen." She's standing beside Cliff, Lo Ren's biggest shredder. They're both scowling, but unlike the others gathered, they're not in wolf form.

"Scardiest?" Roxana laughs, the sound like a trilling bell. "At least he's literate."

"Who are you?" Rylan sniffs the air.

"You don't recognize the dragona princess of New York?" Jewel asks. "Roxana's right. You are an idiot."

Lo Ren snarls, tightening his hold on Jewel.

Blood drips from her throat to the floor, so I send a pulse of energy toward her, healing the place he just punctured. Jewel winks at me.

That was. . .kind of fun. For the first time, ever, I stood up to Rylan instead of dropping my head. It felt. . .right. "You came to talk," I say. "Or you'd be furry. What do you want?"

"When Kamir called me this morning to tell me about your petition," Lo Ren says, "I told him it was a joke."

"I do like making jokes," I say. "But I'm sorry to say you're wrong. We're deadly serious. What do you care, though? You never go below Midtown."

"You're delusional if you think we'll agree to let you bring all these mangy dogs onto our island," Rylan says.

"Kamir told me to kill you all," Lo Ren says. "I figured I'd let a few of the pathetic creatures you bonded join our pack, but now that I'm here. . ." He looks around slowly, his lip curling. "There's no one here I could possibly tolerate."

"Why didn't you already kill her, then?" I toss my head at Jewel. "Planning to beg me to leave New York City again?"

"Beg?" Lo Ren snarls.

"Oh," I say. "Maybe I got it wrong. Didn't you get a video, Izaak? We can let his pack decide whether he was begging."

"The begging was when we threatened to tell everyone how small his wiener is," Roxana says. "But most of the people in here have probably seen it." She turns toward Rylan and mock whispers. "I'm so sorry."

Jewel laughs. "I love her."

"Shut up." Lo Ren's hands start shifting, and claws sink into the soft skin of her neck instead of fingers.

"Let's do it this way," I say. "Kamir wants me dead? Then you fight me. If you kill me, my wolves will move back to Waterbury. If you don't. . ." I don't remind him that I offered the same thing last time, and he turned me down. With this many people around, maybe he'll actually feel compelled to say yes.

"As if that would ever happen," Cliff says.

"You mean your leader being brave enough to fight Xander to save your lives?" Roxana asks. "You're so ugly that I remember you were there last time Lo Ren wouldn't fight him—you were stuck in Jello."

Cliff's already not-pretty face contorts. "Shut up, bitch."

"Wait, you're calling me a female dog?" Roxana asks. "Because that's a compliment coming from you, right?" She winks.

If Cliff was just a little dumber, he'd lunge at her.

"If I fight you," Lo Ren says, "what happens if you win?"

"You're considering it?" Roxana frowns. *Don't do it.* She turns toward me. *Please.*

If he will, I have to.

Her eyes are large—frightened—but she knows how much this matters. If I can spare casualties on all sides, I have to try. She exhales and turns toward the window.

"Oh, please," Bevin says. "There's no way Lo Ren will fight you." She drops down into a wooden chair and glances at her nails. "He's way too scared of you to ever agree. I'm not a wolf, so I can't smell much, but even I can smell his fear."

Why are they standing around talking?

Suddenly, I realize how strange it is—the Manhattan pack came in force. They have twice as many shredders as I do, and he's holding my strongest, most dominant nurturer. For an alpha, Lo Ren's a coward—he proved that last time when he refused to fight me. Or. . .he's not a coward, but he is scared of me specifically. I'm just not sure why.

"They're distracting us," Bevin says. "They're sending wolves to the roof."

Could that be right?

"To slaughter children?" Izaak asks. "If so, they're *disgusting.*"

Lo Ren's smiling. "They should be there, or very close."

"Are you sure you aren't half-demon?" Bevin asks. "Because if your pack follows an alpha who, with twice the numbers, can't face another alpha, they're as deplorable as you."

"Deplorable?" Rylan snorts.

"You have to use very small words with them, Bev." Roxana laughs. "They don't even know what deplorable means." She steps closer to Rylan. "It means that your boyfriend has a tiny wiener *and* he's a bloody disgusting coward to go along with it."

Rylan snaps. She lunges for Roxana, and in that moment, just as my heart stops, Roxana thrusts her hands forward and a massive fireball rips out her hands, burning right through the wolves who leap in front of Rylan. Silvie and two other wolves I don't know very well disappear in a ball of flames.

All the hair on the side of Rylan's head is singed off, but she's alive.

"My wall!" Gavin pops up from behind his counter, his eyes wide, his whole body trembling. "Was that really a fireball?"

"What are you doing in here?" I wave him back. "Get out while you can."

"But my wall!" Gavin looks more concerned about the wall than his life.

He's not the only one who's upset, though. Rylan's clutching her head and keening.

"I *missed?*" Roxana growls. "She was *right there*, and somehow I missed her." She cocks her head, my vicious little dragon smiling at Rylan's distress. "I did make you way uglier, though. You're finally a match for your nasty mate."

Lo Ren's entire face was white, but thanks to Roxana's taunt, his expression contorts into pure, unadulterated rage. Coward or not, if you hurt a wolf's mate, they don't take it well. He's mid-shift when he rips Jewel's throat out.

She slumps to the floor, blood spurting all over the salt and pepper tiles Gavin always keeps so clean.

I hurl energy in Jewel's direction with no finesse, desperately hoping it'll be enough, but I can't focus on her.

Lo Ren's coming right at me.

I shift—the shirt I *just* bought tearing with a loud crack as my bones remodel and fur sprouts. I drop to all fours, already snarling, but Lo Ren's slightly larger form has already reached me.

His teeth snap, but I'm good at twisting, so he only catches part of my shoulder—not even close to a killing blow. Although Lo Ren's keeping me busy, twisting, biting, and snarling, from the corner of my eye, I can see that his other wolves are just as upset. Cliff's shifting, and he's lunging at me too when one of my wolves, Ysandre, leaps over Lo Ren and me and plows into him, teeth bared.

More of Lo Ren's wolves are leaping through the gaping hole that so upset Gavin, but my new pack is rising to meet them, growls filling the room. They may not look very sophisticated or well-educated, and they may not fit the typical New York vibe with their overalls and tractor-decorated clothing, but they fight like stray dogs—vicious and desperate.

It's turning into a bloody, terrible fight, and I'm worried about the pups and mothers on the roof. Lo Ren's not fighting me alone, which means they could kill us all. My shredders are working to give me a fair fight, but as soon as my pack narrows the fight to just him and me, Lo Ren summons another bunch of wolves through the hole.

He's still stalling. He knows getting to the roof will end it.

I'd rather die than go through the agony of losing every pup in our pack one by one. I don't doubt that Lo Ren'll do it. He's an alpha through and through, and that means he'll do anything to win.

Roxana's fighting a very angry and charred Rylan with Bevin's help. Every time the nearly-black wolf gets close, her fangs bared, Bevin bumps her back with a zap. Roxana's pretty decent with the kicks and blows, but she has nothing to take on a wolf's fangs, other than huge fireballs that seem hard to control.

I'm more confident that I can beat Lo Ren, but he's not giving me the chance. He has the numbers to beat us down, one wave of wolves at a time. I wonder how long we'll be able to last before he finally kills us all. . .or I surrender.

I'm circling him again, thinking hard about any other options we might have, when someone changes the game. Instead of lunging at Roxana this time, for the hundredth time, Rylan changes course and lunges for Bevin.

I expect Bevin to knock her back, but something goes wrong. My crazy old friend throws her hands out, but Rylan just keeps coming, her snarling snout rocketing toward Bevin's throat. I freeze, and so does Lo Ren, about ten paces away.

That's when Rylan's fur starts to change.

Starting on her nose, it turns grey. . .and then white. The color change rolls over her, like someone splashed her with a bucket of paint. It's one of the strangest things I've ever seen.

Bevin's back arches, and she howls. As her head falls backward, her arms spread wide and those long, odd black nails sprout from her fingers and grow outward. At least her claws are retractable—but they freak me out every time they show up.

She got her second demon power, finally. The white fur on Rylan must have something to do with that. As Rylan lands on the ground, she collapses, whimpering. She tries to rise, but she looks almost *tired*, like she's weary. Like she's spent.

Lo Ren and I both creep forward slowly until I see what happened.

Rylan's old.

Somehow, Bevin aged her.

We're not the only ones who aren't fighting. Almost all the wolves in Grand Central Gloffee have frozen, watching. Before our eyes, Rylan shifts back to human. The hair on the left side of her head's still singed, blackened right up to the side of her head, but if it weren't for that, and her smell, I wouldn't know it was her.

Actually, even her smell changed. She smells sort of mothball-y now.

Her naked body, curled into a fetal position, is wrinkled. Age-spotted. Feeble. "What have you done?"

When she turns her head upward, her mouth trembles. "What is this?"

"Looks like Bevin's second demon power finally arrived," Roxana says. "And *boy*, it's a cool one." She throws up her hand for a high-five.

Bevin's less excited. "I aged her."

"Think what you could do with wine," Roxana says. "We are so going to monetize this."

Bevin rolls her eyes.

But Lo Ren's even less impressed with Roxana's excitement. "Rylan!" He's shifted too, and he's pulling someone's discarded pants on before going near his mate. They're way too big, but he's determined. I guess our taunts really got to him. When he finally does walk over to her, he doesn't crouch down beside her.

He just stares, wide-eyed. "How could this happen?"

"I'm glad you asked," Bevin says. "It's new to me, but I'm so happy to have so many wolves on which to practice it." She throws her hands out, aging the grey wolf beside her. "Since you were just attacking Jewel, who had *barely* recovered, I figure I know which side you're on." She smiles. "Grandma."

Another wolf turns white and shifts into an old woman.

Bevin's smile widens. "I think I'm actually stealing their life-force when I do this. I'll already live a thousand years, but I wonder how much longer I can go." She glances my way. "Who's next, boss? Lo Ren? Or do we head up to the roof and age them all to death?"

Lo Ren doesn't wait for input. He tosses his head at Cliff. "Bring her." Then he jogs over several fallen wolves and out the hole in the wall. The rest of his pack follows, limping, loping, and bounding away from the carnage.

"You were right," Jewel says to Bevin. "He is a coward."

The second they're gone, Bevin slumps into an armchair. She's never looked better—healthier. But she looks defeated in spirit.

"You alright?" Roxana crouches beside her.

"There's no way I could have done that again," Bevin says. "But I bluffed well, right?"

Roxana drags Bevin against her chest and hugs her tightly. "You did so well, Bev. So, so well."

"Hey, I totally slammed a few of them into the wall," Izaak says. "And I got one with a chair. Did anyone see it?"

Gavin's head pokes out from behind the bar again. "*You* broke those chairs?" He looks like he's aging without Bevin's help.

"Calm down, fam. You'll pop an aneurysm." Izaak smiles. "Did I mention I just landed a big role in a movie?" He makes an air gun and blows it out. "How about I do a free poster or something for your wall, endorsing this place as the best gloffee in New York."

"I really liked those chairs." Gavin still looks forlorn. "But it's not like I could ever really stay mad at you." He smiles. "Next time, though, hide back here with me."

"Next time?" I ask. "Let's not talk about *next time*."

"I think they'll be back," Bevin says.

"Why do you think that?" Roxana asks. "I bet they call the Wolf Council and agree to split, but I think we should demand part of Central Park, at least. Don't you?" She looks so proud, so triumphant.

"They're not our only enemies," I say. "And now that the wolves have dealt with Bevin. . ." I sigh. "I think she's right. If they're even a little smart, when they come back, they won't be alone."

22

IZAAK

One of my earliest memories is Mom coming home with blood spatter all over her clothing, and Dad helping her take off her stained boots, pants, and jacket in the laundry room. She went to shower, and Dad set to work, cleaning. Bleach. Clorox wipes. Anything that couldn't be completely cleaned went into the burn pit.

It felt. . .normal.

That's just what parents did. They went to work. They came home. They cleaned up, and then they helped make dinner for all the kids. The fact that my mom was an assassin didn't seem strange. Clean up the carnage, then make tacos.

I suppose it shouldn't seem odd to me that last night, the Manhattan pack attacked us, and we defeated them, largely due to Bevin's terrifying new demon power, and then they left. We cleaned up. The only thing missing was the tacos.

Now, this afternoon, we're preparing for my first

meet-and-greet with my possible romantic comedy co-leads. No biggie.

"I'm telling you," Xander says. "There's no way for us to practice without humans around. The vampire-fear thing just doesn't work on supernaturals."

After the fight finally ended last night, and after we did emergency clean up—the hillbilly wolves were surprisingly good at replacing glass and tile, given that Xander said their compound wasn't well maintained—I told Bevin and Roxana my good news to brighten everyone up a little, and things sort of spread from there. Four wolves volunteered to help me, but they were just as useless as Xander predicted they'd be. I did wonder whether it was a sort of a wolf-fulfilling prophecy. The alpha predicted they wouldn't be afraid, so they weren't.

Either way, even when I tried my hardest to scare them, it didn't work. In fact, the eight-year-old with the mullet *laughed* at me when I glared, saying I looked like I needed to toot.

Which is how Xander and I wound up going together to my meet-and-greet. Donovan Sommers is just as excited to see me as he was the last time, but he frowns when he sees Xander. "Your manager must have lots of things to do," he says. "He doesn't have to come with you every time."

"Izaak's my top priority," Xander lies.

"Right, but shouldn't you be looking over the contract or lining up endorsements for him?" Donovan looks truly perplexed.

Xander clearly has no idea what a manager's supposed to do, so when he whips out his phone, I realize he's making a note for himself. I can already imagine what it says. *Look into what managers do for actors; line up endorsements? Review contract?*

It makes me smile.

Of course, Donovan was telling me about the two women I'm meeting today, so it wasn't the best time to be smiling.

"What's funny?" Donovan asks. "Do you think Elizabeth's a bad choice?"

I shake my head. "Nothing like that, no. Not at all."

In fact, when I meet Elizabeth, it goes better than any co-worker meeting I've ever had. She's easy to talk to, she's smiley, and she seems genuinely excited to work with me. It could just be that for the first time ever, I'm not terrifying, but I swear, we even have chemistry. Xander seems to be suppressing both my fear-inducing effect *and* my vampiric charm, so I'm actually just interacting.

Her eyes don't glaze. She never shudders, and when I make a joke and she laughs, it feels and sounds genuine.

"This is what it's like," I whisper, "for regular people."

Xander laughs.

"Regular what?" Elizabeth asks.

"Never mind," I say. "Let's talk about the other movies you've done—what you liked, and what you didn't."

"Actually, we have Robin coming in soon," Donovan says. "I'd love to get a few minutes of you two reading the roles before it's time to go."

"Of course." Elizabeth pulls out the script. "Just let me know which scene. I've already read them all."

While Donovan's flipping through the scenes, Elizabeth whispers, "I'm happy to chat with you later—any time you want." She slides a scrap of paper my way. "That's my personal cell."

Of course, as soon as he stops perusing, the scene Donovan picks is the one where Trevor and Helene. . .kiss. My heart starts racing before I even read the first line. I've literally never kissed someone who wasn't reacting to my charm.

I could have kissed a supernatural, I suppose, but it's not common for vampires to mix with anyone but other vampires. Being an aspiring actor, most vampires aren't interested in me. Werewolves aren't interested in vampires *ever,* and most demon-spawn also keep to themselves. No witch or wizard would ever date a vampire, so that's left me largely to date humans.

They're easy to find, but I just keep thinking about my dad.

Does he really love my mom? Or was he just captured by her charm? I really don't want someone who was given no choice. But here, in this moment, yes, Elizabeth and I are acting. Yes, the entire thing is fake.

It still feels like one of the realest moments I've had with any woman.

The closer we get to the part of the scene where they kiss, the more nervous I feel. The fact that Trevor's been lying to Helene about his job, well. It feels. . .terribly real to me. I'm sure my mom lied to my dad about what she did until he was past caring.

"But it's too late," Elizabeth as Helene says. "I couldn't possibly watch a midnight movie. We both have to work tomorrow."

"We can skip work," I whisper. "They'll figure things out without us."

"Maybe you really mean that, but this project matters to me. I've spent more than a month on this launch. I can't possibly miss it."

I find myself smiling at her genuinely—she's really throwing everything into this. "Fine," I say. "You're right. It's just that whether this product launches well or not. . .doesn't seem nearly as important as whether I can spend another few moments with you." I bite my lip, and stare into her eyes.

And then she leans closer. "Do you really mean that?"

It's time. "Of course I do. In fact, at every meeting, at every presentation over the past few weeks, I've been so distracted by your eyes, your hair, your smile—your *mouth*, that I've hardly been able to talk at all."

She inhales then, tilting her head upward.

And I take her jaw with my hand and shift it—

Donovan claps. "Bravo. Very, very good."

It's like my phone alarm going off at four p.m. Very, very unwelcome.

"Robin's waiting just outside," Donovan says, "but we'll be in touch."

Elizabeth stands, winks at me, and ducks out.

"I thought that went really well," I say.

"Honestly, I'm shocked," Donovan says. "I felt like that would be our worst match. She's so. . ." He sighs. "Does it sound bad for me to say vanilla?"

I frown. "She was—"

But then Robin's walking in, and I'm stuck smiling and introducing myself.

"I just *loved* how you played that serial killer." She

tosses her hair. "I mean, you were spine-tinglingly scary, and somehow still hot."

Just what I like to hear. I'm terrifying and yet still hot. Every vampire's MO. "Oh, great," I say.

After that, she kind of checks out. Robin says the right things, but with a strange air of indifference that tells me she doesn't care enough to try. There are several awkward lulls in the conversation before Donovan says, "Why don't we have the two of you read a scene together?"

"Sure," Robin says. "I'm not the best at cold-reads, but that's fine."

"I'm sorry," Donovan says. "My assistant was supposed to send you a copy of the screenplay last week."

"Oh, he probably did." Robin laughs, and the sound grates on my nerves. "I'm just far too busy to read through things before I decide whether to take them."

"But how do you know whether you want to take them," Xander asks, "if you haven't read the script?"

Robin's head turns toward Xander slowly. "And who, exactly, are you?"

"I'm Izaak's manager, Xander Binnigas."

Robin blinks. "Uh-huh." She turns back to Donovan. "What did you want me to read?" She holds out one bored hand.

"How about this scene?"

Blessedly, there's no kiss in this one he chooses. Robin really should have at least read a few pages first, because she's not a strong reader, fumbling over half the dialogue.

When Xander's phone rings, interrupting one of her longer monologues, I almost sigh in relief.

"Sorry." Xander points at the phone and mouths, "Bank."

I nod—we've been worried about financing—of course he has to take it. I wish I could follow him out of the boardroom to see what the bank has to say, but I'm sort of stuck.

"Rude," Robin says.

"It's a big deal we've been working on," I say. "He had to take it."

"It's not even another client?" Robin scoffs. "I'd fire him so fast."

I just bet she would.

Before I can come up with a reason not to, Robin plunges back into the part of the scene we were on, and I cringe a little. I was hoping we were done. If I have to keep listening to her blunder her way through this, I might start hissing and snorting out loud. Donovan chose kind of an important scene—it's when my family inadvertently outs Trevor as the son of the chairman, and Helene feels like an idiot for always commiserating with him about work, paying bills, and scraping by.

That's when I realize it's my turn. "Of course I didn't think you were silly," I say. "I may not totally understand how it feels to rinse out a bread bag, let it dry, and then use it to store other things—" I pause there. "Is this really the best example? Do people really do this? Even poor ones?"

But when I turn toward Donovan, he's scooching away from me.

Shoot.

One glance at Robin and it's clear. She's also very, very nervous. She's moved her chair almost two feet away.

"Xander," I yell. "Where'd you go? I want your input on a line in this scene."

He shoots back through the door, his expression sheepish. "Sorry. Turns out she's fine, but she got called over to ask her mother for some help, and then she had to go right to work. Clark was stuck helping their mom instead."

I want to ask whether Minerva got some answers from her mom about her birth mom, but this is not the time or place. Also, I'm about to lose my big break, because Xander's not doing his job. I widen my eyes and toss my head at the two panicking humans right next to me.

"Sorry." Xander slides his phone in his pocket and sits, his gaze slowly moving from Donovan to Robin. "I know that was rude, but being a good manager means taking care of people, and that's the one thing I'm really good at."

Donovan swallows, his Adam's apple bobbing. "Right." I can almost see his blood pressure lowering. "Yes, that is the most important thing about a manager. Someone who sees the person." He nods, exhaling loudly and dropping his elbows back on the table. "I'm glad Izaak has you."

Robin's frowning, the lines between her brows prominent.

"You'll want to book an appointment for Botox," Xander says. "Yours has clearly worn off—don't want to risk smile lines, or frown lines are even worse, I hear."

"I'm only twenty-five," she says.

"But Botox is preventative," Xander says. "Or that's what they tell me. If you wait, it might be too late."

Robin hops to her feet, clearly much more afraid of wrinkles than she is of me. She's tapping on her phone as she blows through the door.

"She's a terrible fit," I say. "I far preferred Elizabeth."

Donovan shakes his head, like he's trying to wake up or clear the brain fog out.

I'm okay with him being a little foggy, as long as he doesn't start to associate feelings of panic and anxiety with me. Better that he remember something like fine lines and wrinkles as the culprit for his stress.

"I actually *am* late on my Botox appointment." Donovan's whipping out his phone. "Same time tomorrow?" He glances my way. "I liked Elizabeth, but we should at least meet Tiana and April, right?"

"Sure thing," I say. And once he's gone, I add, "Because I just love waking up at three in the afternoon." My yawn nearly cracks my jaw, but I manage to keep alert until we're out the door and in a cab. "Forget Botox. These early afternoons are going to kill me."

"Not just you," Xander says. "I can't keep following you around like I'm actually your manager."

"Speaking of that," I say. "I've been thinking about this. You are organized, you're smart, and you need a job." I wave at two cabs, and they blow right past.

"Uh, no," he says. "There's no way I want to be your chauffeur."

"A car would be nice, I won't lie." I laugh. "But I'm

not asking you to be my chauffeur—I said my *manager*. Are your ears working?"

Xander blinks. "Are you serious?"

"I know we were just saying that to explain why you're there, but think about it. Roxana has photoshoots. I have acting jobs now, thanks to your help. We do need someone to manage our schedules, and who better than the person in *charge* of our schedules, our alpha, right? Plus, you'd be able to provide security and help make sure we're not taken advantage of."

"I guess."

"I'm thinking, since my agent gets fifteen percent, maybe you'd take. . ." I cringe. "Ten?"

"Done." Xander smiles. "I saw that sample contract. Ten percent of this one movie would equal my annual salary for the past year."

I can't help swearing under my breath. "I should've said five."

Xander laughs, and it's a good sound to hear. He hasn't been happy very much lately, and Xander's usually a pretty happy guy.

"I've been thinking," I say.

"Uh-oh," he says. "That must've hurt."

"Rude," I say. "I want a clause in our contract that requires you to be polite to me."

He rolls his eyes.

"I'm serious—I'm the talent."

He pretends to walk away.

I jog to catch up. "But honestly, I've been thinking about you. I know you're stressed with the Manhattan pack attack and—"

Xander looks sick.

"The thing is, you should know that no one blames you for that."

"Talk to Gavin and get back to me," Xander says. "And the husband and two wives of the three wolves who died."

I shake my head. "They aren't upset. Surely you can sense that. You're the good guy here. You're just trying to live your life, and Lo Ren and Rylan were at fault, not you."

"I should've moved us when I could." Xander's not meeting my eye.

"Where? Out to Waterbury?"

He shrugs.

"That's the thing—bullies are everywhere. If you did that, we'd just have new problems there, and my dreams are here. So are Minerva and Clark's. Bevin, too. Do you think she could have a secondhand magic shop in a place that small?"

"I know that people are dying because of what I decided."

"No, people are dying because of what Lo Ren did, and because of what he and his mate decided. They're the bad guys. We can't live our lives at the behest of people who only care for themselves. That's a small world that I want no part of."

We finally get a cab. "I guess," he says as he's climbing inside.

"Do you blame Bevin?"

Xander turns toward me slowly. "For what?"

"I mean, she's got her own problems, and now they've become our problems."

"She descended defending Roxana," he says.

"Alright, then do you blame Roxana?" I hold his gaze.

"Of course not."

"Then you can't blame yourself either. Bevin wants to be good in a world that paints her as the villain. I want to be an actor. You just wanted a pack, and now you have one. A weird one, but a pack is a pack. And Minerva—what about her? Is it her fault that her parents aren't her parents?"

Xander slowly shakes his head.

"You need to stop dragging around all the evils in the world. You're strong, but no one's that strong."

"I'm worried," he finally admits. "I'm worried that between my problems, Bevin's problems, and Minerva's problems, no one could ever be strong enough. I'm worried that we're all going to go down together."

"But think about the good stuff," I say.

"Like what?"

"We're buying a building," I say. "I mean, more you guys than me, since I'm not getting paid until after we sign the contracts. But Minerva's finally getting answers. Bevin's scary powerful, but still a good person, and best of all. . ." I wait for a moment, until I know he's really listening.

"What?"

"You and Roxana," I say. "The two of you are strange, yes. You're maybe the strangest couple I've ever seen."

"Thanks a lot."

"But also, somehow, you're right."

"Maybe mention that to Clark."

I whistle then. "I forgot about his crush."

"He hasn't," Xander says. "That's the real reason he's gone, I think. He must've seen us or something, because he went and told Lionel about us. . .and then he told him every bad thing he could think of about me."

"He didn't."

Xander tells me about his dinner at Roxana's. "Who else could have known that stuff?"

"But at least you're such a goodie two shoes it didn't matter," I say. "I mean, as bad things go, those are pretty weak."

Xander doesn't look happier.

"You two have been friends for a long time," I say. "What he did—it was pretty bad. You're his alpha and his good friend, and he sold you out. But do you think you can forgive him?"

"I'm worried that's the wrong question," Xander says. "I knew it would hurt him to find out about me and Roxana."

"Seriously though, I think I should get credit for this," I say. "I'm the one who pushed you to take that photo with her."

Xander's half-smile is real. "You did, actually. Without that, who knows? Maybe she wouldn't have come down the fire escape. Maybe we'd never have met. Maybe she'd be in Russia with Ragar, I'd still be begging for scraps from Lo Ren, Bevin would never have descended, and you'd still be posing for hemor-rhoid commercials."

"Hey, that was a one-time thing."

Xander laughs. "But truly, that one interaction kind of set us down this path."

"I think we'd have gotten here anyway, no matter

how it went down," I say. "I think we were all destined to be friends."

Xander frowns. "Lo Ren did say something about a prophecy or something when I ran into him that first time."

"I wondered about that, too. Nonsense, probably."

"But the question I don't know the answer to, the one that's been bothering me. . . Will Clark forgive *me* for taking his girl?"

"The one he never held hands with, kissed, or even asked out?" I snort. "He's a real idiot if he doesn't."

"I really care about Clark," Xander says. "You know I do."

"Yeah."

"But the thing that worries me is, if he can't forgive me, we're stuck." Xander sighs. "Because I'm not taking it back. Roxana. . ." He whistles. "She's the real deal, and I do *not* plan to screw this up."

23

MINERVA

I've never skipped a day of work in my entire life.

It's always been the most important thing to me. I couldn't become a guardian without excelling. I couldn't make my dad proud without becoming guardian. And my partner Amber, she needed me, too, so missing shifts was out of the question.

But after leaving my mom's house, I'm planning to skip. I have to research the Angel Council and figure out how I can get in there to see my birth mother. She's the only one I'm sure can answer all the questions I have.

I haven't been walking away from Mom's place for very long when Giggles wings her way over to me. She's settling in on my shoulder, but her claws are just a little grabbier than usual. "Go easy, huh? It's been a rough day." I crane my head sideways to see her better. "And how did you get all the way out here? Did you take the train?"

She coos.

"Okay, but really."

I'm not a normal pigeon. You must have noticed.

"Are you holding out on me? Can you portal me back?"

You're far too big.

Great. My pigeon can do things I can't, and I'm not even talking about flying. "Look, my mom told me a lot of things, and most of them sound totally insane, but I need to look some things up, and the closest library. . ." I realize that the closest library *isn't* in New York City. I'm less than a block from the Scarsdale Public Library right now.

I hang a hard right and start to jog. I'm not sure what time this place closes, but I need to get in before it does. I'm wheezing a little when I reach the front. The woman who checks my ID frowns.

I expect her to insist that I can't bring a bird in, but she looks right past Giggles. My gloffee must have decided that pigeons in libraries aren't normal and covered for me.

A pigeon familiar's not my only problem, apparently. The woman purses her lips and huffs. "Your membership expired six years ago."

"But I still have the card," I say. "You must admire that kind of dedication to reading, right?" I'm still puffing a little, but she begrudgingly waves me through. "Go renew your membership first, or you can't check anything out."

The books I'll be looking at can't be checked out, but I don't bother telling her that. I sneak past the front desk by pointing at the bathroom, and then I hang a quick right toward the archives.

"Miss." An older man waves. "The only thing down there is microfiche and old dusty books."

I nod. "No, I know. I just want to look through some microfiche."

"We close in twenty-six minutes," the man says.

"Of course," I say. "I'll be quick." With a flick of my wand, I whisper, "Oblivisci vidisti me."

The man blinks, frowns, and shuffles away.

I breathe a sigh of relief as I duck past the microfiche to the door marked, "Special Collections."

The normies think it's full of books so old and fragile, they can't be touched often. I'm sure there are a few things like that in here, but by and large, the special collections around the world are actually the books detailing supernatural groups, history, and spellcraft. Anytime a supernatural dies the world over without heirs, their books come to the local library. A lot of them are stupid, and they're rarely organized well, but sometimes you find some gems or even handwritten accounts. I dig around through most everything, organizing as I go. I should probably worry about how I'll get out of here when I'm done, because there's no way I'll find my answer in the next twenty minutes.

I do stop digging through books long enough to text Amber. LET THE CHIEF KNOW I'M OUT SICK.

WHAT ARE YOU REALLY DOING? Amber fires right back.

I'LL TELL YOU TOMORROW. The lying gets easier and easier. I'm sure I can think up a somewhat believable excuse by then.

My mom calls me three times, and Clark calls me

six. Then he starts texting me, and it's annoying enough that I shut off my phone. How am I ever supposed to find answers when I'm constantly being badgered?

Unfortunately, there's very, very little about angel-spawn or the Angel Council. I've finally found *something*, although it's a little hard to read. It was written in Latin quite a long time ago, but if my translation is right, it focuses on the purpose of the Angel Council. It's the most promising thing I've found, and I'm excited. . .when I get some kind of summons from Xander. It's vague, but it feels urgent.

I'm sure he came home and found the wolves running amok. Or maybe the building sale's hit a snag, or it could be about the Manhattan Pack—he made a petition today, I think. Either way, I'm *always* the one having to organize and clean things up.

For once, they're going to have to figure it out without me.

It makes me twitchy, and guilty, and a little panicky, but I ignore the summons and keep looking. The Angel Council allows petitions twice a month, and the next one's in six days. I need to be ready when it opens, and I'm not even sure what to look for yet. I just know that I *have* to meet my mom.

Unfortunately, after six hours, I'm not closer to any real answers.

Sometime between four and five a.m., working a night shift and waking up early catches up to me, and I fall asleep. When I wake up, Giggles is stretching in the small ray of light streaming through the back window. *About time, sleepyhead.*

"You should've woken me up."

She struts toward me. *Not a chance. Your pack is fine, and you needed sleep.*

"My. . .pack?"

I checked on them, back when you ignored them. You didn't notice I left? Her orange eyes narrow. *Typical.*

"What happened?"

Dog fight. Your friend with the red tail fixed it, and the other dogs went home.

"Bevin? Is she okay?"

She has energy stealing power now. Stronger.

Her other demon power must have showed up, finally. "We should get home." As I straighten, I realize that I drooled all over the book I fell asleep on. Whoops. I clean up as well as I can, and then Giggles and I try to sneak out.

I startle a very old janitor, who thankfully doesn't see Giggles either, and then I duck out before she can call anyone over to see what I was doing in special collections this early in the morning. I've barely turned on my phone, half a block from the library, when Clark calls.

"Hello?"

"Where on earth are you?" he asks. "The phone company says your signal just cut out, and I didn't want to report you to the Paranormal Affairs Department, well, for obvious reasons."

"Because I'd kill you?" I ask. "And then dump your ashes in a sewer treatment plant?"

He laughs. "Something like that."

"I went to the library to see how much of what Mom told me was completely insane."

"What library are you at?" he asks. "I'll come get you."

"Actually, can you meet me somewhere?" I ask.

"Where?"

"The Angel Council meets in Fort Tryon," I say. "At the Met Cloisters, right?"

"I think Bevin said that's where she went," Clark says. "But Mom said—"

"Bevin says our aunt's there, and I think it's time we find out whether that's true. Will you go with me?"

"They only take petitions on Wednesdays," Clark says. "First and third."

"I'm aware," I say. "But I found out that normies tromp all over the place Thursday through Tuesday, all day, every day. If we pretend. . ."

"You want to get in. . .as normies?" He laughs. "It's not a terrible idea."

"Right?"

"Should we tell the others?"

Giggles starts chittering. I think she wants me to, but the idea makes me uneasy.

"I think we should talk about this in person," Clark says. "Tell me where you are."

It takes him forty minutes to reach me, even by car. That gives me time to grab a bagel and find a bathroom. I can't do much for my hair or rumpled clothing, but I splash water on my face, at least. Once Clark picks me up, I have to suppress the urge to scream at him about the car.

Dad's car.

His pride and joy.

He's had it this whole time and never told me about it. That hurts more than him getting the car, honestly. I didn't think Clark would keep something like that from me.

But we have bigger things to deal with, and I have the wand Clark never got. Actually, he might be angry about that. "Want to talk about the wand?"

"Why'd you hide it?" His voice is hurt. Probably feels a little like me about the car.

"I just got it a day ago, from the Chief, of all people." I sigh. "He did tell me about it almost a week ago, though."

"The Chief?" Clark turns entirely sideways in his seat.

I grab the wheel. "By the angel, pay attention to the road."

"You were safe." He's frowning, but he turns back while I explain.

"So you didn't have it all this time?" he asks. "And that's why you asked me about it?"

I nod before I realize he can't see me. "Yeah, I just got it—unlike this car."

He shifts a little so I can't see his face, the coward.

"And of course, Mom's being super cagey about why they didn't tell either of us about the wand, too."

"Of course she is," Clark says. "Mom's cagier than I realized."

"I get that I embarrassed her," I say. "And I know that she wasn't too keen on Dad taking on cleanup for his sister's mess."

He drops a hand on mine. "You aren't a mess. You're my sister. And I'm sorry I didn't tell you about the car." He turns to smile at me quickly. "I just wanted to make those three things clear."

It does ease something in my heart, hearing he still thinks of me as his sister. An apology. "You could have told me about the car. I'd have understood."

"But you didn't get a college fund either. I knew when I took it that it wasn't fair." Clark sighs slowly. "I think I didn't tell you, because I'd have had to accept why I thought I deserved it."

"What?" Now I'm confused.

"Dad loved you best. Mom loved me more, but she's. . . It wasn't the same."

I can't even argue with him about that. Mom never loved me much, but Dad loved me enough for two parents, and he did sort of overlook Clark. Maybe that's part of why Mom always favored him. "Families are hard, even when you don't have adoptions and angel-related secrets."

"Right?" Clark's hands shift on the wheel. "But I also understand why you'd want to meet your biological mother. If I'm being honest, I'd like to meet her too. Mom sounds a little unhinged about all of it."

"Right?" I shake my head. "I swear, it's not a good time for any of this, either. How's everyone else doing? Have you talked to them?"

"Wait, who?"

"You got the bat signal last night," I say. "Right?"

"Bat sig—do you mean the panicked demand to come that Xander sent, like he's our boss?" He cringes. "I ignored it. I know what he wants, and I guess I'm not ready to deal with it yet."

"You know what he wants? What does that mean?"

Clark's shoulders slump. "It's between me and Xander."

"He called all of us just to talk to you?"

My brother sighs. "I kind of made a deal with Lionel Sol." He shakes his head. "I was really upset, okay?" When he turns toward me, he looks almost desperate. "You know how much I like Roxana."

I'm not following any of this. "You made a deal with Lionel, because you like Roxana?"

"I've liked her for a long time. In fact, I'd almost say I've liked her as long as I've known her."

"Okay, but—"

"I kind of made a deal with Lionel's dad first, Orion, to try and break Roxana and Lionel up."

"They weren't even really together," I say. "Why would you do that?"

"Still." He shrugs. "I'm the one who put those photos of Lionel in her room. His dad gave them to me."

I slug him on the arm. "You're an idiot."

"I became an unemployed idiot, because Orion was upset about Lionel meeting her through his job—through me. So I helped them, and I got a new job."

"You—" I can hardly believe what he's telling me. "You're telling me that Xander knows about all this, and—"

"It gets worse." Clark sounds *glum*. "Xander has known about that for a long time, but then. . ."

When he tells me what he did to Xander, how he betrayed him to Lionel, I'm truly disappointed.

"It's just that Lionel said he'd get me a new job, and I didn't want Roxana dating Lionel *or* Xander, and I know it was a terrible thing to do, but I was just so angry."

"Stop the car." I lean against the window. "I'm getting out."

"Minerva, wait."

I shake my head. "No, you should be driving

straight back to talk to Xander and Roxana, and you should beg for their forgiveness. They're dating, and you should know how huge that is for either of them. As their friend, you should've been *happy* for them. Heaven knows, no one else in the world will be."

"I know." Clark leans against the steering wheel. "I do know."

"You just—" I don't even know what to say to him. "Get off here." I point. "Drive straight home and beg on your knees. Do that, or I'm getting out, and I'm not talking to you again until they forgive you."

"But—"

I shake my head. "I mean it."

The drive to our apartment building isn't long, but it feels long. Tremendously long. When we finally reach our block, Clark pulls into the garage two buildings down from us. The attendant waves.

"Wait, have you been parking it here, right by me?"

"There's not a garage close to me that had room," he says. "I only use it when I leave the City, so. . ." He trails off as he pulls into his spot. It's even marked: Lucent.

It rankles, realizing that my brother has been lying to me about not only this stupid car, but about everything. "I—it kind of feels like I don't even know you."

He nods, not arguing. "I know. I'm sorry."

"Let's go."

"Should we grab some gloffee first?" He looks like he's trying to find a way to calm me down.

I do need gloffee, but I don't really have time to— that's when I see it. The hole in the front of the shop that has been a fixture here since I came to New York. "What on earth happened?" I jog until I'm standing in front of it. The giant hole was patched with wood sheets, but there are already men in front of it, holding a bunch of power tools.

"Some kind of gas main blew," the man says.

Smells and looks like a normie.

I guess they respond faster, especially on a building that was clearly ruined by supernatural infighting. If I knew what really happened, I'd probably want to stay far away. Although, as it is, I don't know what happened, and that makes me feel terribly guilty.

I should have been here.

But I was too focused on myself.

"Go," I say. "Hurry."

It takes almost half an hour for Roxana to fill us in on what happened. Xander and Izaak are at some kind of meeting for his movie, but apparently Gavin and most of the others are alright.

"We only lost three wolves," Roxana says, "which is still really, really horrible, but I think Lo Ren lost a dozen or so." She looks upset, but at least she doesn't appear to be mad at Clark.

I meet his eye, widening mine. I hope he gets what I'm saying—looks like Xander didn't tell her. That's good. It means he wants to forgive him.

"Not to mention the other thing," Clark says.

"Yeah, that aging trick that Bevin picked up is *whack*," Roxana says. "I really hope she's able to control that one." She shudders. "The last thing any of us wants is prematurely white hair and loads of wrinkles we didn't earn."

The door to my room opens, and Bevin staggers out, rubbing her eyes. "Sorry, guys. After my new parlor trick, I couldn't sleep a wink all night. I finally drifted off for a quick nap."

Roxana glances at her watch. "You were only in there for an hour. You can't sleep more?"

Bevin shrugs. "I tried. Believe me."

"Wait, isn't it almost time for your gala?" Roxana's eyes widen. "When's Ricky supposed to be coming to get you?"

I almost forgot about the guardian fundraiser. I'm supposed to be schmoozing everyone, and I spent zero seconds preparing for *how*. I slap my head. "I should just cancel. I think it's doomed to failure."

"I don't know," Roxana says. "My parents are still mad I walked out on the wedding, but they must have softened some, because—"

"They released her trust fund!" Bevin's bouncing. "The building sale's a done deal. She wired money over this morning."

I can hardly believe it. "Her parents aren't furious anymore? Why not?"

Roxana shrugs. "They're pretty excited about the fireballs I can make, and. . ." She frowns. "Right, you missed the last ones, but I think I killed more wolves than anyone." As if she's just realizing how that sounds, she grimaces. "They were trying to kill us."

"It was even cooler than my trick," Bevin says. "And Gavin pulled his CCTV footage, and we sent it to Roxana's parents, who are really excited. They might actually approve you with a little persuasion."

"Gaining new powers is better than marrying a Russian thug?" I ask. "Who knew?"

"If I had known, I'd have been researching dragona powers long before," Roxana says.

Clark starts toward the door. "I'm going to wait for Xander across the hall. We have some stuff to talk about."

"See that you do find him," I say.

He ducks out.

I shower and use a drying charm on my hair. Roxana and Bevin have only just started working on getting me ready when there's a knock at the door.

Ricky's here.

Ugh.

I'm not even close to ready. I catch Roxana's eye. "Can you chat with him for a minute?"

"You sure you want *her* to do it?" Bevin raises one eyebrow.

It's either the world's prettiest woman, or the demon-spawn friend Ricky doesn't exactly approve of. Neither of them are great options, but that's my life. I suppose he'll have to get used to it. "Fine. You go."

Bevin takes the nail file she was using on her long black talons along with her. I suppose she's trying to tame her new demon mark, but I doubt she'll succeed. That's kind of the point with demon marks. They aren't manageable.

"Okay," Roxana says. "Now, put this on." The dress she hands me is never going to work, not on me.

"Thanks, but that's a pass."

Roxana scowls and shakes her hand. "It's Dior. You don't pass on Dior. Put it on."

"I've seen you wear that one and believe me. My top and your top aren't interchangeable."

She throws it at my head. "Don't rip it, or you owe me three thousand dollars." She pivots on her heel and *leaves*, like that's that. Without someone to help me dress, and worried that she's flirting with Ricky, I yank the slinky black dress over my head and brace myself to look in the mirror.

I have boring brown hair.

I have the figure of a toothpick.

And I have horse teeth.

It's fine—I'm honestly fine with how mousy I look. Did I used to wish that I had the sort of looks that would beckon to hot men from across the room? Yes. Did I spend almost all my extra money on beauty charms until the age of sixteen? Maybe. But I'm an adult now, and I've fully embraced my appearance.

The woman staring back at me from the mirror looks *not like me*.

It's almost disturbing, really. My boring brown hair has become strangely shimmery, and somehow, there are even richly darker strands among the plain old brown. There are also golden, almost luminescent strands. It looks like I just went to the most expensive magical salon in Manhattan and emptied out my savings. My skin's glowing, and the dress, a dress that perfectly fit Roxana, hugs my almost-nonexistent curves in a way that almost makes them look. . .generous.

"Roxana!" My voice, on the other hand, is just as shrill as it ever was. That's almost a relief. "Can you come back for a second?"

"Coming." Roxana's mellifluous voice is, of course, *exactly* the same. "What?" She pokes her head through the door. "See? I told you it would be fine."

"There's something wrong with me," I say.

"I know." Roxana steps inside, after turning back and waving through the door. "When your friend helps you look amazing, you say, 'thank you,' instead of scowling."

"But—"

She steps closer still. "This dress was spelled by one of the top mages in the fashion industry. It shifts to fit its wearer perfectly."

"It—it does what?" It hardly seems fair that the world's prettiest person has this kind of thing. It's like giving a plane to a *bird*. It doesn't need one.

Actually, I want one, Giggles says. *I'm adding that to my Christmas list.*

"Wait, you have a Christmas list?" I'm gaping.

Giggles snorts, turns around, and lies down on the floor of her cage. It is, of course, pristine. My bird poops everywhere but her own cage.

Only idiots poop where they live.

"As if you're ever in there."

"That dress does not go with a pigeon," Roxana says. "Maybe Giggles can stay and hang with me tonight." She holds out her hand.

Shockingly, Giggles glances between us, as if she's weighing her options. Then she, very clearly, coos. But what I hear in my head is, *Popcorn?*

I open my mouth to explain what she wants, but Roxana just answers. "Of course."

My jaw drops. "Wait, did you hear her?"

Roxana blinks. "Of course. She's been talking to me for a while—I'm assuming it's because of the link to Xander. I'm starting to hear all kinds of people." She purses her lips.

"But you're not a wolf. This is not normal. Not at all."

My friend shrugs. "I mean, what's normal, really?"

The sounds that are barely audible through the crack in the door finally register. Bevin's saying, "—ideas for how to deal with demon talons? They pop up at the most irritating times, and I've tried painting them, but that was a bust. No matter what kind of file I use, they won't get shorter or smoother."

Poor Ricky's being interrogated on demon mark mitigation. I slide some black pumps on and push past Roxana. "I don't want to make you late," I say.

"Don't worry about that." Ricky smiles. "They won't start without me."

"Why?" Roxana asks. "Isn't it a big fundraiser?" She snorts, which is not a sound I expected to hear her make. I hope Xander's not rubbing off on her. "Do they wait for every single guardian?"

"No, but I'm actually the keynote speaker this year," Ricky says.

"You didn't mention that," I say.

He shrugs. "They wanted someone with a doctorate in complex restraining spells."

"Wait," I say. "You have a *doctorate?*"

"My dad sort of wrote the book, or at least, the first seminal book on them. It's in my blood."

I can feel it—fate—pulsing behind my ears. "What time's your keynote?" I ask.

He frowns. "Why do you ask?"

"I have a spell I'd like you to take a look at if you have time. I was hoping you might be able to make sense of it."

"I have, maybe, fifteen minutes before I'll be nervous," he says.

"We'll give you two a little space." Bevin drags

Roxana out the front door, and of course it's only then that I think to ask where all the wolves disappeared to. When I was here last, there was a mountain of their stuff and at least two dozen of them running around.

Now?

Nothing.

Not even a fur ball.

I'll have to ask later. Neither Clark nor I could make heads nor tails of the spell in my file, the one Bevin stole from the Angel Council. Maybe Ricky can tell me what it is, and more importantly, what it's supposed to do.

And how it might be related to me.

"Okay, so this might seem kind of strange, but the thing is, the rest of the file I'm working on is classified."

Ricky laughs and holds out his hand. "If you had *any* idea how often I heard that, you would know I'm used to it. The vast majority of the spells I'm called to look at were performed illegally, and I'm never given much detail. Don't worry."

I'm a little nervous handing over the spell. For some reason, my mom's wacky warnings keep ringing in my ears. But I know she's being crazy, and clearly she's not going to tell me anything useful. That leaves me following every lead I have, no matter how strange. "Here."

Ricky flips through the pages quickly—almost too quickly. "I know that one's confusing." I point. "Clark and I did realize, though, that this one is a binding spell of some kind."

"Yes, it certainly is." My boyfriend reaches up

toward the end of my nose, and then he says, "Boop," and keeps on flipping.

It's the first truly irritating thing he's done.

He must really know his stuff, or he wouldn't be so patronizing. He glances at his watch, and then he sets down the stack of papers. "Well, this spell was certainly interesting, but also ultimately totally useless."

"Why?" I want to snatch the pages back. It makes me nervous, somehow, that someone else's holding *my* spell.

"It has the most diabolical mechanism of attachment I've ever seen. It literally functions like. . ." He pauses, tapping his lip. "Think of it like a magical vacuum. Once it's latched on, it would be impossible to remove. At least, until the subject was dead. It would just sit there on whoever it was cast upon, sucking, and slurping, and generally wreaking havoc until every scrap of their magic was exhausted."

"I don't understand."

"Every containment spell functions to either contain or drain, right?" He watches me. "Basic restraining spell theory."

"Okay."

"And this one, well, it's set to full-throttle drain."

"Would it be effective on, say, a nearly-descended demon-spawn?"

"Oh feather yes, it would," he says. "The problem is the casting cost on this one." He whistles. "I don't know a mage in the world who could cast it without guttering."

Guttering—draining your personal magic so low that you die.

"You mean that—"

"It's elegant," he says. "It would probably contain a level six demon-spawn, but if anyone managed to cast it, and that's a big if, they'd die within moments. Seconds, probably. Even with a well or a link."

"Let's say someone did cast it," I say, thinking about what my mom said, that my dad had given up everything he had to help me. . . "What kind of being could you cast it on and *not* kill?"

He laughs. "Are you really asking?"

I shrug. "Just an academic question."

"An akero, maybe? A daimoni? I can't think of anyone else."

Clark breezes through the door a moment later. "Xander's mad, sure, but he felt guilty too, so he said it's fine. He's going to forgive me." He's beaming.

"Oh." I can barely deal with Clark's stuff right now, I'm so deep in the middle of mine. "That's good news, I guess."

"You showed Ricky the spell? Why?"

"He has a doctorate in restraining spells," I say. "Cool, right?"

"I'm just surprised you told him that was cast on you. I thought you guys had only been on a few dates."

Ricky's normally tan and healthy face pales. "This —who said this spell was cast on you?"

"It was in her file at the Angel Council headquarters with a spelled key," Clark says. "We aren't *sure* it was cast on her, but it seems likely, right? Look, her name's printed at the bottom of each page. Well, her initials, anyway."

Sometimes, I really want to punch my brother. "I

339

hadn't told him any of that," I say. "I kept the details vague."

"But this spell couldn't have been cast on her," Ricky says. "The only person on earth that might survive something like this would be. . ."

I wait for him to follow the breadcrumb trail.

"We think Minerva might be angel-spawn," Clark says, turning toward me. "I'm so sorry, Minerva. I thought you'd told him."

I sigh. "Well, I guess he knows now."

"Do you really think you could be angel-spawn?" Ricky looks like I popped him between the eyes. "And what?"

I shrug.

"You think maybe they cast that giant sucking spell on you so you can walk around as. . ." His jaw drops. "As a fumbly, half-human."

I shrug. "No way to know for sure, but we think. . . maybe."

24

MINERVA

"There is one way to know," Ricky says.

"One way to. . ." I can hardly believe what he's saying. I thought the only way I'd ever know for sure whether my mom was telling the truth was to, well, talk to my birth mother. "How?"

"Yes, how?" Clark asks. "Because our mom says that our dad put a spell on her to keep her safe. Could it have been that spell?"

"It would have killed him to cast it," Ricky says. "Anyone who casts the spell I saw. . .they'd die for sure."

"But would this spell keep her safe?" Clark asks. "If it's true, if she's. . .part you-know?"

"If she's angel-spawn?" Ricky winces. "I'm not sure. The spell I saw, if it was actually placed on her, even if she was angel-spawn, I can't see how it wouldn't kill her."

Clark gasps.

"Here's the thing," Ricky says. "I want you to think

about the most basic restraining spell." He points at Clark. "I'll demonstrate. We learn this in Containment 101." He whips out his wand. "Siphon potestas."

My big brother wheezes, his eyes bulging, and he grabs at his neck. He begins coughing, he pales, and he falls back onto the sofa.

"If I didn't release the spell, he'd eventually pass out," Ricky says. "Once he was unconscious, it would stop siphoning, unless I kept feeding power into it. It's keyed to his strength, so the more he tries to fight it, the more he defends against it, the stronger the spell becomes, but it's pulling that power to run from me, the caster."

Clark's still dragging in heavy, labored breaths. "A little warning next time."

Ricky smiles. "Where's the fun in that?"

"How's the one you saw written down any different than the spell you just cast?" I ask.

"That's the wrong question." He shakes his head. "The theoretical spell's inverted for one, so the power that feeds the spell. . ." He sighs. "It's the power being stolen from the person the spell was cast on—it's in a never-ending feedback loop, but that means the spell would quickly exhaust the person it's feeding on and kill them, too."

I blink.

"But that makes no sense," Clark says. "Where would the energy it's pulling even go?"

Ricky's face brightens. "That's the most brilliant part. See, the spell inverts, so the power a spell like that needs to keep going is actually coming from the person it's robbing magic from. It would circulate round and round, siphoning off power forever, if the recipient of the spell had limitless power. Not that anyone does, but let's say you cast it on someone like an akero."

"The spell would get stronger with time?" I ask. "If it kept going?"

"Ding ding," Ricky says. "And the only way that could work is if. . ."

"The creature that was spelled also gets stronger almost constantly," Clark says. "Otherwise, it would sputter out on its own."

"Along with the host's life." Ricky's expression is grim. "I just can't imagine this being cast on anyone— it would mean almost immediate death for the caster and the recipient. *But*, as a theoretical construct?" He shrugs. "This could get the author a PhD. I'd love to meet whoever thought it up."

"But you said you could tell if it was cast on me," I say. "Right?"

"I mean, sure," Ricky says. "The whole thing's woven, right? While most of it's inverted, there would be at least one thread that couldn't be tucked. It would allow some magic to escape in small, tenuous filaments, erratic and inconsistent."

"Magic that would be irregular and hard to control?" I hate how flat my voice is, but here we are.

Ricky shrugs.

"How exactly would you find that one thread?" I ask.

He steps closer to me, his fingers tipping my chin up just a little until I'm looking into his eyes. "Minerva, this spell can't be real. You're not angel-spawn. If this was real. . ." He sighs. "Living with a spell like this would be like walking around with a two-thousand-pound gorilla jumping on your chest. It would be oppressive. It would be demoralizing. It would be like a bottomless pit of evil, feeding on you all the time, always hungry. I know you—it can't be true, okay?"

"But if it was?"

"A talented spellcaster could find that string," he says.

"How talented are you?" I can't stop looking at him, even though I'm afraid.

"I'd be able to find it, if it was real."

"How long would it take you to look?"

"A while," he says. "I couldn't do it tonight. I'm too tired, and we have to leave right now. But I'll try, if you ask me to."

"Can I think about it?" I swallow. "About whether I even want to know?"

"Of course," Ricky says. "You absolutely can."

Clark looks nervous as we walk out the door, and he should. I'm about to traipse into a fundraising gala to try and win over a lot of people who hate me. Traditionally, I've not been amazing at this sort of thing.

The night starts well, aside from the miserable mess about the spell. Ricky doesn't mention any of the insanity from my apartment—not in the cab, not when we enter the gala, and not when he leaves me at the table to give his keynote. As he stands at the front of the room, I'm proud.

I came in on this man's arm.

He's gorgeous. He's brilliant. He's talented. He's powerful. He's a force for good. His speech focuses on the way proper spellwork keeps the world safe, but he also talks about how good spells keep the individuals who have gone too far safe. . .from themselves. He spends quite a bit of time on our responsibility to the humans who were born with daimoni blood. If Bevin could've been here to listen, she'd be impressed by how open-minded and altruistic he is, I'm sure.

He closes out his speech with a line I'll never forget. "The job we have as guardians—it's not for the faint of heart. I think most people know that much. We risk our lives every day. Normies will never know we're doing it, and that's the way we want it. We're not here, on the front lines, for accolades. We're not here for a reward. We're here to save humanity itself. My personal goal when I work to keep Earth safe every night is to help demon-spawn everywhere remember that they're as human as we are. We all have work to do to keep the evil within us contained, but their job is just a little harder. They deserve our support. Thank you."

Everyone cheers when he sits.

I might cheer the loudest, though. "That was amazing," I say. "I was so impressed."

On his arm, I half-wonder whether I might convince some of the people who hate me that I'm not a bad choice. We've barely stood up from the keynote, but I'm optimistic for the first time in a while.

"Ah, Minerva, I thought I saw you." Chief Lumos waves us over. "I've got the Sublime Chancellor here, and I wanted to make sure you met him."

Ricky's smiling as we approach.

"What a great talk, son," the Sublime Chancellor says. "Very introspective for a guardian. I always thought of you as blunt tools, but you seem much more insightful than I realized. Sorry for making assumptions."

"We all do that now and again," Ricky says. "In fact, I hear you met my girlfriend under less than favorable circumstances a while back."

The Chancellor frowns. "Your—oh, the PA Officer whom Chief Lumos was just raving about?"

Ricky nods. "Minerva Lucent."

"And you said I met her. . ." It's obvious the moment he recognizes me. His eyes narrow. His mouth flattens into a line. "You boiled my son like a lobster."

"Come now," Chief Lumos says. "We had other officers on the scene within ninety seconds, and he was just fine less than an hour later."

"Also, I hear he was in a hot tub with not one, but four completely baked humans," Ricky says. "I'm sure Minerva here was embarrassed that her spell went a little awry, but hers wasn't the only mistake made that night. It might not have even been the largest."

"You know." The Sublime Chancellor waves me closer, and he drops to a whisper. "He used to party at least once a week, but ever since that night." He slaps his knee. "He hasn't gone out even once."

"You're saying she did you a favor?" Chief Lumos arches one eyebrow.

"I suppose she did." The Sublime Chancellor grins.

"Alright, Potts," the Chief says. "Let's talk about this more next week over a round of golf. I'll tell you about some of the other miraculous ways Minerva Lucent has turned things around at the Precinct, and once you hear my reasons for recommending her as my replacement, I'm sure we'll convince you."

"I still can't believe you're retiring." The old vampire slaps the Chief's back. I can't think of him as the Chancellor anymore, not now that I know his name is *Potts*.

"It's not my call," Chief Lumos says. "The wife demands it."

"Good for you. The older I get, the less time I want to spend with my wife." They're both laughing as they walk away.

"Ten minutes in, and you've already mended one bridge," Ricky says. "Where should we go next? Wolves? Dragona?"

I scan the room, but literal seconds later, I see something strange. Lo Ren Fang, I recognize. I've met him twice thanks to Xander, and he has a uniquely beautiful face. His mate is just as lovely, but in a very different way. Only, she's not here. He's with. . .his grandmother? His great-grandmother? The woman whose arm he's holding looks utterly wizened.

That's when it hits me.

Bevin said she *aged* his mate. I thought she meant maybe a few winkles here or there. Some grey hair. In my wildest dreams, I never contemplated this. The woman on Lo Ren Fang's arm looks *minutes* from keeling over.

"Wolves?" Ricky asks, following my line of vision. "Alright." He waves at Lo Ren before I can yank his wrist down.

Lo Ren narrows his eyes, but he's definitely looking, which means it's too late to avoid talking to them.

Ricky's dragging me over there when someone else says my name. "Minerva Lucent." The steely voice reminds me of every female villain in basically every Disney cartoon, but especially the movie *Maleficent*. I turn very, very slowly.

"Mrs. Goldenscales." I bow slightly. "So nice to see you again."

Her face is as unlined as her daughter's, but I know she's centuries old. So many things about life are just patently unfair. "I wish I could say the same."

"I'm sorry," I say. "I should have called you when Roxana showed up, but I wasn't sure what to do. She was so. . ." I swallow.

"My daughter insists you were helping her," she says. "But that *help* made our life miserable, and if you thought she needed *help* to stay away from us, what does that say about your view of our parenting?"

My hand's trembling. Roxana's mother is Depends-diaper-level terrifying. "Um, no, it's not like that at all. The thing is, you and your husband are just *the best*. It was Ragar whom Roxana was trying to escape."

"The man we engaged her to?" Mrs. Goldenscales raises her eyebrows. "The man we selected for her?"

"No." I force a laugh. "I mean, it's not like she told you she didn't like him. That's on her."

"Actually, she did." Mrs. Goldenscales crosses her arms.

"I can't feel my feet," I hiss softly, hoping maybe Ricky can save me.

My gallant boyfriend tries. "I think Minerva means to say that—"

"I'd actually like to hear what she has to say directly from Minerva." Mrs. Goldenscales scowls at Ricky. "Unless *you're* the Chief's suggested replace-ment?" She lifts her eyebrows again, and I swear, raising a sword in my direction would be less terrifying.

"Minerva Lucent?" Lo Ren Fang has heard just

about enough, apparently. He prowls his way across the floor to join the little circle forming around me and Roxana's mother. "You're part of Xander's abomination of a pack."

"I, well." I swallow again. "The thing is—"

"Wait," another voice says. "Xander Binnigas?" This time, it's a mage. I don't know him, but I recognize the bulge in his robe. Only idiotic wizards store their wands down there. As if any girl wouldn't realize it was his wand, not his *wand*.

"I was talking to her first," Mrs. Goldenscales says. "The rest of you can wait your turn."

"What made you think you could be bonded by a werewolf?" someone asks.

"Should the city worry that if you're bonded to an alpha wolf, he'll be making the real decisions for the Paranormal Affairs Department?"

"How could you align with a demon-spawn in good conscience?" someone else asks.

"Is it true your demon-spawn friend can steal the life force of any supernatural?"

The questions come so fast and so furious that I can't even tell who's asking them anymore.

"Are you really planning to stay here and challenge the Fang wolves?" a short woman at the front asks. "Don't you care how many people die for you?"

"What about the Demon Council?" a man asks. "Don't you think they have an obligation to keep their newly descended demon-spawn in line? Why are you supporting an insurrection?"

"Why do you want to be Chief?" another man asks. "Is it so that all your friends won't be prosecuted for their misdeeds?"

"Is it true your boyfriend's a vampire who pretends to be an actor so he can drink the blood of untold numbers of extras and movie-goers?"

"Stop," I say. "My boyfriend's right here. He just gave the keynote. He's a guardian—a mage—not a vampire."

That shuts them up.

"I do have a best friend who's demon-spawn, and she's one of the best people I've ever met. Another friend of mine's a vampire. He's an actor, but not so he can drink as much blood as possible. He's an actor because he wants to make people smile. It's hard for a vampire, making people smile in spite of the innate fear they feel around him. Like my demon-spawn friend, my vampire buddy's a good person."

The murmurs have restarted, but I'm not about to let them grow again. "It's like cancer, this gossip." I look around the room, daring them to challenge me. "You just listened to an inspiring keynote about battling the evil in all of us, and you thought to your-selves that Ricky was talking about someone else, not you." I pause and look around again. "But you're wrong. He was talking about you. We all have evil inside us, and unless we're constantly fighting it back, it's winning."

"You're bonded to a werewolf," Lo Ren Fang says. "How's that for evil? You're not even a shifter."

"I'm not," I agree. "But there weren't werewolves here at all until the akero came. There weren't vampires or dragon-shifters or mages. All of these things were new on earth at one time, just like this pack is new now. If we hate everything new, if we decry anything different, what kind of world will we have?" I pause for a beat. "A boring one, that's what."

"Or a safe one," a gravelly woman's voice says. "Because your so-called demon-spawn friend, the one with the big heart? She did this to me." The people step aside as a very old woman hobbles toward me. It must be Rylan, Lo Ren Fang's mate.

"You were trying to kill her at the time," I say. "Along with my friend Roxana."

Hag Rylan lifts her chin. "The dragona should die. She's lying with a werewolf. It's filthier than bonding non-wolves to a pack."

"I'm not sure any *lying* has happened yet," I say. "They barely started dating, and if you knew how awkward Xander was. . ." I shake my head. "Doesn't matter. The point is that—"

"You're saying that *my daughter*'s the abomination? I nearly burned that wolf to cinders when he walked into my home." Mr. Goldenscales is such a small, nondescript-looking man that I almost always forget to notice him, at least until he talks.

His voice booms like thunder on a drum.

"Yes, how dare you say my daughter's not good enough for a *werewolf*," Mrs. Goldenscales says. "And then you casually admit you were trying to kill her, like that wasn't an act of war?"

It looks like the dragona king of New York City's about to shift right here.

"I'm sorry," Ricky says, at my side. "This was—I'm just, I'm really sorry."

I shake my head. "The whole thing's a mess, but it's not your fault. I knew it might go like this. I'm just sorry I dragged you into it."

"No, not that." He tosses his head toward the corner of the room. "I'm sorry about *that*."

At least a dozen armed militia-mages are marching this way. It's probably for the best that he called in the cavalry. It looks like the dragona and the werewolves are about to kill one another.

"Smart move, calling them." It's sad, but this is what our communities are like. They fight constantly. "I mean, I'm sorry I caused the fight, but better safe than dead."

Ricky looks terribly sad.

"What am I missing?" The militia-mages are slowly working their way toward us, stunning, zapping, and generally terrorizing all the many, many agitated super-naturals separating them from where we're standing.

"They're not here to mediate fights," Ricky says. "They're here. . ."

"For what?"

Ricky looks *wrecked*. His eyes are full of regret. His wide, broad shoulders are slumped. And his mouth— it's twisted painfully. "Minerva, I'm so sorry, but an angel-spawn ascending is just as dangerous as a demon-spawn descending. If there's any chance that what you suspect is true. . ." He gulps. "I had to report it. I'm sure it's not the case. I'm sure you're just you, but they have to run some tests just to make sure."

Of course.

This is just how my life goes.

The militia mages, the trained magic-SEALS, coming at us like a freight-train? They're coming for *me*.

I should have known.

As they get closer, I realize that I know one of

them. At the very front, with a massive, glittering golden sun embroidered on the chest of his robes, Lionel Sol's holding a shimmering, shining wand. It's brighter than any I've ever seen.

Except the one I have hidden away in my pocket.

Now that I've thought about it, I can feel Dad's old wand, pulsing. I reach down and pull it from the hidden corner of my borrowed dress, and now that I'm holding it, my entire arm starts to glow like a lantern. "I hear you're coming for me."

Part of me wants to go with them.

They'll have answers.

They'll be able to tell me, like Ricky didn't, what I really am, and maybe even where I came from.

Or what's wrong with me.

The militia-mages, led by Lionel, freeze. Their eyes widen, and their wands droop at the end.

"The thing is, I'm not interested in going anywhere with you." When I look around, I notice that Lo Ren Fang and his mate are gone. In fact, they've been gone for several minutes now. I'm not sure where they went, but it's a weird time for them to disappear.

There's a strange sort of popping sound, and Giggles bursts into view in a flash of bright light near my shoulder. She's larger, and almost unbelievably, even fatter than usual, and her beady orange eyes are gleaming. *Your friends need you. Xander won't call, because you didn't come last time.*

"I'm a little busy here," I say.

You asked for a ride last time, Giggles said. *And I realized, I can probably give you one, but only if I'm a little bigger. So.* She spreads her wings and flaps, and people on either side go flying.

"What is that?" someone asks.

"It's her pigeon familiar," Lionel says. "But why's it so large?"

"She bonded a pigeon?" The militia-mage behind him's frowning. "Why would anyone do that?"

Giggles coos, and then she hisses, and then she dives toward me. But one of the militia-mages is faster. He whips his wand at her and chants, "Perdere."

It's a vicious spell—an exploding damage spell, meant to maim or destroy. Fury rises up inside of me, and I move without thinking, throwing a counter spell to defend my little feathered rat. She may stink, and she may poop too much and in all the wrong places, and she may be uncomfortably large, but she's *my* feathered rat, and. . .

I love her.

"Invertere," I shout.

My spell hits too late—his strike already hit Giggles. Feathers spray outward, and she falls backward, careening toward the ground. But then my casting clicks into place and some portion of the damage inverts, flying outward from Giggles and back at the caster.

He explodes on the spot, nothing but pink mist.

My jaw isn't the only one dangling open.

"What did you just do?" Ricky asks.

"He started it." I sound like a small child. "I mean, I just inverted his spell."

"You can't invert spells," Lionel says. "Magic doesn't work that way."

"Mine does." I look right at Ricky. "Someone told me just tonight that you *could* invert a spell, theoretically anyway. One thing you can't do, however, is undo a betrayal. Once you've picked the wrong side, you're kind of stuck there."

I feel a tingling in my hands and feet then, and I know.

Xander needs me.

My pack needs me.

For better or for worse, I am whoever and whatever I am. The Illuminae may want to investigate me, but they won't do it under dodgy circumstances or illegal methods. "If you want to take me in," I spit at Lionel, "get a warrant and present it to my boss. Don't show up at a party and attack my sweet little innocent familiar." I bend over, gather Giggles up in my arms, and chant, "Nullus locus est sicut domus."

For a split second, nothing happens, like always.

Then light begins to gather from all corners of the room, rushing toward me like dogs chasing a ball. I press Giggles' limp body against my chest, and then there's a much bigger popping sound, and I know I'm taking us both home.

25

ROXANA

I once stabbed someone. . .with a plastic knife.

My seventh birthday was right around the corner when Mom and Dad decided we should take a family trip. They talked about a lot of possible locations before settling on Bermuda. It was a quick flight—via dragon wing—but the real draw was that Bermuda allegedly had pink sand beaches.

Mom wanted to see them.

She also wanted us to spend more time as a family, and that meant bringing all my brothers, too. In the end, seventeen of my brothers decided to come, and that meant that Mom didn't need to bring a single guard. Who would attack eighteen of the largest and most powerful dragona males in North America on holiday in Bermuda?

No one. That's who.

It was a flight of nearly four hours. Normally Dad would carry Mom and me, but this time, I had seventeen other options. I wound up selecting the same brother I virtually always chose when given the opportunity. It wasn't the brother closest to my age, Sebastian. He liked to poke me until I squealed. Not physically, of course. Mom would have shut that down immediately. But he'd badger me, tease me, and generally give me a hard time about everything.

I didn't choose my oldest brother either, Mateo. He was so bossy and so officious that I wanted to spit in his eye within minutes of most interactions. The other fourteen brothers who came along ranged from considerate to overprotective, but most of them were just fine.

But one brother in particular always made me laugh.

Most dragona males spent a lot of time in their dragon forms. It felt safer, less vulnerable, and frankly, they just liked it. Luka, though, spent a lot of time as a human, at least, when I was young. He used to hide behind things and jump out and scare me. For someone who was coddled in every way, it was terribly exciting. He would spray me with water when I wasn't paying attention. And he'd bring me small things he saw that I might like. He was, essentially, the perfect brother for a small dragona female, in practically every way.

Sadly, that also made him the perfect *fiancé* to another dragona, and on my fourteenth birthday he was shoved to the altar by Mom.

But on that trip, he was my ride.

I looked forward to lots of fun flights over perfect beaches, water fights, swimming, and quite a few delicious snacks. Luka actually paid attention to what I liked, which meant he was great at figuring out what things I might like to eat, even in strange places. I think because Luka was coming, Mom wasn't paying much attention to where I was or what I was doing, which made it a real vacation for her.

On our third day, Dad had been called away to talk to Mateo about some world domination problem, and I was left entirely with Luka, which was just fine by me. We enrolled for a cupcake decoration class, and I was looking forward to it. The sample cupcakes showed a lion, an elephant, a seal, and a bear, and I wanted to make one of each. Only, when it came time for our class, Luka wasn't anywhere to be found.

Sebastian came instead.

He wasn't in human form, either. He came as a great, hulking golden beast, which meant he couldn't come anywhere near the normie cupcake decorating hut. When I saw him, hunched back by the copse of palm trees, I started to cry. I was old enough to understand that normies couldn't see him, so I swallowed my frustration and trotted over to see what was going on.

"Luka had to go with Dad, so I'll watch you from here."

"I don't want to do it alone." I was turning seven in four days, and I was scared to be in a decorating class with a half dozen normies alone.

Sebastian rolled his eyes. "Stop being such a baby. You're the one who wanted to do that dumb thing, so go do it."

Which is how I got stuck in that stupid class alone, and feeling like a baby. I should have known that Sebastian would rather have died than try to pipe frosting out of a small tube in the shape of a lion's mane.

I felt childish and scared.

That's my excuse.

The little boy next to me, Remy, stole my yellow frosting and squeezed it into several ugly little poop-shaped piles.

"Cupcakes are dumb," he said.

It sounded an awful lot like what Sebastian had just told me, which just made me feel dumber.

"But I wanted the yellow," I said. "I need it for my lion."

"Lions are as dumb as you." He stuck out his tongue.

But that was fine. I reached for the grey. I could do my seal next. Only, he got there first. When he turned the grey frosting into a bunch of smaller blobs, laughing, I balled my hands into fists. "I wanted to make a seal."

"Seals are dumber than you."

He wasn't very original, but two other kids in the class sitting on the other side of the table laughed. None of the adults were even paying attention.

Dumber than a seal. Dumber than a lion. A big, fat baby who no one wanted to deal with. That's exactly how I felt. So when the kid yoinked the brown frosting too—which maybe he should have started with, since he was making everything into poop—and I couldn't even decorate the bear head?

I was *livid*.

I knew what he would say, that I was dumber than

a bear. I braced myself for it. "Why did you take the brown?" I asked. "I wanted to make the bear."

"Because," the little boy said. "You're like a big, stinky pile of poop, so I had to use the brown to make *you*."

I was *fuming* by then, and I'd had more than enough. I picked up the white plastic knife next to me, the one they gave us to smooth out the seal's body, and the lion's face, and I jabbed it into his shoulder.

That's the first time I learned that fits of violent rage are *not* widely considered to be acceptable among normies. It was quite a mess for my mom and dad to clean up. Even though a plastic knife wielded by a six-year-old did almost no damage, I managed to slice his arm a bit, and I'm sure they had to pay out a substantial settlement. After that, I never left Dagobar tower without a physical bodyguard next to me, be it one of my brothers or another New York dragona at my side at all times.

Which is why I'm so utterly useless at fighting.

I've never, ever, *ever* needed to raise so much as a finger. All my stabbing-fury situations were immediately stolen by the *very* violent, *very* capable dragona males who stood perpetually at my side.

"I can't do it," I say. "I mean, I know I *have* made fireballs, but unless someone is right in front of me, threatening, I can't make one."

"I'm not asking you to," Xander says. "I just want you to think back to that moment you did."

"Wait, which one?" I ask. "The first one? Or when I missed Rylan's ugly mug?"

"Either one, really," he says. "But Rylan might be more fresh."

"Okay."

"Try to remember what *exactly* you were thinking and feeling when you created that fireball."

"I wasn't thinking," I say. "In fact, I wasn't thinking either time. I was reacting."

"To what?" Xander's smiling now.

"Fear, I guess. I felt threatened both times, and I just had to do something."

Xander throws a knife at my face, and I blast it with a tiny fireball, which melts the knife, and blows on past, incinerating the tree behind him.

"Holy wings of fire," I say. "How did you know that would work?"

Xander shrugged. "We'd tried a hundred things that didn't."

"What would you have done if it *didn't* work?" I can still see that knife hurtling toward me.

"Find a new girlfriend who wasn't horribly disfigured?" Xander winces.

I have half a mind to throw a fireball *at him*. "Are you kidding? You better be kidding."

Xander steps closer and pulls another knife from his pocket. He hands it to me.

I step back. "No thanks. Not great with knives."

He shoves it into my hand, pressing down forcibly. "Check this one out."

When I do, I realize that it's plastic—high end plastic, but plastic all the same. When I press on the blade, it collapses. "That was a *toy?*" Now I'm more upset.

"You'd have gotten a black eye, or maybe a broken nose, but Clark could fix both of those."

"Are we talking to him now?" I can't help

compressing my lips. I've been acting around everyone else like nothing happened, but with Xander, I don't have to pretend.

Xander shrugs. "I am. You can decide for yourself, but here's the thing." He sighs. "He's liked you a lot for a long time, and I knew that when I started thinking about you. . ." His face flushes. "I'll just say that I didn't think about you like a good friend of someone who liked you should be thinking about you."

That makes me smile. "Your guilt means he gets a free pass for being daimoni-poop?"

"Who taught you to swear?" Xander's eyes are dancing. "I'm going to guess it was your grandmother."

"Nice try," I say. "Never met her. She had my mom so late in her life that she only lived a few hundred years after."

Xander shakes his head. "Wolves live a long time—two hundred years, in many cases, but nothing like you scaly monstrosities."

"Your sweet talk always makes me swoon." I've arched one eyebrow. "But could we focus?"

"On?"

"I've now made three fireballs, but now that I know your knives are fake, what did you think—"

"You can do it whenever you're really scared. When you feel backed into a corner, you explode. Which means you have some kind of aversion to it that's keeping you from doing it whenever you want. Once we figure out what that is, you'll be ready to flame anyone and everyone at a moment's notice."

And that's when the itching hits. My hands clench, and my toes curl as a wave of intense itching hits me from *all* my scaly places. It happened the day before too, but the adrenaline from the fight delayed it some.

"That's a good reason to forgive Clark, right there," Xander says, "since he's the only one who seems to know how to make your dragona cortisone cream." He pulls out his phone, and I can feel through the bond that he's texting him to ask for more. I'm starting to understand more and more about the bond, just like I'm figuring out how to use my previously nonexistent powers, one small bit at a time.

"Why do fireballs make me itch?" I ask. "It's so irritating. Can you imagine if I'm in the middle of a real fight, and I'm blasting the bad guys, and then I have to say, 'Can you hold on for a minute? I have some scratching to do'?"

"It didn't happen last time," he says. "I'm not too worried about it."

"But it did," I say. "It was only delayed a few moments, but luckily that was enough. What if it gets worse with every fireball?"

"Let's worry about our current issues before we start obsessing over future ones." He hands me the ointment, and I slather it on the places I can reach before handing it back.

He's always understood me through the bond—probably a wolf thing—but he knows right away what I want, positioning himself right behind me before lifting my shirt just far enough to reach the scales on my back.

"You know that it's only my back," I say. "People can see it—my bare back won't kill anyone."

"Speak for yourself," he mutters.

Moments later, a jogger stops and heads our way.

"Do you need help with anything?" he asks brightly. "I noticed that guy was using some kind of ointment. There's a pharmacy right around the corner. I can run grab whatever you need."

"Buzz off, loser," Xander says. "I'm literally right here helping her."

"Yeah, my boyfriend has it under control, thanks," I say.

The men working on the retaining wall for the flowerbeds circle around seconds later, offering to do the same.

"We're fine," Xander snaps.

The window washer from across the street, two delivery guys, and a lady who walking her two bulldogs stop next.

"Alright," I say. "You were right. Sorry for being so annoying."

Xander shrugs. "Just the price you pay to be you."

"And the price you pay to be my boyfriend."

That word always makes him smile, and that makes me grin back.

We spend another hour in the park, and Xander springs a few irritating things on me, like firecrackers, a fake gun, and a very large bug, but I manage to figure out how to make fireballs on command instead of as a reaction. I also set fire to a bush, incinerate two planter boxes, and melt a bench into slag.

"The city should bill us or something," I say.

"Now that you have your trust fund, don't be so eager to blow it all in one afternoon." Xander's smiling, though. It might not have been a conventional date, but it was a productive afternoon, and we spent it together.

He also managed to find the same place he bought our shirts before, and he buys another one. "Maybe get two," I whisper. "The second one's half off, and. . .werewolf problems."

He's laughing, but he buys a second.

I slide my fingers into his, and we walk down the street, almost like a normal couple, if we can pretend we didn't just destroy a fairly substantial corner of Central Park while "training" me.

"Don't worry," Xander says. "Since Clark's feeling guilty, he'll be happy to come repair whatever he can with his magic, and I don't have to feel bad about asking him to do it."

"Did you talk to the Wolf Council again this morning?" I ask.

He sighs, but I can sense that's a yes.

"What did they say?"

"They said that the longer we *survive* inside of the Manhattan area, the stronger our claim, which basically supports what Lo Ren said. Making a claim was useless. They're going to let us battle it out." I sigh. "They also mentioned that to have a real claim, I need to own property inside the staked geographical area. I may have lied and said that I already do."

"Well, let's make it true," I say. "My trust funds are verified at the escrow office. I bet if we call my dad, we can move the close forward."

"Move it up, how?"

"My dad's a major stakeholder in PNC." I bite my lip. "Or did I not mention that?"

Xander shakes his head and chuckles. "Well, now that we're doing two million each, that's easier. I just got verification the wolf pack's money is in my account, but I think it takes time to clear."

"Let's simplify it. Bevin and I can pay the down payment, and then you can repay me later if you want. I honestly feel a little bad taking all those wolves' life savings."

Xander frowns. "But what if the money doesn't post, or what if—"

"Then I'll own a building with Bevin. So what? You can still pay rent, and I'll get to say things like, 'if your rent is even *one* day late, you dirty dog. . .'" I can't help bouncing a little bit. "Or, wait, maybe I get some overalls and carry a plunger, and I can grumble and wave it at people."

"Where are you getting your information on landlords?"

I laugh. "Television—apparently *bad* television."

"You'd be the hottest landlord I've ever seen," he whispers, his eyes intent on mine.

My heart races a little, and I curl my hands around the collar of his black leather jacket, pulling him closer. "Show me."

His half-growl before he kisses me should bother me. I hated how Ragar pushed people around, most notably me, but I *love* it when Xander acts possessive, growling or scowling at other guys. It makes me like him *more*, not less. Maybe it's because I know he'd never actually force me into doing anything.

I feel safe around him.

Not bludgeoned or forced or changed.

He likes me exactly as I am, flaws, shortcomings, and beauty all together. He knows about the nuisances of being with me, and he snarls about them sometimes, but then he smiles and tells me I'm beautiful.

When he wraps his arms around me, and when he presses his lips against mine, I can almost pretend that we really are safe. We're all going to be alright, no matter what groups want to kill us, no matter what horrible councils or miserable leaders want us dead.

Of course, it's easier to kiss my hot, hilarious, powerful alpha werewolf boyfriend when the phone in his pocket isn't ringing nonstop. I finally pull away. "Who on earth is that?"

Xander looks mad enough that he might go furry when he yanks the phone from his pocket. "It's Bevin." He swears. "Hello?"

"Hey, Z. I'm at the escrow office right now, and they've discovered that there are *squatters* living in the building we're thinking of buying. They said that we'll need to notify the bank and take *measures* to ensure they're gone before we can close. If we don't, we run the risk of having to deal with them ourselves, and that can be a long and miserable process."

"Uh."

Thankfully Xander keeps his volume so high that I can hear what she's saying too, because he looks worried. "Bevin, can you ask them if we could move the close up, now that we have the downpayment sorted?"

"What?" Bevin asks. "I'm not sure—"

I take the phone and explain.

Ten minutes later, after a call from my dad, who's more than willing to help once I send him a video showing him how great I've gotten with fireballs, we have a signing set for one hour from now. What's more, he got them to release the hold on Xander's funds so we can all go in for two million each, like we wanted.

"Who knew your dad could make things so easy?" Xander snaps. "It's like. . ." He laughs. "Well, I guess it's like magic."

"He was actually kind of proud of me for buying a building. I think he thought I'd blow my trust fund on a whole building's worth of clothes, shoes, and jewelry."

"I heard when he said that 'even when this thing with the werewolf ends, real estate's always a good investment.'"

"You should turn the volume on your phone down," I say. "Sorry."

"It's fine. That didn't sting nearly as much as when he said, 'Since you own the building, you'll be able to kick him out. Clean break.'"

I can't help my chuckle. "My dad's a pragmatist, but we didn't do that. He listened when I told him to get your money released from the hold."

"He sure was shocked I had two million dollars," Xander says.

"He was." I can't help my smile.

"And he should have been. It's not even mine." Xander shakes his head. "I know the Waterbury pack is a little rough, but having a pack at all. . ."

I press my head against his hard, wide chest, and I wrap my arms around his torso. "You are a wonderful alpha, Xander, and I'm not the only one who thinks so."

He stands like that for longer than I thought he would. Maybe that means he needed to hear it. Then we walk to the bank, wearing our matching dog shirts, and we sign a lot of paperwork. Two hours later, Bevin, Xander, and I own a building.

"Does anyone feel a little bad for leaving the other three out?" Bevin's worrying her lower lip with her teeth. "I mean, Minerva and Clark were going to raid their retirement funds, which sounded bad but they were ready to do it, and Izaak's so proud that he's about to get a big paycheck."

Xander shrugs. "Like you said earlier, if they want to be part owners, they can pay us back later."

"But it's our names on the paperwork," I say. "Hopefully that's okay because we need to convince the wolf council that we're here to stay."

"We will." Bevin takes the folder and stands up. "We're a lot tougher than they thought."

On our way back to *our* building, I can't help worrying a little. "What's our plan, though? I mean, the wolves and the demon-spawn are still mad at us, right?"

"I think Lo Ren brought maybe a third of his wolves last time," Bevin says. "What happens when he comes with all of them? They've held back because they think I can lay waste to lots of them with my new power, but I can't. So, then what? Roxana can't take them all out with fireballs."

"I'm actually worried about something else." Xander kicks a smashed can, and it skitters along the pavement before clattering into the edge of a building.

"What?" Bevin and I ask at the same time, both of us turning toward him.

"What happens when Lo Ren realizes that he's not our only enemy?"

"The demon-spawn and the werewolves don't talk," I say. "I know you were worried, but if they were going to work together, I think they already would have."

"But what if they did?" Bevin asks. "The other demon-spawn would be able to tell them that while my power's terrible, there's never been a demon-spawn who could use something like that against multiple opponents at once."

I blink. "Are you suggesting that—"

"I think they're going to attack us together. That's the only way to address Bevin *and* my new pack." The line of Xander's mouth, my sweet, happy jokester, is as flat as I've ever seen it.

We're all worrying as we walk up the stairwell, but Xander manages to broadcast the good news to the other wolves right away. *You can all come talk to me about signing leases. We have seven open units now. Everyone else will need to find different accommodations or wait to see whether we can free up the other units.*

We could expedite the departure of the existing tenants, a voice that sounds decidedly like Jewel says.

"That feels rude," I say.

"Wait," Xander says. "Did you hear that?"

I frown. "Should I not have?"

"Hear what?" Bevin asks.

"See?" He's smiling. "She didn't, but you're starting to pick up on some of the wolf chatter."

"No fair," Bevin says. "I'm bonded, too."

"I wonder why I'm hearing it now," I say.

"Did you two. . ." Bevin lifts her eyebrows.

"Not yet," Xander says, at the same time as I say, "None of your business."

"I mean, it kind of *is* my business." Bevin's eyebrows bob. "Since I'm part of your pack, and you may be my new alpha's *mate*." Now she's really smirking.

"Hey." I'm really frowning now. "What's she talking about?"

Xander's face turns bright red.

"Wolves become official mates only after consummation," Bevin says, "or that's what I heard."

Thankfully, the ringing of my phone saves me from further discussion on that. "Hello?" I point at the phone and start walking toward my apartment, which is now actually kind of mine for the first time. I may not have my name on the lease, but I do own the building.

It feels nice.

"Roxana." It's *Lionel*. I definitely should have checked my caller ID before hitting talk.

"Oh."

"Not happy to hear from me?"

I shrug.

"Listen, we need to talk."

"So do it," I say. "Talk."

"That mess at your parents'. . ." He sighs. "I'm sorry about that. I never apologize, but I feel like I should. So there it is—I'm really sorry. And believe me, I understand the desire to rebel better than anyone. I swear, I do. So the wolf—"

"Lionel, you and I are not a good fit."

"We don't know that," he says. "In fact, that night I was going to tell your parents that I'd be fine with you, you know, doing your filial duty and having some eggs while we were together. That wouldn't even bother me. Well, I mean, it would, it *really* would, but I'd be able to get past it. Do you think your wolf could?"

"Lionel," I say, "I'm hanging up." And then I do.

He calls back three times, but I don't answer again. I'm finally standing in my own apartment, and it looks like an *ant hill*. "What are all of you doing?"

Wolves are streaming in and out, carrying boxes, bags, and small pieces of furniture.

"We're so sorry to have imposed," a man with longish hair says. "Thanks for letting us store things here."

"You're going to your new apartments?" I ask.

"The Alpha's assigning us places to live," a little boy with dark hair and eyes says. "I want the one with the window seat."

The man tousles his hair. "But we'll take any one we're given and say thank you."

Although they're not wealthy or very sophisticated, the wolves are efficient and polite. Within half an hour, they've brought in all kinds of things, and no one's standing on the street or milling around in the halls. In fact, a woman with short hair shows up with disinfectant spray and starts mopping the hallway floors. "We're sorry for the inconvenience." She's smiling as she ducks through the door.

Where was all this frenzied cleaning back at their pack compound? Or are they just energized now because they have an alpha?

Bevin's gone, so I can't ask her. I'm not sure where she went in all the chaos, and Xander's drowning in wolves and paperwork. I'm organizing my closet, which I've been needing to do since my mom started sending me clothing, when Minerva finally comes home again.

"There you are," I say. "Are you alright?"

She's pale, and she looks tired. Really, really tired.

"In the last day, you've missed a *lot*." It takes a while, but I get her caught up on the wolf attack, the building purchase, and my new fireball powers.

Bevin wakes up somewhere along the way—apparently she was up all night, and didn't sleep at all before the building close, so she nodded off for a nap in Minerva's room. It's good she got at least an hour of sleep this afternoon.

We spend the next hour in a frenzy, getting Minerva cleaned up and ready to meet Ricky, but when he arrives, she's still a twirly mess. I can't tell whether she's guilty about missing the whole battle, nervous about Ricky, or worried about her birth parent situation.

Either way, it looks like she and Ricky could use a little space, especially when she decides to show him the spell from her file. Bevin and I duck out, but Bevin's as curious as I am.

While we head down toward Grand Central for some gloffee, she asks, "Do you think she'll tell him that she thinks she's angel-spawn?"

I shrug. "Who knows?"

"I'd be nervous to do it," Bevin says. "I wish I could pretend I wasn't demon-spawn."

"Being part akero's probably a little different." Both of us stand in the stairwell for a moment, a little jealous. How would it feel, to be part angel? I wonder whether Bevin's thinking the same thing as we jog down the stairs.

When we reach Grand Central Gloffee, I'm absolutely *floored*. The shop looks like it was never touched. "How'd you fix this so fast?"

Gavin practically jogs to our side. "What can I get you?"

I frown. "Gavin, that hole's just *gone*?" I think back to when we walked up not that long ago—it was covered with boards, and men were out there clearing debris. "It was a disaster a few hours ago."

"You didn't know?" He blinks. "Your boyfriend came by with a team—they cleaned it up and magicked the repairs."

"My boyfriend—" My eyes widen. "Do you mean Lionel? But you know I'm dating Xander."

"Dragona royalty are different." Gavin shrugs. "Your personal life's your business, but. . ." He pretends to zip is mouth closed. "If anyone asks, I'm just happy you're happy."

"I'm not dating Lionel Sol," I say. "If he comes by again—"

"If Simba the Lion King comes by wanting to repair damage to my shop, I'll let him," Gavin says. "And then I'll say thank you. If that upsets you, well, that's between you and Lionel Sol." He turns toward Bevin. "Gloffee?"

"Yes," Bevin says. "I'll have a glachiatto, dragona, a muffin, and whatever kind of sandwich you have."

"You know that's from glaffour berries fed by your friend here?"

Bevin smiles. "Of course I do. Why do you think I like it so much?"

"Aww," I say. "Thanks."

Bevin smiles. "It is on the house, right? To thank Roxana for the repair?"

"Of course," Gavin says. "And I heard you two bought something today."

I roll my eyes.

"A good word with your other boyfriend would be appreciated," Gavin says. "I hear he's handling negotiation on all the leases."

"Poor Xander," Bevin says, the second Gavin's gone. "Do you feel a little guilty, making him do all the paperwork and arguing?"

I shake my head. "Not in the slightest. If you left it to me, they'd be signing leases in crayon." I can't help my laughter. "I'm fit for nothing but bankrolling things like this."

"There's time to turn you into a real person yet, Roxana Goldenscales."

"That's what I'm afraid of," I say.

"I'm actually pretty proud of how far you've come." Bevin's eyes lift, and her head turns.

I follow her line of sight to see what she's watching, and I notice Minerva stroll past us and down the street, arm-in-arm with her hunk. "She polished up pretty well."

"My magicked Dior works wonders," I say.

"When did you say I could borrow it?"

"Any time." I can't help my smile. I always wanted this—friends who borrowed my stuff. People to chat with. Makeovers, boyfriends, all of it.

When Gavin brings Bevin's glachiatto, he also brings me a glespresso, a glafficino, and a pumpkin spice muffin. "I know you said you didn't want anything, but I also heard you haven't settled on a favorite gloffee yet. . ."

"Thank you." It's nice to have friends.

"They're werewolf flavored, for obvious reasons." At least he knows which one is my real boyfriend.

I've just taken my first sip when someone calls Bevin's name.

We both turn, but Bevin's face falls.

"Everything okay?" I have no idea who the woman is.

Bevin shakes her head. "What do you want, Soki?"

"Wait, that's your sister?" I'm surprised, because she looks nothing like Bevin. She has olive skin to Bevin's fair skin. Her hair's ebony instead of blonde. Only their eyes are almost the same shade of blue, but not quite. Soki's are icier—crazier too—by a wide margin. The red horns poking up through the hair on her forehead are small, but they're the exact same color as Bevin's tail. They shine in just the same way, too.

"She won't be here long," Bevin says.

"You're right," Soki says. "I won't." She takes two more steps and crouches in front of Bevin, staring intently at her nails. "Black."

"What do you want?"

"You should be thanking me, sister." Her words are the barest whisper. "I came here to plead with you one last time."

Bevin's jaw is set. "Again, I'll say *no*."

Soki sighs. "It's a big mistake. They're done waiting."

"Because they heard I finally got my second power."

"That's a higher-level power," Soki hisses. "Can you really steal people's life force?"

"I can age them," Bevin says.

Soki pops to her feet with a hiss. "Same thing."

She's *stealing* people's life force? That's why they age?

"I bet you couldn't sleep at all after you did it." Soki clenches her fist, and tiny flames dance up her arm. "I hate that all I got were these dumb flames, and you got—"

"Flames were your first power," I say. "This was my second. And you were wrong about it not coming because of my bond to the werewolf. It did show up, just later."

Soki narrows her eyes. "The stronger the power, the longer it takes to appear."

"Did you come by to yell at me?"

Soki shakes her head, her hair shimmering in the incandescent lighting. "I came, against my better judgment, to. . ." She clears her throat and drops to a whisper again. "To warn you."

"About what?" I ask.

"Shut up, dragon whore," Soki says. "I'm here to warn my sister. You can burn for all I care."

"Burn?" I snort. "Unlikely."

"The Demon Council wants your powers, or they want you dead," Soki says. "And they're not waiting any more. You're their top priority, and they're willing to do whatever it takes to get what they want."

It sounds like she's saying they're coming for us. "Are they—"

Soki flings her hand at me, and my head slams into the back of the sofa. "I'm not talking to you."

Bevin stands. "Don't hurt my friends." Her eyes are pretty intense. "Or I'll hurt you double—that's a promise."

"I won't be able to help when they come," Soki says. "I'll have to follow them."

"Which is precisely why I never will. Taking orders from the devil? Pass."

"They're coming *soon,* Bev. I really wish you'd reconsider, but I think you're about out of time," she says. And then she walks out the door.

26

MINERVA

My most prized possession for the majority of my life was an akero feather.

But I never could remember where it came from.

I remember getting lost at an early age, and I remember walking around for hours, and I vaguely recall falling asleep. When I woke up, I was on my own front porch. I had a feather clutched in my hand when I woke, but I never knew where it came from. Dad said it was very valuable, and he bought me a special safe to keep it in.

I used to pretend that an akero had saved me that night. I made up all sorts of stories, and in each one, I was special—important.

Precious.

That was a feeling I never had in any other aspect of my life, but I always felt like the existence of that feather meant that I was destined for greatness. It's one of the reasons I felt so *sure* that trading it for the fire lizard to make my lifelong dream more likely would work.

It couldn't have been for nothing, right?

After light floods the room, and after the popping sound, my whole world goes white. I finally remember —that night, I didn't get lost. I wasn't simply tired or crabby. I had been just fine when Mom and Dad took Clark and me to the carnival. I wanted popcorn, and Dad bought it for me. I wanted cotton candy, and Mom had caved on that one, too. I had begged to ride on a carousel, and they agreed to that, too.

I loved the carousel *so* much that I begged to do it again.

Dad had gone to buy another ticket when Clark started jumping up and down. "I have to pee." He was whining, clearly distressed, and Mom knew he wouldn't make it until Dad came back.

"I don't wanna go in there." I scrunched up my face. "The toilets sound like monsters roaring."

Mom groaned. "It's fine. Just come."

I shook my head and set my jaw. "I hate them."

"Fine, then you wait here," she said, pointing at the concrete border around the planter near the bathroom. "I'll be just a few feet inside, helping your brother go to the bathroom. Call out if you need me."

Only, I couldn't make a peep.

The man who came for me clapped his hand over my mouth. When he dragged me off, I screamed as much as I could, but no one could hear me. Not even my mother, who was quite close. There was another man waiting just over a fence, and they both wore dark, heavy boots that clunked, and black hats that partially covered their faces. Once we cleared the edge of the carnival, the first man cast a silence spell on me. They spoke quickly in a language I didn't understand.

There were a few words I could make sense of.

"Kill her."

I heard them say it, and my heart raced. "Don't kill me," I said. "Please don't." But no words emerged. No matter how loudly I tried to scream, no matter what words I tried to form, none came out.

Until they did.

"Help!" I shouted. "I've been kidnapped. The men want to kill me! HELP!"

I wasn't very old, but my voice was quite loud, louder than I expected it could be. The men's eyes widened, and they lunged for me.

"How is she making noise?" The man who covered my mouth before did it again, and I bit his hand.

"Little devil," the other man said. "She deserves to die."

The man whose hand I'd bitten pulled out a large knife and pressed it against my throat. "This knife should work. It's spelled to kill even creatures like her."

The blade pressed against my neck burned like molten lava. I felt it in my soul, and a scream tore out of me.

"Shut her up," the second man yelled. "Do it quick."

As the man holding me pressed the blade harder against my throat, I felt something explode inside of me, and something else unfurled.

My wings!!

I flapped them as hard and as fast as I could, and I flew upward into the air, banging my head hard on the ceiling above us. It hurt, but nothing like that blade had. I redirected, my wings rapidly fluttering, and I darted through a window, the glass shattering around my face and shoulders. The shards sliced my skin, but the cuts healed as fast as they were made.

I shook it off, and I flew.

Higher, faster I went, the air cooling, the stars sparkling, and the wind whipping my hair around my eyes. "What's going on?" I asked. "Who am I, and what am I doing?"

You are mine, a strange voice spoke. *Call me, and I will come.*

My wings beat harder, and I shot even higher. Who was that? What did he want? Why did he say I was *his*? I was excited, but I was also inexplicably afraid. He said I belonged to him, but Mom and Dad said people can't own people.

Call for me, child.

But I didn't.

I didn't call him ever. I just flew, and flew, and flew, and then I recognized something. The park by my house. It's easy to spot, because there's a large tree next to a pond, and beside that, there's a sandbox with a tire swing on the edge. Next to the swing, there's a tennis court, and beside that's the best part of all—a playground area with a blue tube slide and a red bumpy slide. Beside the slides, there's a row of monkey bars, and they're my favorite place to be.

I'd sit on top of them for an hour sometimes, staring at the clouds.

I knew where I was.

I slowed down, my wings flapping less frantically, and I aimed for the road that curved by the big willow trees, and I followed it all the way down, until I hit the road with the weird name. I followed that one until the blue house with the wheelbarrow full of flowers out front.

And then I reached my own front porch.

When I finally landed, my dad was waiting with open arms. "I'm so glad you're alright, sweetie," he said. "I'm so glad you came back to me." His voice, I knew. His voice, I trusted. He loved me—I knew it in my bones. I knew it in my feathers. I knew it in my heart.

"Where else would I come?" I smiled.

"Well, speaking of that, we have a decision to make." He brushed one hand down the side of my dark blue wings. "You found your wings again."

"Again?" I asked. "Did I lose them before?"

He was still smiling. "A few times now, but each time, when we talk, you decide you'd like to lose them one more time. See, you're just full of magic, Minerva." He tapped the center of my chest with his pointer finger. "So full that it just explodes out of you. That means we have two options."

"Is this why the man was calling me?"

"The men at the carnival?" Dad lifted his eyebrows. "We caught them." His lips were a flat line.

"Not them," I said. "Another man. One I didn't know, one who spoke to me in my mind. He said I was his."

Dad froze, like we were playing hide-and-seek.

"He told me to call him and he'd come."

"Did you do it?" Dad's eyes looked almost panicked, like the time I knocked over a glass vase and walked through the tiny glass pieces. "Did you call him?"

I shook my head. "I didn't know him. You said never to talk to strangers."

He exhaled a lot, and then he hugged me tightly against him. "That man—he's your father, Minerva."

"No, you're my father."

Dad's eyes looked sad. "I'm your father, of course I am, but I'm your father because I chose it. He's your actual father, and if you call him, he will come. I'm just not sure what he'll do if he finds you."

"You think he'll hurt me," I said. "You always get that look on your face when you think something bad will happen."

"I'm scared that he might kill you." His eyes were so serious.

I reached up and brushed at the wrinkles in his forehead. "Killing someone means they don't smile ever again?"

"It means they stop breathing here on Earth. Their bodies stop working. They might live somewhere else —we don't know."

"Does my other dad know what happens?" I asked. "Why would he want to do that? Does he not like to see me?"

My dad's shoulders slumped. "Your other dad sees you as a risk. Your life could cause some problems for him. I think he sees you as a mistake."

"Am I a mistake?"

A single tear runs down my dad's cheek. "I don't know everything." He chokes, but he clears his throat with a cough. "There are a lot of things I don't know. But I do know one thing for sure, Minerva."

He lifts my chin with one finger until I'm looking right at him. "I know that you are the most beautiful, most bright, most miraculous child I have ever met. You bring more light into the world than anyone else, and I can't believe in a world where you're a mistake."

I'm crying too, then. "Okay." If Dad likes me, I can't be that bad.

"I would like you to let your mother and me hide your wings again. I would like you to let us dim your light, but only to keep you safe. I won't do it if you don't want me to."

"Who's looking for me?" I asked. "It's just my other dad?"

My dad nodded. "And his helpers."

"To kill me."

He shrugged. "I'm not sure, but maybe."

"Okay," I said. "You can do it."

A few moments later, a bright and shining woman landed next to me. "Hello, Minerva," my mother said. In that moment, I suddenly remembered her. She looked so much like my dad. She was tall, and she was stately, and she was bright.

She glowed like a lantern.

And her wings—they were bright blue, just like mine.

She wrapped her arms around me, much as my father just had, and she kissed my cheeks. "You are so beautiful," she told me. "And your wings are spectacular." She ran one finger over the edge of them, and for the first time, I noticed the difference between her wings and mine. The color of blue was the same, a dark, bright blue, like the starry night sky, but the tips were different. My other mother's wings were solid blue.

Mine were silver edged.

"How did you like flying?" she asked softly. "Did it bring you joy?"

I nodded. "Do you love it, too?"

She closed her eyes and looked up at the sky. "More than almost anything else in the world."

"More than me?" I asked.

Her eyes shot open. "Not more than you—nothing, more than you." She smiled then, but it was sad. "I hate coming here for this. I wish you could keep your wings always. I wish you could fly all the time, like you were made to."

"Why can't I?"

"If you keep flying, they'll put you in a cage," she said. "Or worse." She winced, like it hurt to think about that.

"They'll kill me."

Her eyes widened, and she turned toward my dad.

He shrugged. "She asked."

"Do you understand why I'm here?"

"To hide me again," I said. "Dad said you had to dim my light to keep me safe."

"That's true," my other mother said. "And I will miss you every single day you're hiding, but at least I'll know you're still shining."

"Just not as brightly as you." I looked at the aura around her, glowing like a small moon.

"Just as sparkly," she said. "But maybe not something everyone can see."

"Special people will see it," my dad said. "They

always do." He crouched down beside me but looked at her. "Did you bring it?"

My other mother nodded. "I have the feather."

"How many do you have left?" Dad asked.

"This is my last one, but I have a plan to get more." My other mother and my father started chanting then, and I saw them appear. Clear as the clouds in the sky. Bright as the light of the porch. Real as the hand in front of my face, neon blue chains appeared out of nowhere and wrapped themselves around my wings, clamping them against my body.

The chains tightened more and more, until I could barely breathe.

"It's going to last longer this time," my other mother said. "I came up with a way to invert it, a way to make it harder to unravel."

That was the last thing I remembered before everything went black, but I was still clutching the brilliant white feather in my hand when it happened. Something's pecking my face when the light begins to come back.

Wake up, idiot. Giggles has sliced open my hand.

"Hey, stop pecking me." I'm clutching something in my hand, but it's not a feather. It's harder than that. I blink and blink until my eyes work well enough that I can make it out.

It's my wand.

So basically, I'm still clutching a feather, just in a wooden container. "Where are we?" I sit up, blinking more, trying to make sense of what just happened. All around me, there are bright lights and honking horns.

My favorite spot. I couldn't bring you far.

"Your favorite spot is a little paved area between

two roads?" I stand up, brushing off the horribly expensive black dress Roxana loaned me. "Where are we—" That's when I see the road sign. "We're in *Queens*?" I groan. "Whose favorite spot is in *Queens*?"

Pigeons love it here, Giggles says. She flies a few feet away to land underneath a large green sign that reads: Pigeon Paradise Park.

I suppress my groan. "It's going to take me *an hour* to get back to our apartment from here."

I know, Giggles says, *And that's good. All the bad people have come* again. *You'll be safer here.*

"All the—" I'm spluttering. "Giggles, if the bad people are attacking, we need to go right away! What about our friends?"

Let them fight. You should stay safe.

Of course my familiar's a coward.

Giggles splutters. *I am* not. She swoops past me, grabs my wand in her beak, and then there's a loud pop and flash, and she disappears.

"Hey," I shout. "Where did you go?" Of course, the featherbrain doesn't reply. She's either ignoring me, or she's so far away she can't hear me, and I'm not sure which is worse.

Without a purse, a credit card, or an ID, it takes me a half-dozen tries before I find someone willing to swipe their card so I can get on the city bus. I'm not thinking happy thoughts about humanity, but I am finally on my way home.

I just hope by the time I finally get there, I have a home left.

27

XANDER

I had no idea I was in a honeymoon period until suddenly, I wasn't.

"Of course we can't share," a woman with pink hair screams. "You always say you'll do half the chores, but you never do any of them."

"That's because your version of 'half the chores' is having me do the dishes, the laundry, and the bathrooms," the woman with very crooked teeth says. "While you vacuum and dust!"

"It's fine," I say. "You don't have to share. One of you can take this apartment, and one of you can find another place that—"

"Oh, ho, that's not going to be me," crooked teeth says. "Not this time. I always let you have your way."

I'm not the only one looking from one very angry mother to the other and back again. The kids are doing the same thing. It feels like we're watching a somewhat depressing tennis match that might break into a hockey brawl at any moment.

"You have to do something," Jewel whispers. "This is precisely the reason wolves need alphas."

"It looks like they all need their mothers to give them a firm spanking," I say. "I don't see why I should—"

"Even more than a normal human, wolves are prone to fights," Jewel says. "The smallest insults can lead to huge blowups, and Randi and Cheryl have been at each other's throats for a long time."

"You seemed to get along before," I say. "I don't understand why—"

"We were displaced," Jewel says. "We were beggars, basically, and we didn't want to scare you off."

I drop my chin in my hands. "Cheryl has four kids. Randi has two. Cheryl gets the apartment, which is a two bedroom—in New York, that's huge. Randi, I hope you can find a place—our real estate agent offered to help anyone who was still looking."

I expect Randi to throw her cold gloffee at me, but instead, they both shut up. Randi inclines her head in a half-bow, and they step apart. "You can stay with me until you find a place," Cheryl says. "We'll stay in the bigger bedroom, and you can have the smaller one."

"Thanks," Randi says.

I feel a little guilty, after all their arguing, that it was such a simple fix. "I do also plan to do a review of the apartments that are still occupied—there are six— and hopefully some of those tenants will opt to move."

"We can help them make the right decision." Cheryl tosses her head at Randi, who grins.

"No, no, even frustrated single moms are not allowed to *encourage* other tenants to move. We're going to keep things polite and civil." As I say the words, I feel something strange, like the order is settling in.

Both Randi and Cheryl look disappointed, but neither argues.

"Alright," I say. "How many in the pack don't have homes yet?"

Jewel's reviewing a list. "Two families found an apartment within a one block radius already." She frowns. "We filled all seven empty apartments."

"One for the single women—all six of them," I say. "One for the single men." I frown. "Do you really think eight single guys can share one apartment?"

"The four who cause all the problems will be finding another place," Jewel says. "The remaining eight will be fine with four in each room. Trust me."

"That means we have, what? Five families and three couples who still need places to stay?" My head hurts. "This is complicated."

"We knew it would be," Jewel says. "None of us regret our decision."

When I look around the room at the families that still don't have homes, and the ones that do, but have no furniture yet, I can't help feeling guilty.

Bevin and Roxana burst through the front door.

"Oh," Bevin says. "You're still here." She looks around in alarm. "Do all these people still not have a place to live?"

"We're working on it," I say.

"Maybe we could arrange for a few ghosts to haunt the apartments that are left," Bevin says. "Then any normies who are still here will move along."

"I like you," Randi says.

"Me too," Cheryl says.

Bevin glances at me, and I shake my head. "No ghosts."

"Fine." When Bevin folds her arms, she sure looks like she's holding a grudge. Also, I don't feel like my injunctions against scaring the existing tenants will work on Bevin or the others like they do for the wolves.

I *guess* that's good?

"We came up because Soki paid us a visit," Roxana says. "She said an attack's eminent."

"Soki?" Jewel asks.

"My twin sister's sort of the opposite of me," Bevin says. "Where I've tried to be a good little girl, she loves being bad. Except, sometimes she feels a little guilty, given that we're related."

"She warned you?" I ask. "I mean, that's nice."

Bevin shrugs. "Maybe. Or maybe the Council told her to try one more time to get me to surrender."

"Which Bevin's obviously not doing," Roxana says. "But that's bad for us."

"The Demon Council heard about my little parlor trick," Bevin says. "Now they want me to join them even more than they did before."

"They can't have you," Randi's son, Edmund says. "You're ours."

"Exactly," I say. "And wolves don't share."

"Which is kind of our other problem," Roxana says. "What happens if the demon-spawn and the wolves attack together?"

"I'm worried about that too," I say. "Neither the wolves nor the demon-spawn are stupid, and they'd both be virtually assured a win if they hit us at the same time."

"We're going to be alright," Jewel says. "We trust you."

"I'm not sure you should," I mutter. "I have no plan."

"We know about your last plan," Jewel says, "and we veto it."

The other wolves in the room freeze.

"You know what about last time?" Roxana's frowning as she looks around the room.

Jewel's still staring at me. "We know what you planned to do before, and we're all against it."

I blink. "Before?"

"When Lo Ren and his wolves came," Jewel says. "We could all feel your intention, to offer yourself to him, if he would spare us."

Now I'm the one who's surprised. "It was the only solution that made sense."

"Xander Binnigas!" Roxana's eyes are flashing when she rounds on Jewel. "You must be kidding about that, right?"

Jewel looks just as upset. "When you met us, I know what you thought. You thought we were a charity case, but that you were even worse."

"That's not true," Randi says. "Our alpha is the best."

"I didn't tell you back then, because I didn't trust you yet," Jewel says, "but we're not a normal pack."

"What was the first clue?" Roxana asks. "The peeling paint? The rats? Or maybe the overalls?"

Jewel's half smile warns me that she's not a normal woman. Roxana's criticism would've upset most any other woman I've met.

"Very few wolves would be fine with me dating a

dragona," I say. "I could tell that you were a more understanding group as soon as you came, and frankly, that's the only reason I accepted the bond."

"We knew you wanted to save your brother," Roxana says. "And that other wolves were nearing fray as well. But surely having an alpha for a while has reset them, or whatever. Maybe he could release you, and you could all leave."

"We aren't going anywhere," Jewel says. "No more than you are."

"And it's more than Pat and his fray or a rat problem," Cheryl says from the corner. I didn't even realize she was still here.

"What are you talking about?" Roxana asks.

"We're sort of. . ." Randi coughs. "We're a poorly run pack that was without an alpha for over a year, which you know. You saw our pack headquarters, and you probably knew our last alpha wasn't the best either. We bonded him in a similar situation to you."

"I feel terrible that you sold your compound and gave me all the proceeds," I say. "I bet Roxana would be willing to—"

"Of course I would," Roxana says. "We can give you all your money back, if you want to go. It would be the safest move. We have a lot of people who want us all gone."

"We don't want that money back," Randi says.

"Not at all," Cheryl says.

"And after our first paycheck, we'll all be giving twenty percent of our income to you," Jewel says, "and it's only that low because we're paying for our own housing."

Really? "I don't want that," I say. "Keep your money—I'll find a job soon."

"Being an alpha *is* your job now," Jewel says.

"I'll support myself," I say. "Trust me."

The room fills with murmurs.

"We're a bunch of rejects," Jewel says. "My pa—when he started this pack, he was already sort of. . .eccentric."

"He was obsessed with birds," Cheryl says. "My dad told me that."

"It's true," Jewel says. "He spent all his free time bird-watching. It's not a normal thing for an alpha to do. And he started to collect wolves who. . .didn't have a place."

"They were weirdos," Cheryl says. "My dad said that."

"Okay," I say. "But—"

"I'm not done," Jewel says. "You should know that we think you're worth fighting for—worth dying for—but you may not feel the same about us once you know everything." She glances around the room, and I can tell they've talked about this. "After we explain, if you want us to go, we will."

I frown.

"One of the families in our pack—the Thorns—has only a father," Jewel says.

"Alathea's the little girl," Bevin says. "I met her and her dad."

Jewel nods. "She's not a wolf. Her sisters are, but her mother was a normie, and she lived with us. . .right up until she died of cancer last year."

Halfies and non-wolves are not accepted in packs. They just aren't. I have no idea what to say about that, except that I wish I'd found such a weird pack when I was young.

"Stan's obsessed with musical theater," Randi says.

"Rachel knits. Caps. Booties. Blankets. You name it, she's knitted it," Cheryl says. "Her kids had so many knitted things, they started trying to sell them on the side of the road."

"The Drummonds are extremely religious," Randi says. "They spend all day Sunday reading the Bible and singing, unless pack duties preclude it."

Jewel nods. "And the—"

"Stop," I say. "Do you think I'd decide you weren't worth dying for, because you're all strange?"

Jewel drops to her knees in front of him. "My dad formed this pack of weirdos, and then he died a decade ago. It took us over a year to find another alpha, and when we did, he was as strange as we were. It felt like it was meant to be, but he wasn't strong. Within a year, he died. We've had two alphas since then, one who hated us all—we tricked him—and one who was insane and weak, a deadly combination with wolves."

"I'm sorry we didn't tell you," Randi says. "We—" She looks down at her feet. "We needed you too much to risk it."

"We were hoping that if we explained," Jewel says, "that you'd understand why we appreciate *you* as our alpha. That's why we knew an alpha who would date a dragona, bond a demon-spawn, and yet, be strong enough to face off against Lo Ren Fang, was *exactly* the alpha we need. We hoped you'd stand up and fight to the bitter end. Because this is life and death for all of us, too. We love you *and* we need you." She looks around the room, and so I follow her eyes.

Every wolf in here is nodding.

And the ones listening in on the conversation through the bond are agreeing as well.

"We need you, Xander," Jewel says. "Just as you are."

I waited my entire life to have another wolf say that to me, and now I might get them all killed.

"It's precisely *because* you're such unique wolves that I can't just let you wait here." I make a new plan. "Bevin, you said your sister warned you?" I've had a very uneasy feeling since she came up here, and it's not going away. "Jewel, who'd you say has an apartment already, one that's not in this building?"

"The Garretts and the Blumes," she says. "Why?"

"Randi and Cheryl, you're in charge of getting every single one of the children to either apartment—the Blumes' or the Garretts'. Now."

"But we just sent people to their new homes," Jewel says.

"Which means we need to hurry." I push the command out to everyone this time. "Evacuate all the children to the Blume and Garrett apartments immediately. Cheryl and Randi will coordinate and guard."

The good thing about wolves is that they know how to obey an order, as long as it's direct and coming from their alpha. I may not have gotten a guidebook, but some of the stuff comes along naturally with the bond—giving orders is apparently one of those things.

I'm walking people through details when Clark calls. "Xander?"

"Hey," I say. "I'm glad you called. Bevin's sister Soki came by not that long ago and told us—"

"I'm two blocks away, and the roads are barricaded. They're evacuating humans north."

"What?" I look around—it may be too late to get anyone out. "Why?"

"I've seen four demon-spawn so far, and I think there may be more," he says. "It looks like they're moving in pairs toward you guys."

"Stay where you are," I say.

If we die, I'll rest easier knowing Clark didn't die with us.

"No way," he says. "I'll find a way through. Hang on until I do."

That's cute, like he thinks our success will hinge on his help. "Be safe." I hang up. "Your sister wasn't lying," I say. "They're coming now."

"This time, let's meet them in the street," Roxana says, flexing her hands like she's preparing to hurl some fireballs. "I felt really bad when we trashed Gavin's place last time."

"Yeah." Bevin's smirking. "It's sad when your whole harem has to kick in on repairs."

"What does that mean?" I ask.

Roxana's blushing. "Just ignore her."

"Change of plans," I say and push internally. "Take everyone to the roof."

"Eh." Roxana drags out this weird sort of squeaking sound that reminds me of my mother when she was uncomfortable about something.

"What?"

"Last time the wolves were headed up there, and they meant to use the kids as collateral."

"Do you want to hang back and protect them?" I ask.

"Bevin should stay with them," Roxana says. "She's who they want, and she's super powerful now."

"That's why I can't go with them," Bevin says. "They'll keep looking until they find me."

"We'll go," Randi and Cheryl say.

"And us." Harry's a pretty big shredder. He catches Liam's eye, and they both nod.

"I want at least ten shredders up there with them," I say.

"Then who's going to fight with you?" Jewel asks. "Were you listening at all? We won't leave you undefended."

"I've been training," Roxana says.

"And I'll be there too," Bevin says.

"Don't forget me." Izaak looks wide awake when he shoots through his bedroom door, and again, he's dressed in all black.

"You can fight in other colors," I say. "In fact, lime green would make you easier to spot. That should be our pack color."

"Black doesn't stain," he says, "when it's covered with the blood of my enemies."

"This is the coolest pack ever," little Edmund says from behind the end table. "I want to wear black, too."

"You're not even supposed to be in here," Randi says.

"Fine," he says. "Then I'll wear lime green."

His mom rolls her eyes. "As if it's the color that's the problem."

The poor little guy grumbles as she hustles him out the door.

"Wait," I say. "Instead of the roof, bring all the kids here, to my apartment and the one across the hall."

"Smart," Jewel says. "If they hit the roof first, we'll be able to slow them down en route. If they come from the bottom like we expect, same thing. Either way, we'll have two floors to stop them."

I shrug. "A battle strategist, I'm not, but I think it's our best bet."

We all head down the stairs together, and by the time we reach the bottom, we've been joined by a dozen other shredders. Eight men, six women. That, with the three who came with us. . .sixteen shredders including me, a vampire, a dragona who can't shift, and a level two demon-spawn. I don't know how many demon-spawn they send to try and force membership on a truant level two, and I don't love not knowing what we're up against.

The demon-spawn probably know how many wolves are in our pack. It's not a secret. They'd bring enough to be sure to win. And I can't offer to sacrifice myself, not for them. They only want Bevin, so I need another plan. I'm frantically rolling through options as I stomp through the center of Grand Central Gloffee when Giggles explodes into the space above my head, flapping her wings furiously and chittering. I have no idea what she might be saying, but I can make out the general sense.

"Minerva's on her way?" I ask. "Is that what you're saying?"

"Tell her not to come," Roxana says. "We're being attacked. It's not safe here."

Giggles flutters down and lands on Roxana's shoulder, digging her tiny claws into a patch of golden scales.

"Hey," Roxana says. "Those already itch. Be careful."

Giggles wraps her talons around the corner of the scales and starts to scratch at them.

Roxana spins in a circle. "That hurts. Knock it off!"

Again, Giggles starts chittering, and I somehow understand that she's filling in for Minerva. I'm not sure *how* I can understand what a pigeon's saying, but here we are.

"As if you could do anything to help," Roxana says. "Be a good girl, and fly up to our apartment. There are lots of kids in there you could entertain who are probably very scared right now."

Giggles explodes off Roxana's shoulder as we near the exit onto the street, and as I reach for the doorknob, she bursts into flames.

"Not again," Gavin says. "I thought you were going outside."

"We're trying," I say. "Where's Clark when you need him to put out a fire?"

Gavin's hefting a fire extinguisher when Giggles, the formerly-pigeon-ball-of-flame, drops to the ground with a rather large crash.

"Ugh, my tiles!"

"Hello," Bevin says. "Focus. That's a living creature."

"It *was* a living creature," Gavin says. "Now it's collateral damage from the stress of yet another attack." He frowns. "So far, not loving the new building management."

"Growing pains," I say. "And I think she's still alive." I'm staring at the pile of blackened char that used to be Giggles, and I'm not sure, but it's moving a little bit, I think. The movements grow more obvious, the charred remains rocking back and forth, sort of like an egg that's about to hatch.

And then, with a loud pop, the ashes around her tiny body explode, covering all of us with a fine layer of black soot. The creature that unfurls its wings to stand at full height is much, much larger than Giggles. It's at least five times her former mass. Maybe more.

Its wings are a bright, flaming rainbow of orange, gold, and the brightest scarlet. "I'll help until Minerva arrives," Giggles-not-Giggles says.

"You can talk aloud now?" Bevin asks.

"I could always talk, but only Minerva and Roxana were evolved enough to understand me, so I had to evolve again for the rest of you idiots." She shakes off like a dog leaving a lake, and somehow grows larger yet again.

Rays of light are definitely streaming from her like she's a shedding lamp.

"What *are* you?" Roxana asks.

"I'm Giggles," she says. "But enemies might call me a firebird."

"Mother *feather*," Jewel says. "This is so cool."

Clark bursts through the back door, heaving and wheezing. "Oh, man. There's a lot of demon-spawn out there." He looks around the room, his eyes stopping on the enormous bird in the center. "What's going on in here?"

Roxana spreads one arm downward. "This is Giggles 2.0."

"Oh, no." Clark doesn't look *nearly* as excited as the rest of us. "This is bad, guys. Very, very bad."

"Why?" I ask. "She said she's going to help us until Minerva can come."

Clark grimaces. "The thing is, to get through the barricade, I had to circle around, and although I did sneak through the bottom. . ." He exhales. "I was *barely* ahead of a large pack of wolves. Unfriendly, aggressive wolves. Their leader was massive, and someone else called him Fang."

Holy feathered overlords, we're so screwed.

28

ROXANA

The last time *Fang* showed up, he brought maybe half his wolves, or that's what Xander said. But this time? It sure looks like they're all with him. Clark saw dozens and dozens and dozens of them, most of them ready to fight in their wolf forms. He set a magical barricade—like a forcefield—but he's not sure how long it'll buy us. From the front window, I can see wolves filling the street for dozens and dozens of yards to the south.

"Demon-spawn coming from the north," I say. "Wolves to the south. We're screwed."

Clark nods. "It's really bad news all around, but I think I found us a way out. If you head over the roof, you can drop planks to the next building over, and I'm pretty sure I can distract them long enough to get almost everyone out. I brought—"

"We aren't running," Xander says. "The only way we're ever going to be safe is if we face the bullies now. Today."

"*Safe?*" Clark asks. "Or *dead?* Because there's no

way that I can kill even a quarter of the wolves I saw earlier, and I have no idea what the firepower of the demon-spawn might be. I'm sure they brought their best."

"They've underestimated us," Giggles says.

A *pigeon*'s telling us that the villains have underestimated us. "I've gotten better with my fireballs," I say. "Even if they itch me into an early grave, I'm not letting man or beast harm my family. I'll torch them all one at a time for as long as it takes—dragons never give up."

"I did bring more lotion." Clark tosses it to me.

Xander catches it and hands it off to me. "Maybe you can reapply it between fireballs."

Giggles wings her way up into the air, and watching her move in this form is bizarre. It's nothing like she usually looks. Only her bright orange eyes look the same. "We should go. Waiting gives them time to get organized."

A battle-directing pigeon. I'm just. . .I have no words.

"They clearly coordinated the attack," Clark says. "Which is unheard of—werewolves and demon-spawn working together?" He shakes his head. "You must've really scared the wolves the other day."

That's an interesting perspective—are they really scared of us? Could that be their reason for attacking together? If it is, that makes me a little proud. We've always been a strange group, but at our heart, we aren't killers. I doubt Bevin's ever killed anyone, and Izaak has killed before—a demon-spawn too—but only after the jerk bashed his head in first. It took almost all the energy Xander had to keep him alive.

"The block I placed is almost gone," Clark says. "We're running out of time."

Magical strength or not, Clark's no killer either. Xander told me the truth about his famous demon-spawn kill in college. The demon-spawn who were attacking their dorm drank a concoction he'd made. It was supposed to clean their nasty floors so well that they'd be sure to get the security deposit back. Apparently it was also toxic to demon-spawn, but the scent Clark used smelled like lemons. Unless Clark brought that same floor cleaner, I'm not sure what help he'll be in a battle.

And Giggles is a *pigeon*, for heaven's sake. Pooping and pecking trash is her normal behavior. There's no way she's going to do much, even with a new outfit.

She glares at me and poops immediately.

The second her poo hits the ground, it ignites, burning like a Molotov cocktail. "Giggles two point oh isn't a *regular* pigeon." She fluffs her feathers, and then she flies right through the glass window above the door like it's not even there. Before any of us have exited, Giggles opens her mouth and squawks. The shock waves of her squawk knock half a dozen wolves into the air to the left, and they plow into three demon-spawn who immediately react.

The tall demon-spawn with green skin grabs the wolf that hit him and a strange yellowish gas explodes around them. The wolf yelps. Meanwhile, the short, squatty demon-spawn with tentacles for hands sprays some kind of watery liquid at the two wolves careened into him. The demon-spawn with glowing red eyes hisses and bellows, but he doesn't attack the three wolves that crashed in his area, at least.

Xander shoves through the front door, roaring as he shifts into his wolf form—and we lose a second shirt. I swear, our couple shirts are just doomed. He's so beautiful as a wolf that I wish I could grab him around the neck, yank him back, and just pet his multi-colored ruff. That's the kind of thing he should be doing, not attacking and killing other supernatural creatures.

They forced us into this.

Jewel, her brother Pat, and Clark speed through the doors next, Izaak, Bevin, and a bevy of other wolves on their heels. I finally push through along with the last few wolves. Lo Ren Fang's wolves howl, and the demon spawn opposite them hiss, jeer, and shout.

Xander, unsurprisingly, heads toward the demon-spawn first. They're the wild cards, the most danger-ous, because we don't know what precisely any of them can do. He's almost reached the trio at the front who are dealing with hissing, growling, and whim-pering wolves when he slams into something—an invisible wall.

Clark's barrier.

"Hello and welcome." The mass of demon-spawn waiting on the north side of the street part, and the man who came for Bevin the last time saunters down the line. Aquarius something or other. "I'm so pleased to see you at the front, wolf." When he smiles, it's even more pronounced than before—his *otherness*. He's ancient and he's youthful. He's tall and he's slender, but somehow he's also powerful. His hair's silver, but not the silver of age. It's silver like Christmas tinsel or tacky bling on a child's sneakers.

"I can't say I'm pleased to see you again," I say. "I

doubt Xander could either, if he could talk while furry."

"But you see, if he hadn't come, we wouldn't be able to kill him," Aquarius says. "I just wanted to remind my people, and yours, that killing that beast is our only goal here tonight. Until recently, we had planned to kill you all." He gestures around. "And the other wolves bonded to the ill-fated Binnigas pack can die. . .or not." He shrugs. "Except that one." He points at Bevin. "She must be kept alive."

"Why?" I ask. "Last time you said you wanted her dead."

"That was before she manifested a supreme power."

"A supreme power?" I suppress a snort. "Why can't you people use words that don't sound like the ready-made butt of a joke?"

His girlfriend shimmers to life next to him. "It's no joke, dragona. Bevin Bahar can literally steal the life-force of other creatures, and once she knows how to use it, she'll have the power of eternal life or imme-diate death." She beams. "It's the power of a god."

"And once a demon-spawn has manifested a supreme power," Aquarius says, "every future descent yields the same." He beams. "No spawn has ever mani-fested a supreme power before descent number five."

"The Illuminae needed over a hundred mages to destroy Orpheus," Aquarius Silvertongue's girlfriend Violette says. "Bevin Bahar *will* Descend. She will break the angelic shields on Earth and finally usher in the Rise. That's her destiny, and you can't fight what is prophesied."

"The only thing we're breaking is you." I fling my

hands forward and the largest fireball I've ever made explodes outward. I flinch a little as it strikes the invisible wall, but I shouldn't have worried.

It punches right through, exploding right in Aquarius and Violette's smug faces. The other demon-spawn around them shrink back, and as if that finally broke the barrier, they all surge forward.

Right into Xander.

Whom they clearly do mean to kill.

Without any direction, we all fall in behind Xander, Izaak beside me, Clark on the far side of him, and Bevin to my left. Our wolves hold the south side, facing off against the other wolves in a frenzy of snapping teeth and snarling lunges.

The problem with fighting demon-spawn, I quickly learn, is that without knowing their power, you can't fight it. One moment, I'm flinging fireballs, and the next, I'm thrashing through a massive pile of slippery noodles. Beside me, Bevin's battering her way forward, as a column of wind whips through her hair. Izaak's *faster* than I realized, Bevin's vicious, aging several bizarre-looking demon-spawn, and once I extricate myself from the noodle pile, I manage to keep up a fairly consistent volley of tiny fireballs.

It keeps the demon-spawn a dozen paces back, at least.

In between fireballs, I notice that we're outmatched on the wolf side, four or five to one. "The wolves are struggling," I say. "I'm worried they'll all be destroyed."

The first one dies—I can feel it. I stumble, and then I feel another go down.

"I've got this," Giggles says from above us. Seconds

later, a massive flock of pigeons swoops down from the top of our building and flutter their way toward the wolves. We all freeze—demon-spawn and wolves alike —watching to see what two hundred pigeons might possibly do.

Giggles whistles shrilly, and all the pigeons blocking out the glow from the streetlights above us hover over the wolves, their tiny wings beating wildly, and then she shrieks, and they all poop.

"Are you kidding?" Aquarius shouts. "Poop?"

Giggles swoops overhead, her massive orange wings flapping hard and fast enough that I can feel the wind, and then the poop, just as it starts hitting the wolves below, *explodes.*

Wolves howl and catch fire. But the other wolves have identified the pigeons as an actual threat, and they're leaping into the air, tearing them into fluffy feathered shreds. The ones who didn't get caught wing their way higher and circle around, heading back to drop another round.

Lo Ren Fang, enraged by our newest attack, surges forward, pushing hard for the wolf leading Xander's pack against them—Jewel. His jaws snap around her throat, and then he clamps down, offering no mercy. Blood sprays, but he shifts, clamps down again, and shakes harder, removing her head from her body.

Wolves in our pack howl in unison, their nurturer gone.

Xander, Bevin, Clark, and Izaak all turn around, and all but Xander have teary eyes. I wipe at mine, and I scream. I clamp my hands into fists and I dig deep, preparing the biggest fireball I can to eradicate Lo Ren Fang entirely.

But I'm too late.

Bevin leaps over two slumped spawn bodies and then shouts loudly, her hands flung outward, and Lo Ren Fang's body flexes. A horrible screaming whine erupts from his mouth as he ages in front of us. He turns grey, then white, and then he begins to shrink in on himself.

Even then, she doesn't stop.

Lo Ren begins to spasm, and then his body collapses and crumbles to ash. Giggles flies overhead, her great wings beating against the pile of Lo Ren Fang until he's gone. Her shrieking sounds like a battle cry, but Bevin falls to her knees, tear-streaks running through the grime on her face.

The world sucks inward, like we're all being pulled toward Bevin, and then explodes outward, flinging us all away. One glance at the demon-spawn shows that they've all dropped to their knees like they're worshipping her. Murdering someone apparently resulted in a third descent for my friend, and the demon-spawn got to see it happen themselves.

Bevin's eyes have changed—they've turned bright yellow, and they're slitted like a cat's.

When she stands up again, she's taller, too. Much taller.

But if we thought the death of their alpha would gut the wolves, we were wrong. They surge forward, snarling louder, snapping more viciously, and churning toward us, heedless of the carnage around them.

"Kill their alpha!" Aquarius looks utterly unhinged, but apparently that was just the incentive he needed to really turn up the heat. He lifts his hands and spreads his fingers. Lightning strikes dance overhead and then arc between his hands, and he smiles.

It's utterly terrifying.

Even with Bevin and my firepower, we really are unmatched here. Xander's fear hits me like a lance, and I'm not the only one who can feel it. We know Bevin can't pull her trick over and over. Between the spawn she's already drained and killing Lo Ren Fang, I doubt she can do much of anything else.

Which means Xander's fear is likely right.

We're all about to die.

My arms and legs are itching like fire, everywhere. Once I start scratching, I can't seem to stop. Blood's pouring down my arms and soaking my stupid shirt.

"Roxana." Izaak grunts. "All that blood's really distracting. Do you have to—" When he turns toward me, his eyes widen and he coughs. "You're—Roxana, you need to *run* back inside. Right now." He shakes his head. "You look—you look bad."

One downward glance shows that I've turned the skin on my body into a strange mess that most closely resembles very bloody hamburger.

And still, I can't stop scratching.

I'm so bloody hot, and the *itching*. By the akero, the *iiiiitching*.

Aquarius claps his hands together and a strike of lightning hits inches away from Xander. That aluminum foil headed freak's beaming, and I know his next strike won't miss. The idea of Xander dying, after how far we've come, after the group we've formed, after the family we've created, it fills me with a rage so deep, and so strong, and so hot, that I finally stop scratching.

Instead, I ball my bloody hands into fists, and I pull on all the magic I can feel from Xander, from the pack, and from deep inside myself, and I shove it as deep down inside as I can, until the fire inside me is *raging*, and then I release it. Instead of firing out of my fingers like usual, it explodes in every direction.

And so do I.

My body expands, and smoke swirls, and the fire inside me *grows*, and suddenly I'm looking down on everyone around me. They're much, much smaller than they were. . .

Because I'm a massive, scarlet-tinged, golden dragon.

And I'm about to *fricassee* every demon-spawn and every wolf that wants to hurt my family. I open my massive mouth to scream, but instead of rage, molten hot lava erupts, and strikes the horrible octopus creature beside Aquarius.

"Burn, *bwitches*," I say.

"Bwitches?" Izaak asks. "Is that really what you meant to say? Or is it hard to talk as a dragon?"

I turn to scowl. "Mwah mouth ish full of teeth," I say. "Can't you wet anyfwing go?"

"Wet it go?" Now Izaak's actually laughing.

When I turn back to look at the demon-spawn, Aquarius's stupid girlfriend has disappeared, the bwitch, and he's *running*. What kind of leader *runs* when a new threat appears?

Not today, tinsel head.

Thankfully, his stupid silver-foil hair makes him easy to spot from above.

I launch into the air, my massive wings beating slowly, but the air they displace is no joke. It knocks the wolves backward like tumbleweeds in West Texas. I swing around a little clumsily, bumping the corner of a building and crumbling the balcony off not one, but two different rooftop apartments. Luckily, they're not part of our building.

"Oops," I say.

But then I see him—Aquarius. He's at the back of the group now, still sprinting away from the fight. I'm shooting toward him like a fiery arrow, ready to incinerate the entire block to make sure I get that stupid invisible bwitch too, but then a dozen other dragona drop from the clouds above.

They're roaring, and they look angry.

Luckily, I know three of them.

"Sebatchen," I shout as clearly as I can. "Stand down. Itch your sister—Roshana."

Sebastian wheels backward, knocking into two of the others in his line. "Roxana?" His eyes narrow, and he shakes his head. "Females can't shift." He tilts his head. "I've never seen that combination of colors, though. Could you—could it be her?"

I realize he's asking Mateo.

"Sebatchen can't ever put the tchoiwet seat down," I hiss. "And Mateo aways eats ssso much his tumach hurts. Now, hewp me or get out of heyuh."

It takes a few more insults before they believe me, and by the time they finally do, stupid Aquarius is *gone*. But before I can decide what to do about it, Dad and all my other brothers, plus half the guard for the night, wing their way toward us. "What's going on?" Dad asks.

"Itch me," I say. "Roshana."

Luka must be visiting, because he spins around me,

dipping up and down with animation. "Roxana! Best day ever. Now we can fly together." Mom and Dad never let him take me out—far too dangerous.

I've never seen Dad smile in his dragon form, but it's glorious when he does. "Roxana!"

How do they all talk so well? "I need to pwactice tawking waiter," I say. "But wight now, my fwiends aww stwuggwing down there. Come hewp?"

Dad's the first one to angle down. "This will be fun."

The others follow immediately, much better fliers than me. The wolves have rallied, and even without their leader, the demon-spawn are still fighting below.

Until three dozen dragona show up, ready to roast our enemies.

Moments later, the fight's over.

The guardians show up right after, conveniently too late to do anything other than register Bevin's third descent and issue her a stern warning. I'm sure that's intentional. They're too small a force to intervene in wars, but once it's over, they appear and register any new demon-spawn descents. Once I'm sure they won't try to detain Bevin for her supreme powers or for murdering anyone, and once I'm sure Lo Ren's pack and the demon-spawn are actually gone, I find my dad.

As the largest dragon here, he's easy to spot.

"I weawy appweciate yower hewp," I say. "But can you tewl me how to shift back?" I toss my head at my friends. "I need to be hooman again."

Dad's still smiling. "The first time can be tricky. Close your eyes and breathe in and out a few times, and then release all the heat. Curl slowly back inward, and your body will follow."

I listen, only, it doesn't work.

Half an hour later, I'm still scaly, and I'm starting to panic. "Ish it diffewent for femawes?" I ask. "I'm schtuck."

Dad tosses his head. "Come home with us—we'll help you."

They sure will, right into never coming back. I was worried before that they might try to pressure me to come home. Now that I can shift—the only female dragona who can shift in the world—they'll try even harder to force me back. "Awl figuwe it out." I frown. "Fwanks for youw hewp, but you can go home."

Luka looks like he wants to argue, and Sebastian starts to, but Mateo and Dad exchange a glance, and then Dad says, "You know where we are when you change your mind." Then they all launch at almost the same time, winging their way across New York's night sky.

Suddenly, I'm the only dragon left in the middle of the street in New York. Xander has shifted and dressed, and he's walking toward me. He drops a hand on my leg and smiles. "This is. . ." He shakes his head. "You're *spectacular*."

At least my boyfriend thinks it's cool.

"You saved us all."

"I'd say you were pwetty gweat too," I say.

"Not great enough." His expression darkens, and I think about Jewel and the others we lost—thanks to the bond, I felt each loss. I'm sure Xander blames himself even more for each and every one.

"Don't take the darkness pushed on you from

others," Bevin says. "There's more than enough bad in the world. We can only accept blame for the mistakes we've made."

"Wook who's bwiyiant now," I say.

"Wook who has a wisp." Bevin's smirking, and I'd normally sock her on the shoulder, but I refrain.

"Schtuff it," I say.

"That was pretty amazing," Bevin says. "Almost like we're changing into whatever our pack needs."

Giggles flies around my head and flutters over to land on my shoulder. She's a pigeon again. *Minerva's here.*

"What?" My head whips around, but even with my dragon-eyesight, which is quite good, I don't see her.

"Are the guardians gone yet?" a small voice asks.

I finally spot her, crouched behind a trash can. When she stands, I realize she's glowing softly.

"Um," Xander says. "Did you swallow a lightbulb? Or is this somehow related to you missing a *second* fight entirely?"

"It might take a while to explain," Minerva says. "But remember how we hid Roxana?"

"We're going to be doing the same thing for Minerva," Clark says. "She's been outed, and now the Illuminae want her dead."

Never a dull moment when you're a magical misfit.

And I wouldn't have it any other way.

****

I hope you loved My Itching Scales! I'm sorry it was a little slow being written. As you may have noticed, I combined the plot of TWO books into one. Then I proceeded to write almost every single thing I'd plotted for one book, and now I can only charge readers for one. . .so it took me the same amount of time and costs for editing and audiobook creation. . .

I am brilliant. A marketing MAVEN.

BUT hey, I'm putting out a series that has never sold well, because I love you. I plan to write the final book some time in 2025, but I'll have to squeeze it in again, so I'm making no promises. I do plan to brilliantly combine two books into one again, hopefully somehow shortening the story in some places so I don't pay twice and get paid once... we'll see. As always, the story always comes first.

If you want another book to read after this, can I suggest My Queendom for a Horse (my horse shifter!) or Ensnared (my dragon shifter!) I think you'd like either of them, but they both have more romance than this one does, so your mileage may vary. THANKS for the support! I appreciate you so much!!

ACKNOWLEDGMENTS

To my readers: YOU ARE EPIC. I love you so much.

To my kids: YOU ARE ANNOYING. I love you so much anyway.

To my husband: You are FABULOUS AND HANDSOME AND I LOVE YOU. Thank you for putting up with me.

To my yaaaappy dogs, my demanding horses, my very busy cats, and my idiotic (but cute) chickens. You already know I love you, and last I checked, you were all illiterate. For me to include gratitude for something illiterate? That's true love, right there.

I have five kids, eight horses, four dogs, two cats, and thirty chickens that my HOA does NOT know about... I have one husband, and I'm guessing you can already tell that he's a saint. I tried to find a publisher for years for my books, but after being told over and over that they weren't something anyone wanted to read, I decided to test that myself. I've been indie since 2018, and I've never looked back. I kickbox almost every day (to address my excess cookie-making), so if you don't like my kids, my cookies, or my books, maybe don't tell me in person.